big
NATE

RELEASE
THE HOUNDS!

Complete Your *Big Nate* Collection

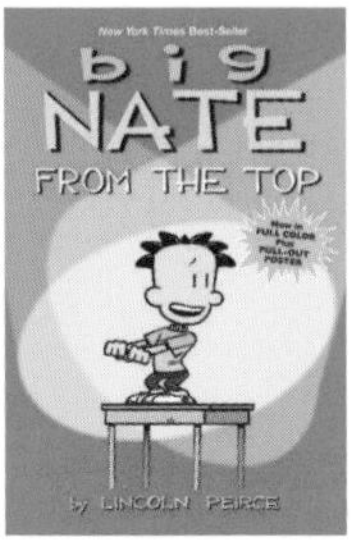
big NATE
FROM THE TOP
by LINCOLN PEIRCE

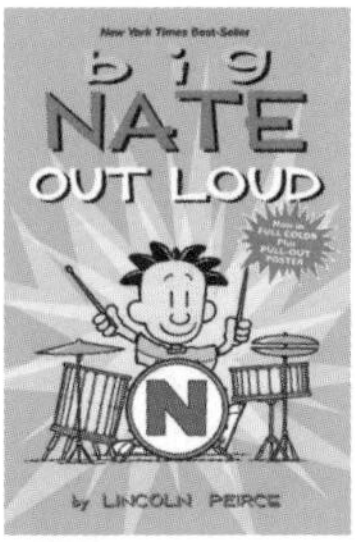
big NATE
OUT LOUD
by LINCOLN PEIRCE

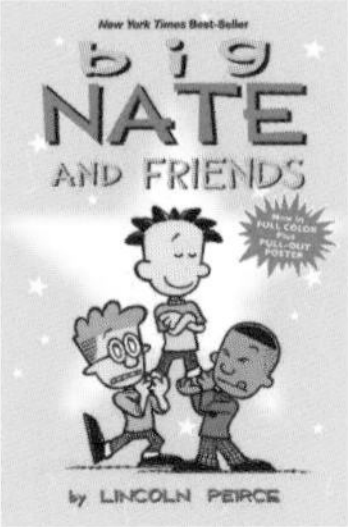
big NATE
AND FRIENDS
by LINCOLN PEIRCE

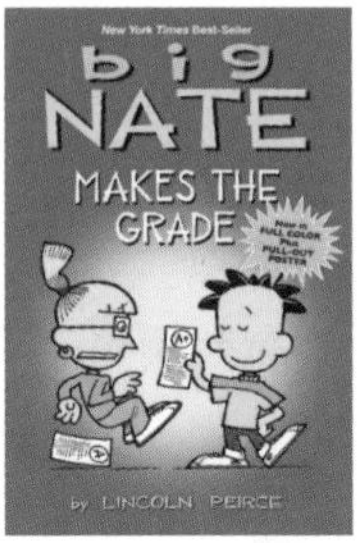
big NATE
MAKES THE GRADE
by LINCOLN PEIRCE

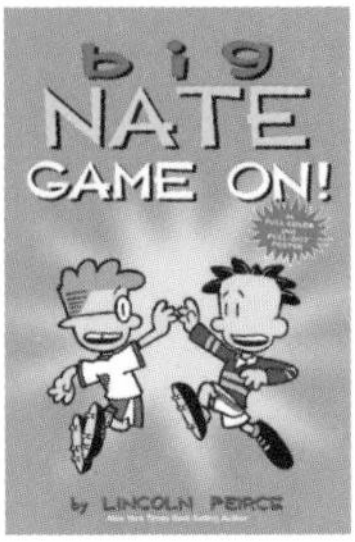
big NATE
GAME ON!
by LINCOLN PEIRCE

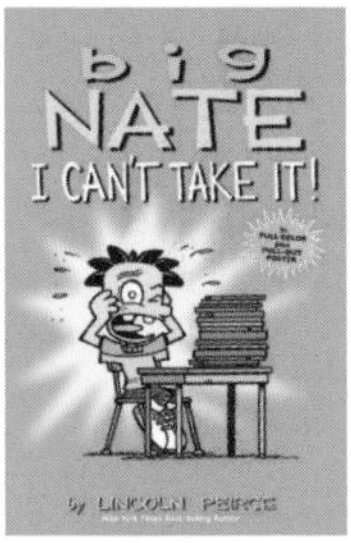
big NATE
I CAN'T TAKE IT!
by LINCOLN PEIRCE

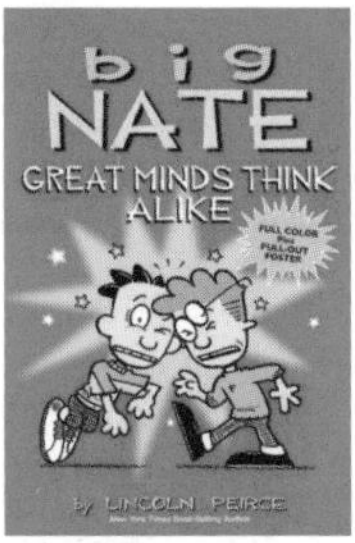
big NATE
GREAT MINDS THINK ALIKE
by LINCOLN PEIRCE

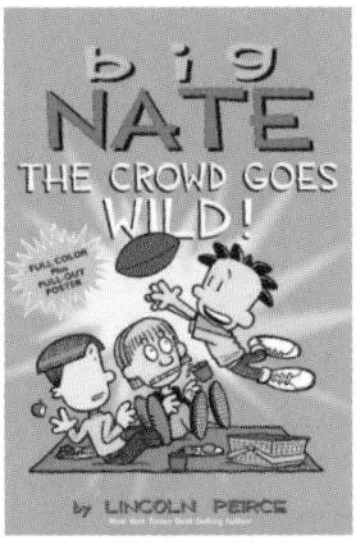
big NATE
THE CROWD GOES WILD!
by LINCOLN PEIRCE

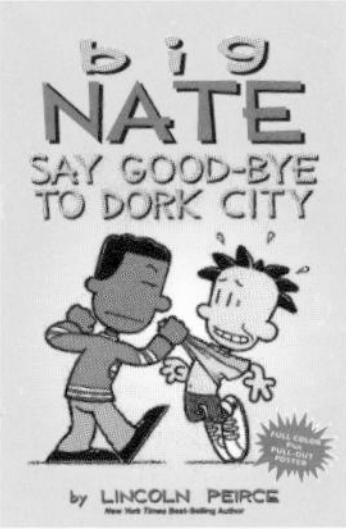
big NATE
SAY GOOD-BYE TO DORK CITY
by LINCOLN PEIRCE

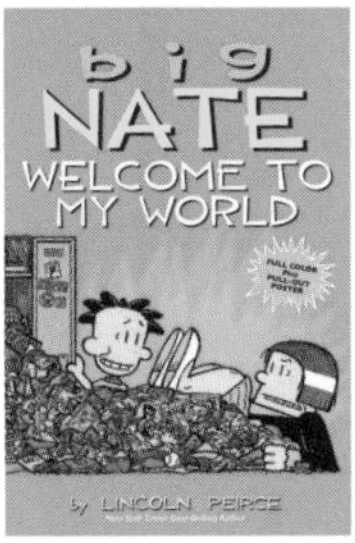
big NATE
WELCOME TO MY WORLD
by LINCOLN PEIRCE

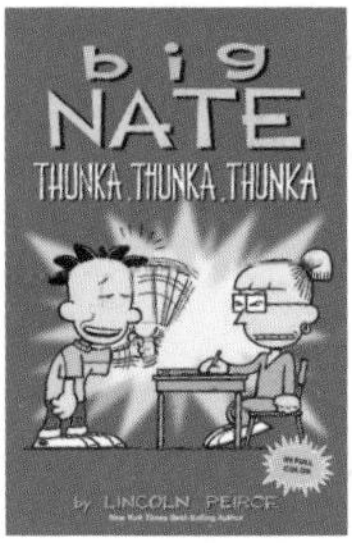
big NATE
THUNKA, THUNKA, THUNKA
by LINCOLN PEIRCE

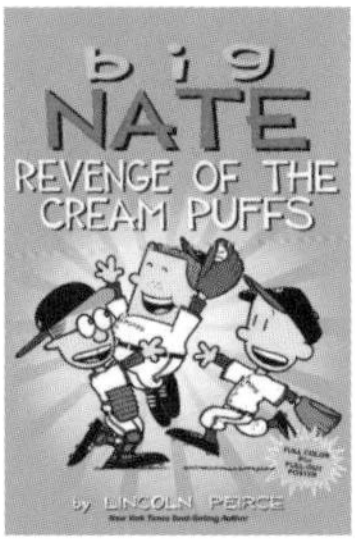
big NATE
REVENGE OF THE CREAM PUFFS
by LINCOLN PEIRCE

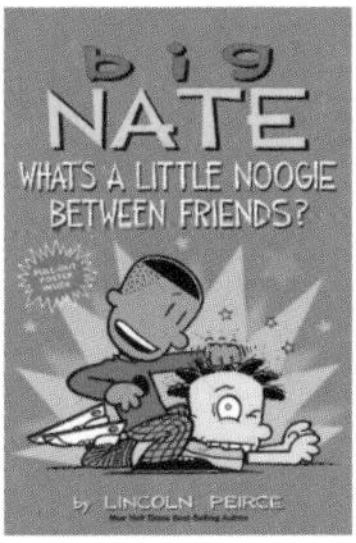
big NATE
WHAT'S A LITTLE NOOGIE BETWEEN FRIENDS?
by LINCOLN PEIRCE

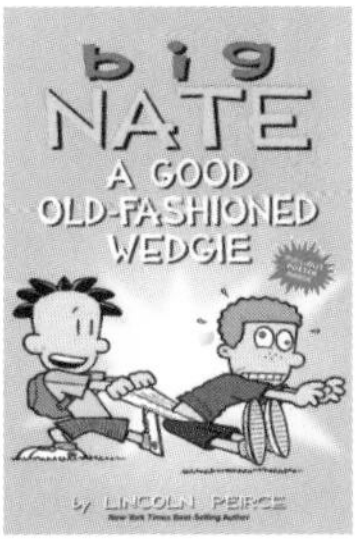
big NATE
A GOOD OLD-FASHIONED WEDGIE
by LINCOLN PEIRCE

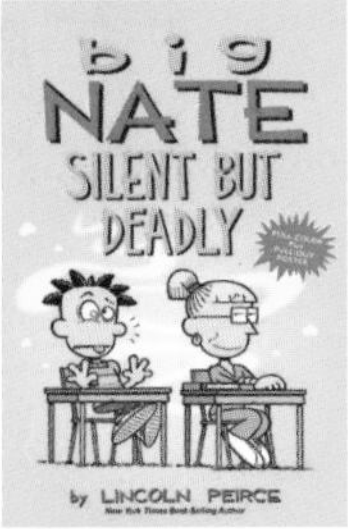
big NATE
SILENT BUT DEADLY
by LINCOLN PEIRCE

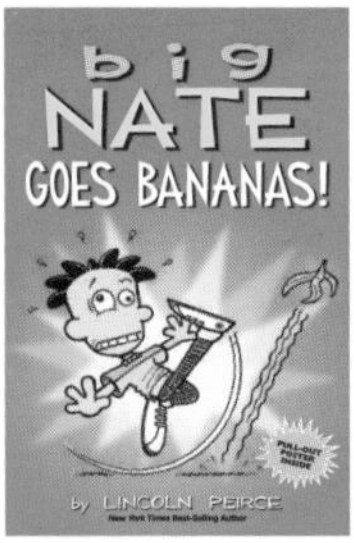
big NATE
GOES BANANAS!
by LINCOLN PEIRCE

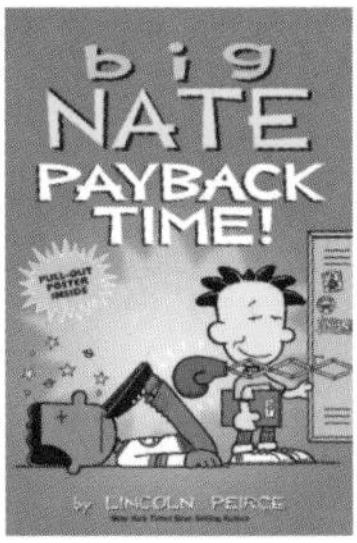
big NATE
PAYBACK TIME!
by LINCOLN PEIRCE

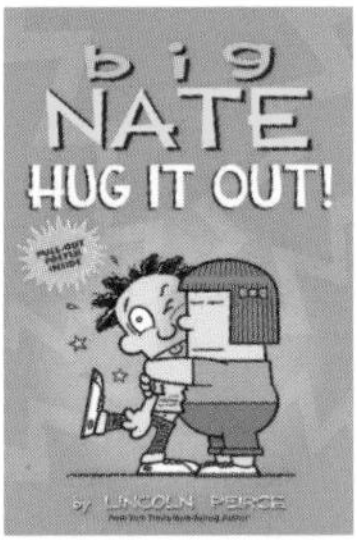
big NATE
HUG IT OUT!
by LINCOLN PEIRCE

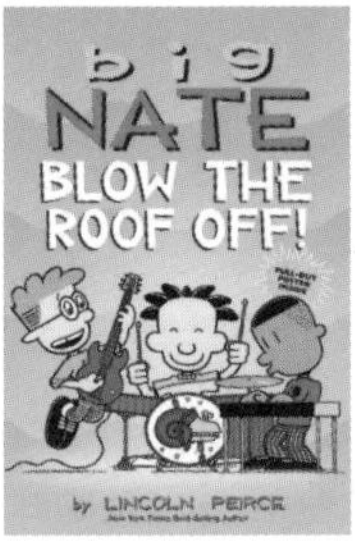
big NATE
BLOW THE ROOF OFF!
by LINCOLN PEIRCE

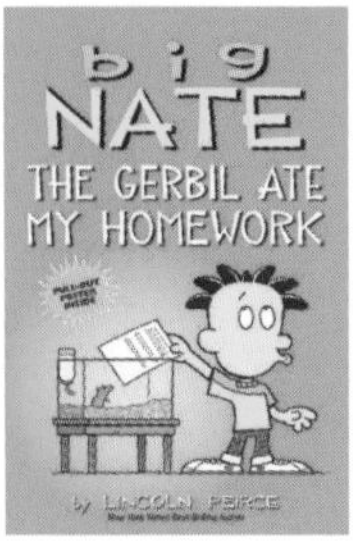
big NATE
THE GERBIL ATE MY HOMEWORK
by LINCOLN PEIRCE

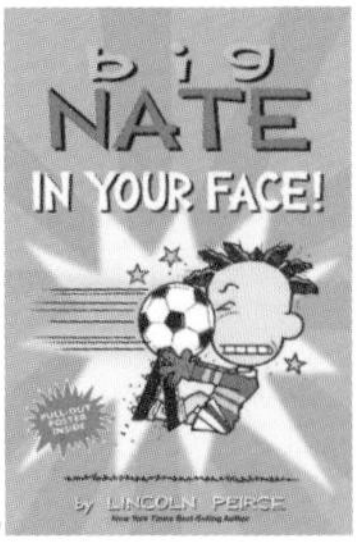
big NATE
IN YOUR FACE!
by LINCOLN PEIRCE

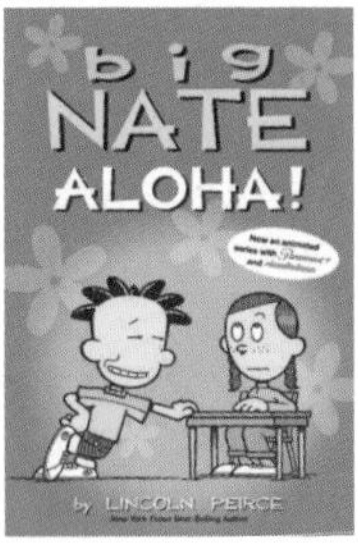
big NATE
ALOHA!
by LINCOLN PEIRCE

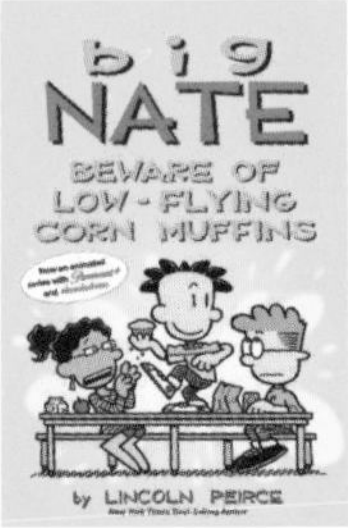
big NATE
BEWARE OF LOW-FLYING CORN MUFFINS
by LINCOLN PEIRCE

big NATE
RELEASE THE HOUNDS!

by LINCOLN PEIRCE

Andrews McMeel
PUBLISHING®

8

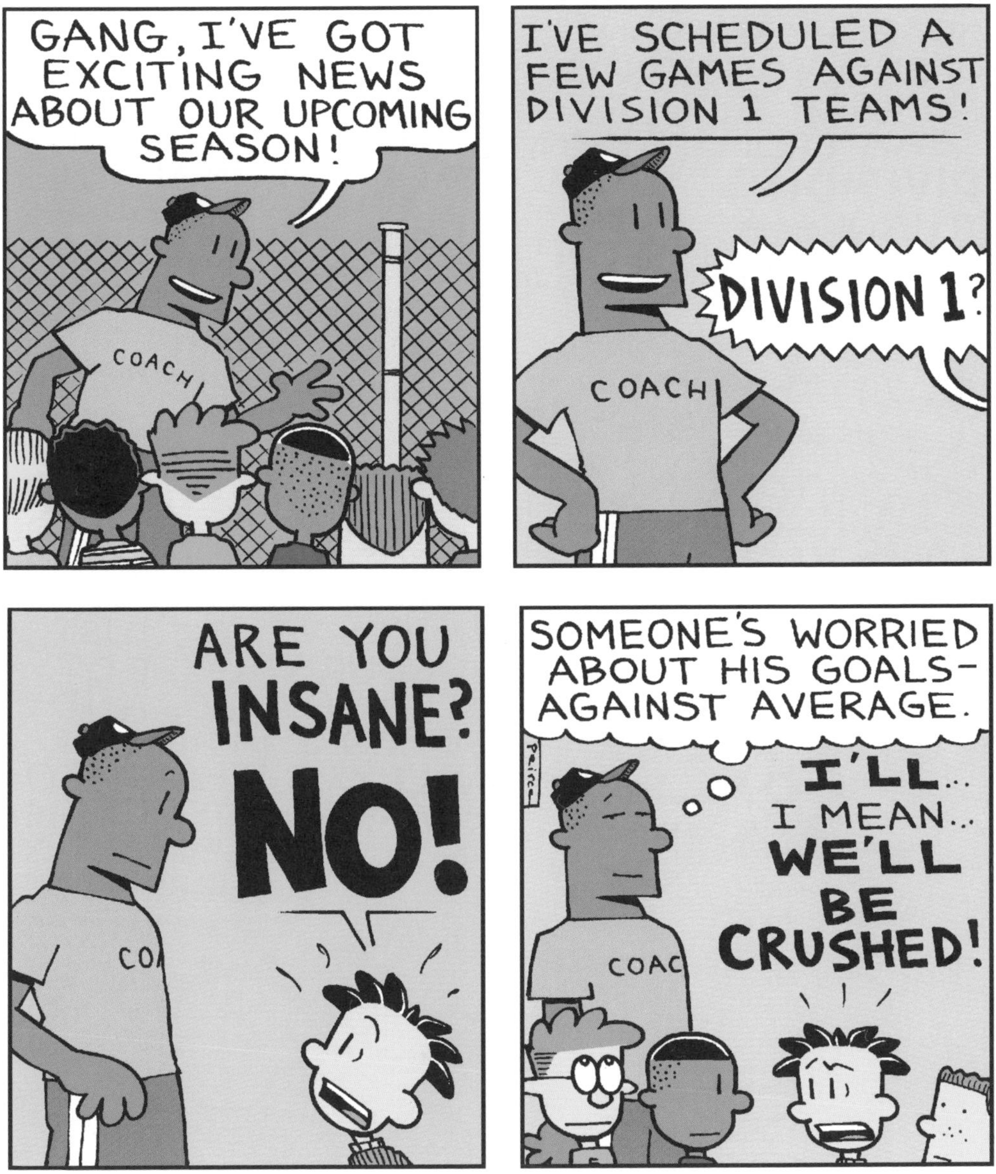
GANG, I'VE GOT EXCITING NEWS ABOUT OUR UPCOMING SEASON!
COACH
I'VE SCHEDULED A FEW GAMES AGAINST DIVISION 1 TEAMS!
DIVISION 1?
COACH
ARE YOU INSANE? NO!
SOMEONE'S WORRIED ABOUT HIS GOALS-AGAINST AVERAGE.
I'LL... I MEAN... WE'LL BE CRUSHED!
Peirce

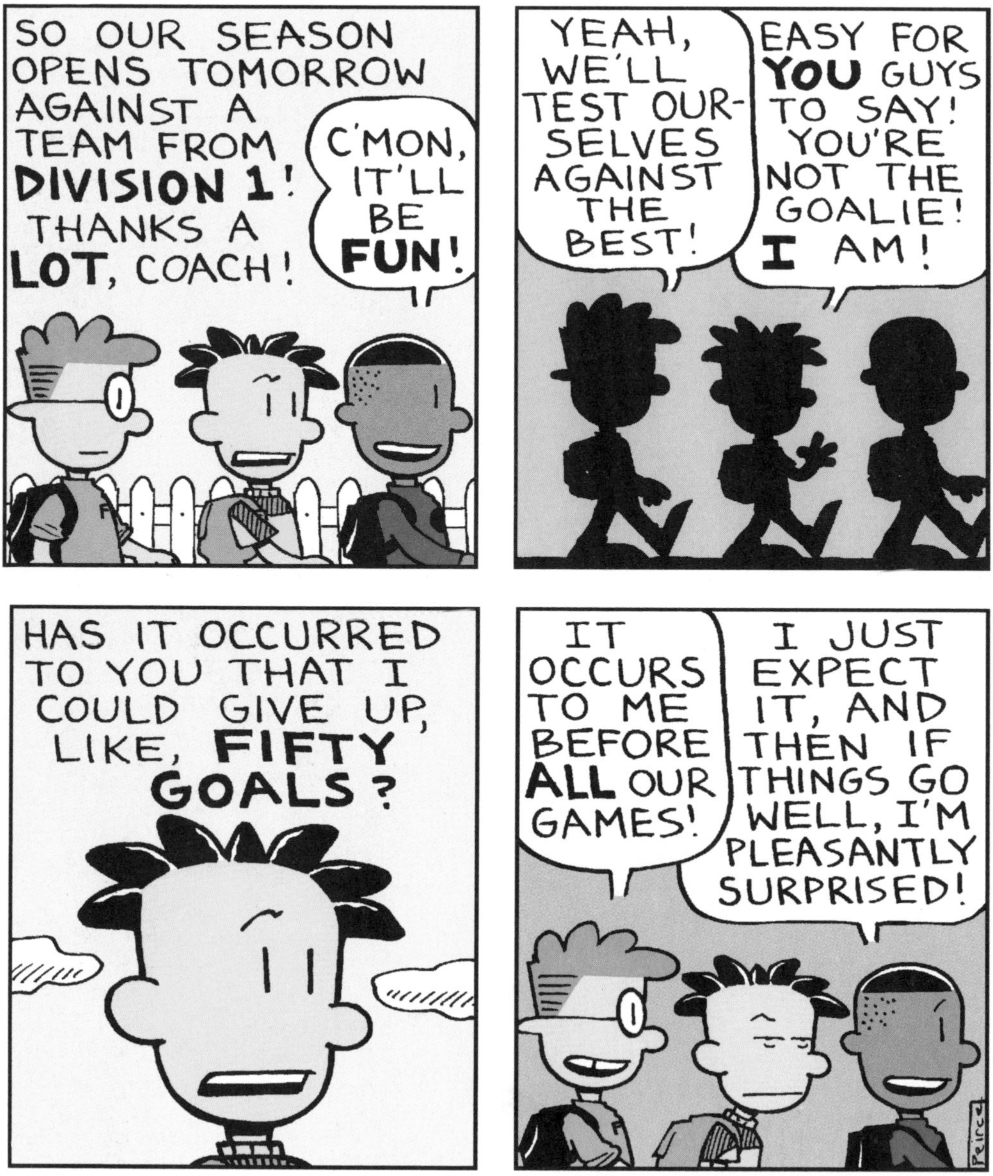
SO OUR SEASON OPENS TOMORROW AGAINST A TEAM FROM **DIVISION 1**! THANKS A **LOT**, COACH!
C'MON, IT'LL BE **FUN**!
YEAH, WE'LL TEST OUR-SELVES AGAINST THE BEST!
EASY FOR **YOU** GUYS TO SAY! YOU'RE NOT THE GOALIE! **I** AM!
HAS IT OCCURRED TO YOU THAT I COULD GIVE UP, LIKE, **FIFTY GOALS**?
IT OCCURS TO ME BEFORE **ALL** OUR GAMES!
I JUST EXPECT IT, AND THEN IF THINGS GO WELL, I'M PLEASANTLY SURPRISED!
Peirce

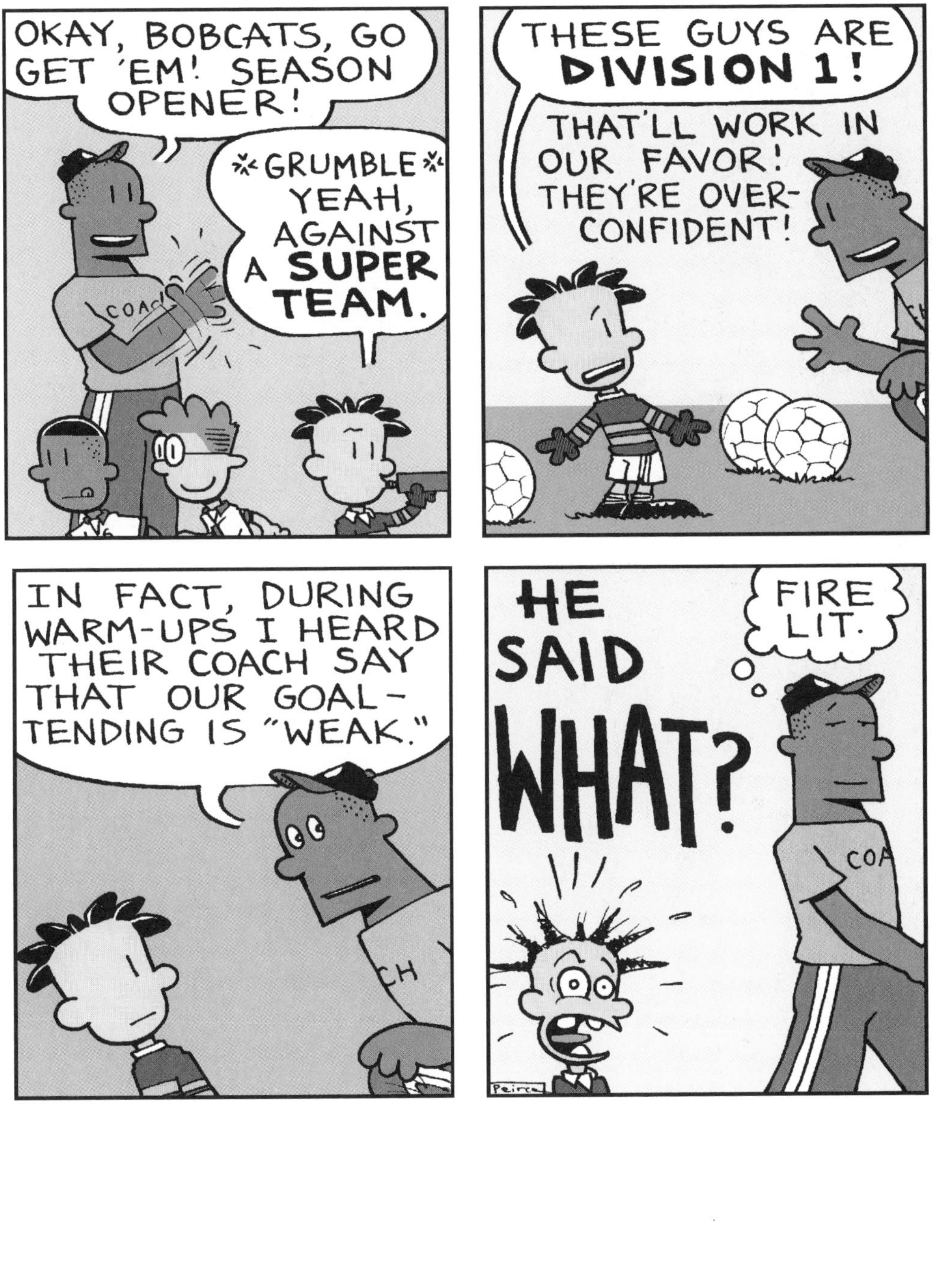
OKAY, BOBCATS, GO GET 'EM! SEASON OPENER!
GRUMBLE YEAH, AGAINST A **SUPER TEAM**.
THESE GUYS ARE **DIVISION 1**!
THAT'LL WORK IN OUR FAVOR! THEY'RE OVER-CONFIDENT!
IN FACT, DURING WARM-UPS I HEARD THEIR COACH SAY THAT OUR GOAL-TENDING IS "WEAK."
HE SAID WHAT?
FIRE LIT.
Peirce

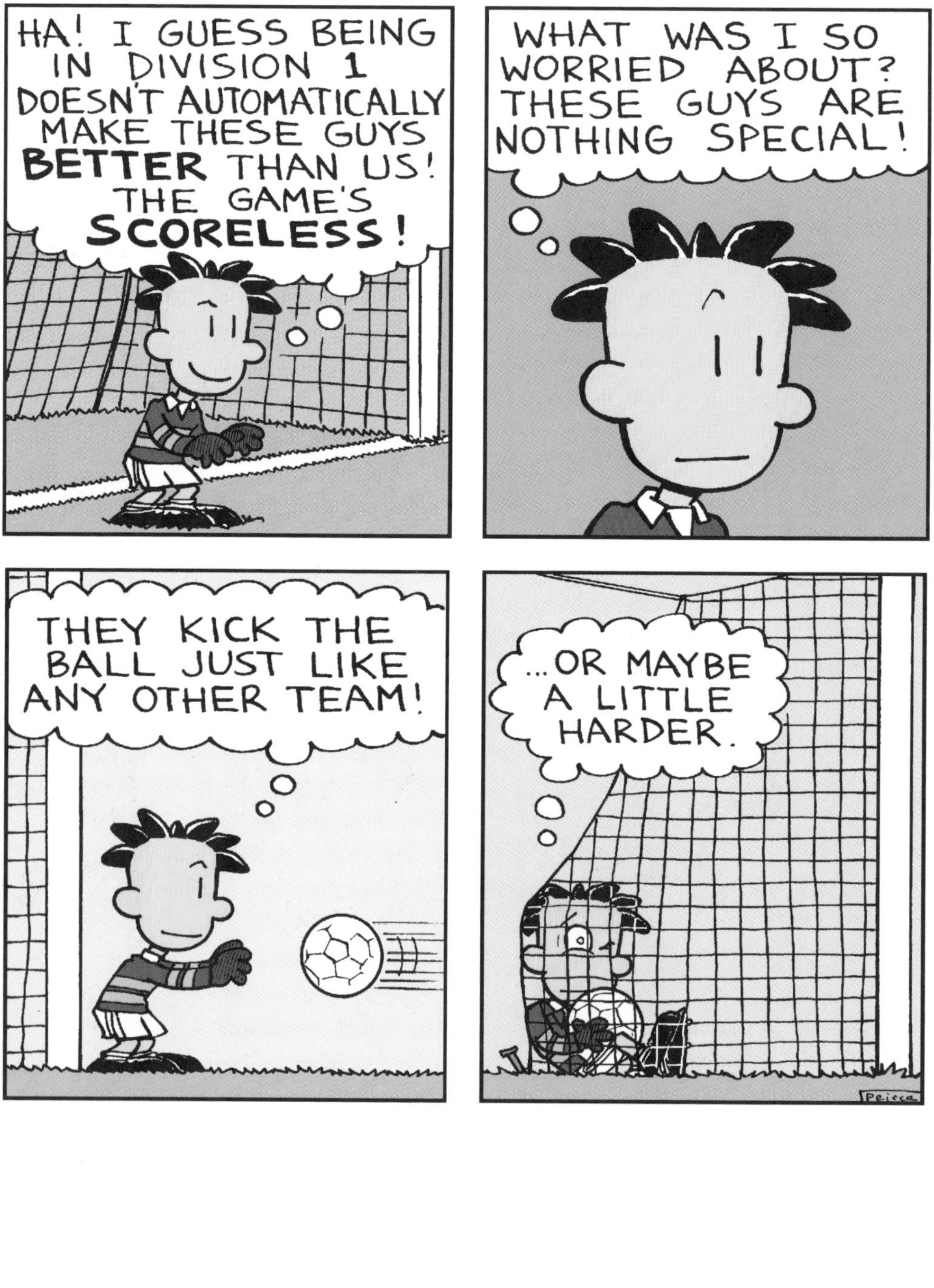
HA! I GUESS BEING IN DIVISION 1 DOESN'T AUTOMATICALLY MAKE THESE GUYS **BETTER** THAN US! THE GAME'S **SCORELESS**!
WHAT WAS I SO WORRIED ABOUT? THESE GUYS ARE NOTHING SPECIAL!
THEY KICK THE BALL JUST LIKE ANY OTHER TEAM!
...OR MAYBE A LITTLE HARDER.
Peirce

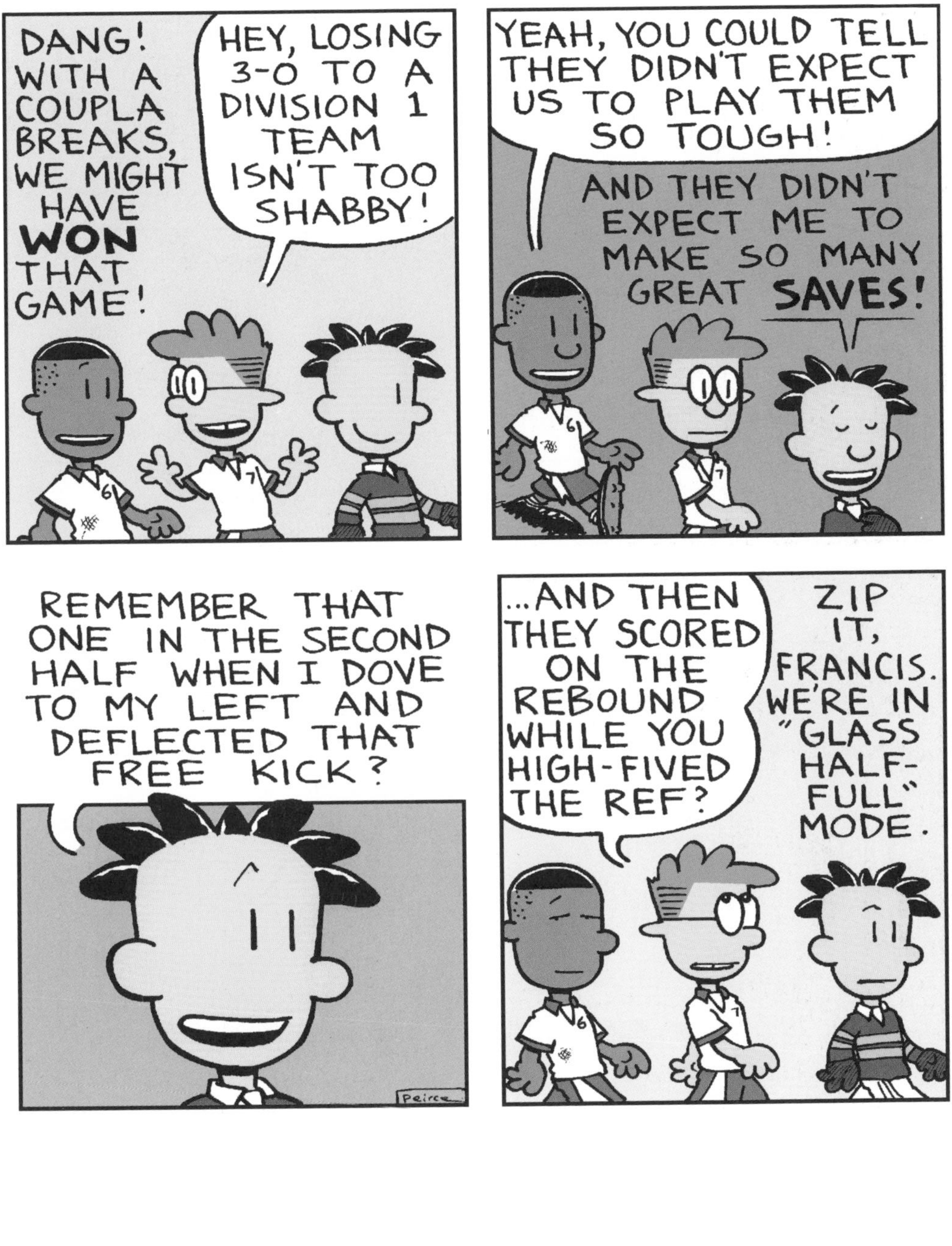
DANG! WITH A COUPLA BREAKS, WE MIGHT HAVE WON THAT GAME!
HEY, LOSING 3-0 TO A DIVISION 1 TEAM ISN'T TOO SHABBY!
YEAH, YOU COULD TELL THEY DIDN'T EXPECT US TO PLAY THEM SO TOUGH!
AND THEY DIDN'T EXPECT ME TO MAKE SO MANY GREAT SAVES!
REMEMBER THAT ONE IN THE SECOND HALF WHEN I DOVE TO MY LEFT AND DEFLECTED THAT FREE KICK?
Peirce
...AND THEN THEY SCORED ON THE REBOUND WHILE YOU HIGH-FIVED THE REF?
ZIP IT, FRANCIS. WE'RE IN "GLASS HALF-FULL" MODE.

GREAT GAME, BOYS! AND WHAT A GOOD LEARNING EXPERIENCE!

YOU DISCOVERED YOU CAN GO TOE-TO-TOE WITH A DIVISION 1 TEAM! IF EVER A LOSS FELT LIKE A WIN, THIS IS IT!

YOU KNOW WHAT **ELSE** MAKES A LOSS FEEL LIKE A WIN? GUMMI BEARS!

EVERY TEAM NEEDS A CHAD.

NO GUMS, NO GLORY!

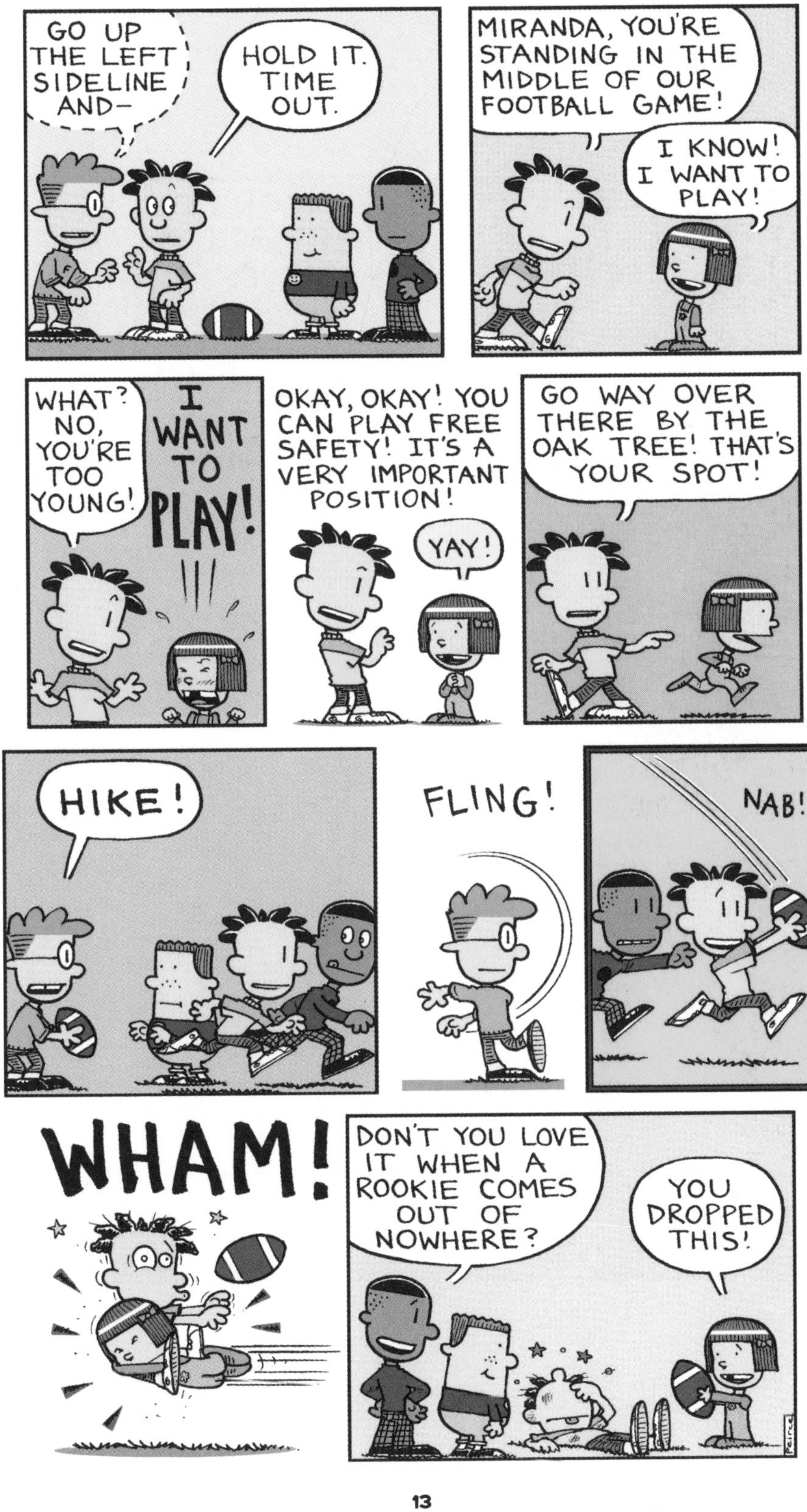
GO UP THE LEFT SIDELINE AND–
HOLD IT. TIME OUT.
MIRANDA, YOU'RE STANDING IN THE MIDDLE OF OUR FOOTBALL GAME!
I KNOW! I WANT TO PLAY!
WHAT? NO, YOU'RE TOO YOUNG!
I WANT TO PLAY!
OKAY, OKAY! YOU CAN PLAY FREE SAFETY! IT'S A VERY IMPORTANT POSITION!
YAY!
GO WAY OVER THERE BY THE OAK TREE! THAT'S YOUR SPOT!
HIKE!
FLING!
NAB!
WHAM!
DON'T YOU LOVE IT WHEN A ROOKIE COMES OUT OF NOWHERE?
YOU DROPPED THIS!

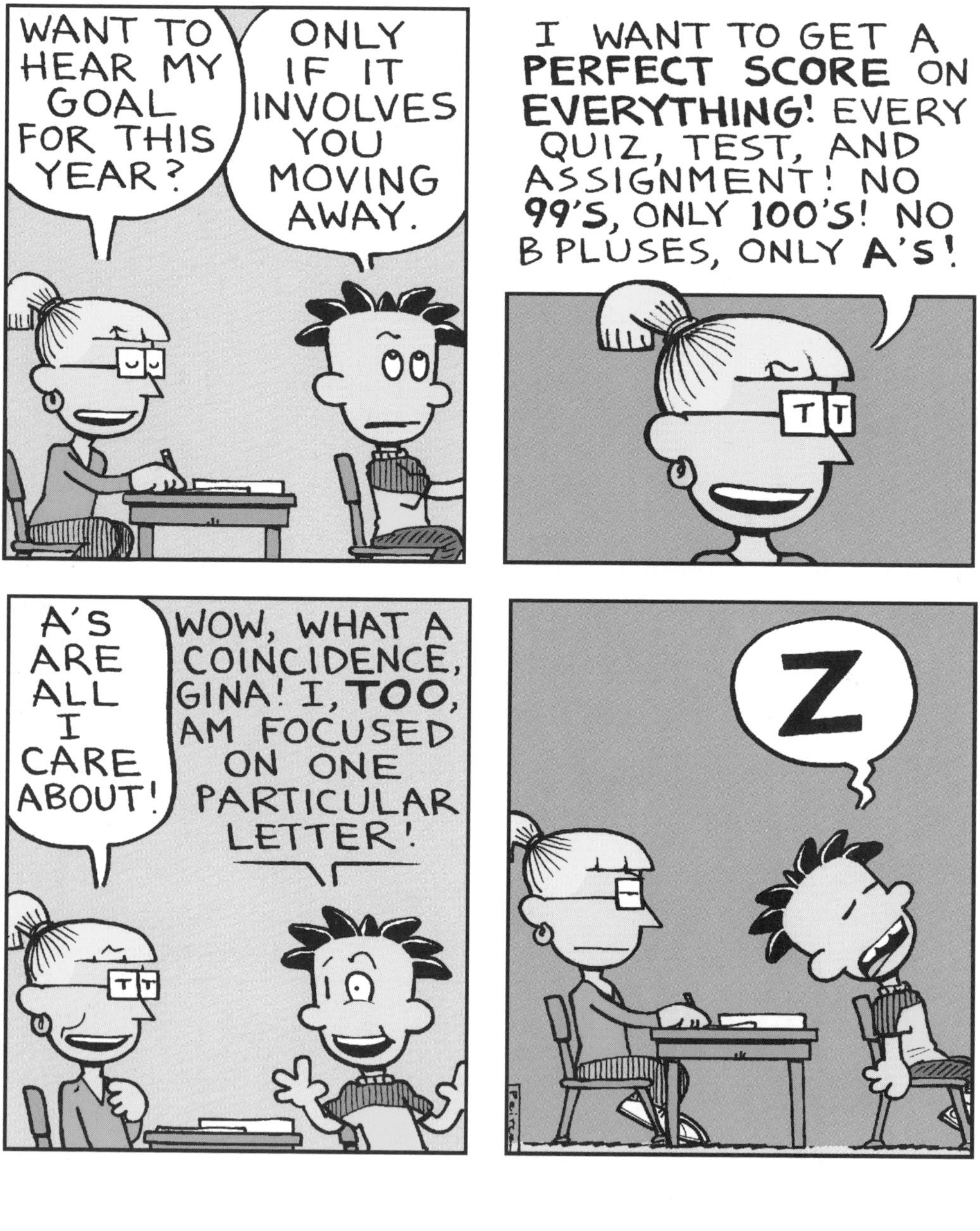
WANT TO HEAR MY GOAL FOR THIS YEAR?
ONLY IF IT INVOLVES YOU MOVING AWAY.
I WANT TO GET A **PERFECT SCORE** ON **EVERYTHING!** EVERY QUIZ, TEST, AND ASSIGNMENT! NO **99'S**, ONLY **100'S**! NO B PLUSES, ONLY **A'S**!
A'S ARE ALL I CARE ABOUT!
WOW, WHAT A COINCIDENCE, GINA! I, **TOO**, AM FOCUSED ON ONE PARTICULAR LETTER!
Z

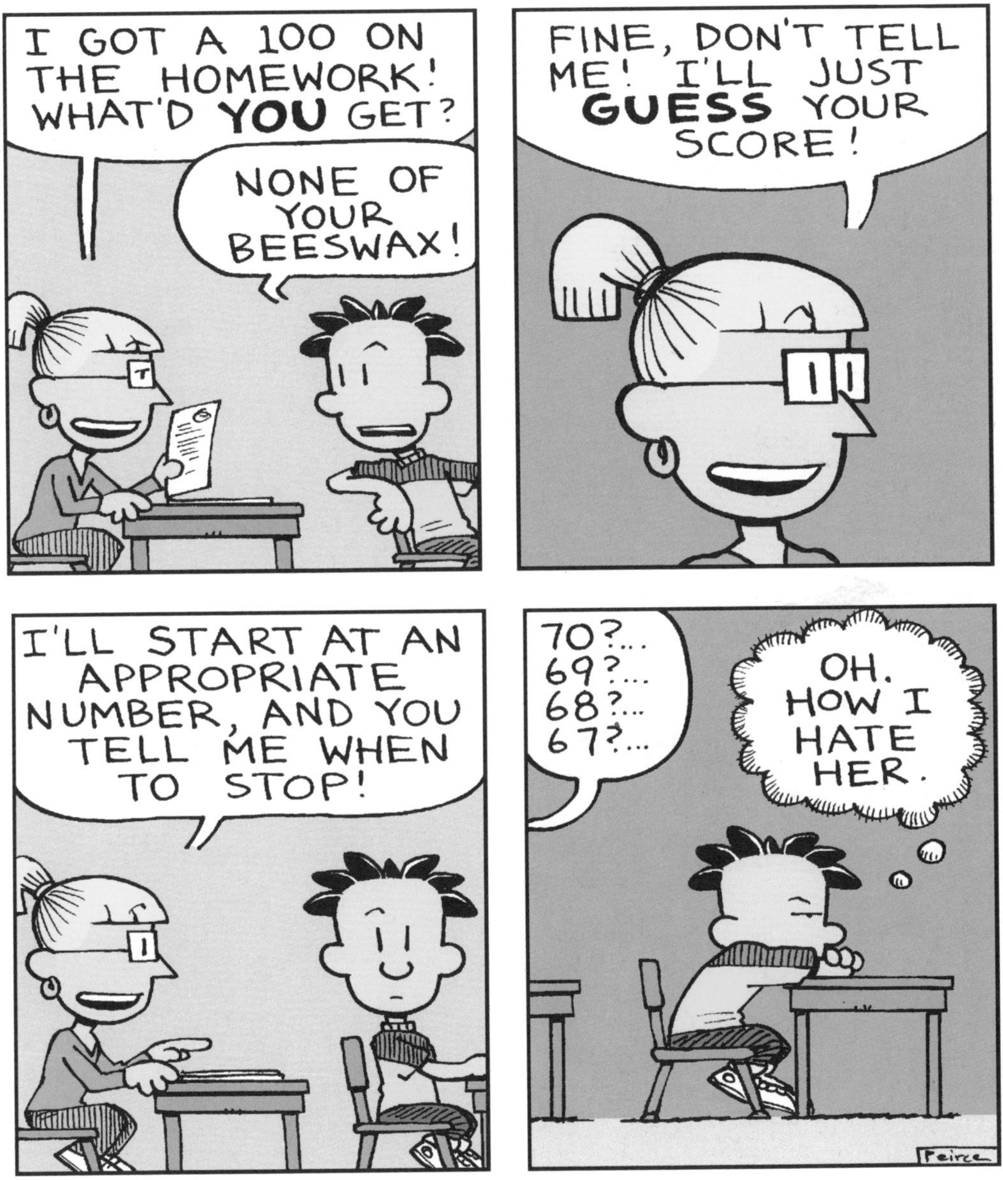
I GOT A 100 ON THE HOMEWORK! WHAT'D **YOU** GET?
NONE OF YOUR BEESWAX!
FINE, DON'T TELL ME! I'LL JUST **GUESS** YOUR SCORE!
I'LL START AT AN APPROPRIATE NUMBER, AND YOU TELL ME WHEN TO STOP!
70?... 69?... 68?... 67?...
OH. HOW I HATE HER.
Peirce

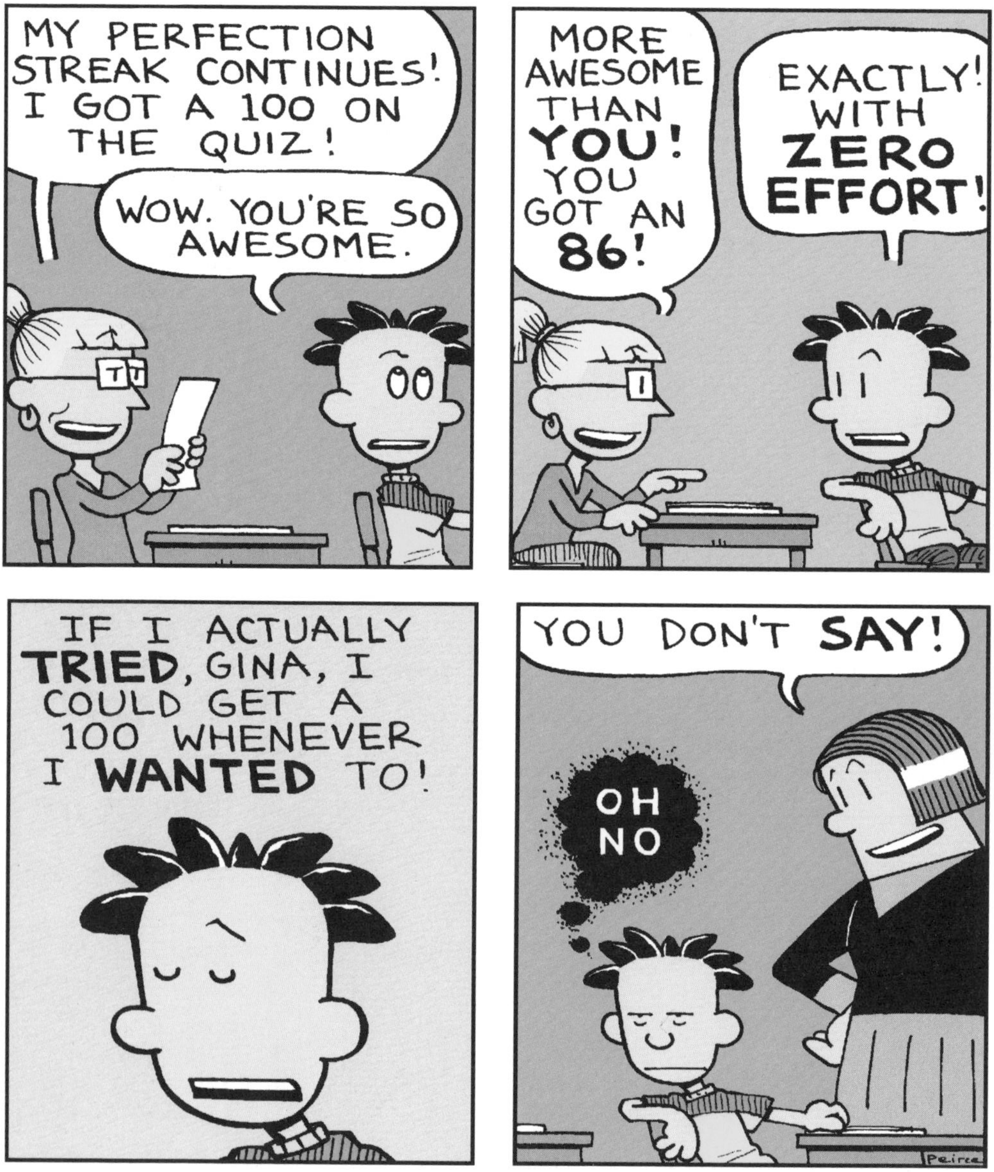
MY PERFECTION STREAK CONTINUES! I GOT A 100 ON THE QUIZ!
WOW. YOU'RE SO AWESOME.
MORE AWESOME THAN **YOU**! YOU GOT AN **86**!
EXACTLY! WITH **ZERO EFFORT**!
IF I ACTUALLY **TRIED**, GINA, I COULD GET A 100 WHENEVER I **WANTED** TO!
YOU DON'T **SAY**!
OH NO
Peirce

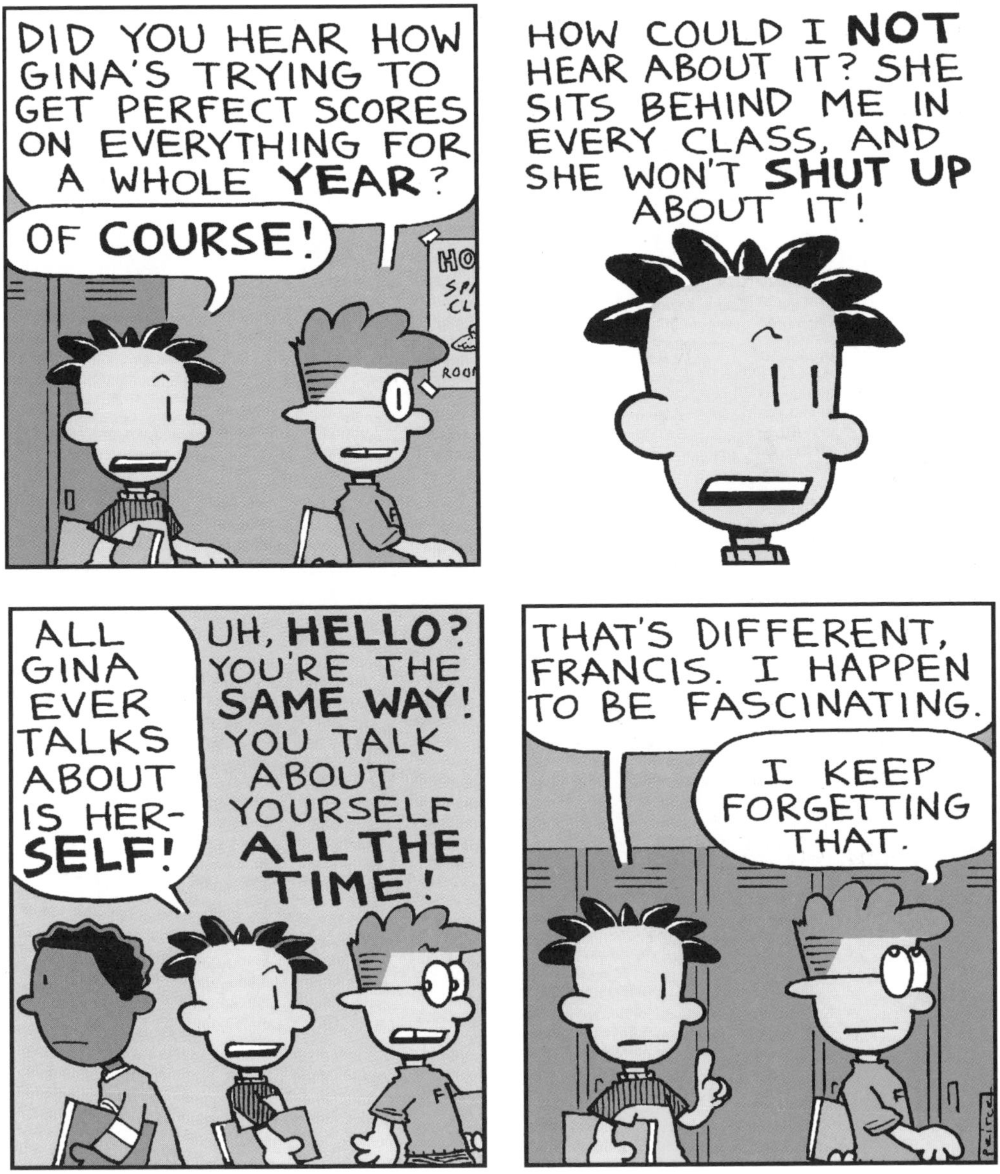
DID YOU HEAR HOW GINA'S TRYING TO GET PERFECT SCORES ON EVERYTHING FOR A WHOLE YEAR?
OF COURSE!
HOW COULD I NOT HEAR ABOUT IT? SHE SITS BEHIND ME IN EVERY CLASS, AND SHE WON'T SHUT UP ABOUT IT!
ALL GINA EVER TALKS ABOUT IS HER-SELF!
UH, HELLO? YOU'RE THE SAME WAY! YOU TALK ABOUT YOURSELF ALL THE TIME!
THAT'S DIFFERENT, FRANCIS. I HAPPEN TO BE FASCINATING.
I KEEP FORGETTING THAT.

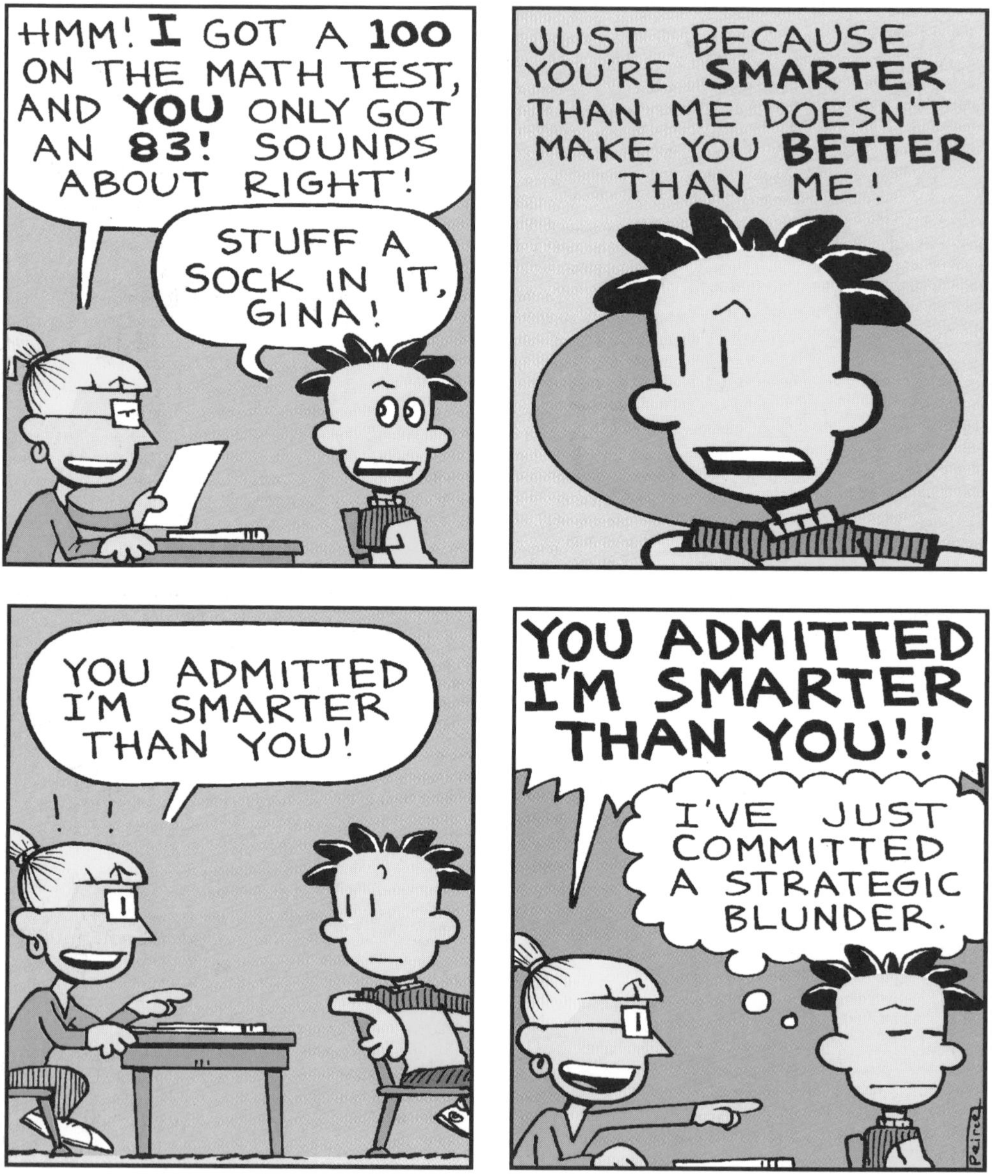
HMM! I GOT A 100 ON THE MATH TEST, AND YOU ONLY GOT AN 83! SOUNDS ABOUT RIGHT!
STUFF A SOCK IN IT, GINA!
JUST BECAUSE YOU'RE SMARTER THAN ME DOESN'T MAKE YOU BETTER THAN ME!
YOU ADMITTED I'M SMARTER THAN YOU!
! !
YOU ADMITTED I'M SMARTER THAN YOU!!
I'VE JUST COMMITTED A STRATEGIC BLUNDER.
Peirce

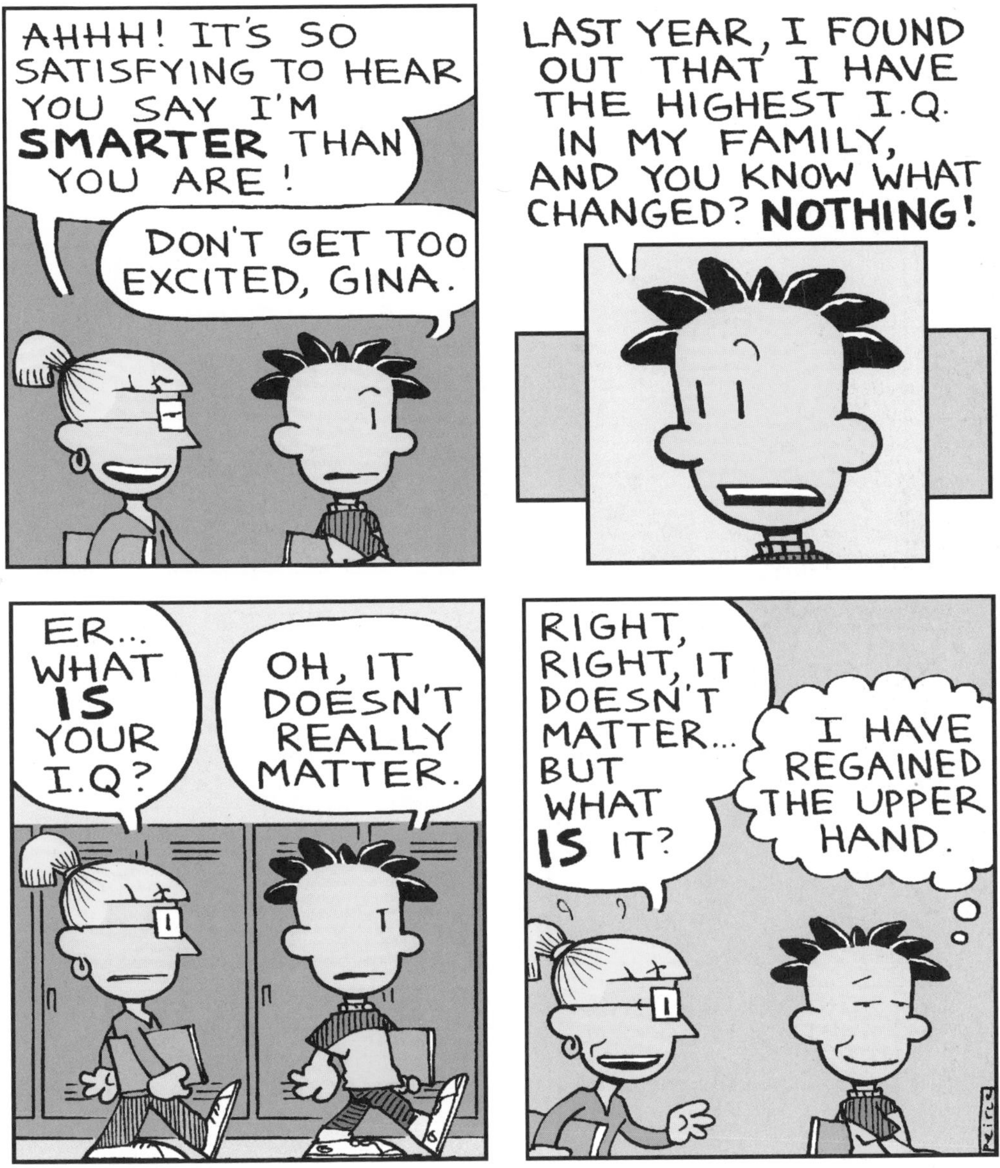
AHHH! IT'S SO SATISFYING TO HEAR YOU SAY I'M **SMARTER** THAN YOU ARE!
DON'T GET TOO EXCITED, GINA.
LAST YEAR, I FOUND OUT THAT I HAVE THE HIGHEST I.Q. IN MY FAMILY, AND YOU KNOW WHAT CHANGED? **NOTHING!**
ER... WHAT **IS** YOUR I.Q?
OH, IT DOESN'T REALLY MATTER.
RIGHT, RIGHT, IT DOESN'T MATTER... BUT WHAT **IS** IT?
I HAVE REGAINED THE UPPER HAND.
PEIRCE

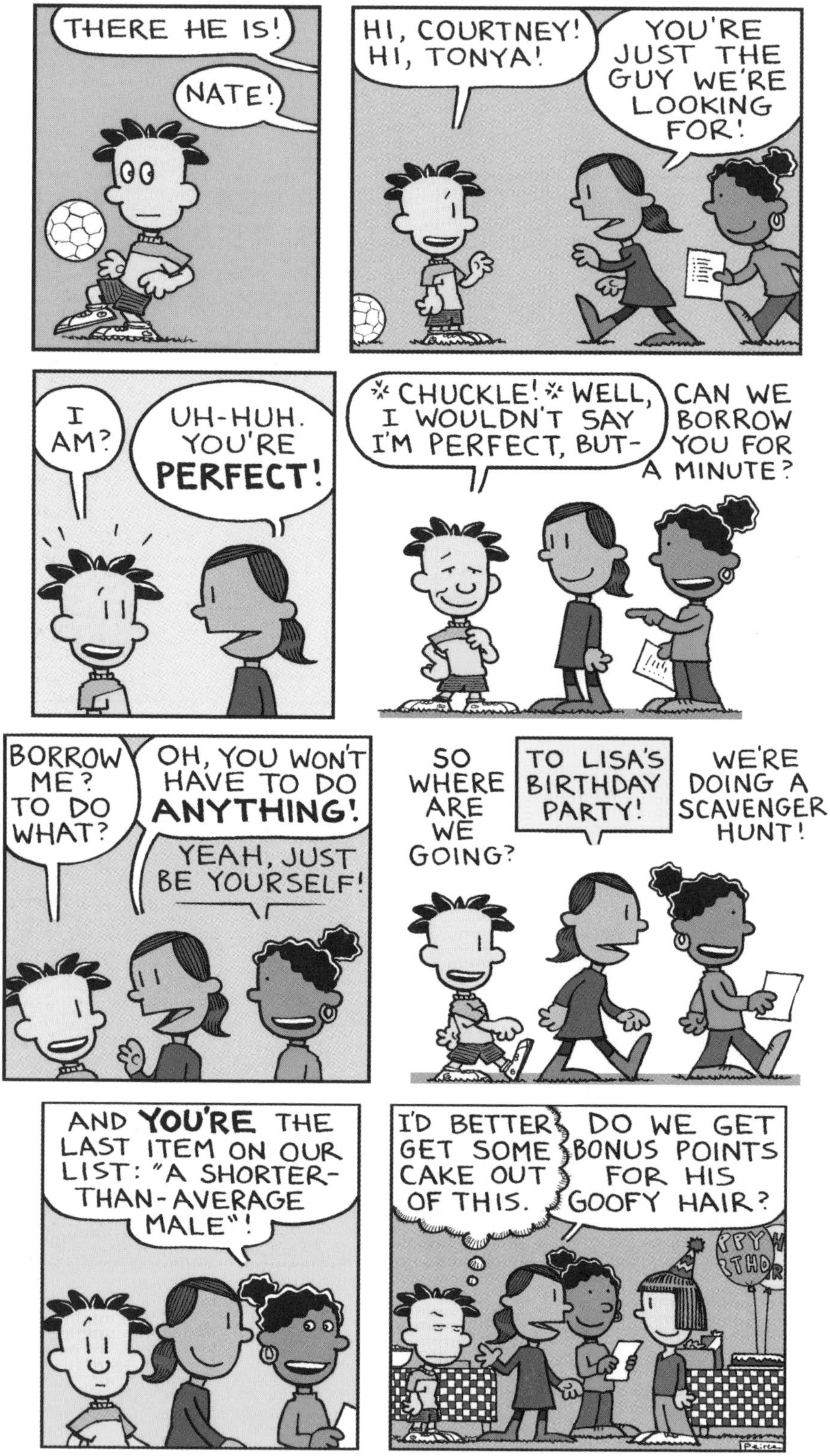
THERE HE IS!
NATE!
HI, COURTNEY! HI, TONYA!
YOU'RE JUST THE GUY WE'RE LOOKING FOR!
I AM?
UH-HUH. YOU'RE PERFECT!
CHUCKLE! WELL, I WOULDN'T SAY I'M PERFECT, BUT-
CAN WE BORROW YOU FOR A MINUTE?
BORROW ME? TO DO WHAT?
OH, YOU WON'T HAVE TO DO ANYTHING!
YEAH, JUST BE YOURSELF!
SO WHERE ARE WE GOING?
TO LISA'S BIRTHDAY PARTY!
WE'RE DOING A SCAVENGER HUNT!
AND YOU'RE THE LAST ITEM ON OUR LIST: "A SHORTER-THAN-AVERAGE MALE"!
I'D BETTER GET SOME CAKE OUT OF THIS.
DO WE GET BONUS POINTS FOR HIS GOOFY HAIR?
Peirce

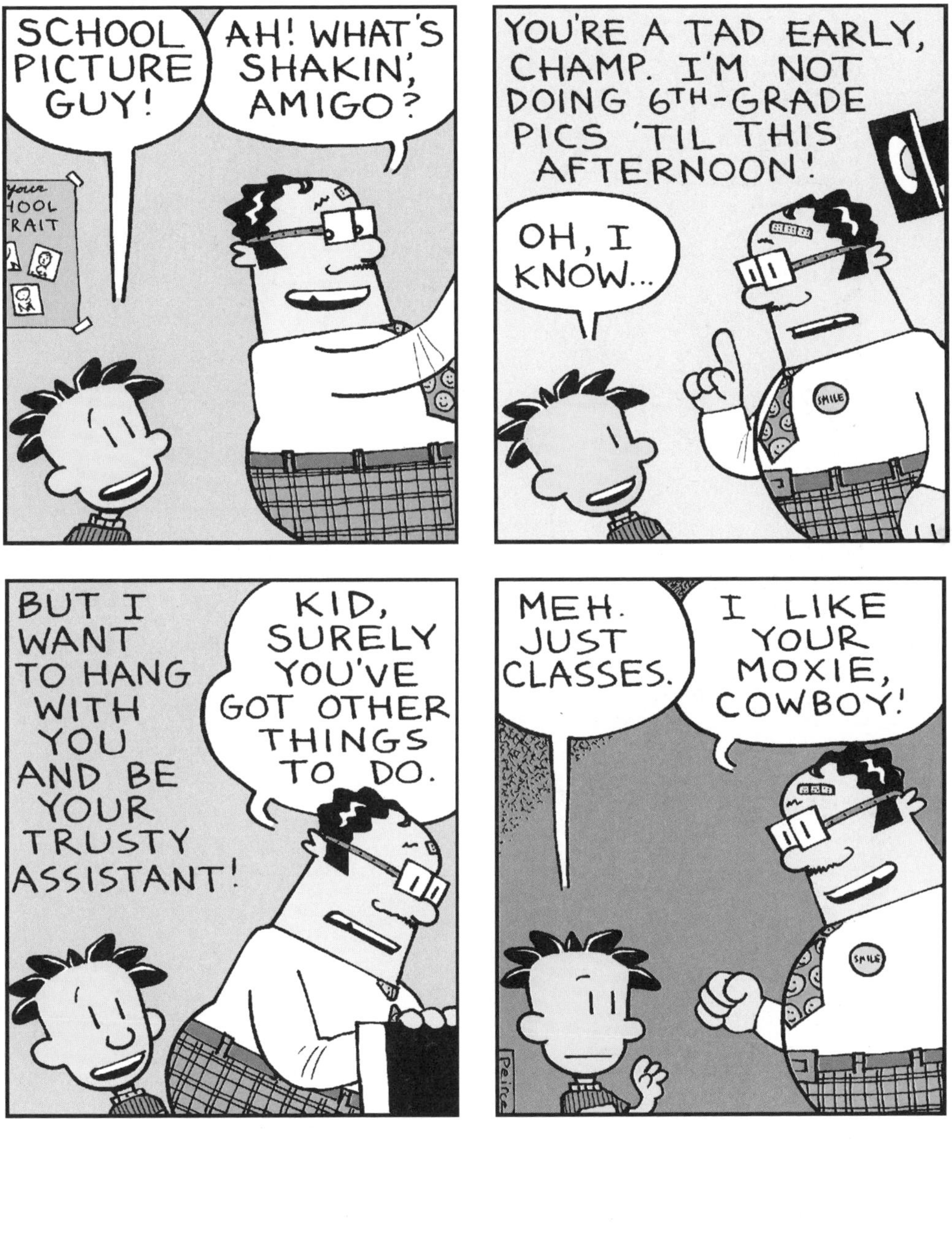
SCHOOL PICTURE GUY!
AH! WHAT'S SHAKIN', AMIGO?
YOU'RE A TAD EARLY, CHAMP. I'M NOT DOING 6TH-GRADE PICS 'TIL THIS AFTERNOON!
OH, I KNOW...
SMILE
BUT I WANT TO HANG WITH YOU AND BE YOUR TRUSTY ASSISTANT!
KID, SURELY YOU'VE GOT OTHER THINGS TO DO.
MEH. JUST CLASSES.
I LIKE YOUR MOXIE, COWBOY!
SMILE
Peirce

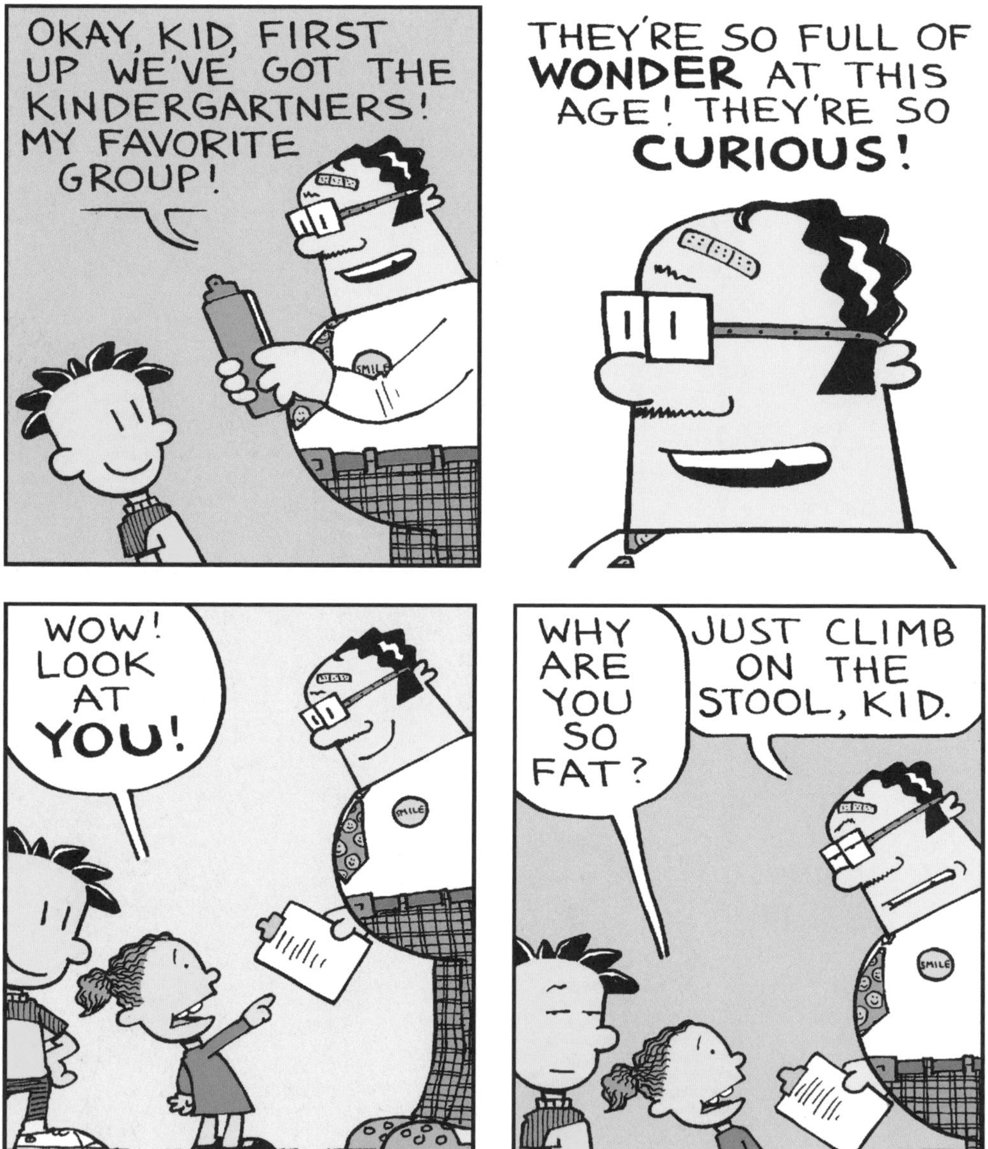
OKAY, KID, FIRST UP WE'VE GOT THE KINDERGARTNERS! MY FAVORITE GROUP!
THEY'RE SO FULL OF **WONDER** AT THIS AGE! THEY'RE SO **CURIOUS**!
WOW! LOOK AT **YOU**!
WHY ARE YOU SO FAT?
JUST CLIMB ON THE STOOL, KID.

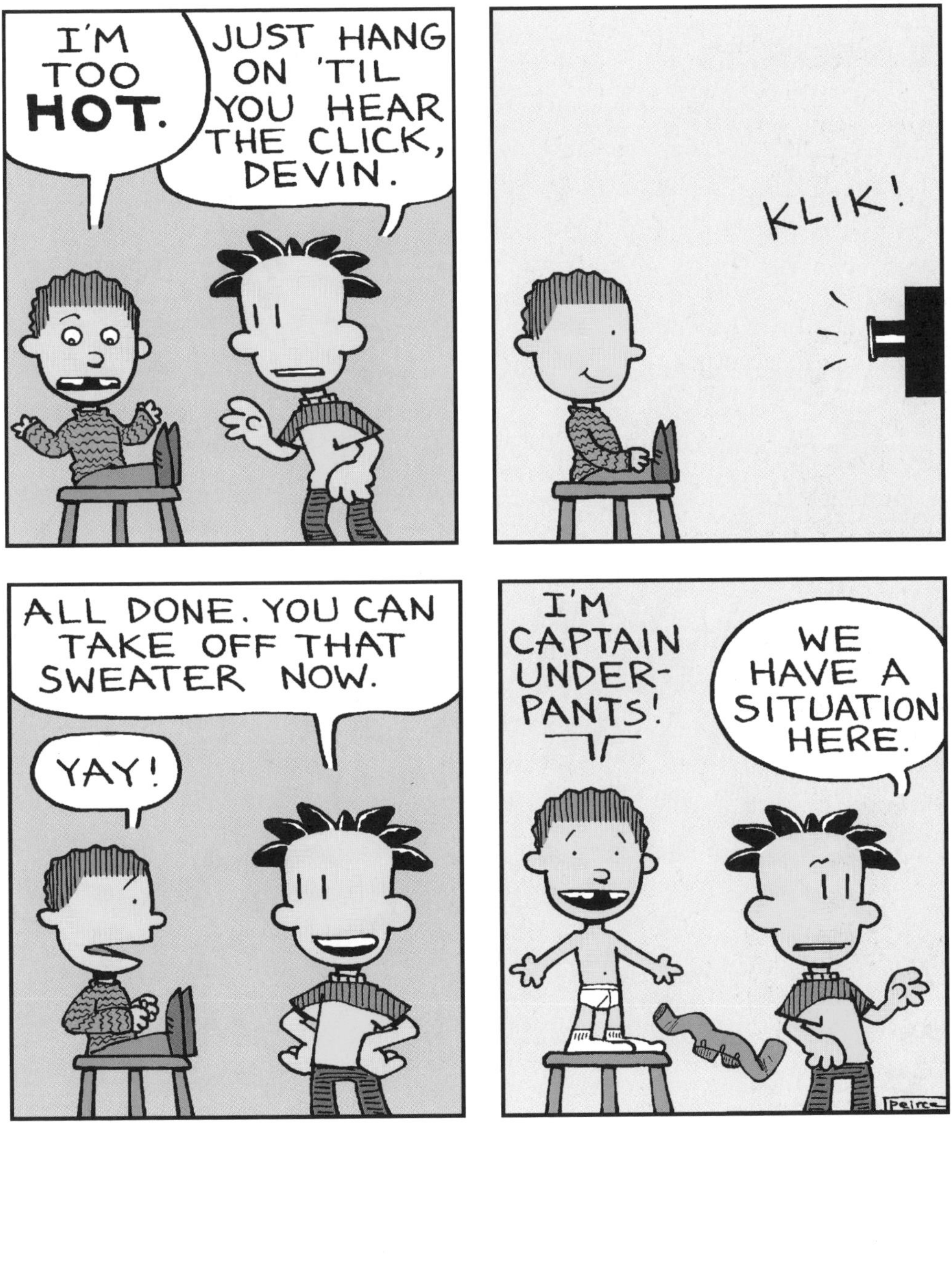
I'M TOO **HOT**.
JUST HANG ON 'TIL YOU HEAR THE CLICK, DEVIN.
KLIK!
ALL DONE. YOU CAN TAKE OFF THAT SWEATER NOW.
YAY!
I'M CAPTAIN UNDER-PANTS!
WE HAVE A SITUATION HERE.
Peirce

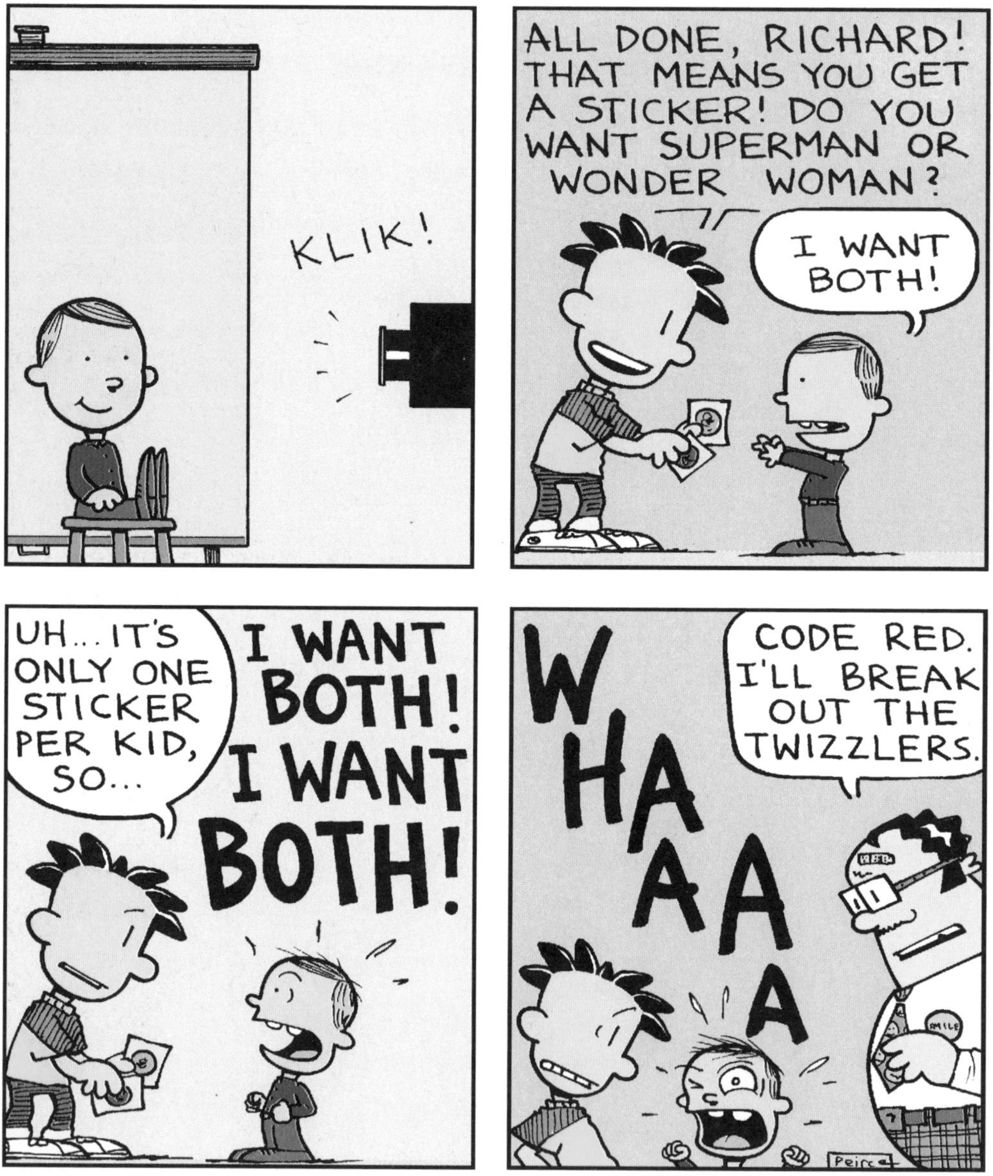
KLIK!
ALL DONE, RICHARD! THAT MEANS YOU GET A STICKER! DO YOU WANT SUPERMAN OR WONDER WOMAN?
I WANT BOTH!
UH... IT'S ONLY ONE STICKER PER KID, SO...
I WANT BOTH! I WANT BOTH!
WHAAAAA
CODE RED. I'LL BREAK OUT THE TWIZZLERS.
SMILE
Peirce

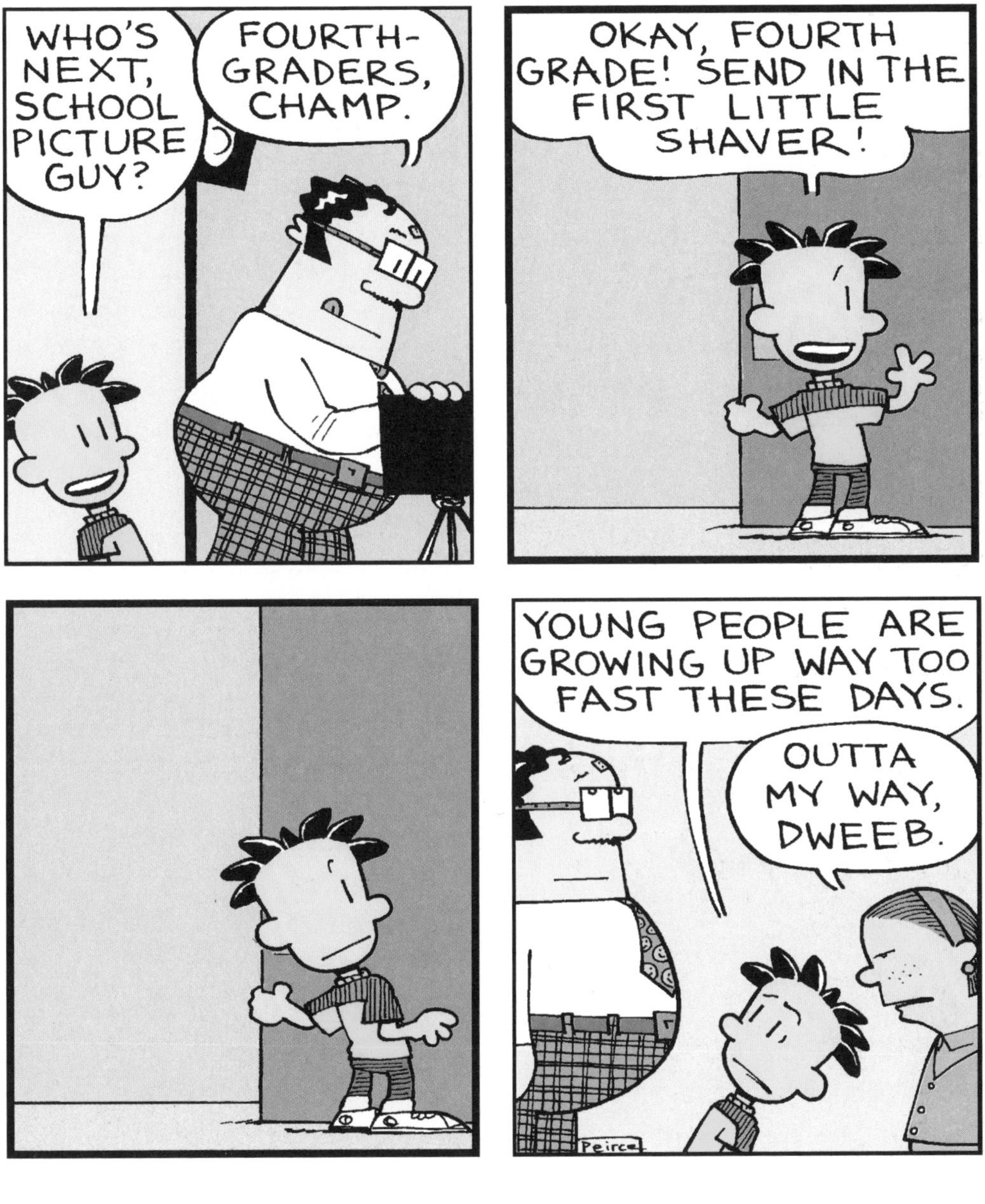
WHO'S NEXT, SCHOOL PICTURE GUY?
FOURTH-GRADERS, CHAMP.
OKAY, FOURTH GRADE! SEND IN THE FIRST LITTLE SHAVER!
YOUNG PEOPLE ARE GROWING UP WAY TOO FAST THESE DAYS.
OUTTA MY WAY, DWEEB.
Peirce

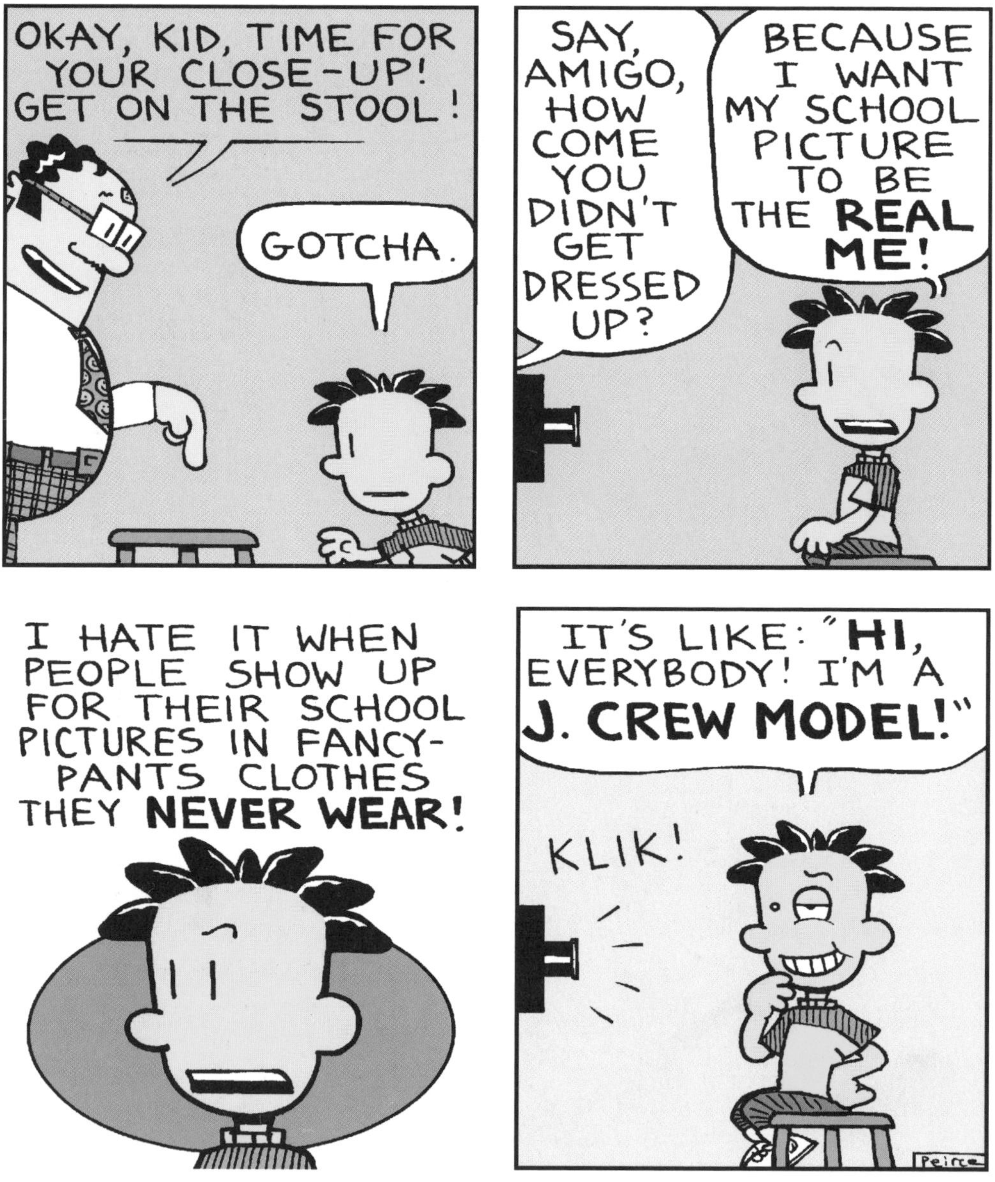
OKAY, KID, TIME FOR YOUR CLOSE-UP! GET ON THE STOOL!
GOTCHA.
SAY, AMIGO, HOW COME YOU DIDN'T GET DRESSED UP?
BECAUSE I WANT MY SCHOOL PICTURE TO BE THE **REAL ME!**
I HATE IT WHEN PEOPLE SHOW UP FOR THEIR SCHOOL PICTURES IN FANCY-PANTS CLOTHES THEY **NEVER WEAR!**
IT'S LIKE: "**HI**, EVERYBODY! I'M A **J. CREW MODEL!**"
KLIK!
Peirce

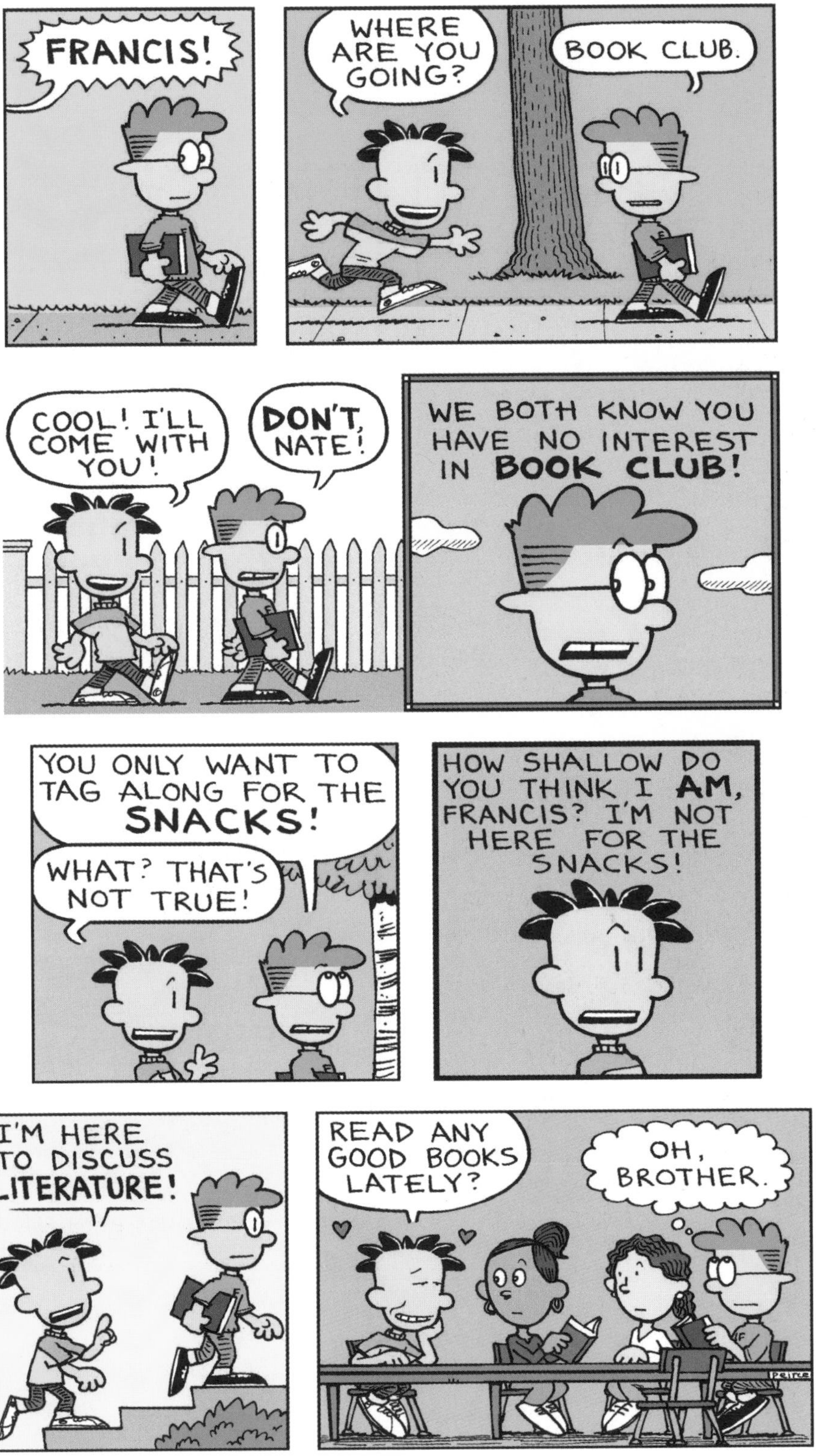
FRANCIS!
WHERE ARE YOU GOING?
BOOK CLUB.
COOL! I'LL COME WITH YOU!
DON'T, NATE!
WE BOTH KNOW YOU HAVE NO INTEREST IN BOOK CLUB!
YOU ONLY WANT TO TAG ALONG FOR THE SNACKS!
WHAT? THAT'S NOT TRUE!
HOW SHALLOW DO YOU THINK I AM, FRANCIS? I'M NOT HERE FOR THE SNACKS!
I'M HERE TO DISCUSS LITERATURE!
READ ANY GOOD BOOKS LATELY?
OH, BROTHER.
peirce

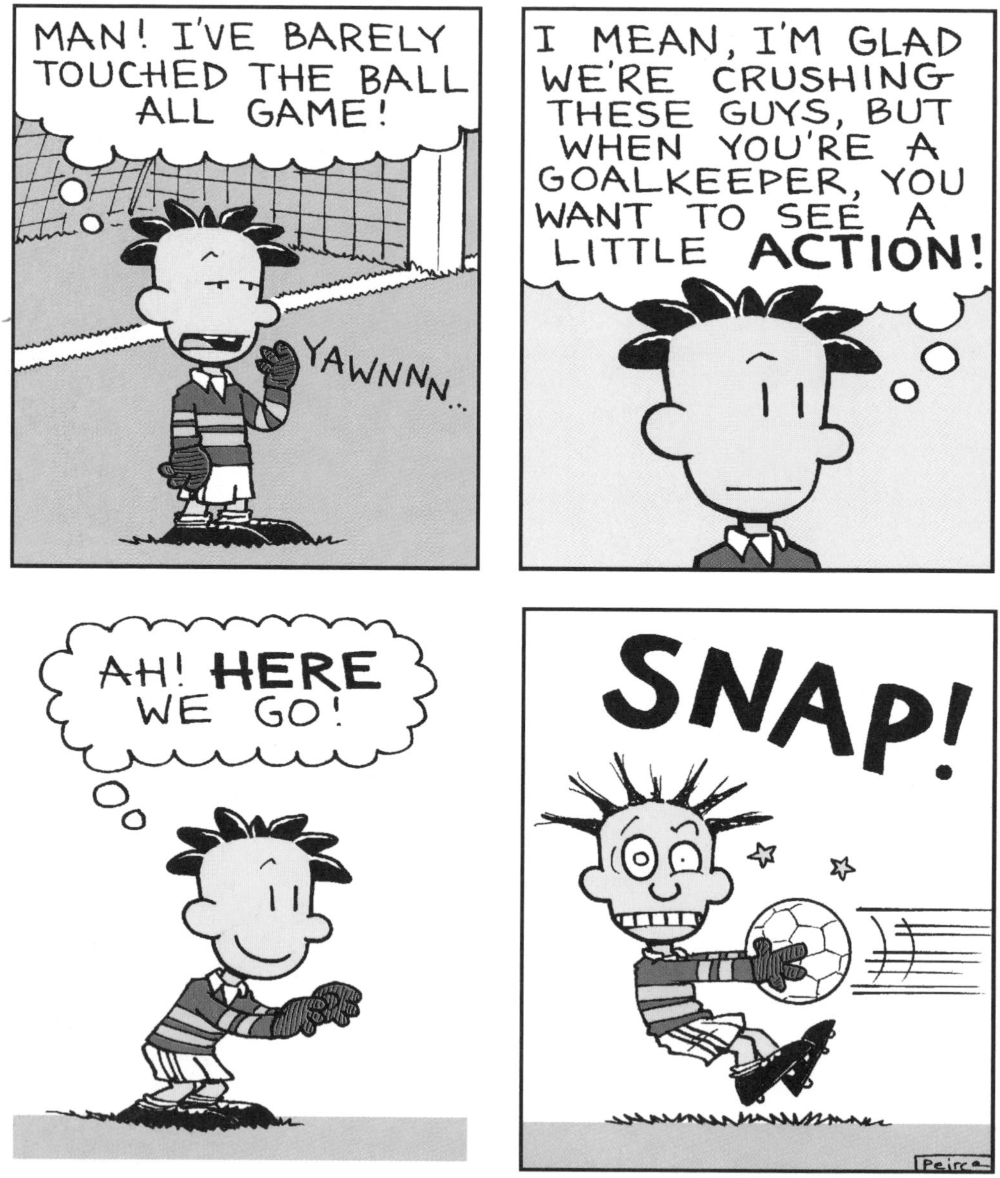
MAN! I'VE BARELY TOUCHED THE BALL ALL GAME!
YAWNNN...
I MEAN, I'M GLAD WE'RE CRUSHING THESE GUYS, BUT WHEN YOU'RE A GOALKEEPER, YOU WANT TO SEE A LITTLE **ACTION**!
AH! **HERE** WE GO!
SNAP!
Peirce

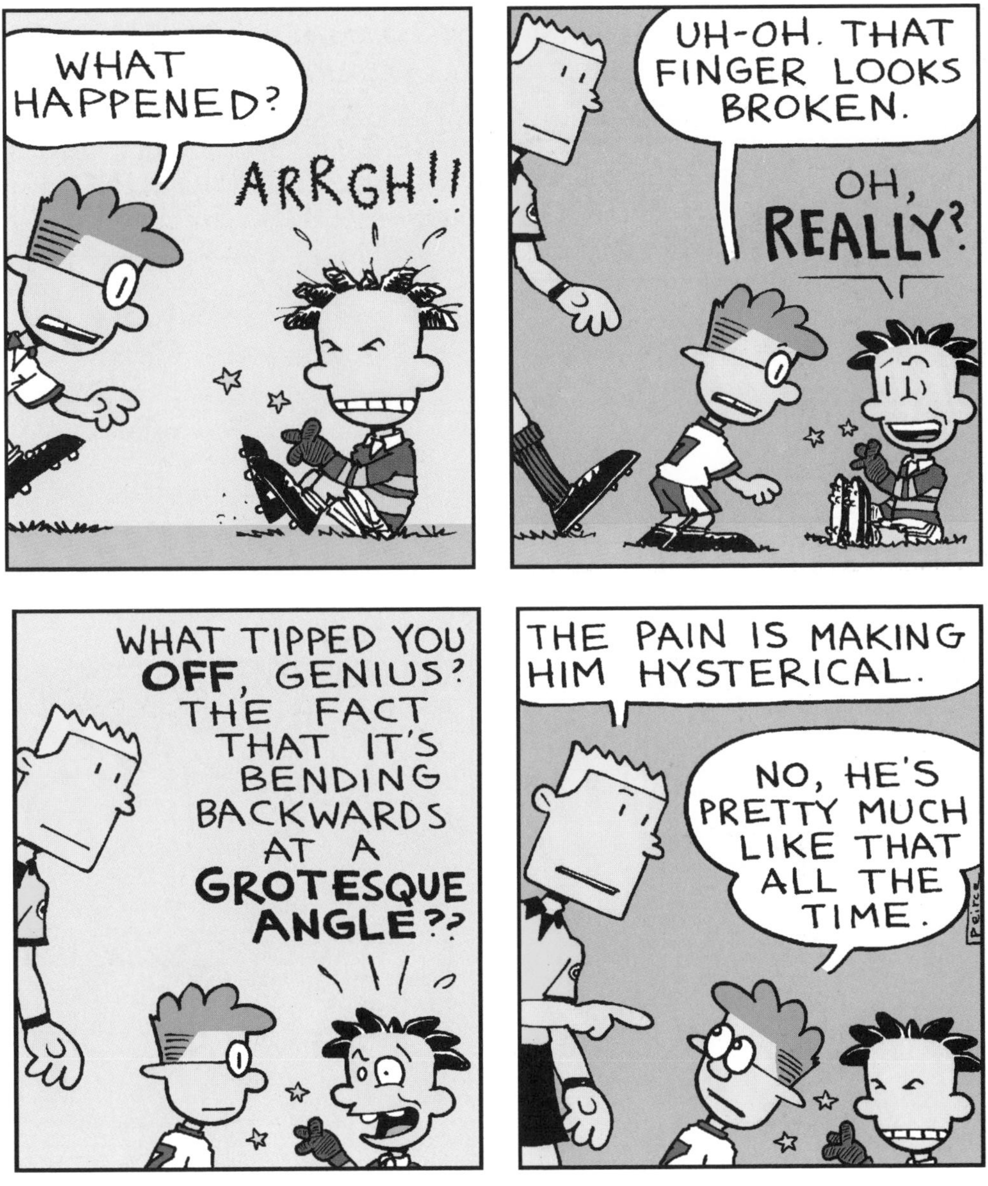
WHAT HAPPENED?
ARRGH!!
UH-OH. THAT FINGER LOOKS BROKEN.
OH, REALLY?
WHAT TIPPED YOU OFF, GENIUS? THE FACT THAT IT'S BENDING BACKWARDS AT A GROTESQUE ANGLE??
THE PAIN IS MAKING HIM HYSTERICAL.
NO, HE'S PRETTY MUCH LIKE THAT ALL THE TIME.
Peirce

IT'S A NICE, CLEAN BREAK. IT SHOULD HEAL QUICKLY.

OKAY. HOW MUCH SCHOOL WILL I MISS?

YOU SHOULDN'T HAVE TO MISS **ANY** SCHOOL. YOUR ONLY PROBLEM MIGHT BE SOME ITCHING UNDER YOUR SPLINT.

OH.

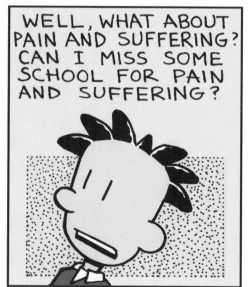

WELL, WHAT ABOUT PAIN AND SUFFERING? CAN I MISS SOME SCHOOL FOR PAIN AND SUFFERING?

THAT WOULD BE A FAMILY DECISION.

DAD?

NO.

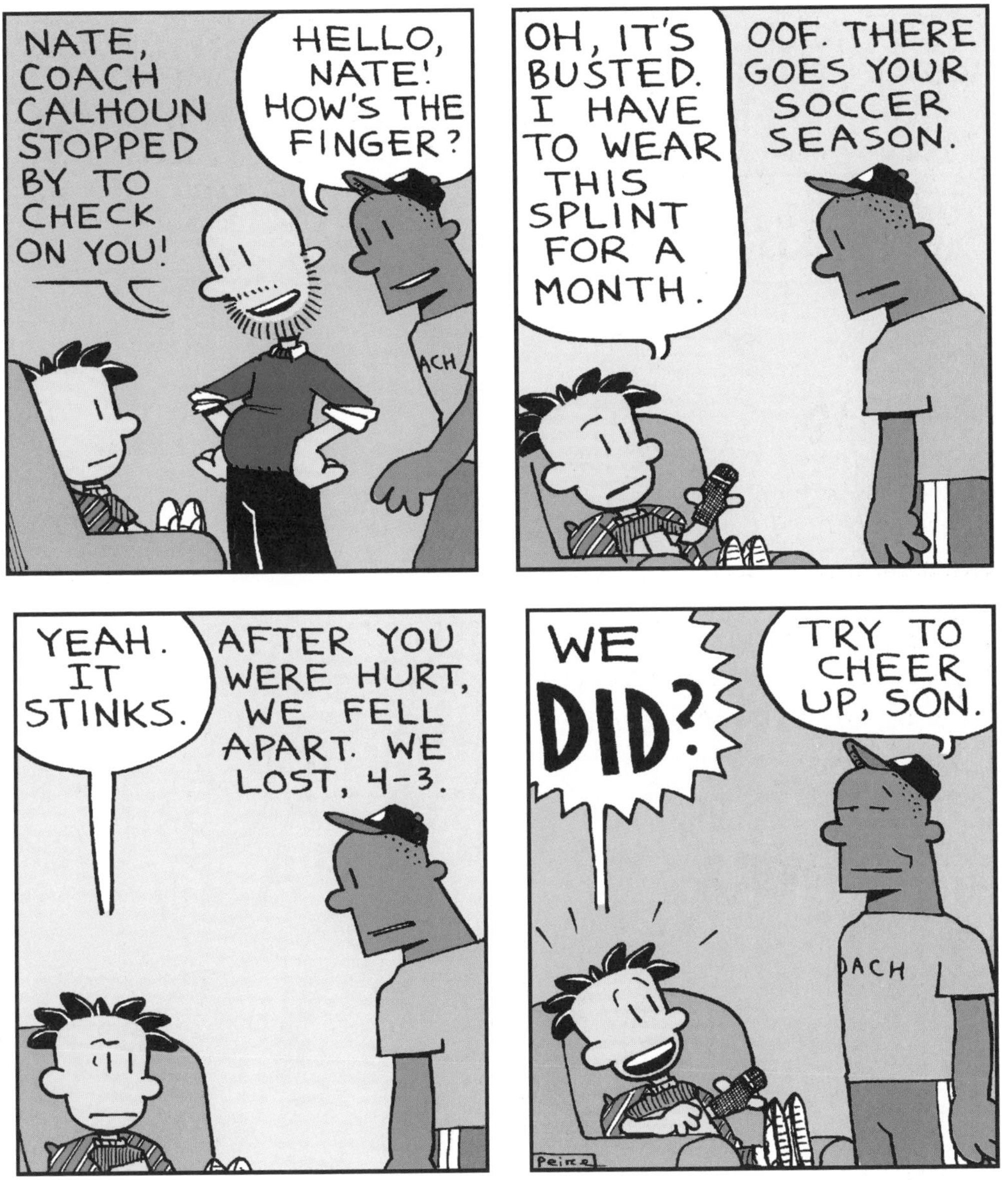
NATE, COACH CALHOUN STOPPED BY TO CHECK ON YOU!
HELLO, NATE! HOW'S THE FINGER?
ACH
OH, IT'S BUSTED. I HAVE TO WEAR THIS SPLINT FOR A MONTH.
OOF. THERE GOES YOUR SOCCER SEASON.
YEAH. IT STINKS.
AFTER YOU WERE HURT, WE FELL APART. WE LOST, 4-3.
WE DID?
TRY TO CHEER UP, SON.
ACH
Peirce

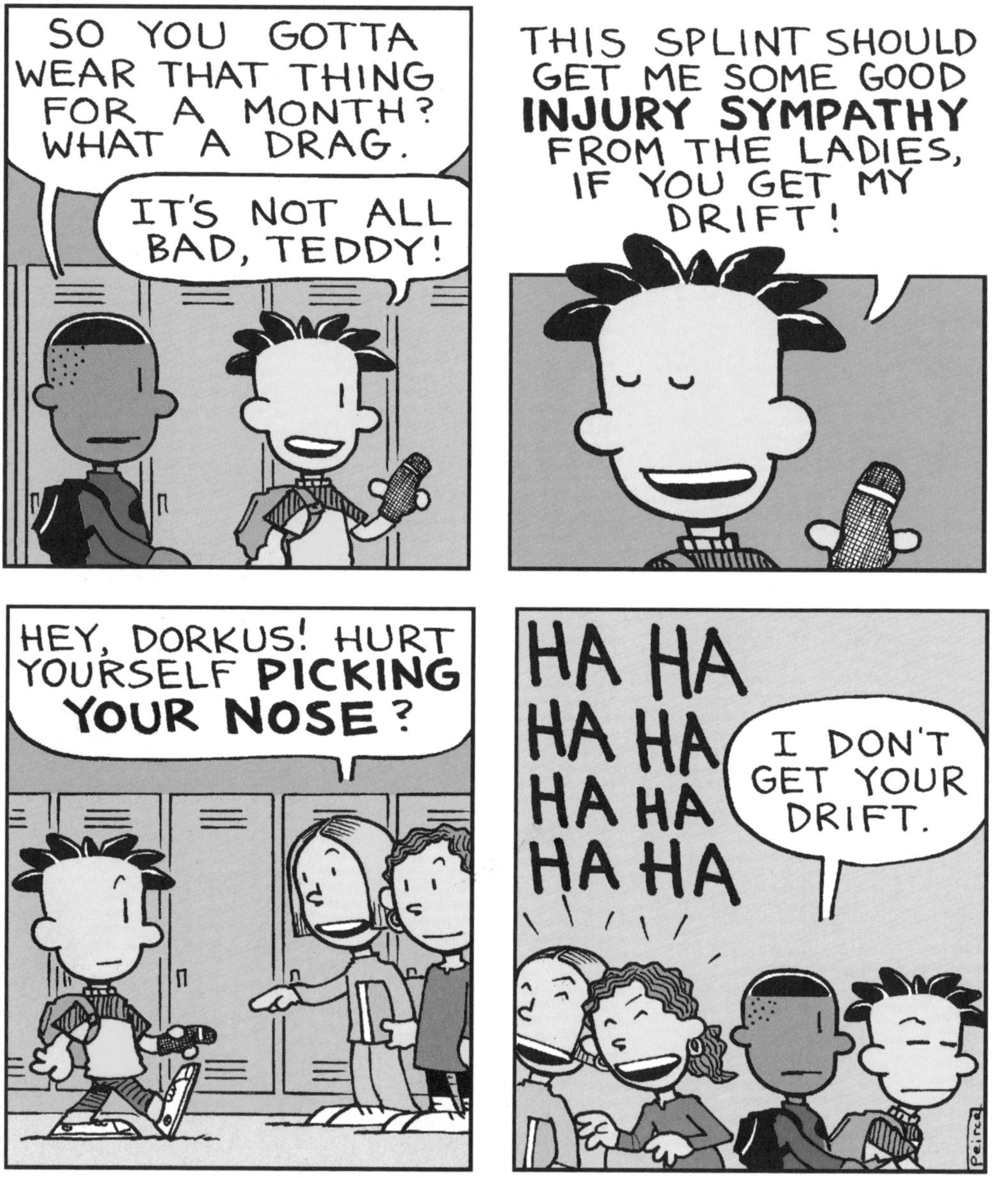
SO YOU GOTTA WEAR THAT THING FOR A MONTH? WHAT A DRAG.
IT'S NOT ALL BAD, TEDDY!
THIS SPLINT SHOULD GET ME SOME GOOD **INJURY SYMPATHY** FROM THE LADIES, IF YOU GET MY DRIFT!
HEY, DORKUS! HURT YOURSELF **PICKING YOUR NOSE**?
HA HA HA HA HA HA HA HA
I DON'T GET YOUR DRIFT.
Peirce

YOU PROBABLY HEARD ABOUT THE GAME YESTERDAY.

THAT WE LOST? YEAH.

WE LOST BECAUSE OF **ME**! AFTER YOUR INJURY, COACH MADE ME PLAY GOALIE!

TURNS OUT THAT IN ADDITION TO CLOWNS, ROLLER COASTERS, AND GREEK YOGURT, I'M ALSO AFRAID OF SOCCER BALLS!

YOU GAVE IT THE OL' COLLEGE TRY, CHAD.

COLLEGE! THAT'S **ANOTHER** THING THAT FREAKS ME OUT!

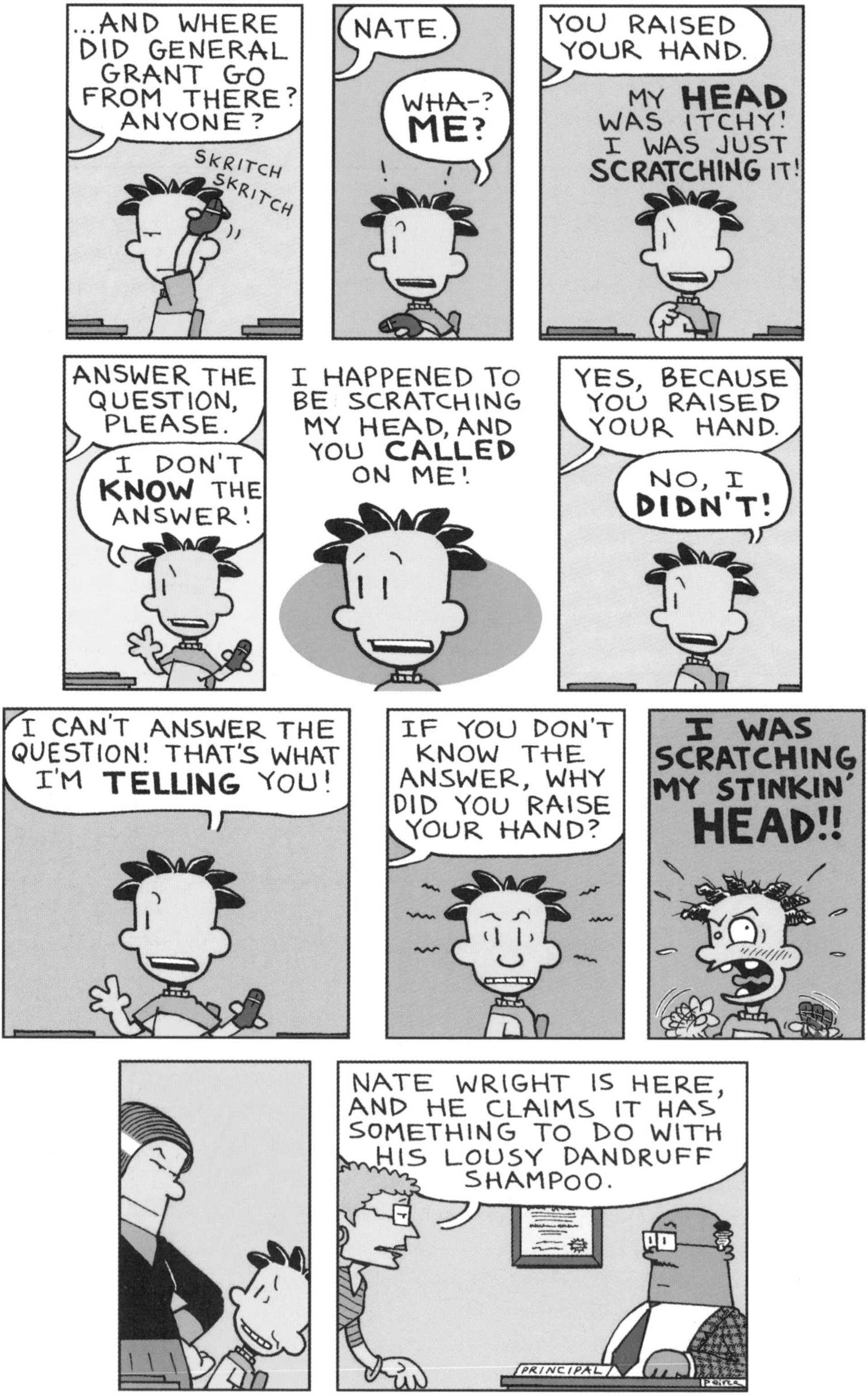
...AND WHERE DID GENERAL GRANT GO FROM THERE? ANYONE?
SKRITCH SKRITCH
NATE.
WHA-? ME?
YOU RAISED YOUR HAND.
MY HEAD WAS ITCHY! I WAS JUST SCRATCHING IT!
ANSWER THE QUESTION, PLEASE.
I DON'T KNOW THE ANSWER!
I HAPPENED TO BE SCRATCHING MY HEAD, AND YOU CALLED ON ME!
YES, BECAUSE YOU RAISED YOUR HAND.
NO, I DIDN'T!
I CAN'T ANSWER THE QUESTION! THAT'S WHAT I'M TELLING YOU!
IF YOU DON'T KNOW THE ANSWER, WHY DID YOU RAISE YOUR HAND?
I WAS SCRATCHING MY STINKIN' HEAD!!
NATE WRIGHT IS HERE, AND HE CLAIMS IT HAS SOMETHING TO DO WITH HIS LOUSY DANDRUFF SHAMPOO.
PRINCIPAL
PEIRCE

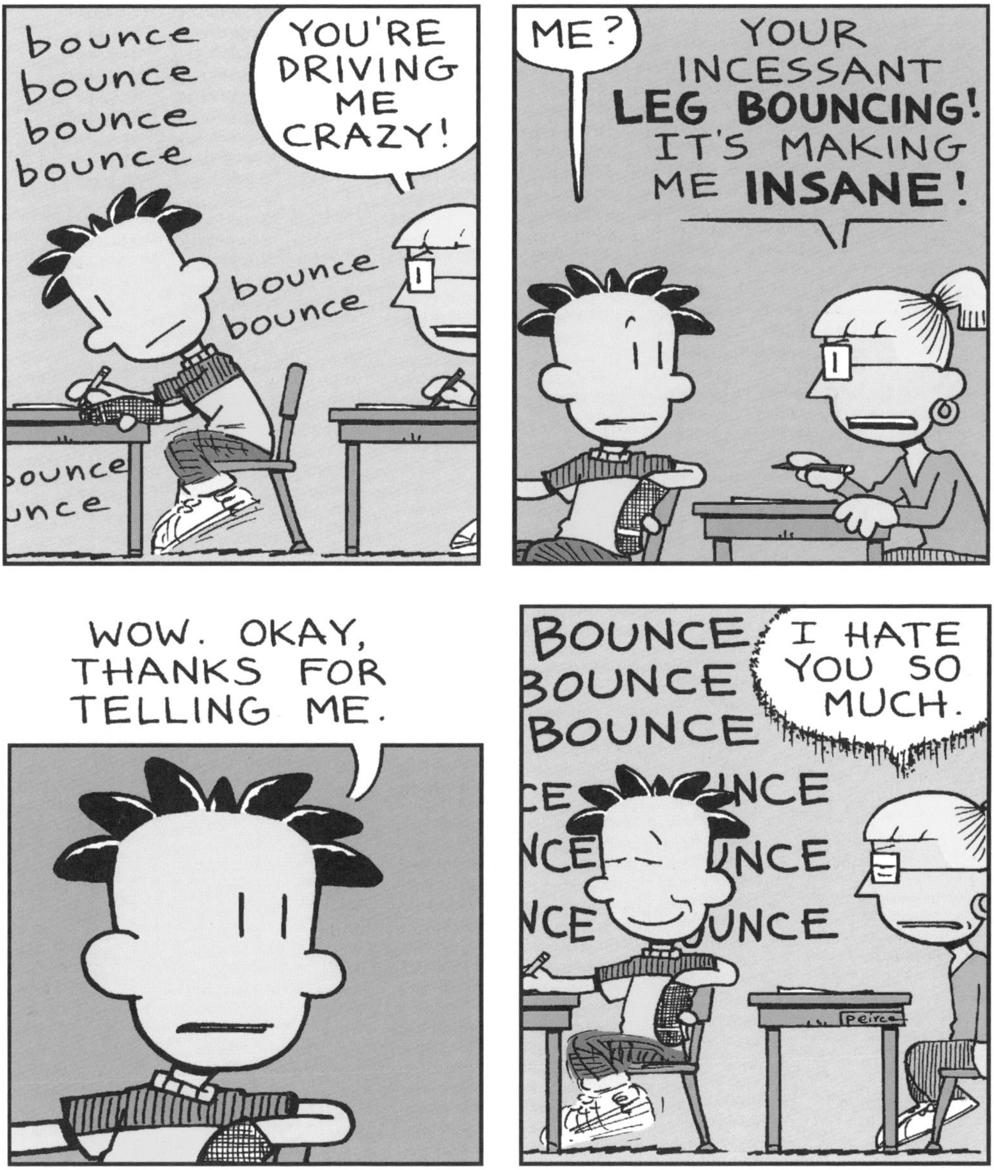
bounce
bounce
bounce
bounce
YOU'RE DRIVING ME CRAZY!
bounce
bounce
ME?
YOUR INCESSANT LEG BOUNCING! IT'S MAKING ME INSANE!
WOW. OKAY, THANKS FOR TELLING ME.
BOUNCE
BOUNCE
BOUNCE
I HATE YOU SO MUCH.
peirce

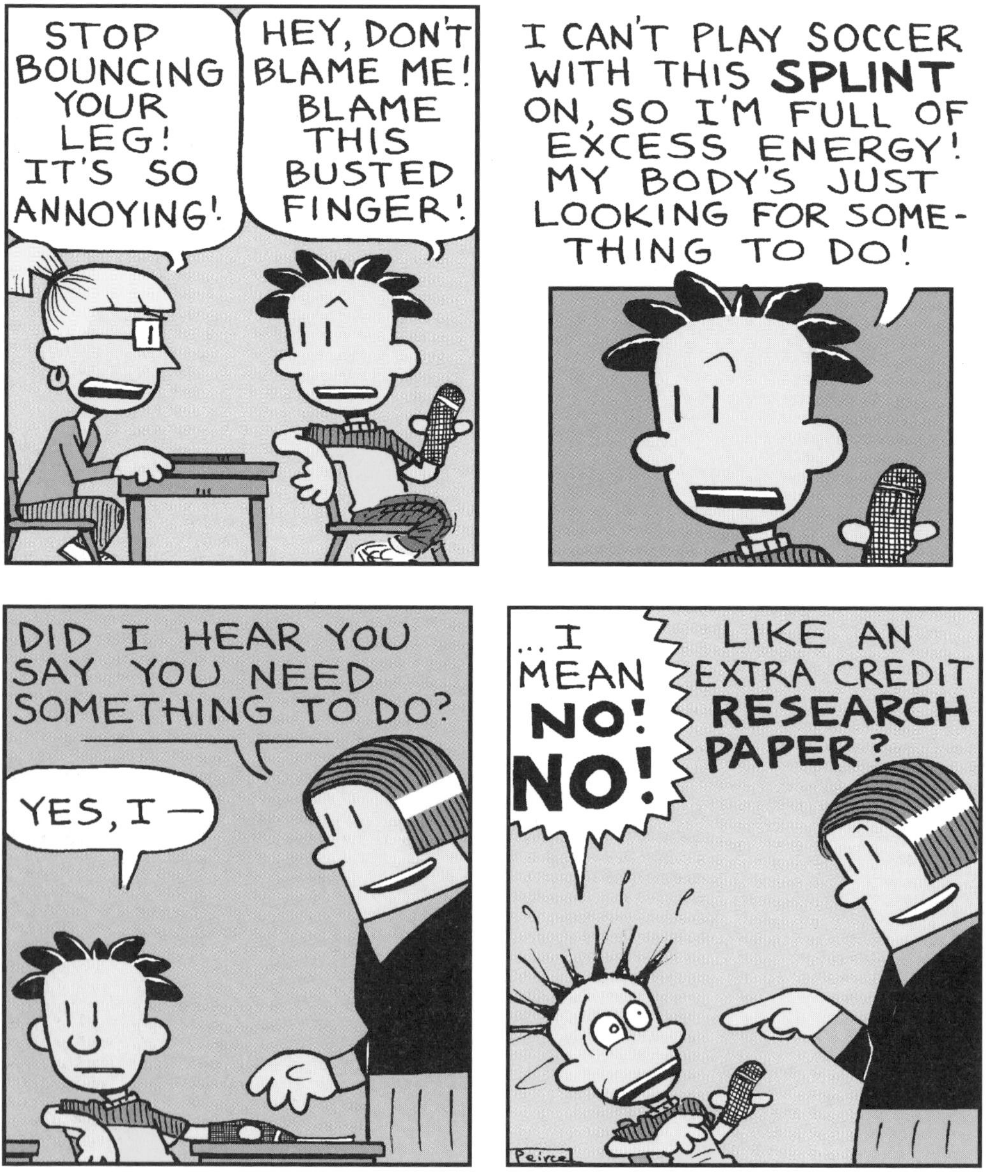
STOP BOUNCING YOUR LEG! IT'S SO ANNOYING!
HEY, DON'T BLAME ME! BLAME THIS BUSTED FINGER!
I CAN'T PLAY SOCCER WITH THIS **SPLINT** ON, SO I'M FULL OF EXCESS ENERGY! MY BODY'S JUST LOOKING FOR SOME-THING TO DO!
DID I HEAR YOU SAY YOU NEED SOMETHING TO DO?
YES, I —
LIKE AN EXTRA CREDIT **RESEARCH PAPER**?
...I MEAN **NO! NO!**
Peirce

MRS. GODFREY, THIS ISN'T FAIR!

WHAT ISN'T FAIR?

MAKING ME DO AN EXTRA CREDIT RESEARCH PAPER!

NATE, EXTRA CREDIT ISN'T A **PUNISH-MENT**!

THEN WHAT IS IT?

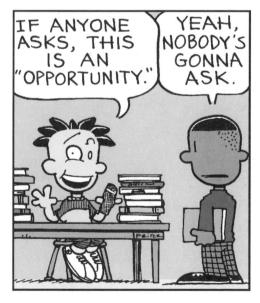

IF ANYONE ASKS, THIS IS AN "OPPORTUNITY."

YEAH, NOBODY'S GONNA ASK.

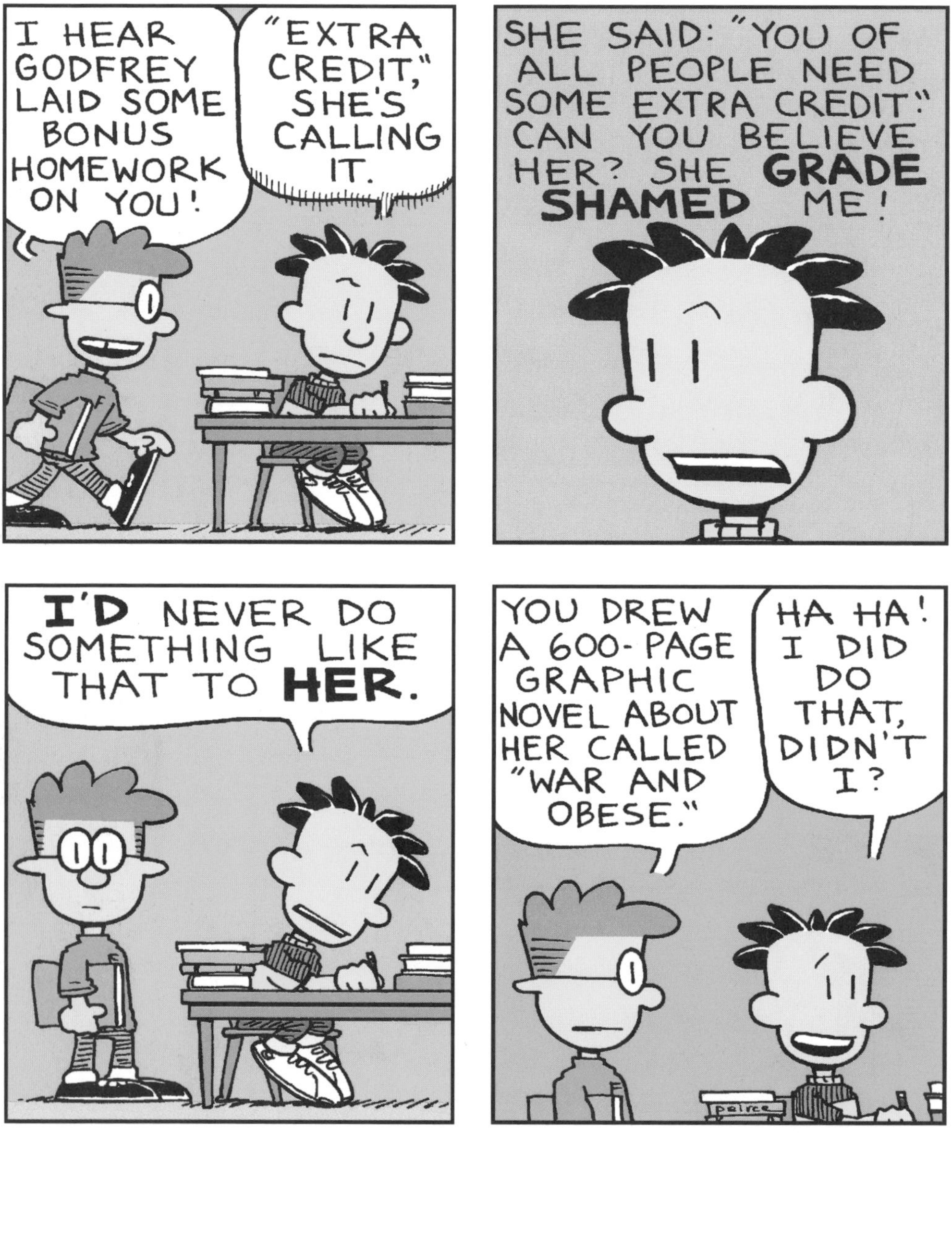
I HEAR GODFREY LAID SOME BONUS HOMEWORK ON YOU!
"EXTRA CREDIT," SHE'S CALLING IT.
SHE SAID: "YOU OF ALL PEOPLE NEED SOME EXTRA CREDIT." CAN YOU BELIEVE HER? SHE **GRADE SHAMED** ME!
I'D NEVER DO SOMETHING LIKE THAT TO **HER**.
YOU DREW A 600-PAGE GRAPHIC NOVEL ABOUT HER CALLED "WAR AND OBESE."
HA HA! I DID DO THAT, DIDN'T I?
peirce

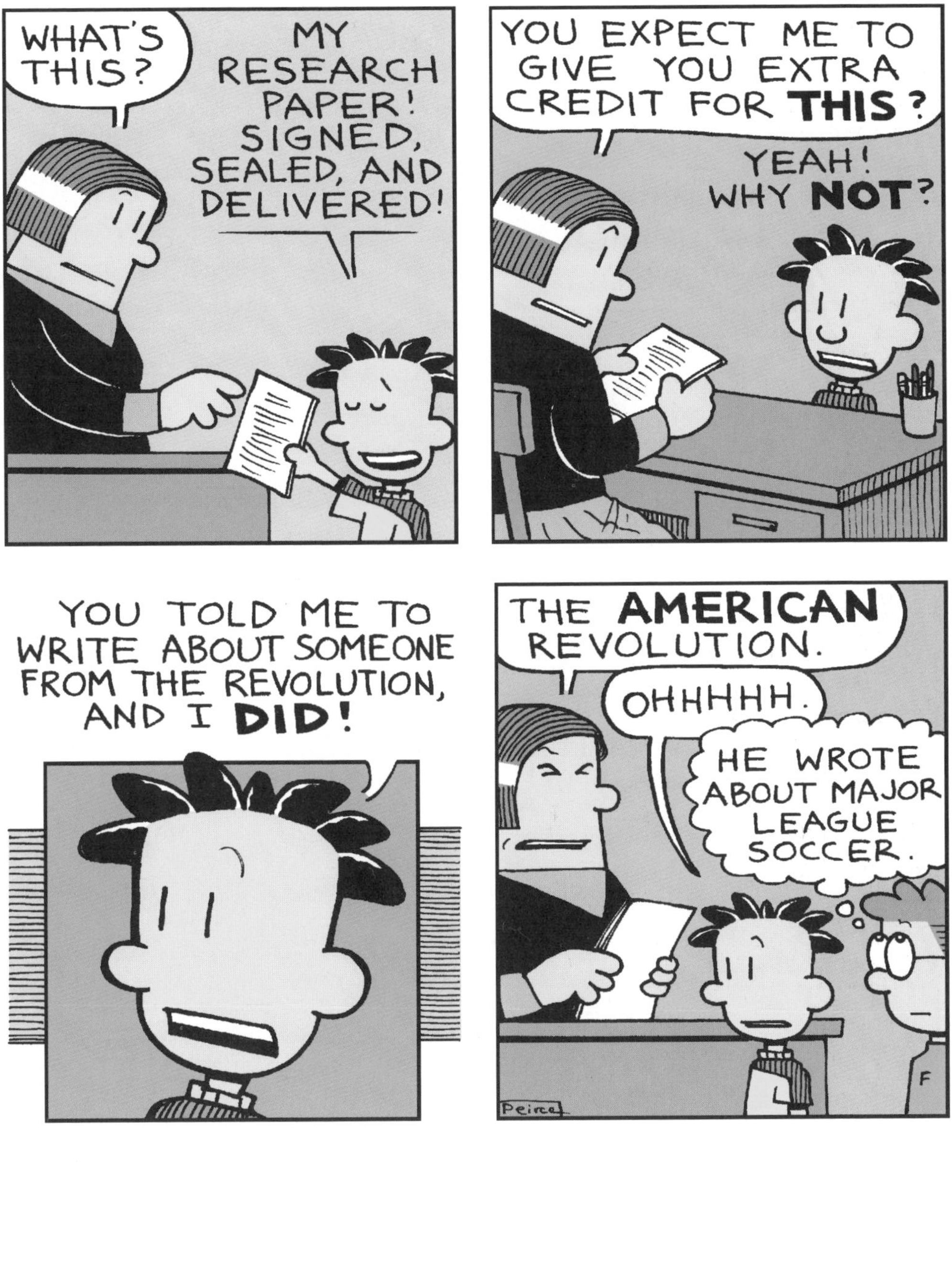
WHAT'S THIS?
MY RESEARCH PAPER! SIGNED, SEALED, AND DELIVERED!
YOU EXPECT ME TO GIVE YOU EXTRA CREDIT FOR **THIS**?
YEAH! WHY **NOT**?
YOU TOLD ME TO WRITE ABOUT SOMEONE FROM THE REVOLUTION, AND I **DID**!
THE **AMERICAN** REVOLUTION.
OHHHHH.
HE WROTE ABOUT MAJOR LEAGUE SOCCER.
Peirce

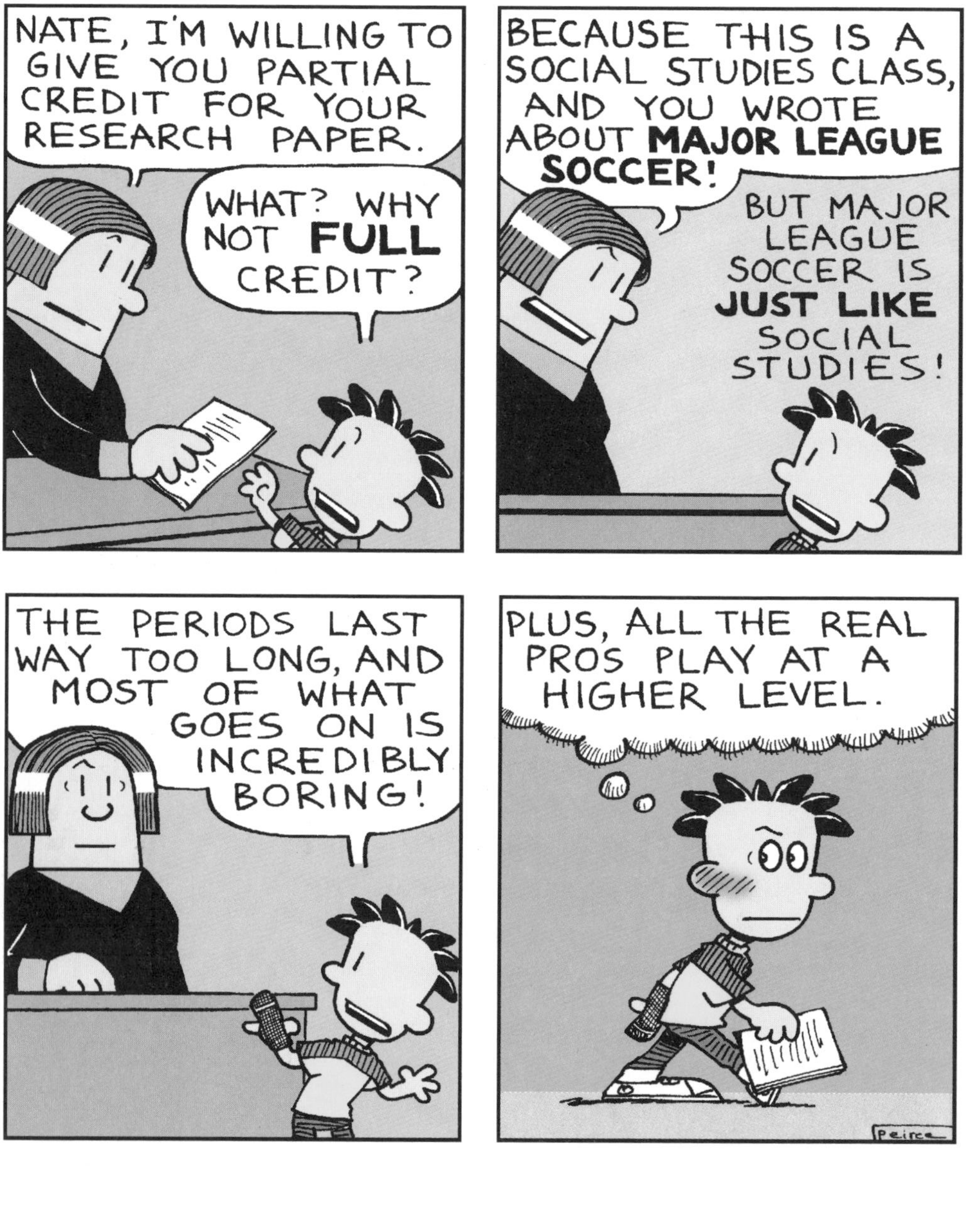
NATE, I'M WILLING TO GIVE YOU PARTIAL CREDIT FOR YOUR RESEARCH PAPER.
WHAT? WHY NOT **FULL** CREDIT?
BECAUSE THIS IS A SOCIAL STUDIES CLASS, AND YOU WROTE ABOUT **MAJOR LEAGUE SOCCER!**
BUT MAJOR LEAGUE SOCCER IS **JUST LIKE** SOCIAL STUDIES!
THE PERIODS LAST WAY TOO LONG, AND MOST OF WHAT GOES ON IS INCREDIBLY BORING!
PLUS, ALL THE REAL PROS PLAY AT A HIGHER LEVEL.
Peirce

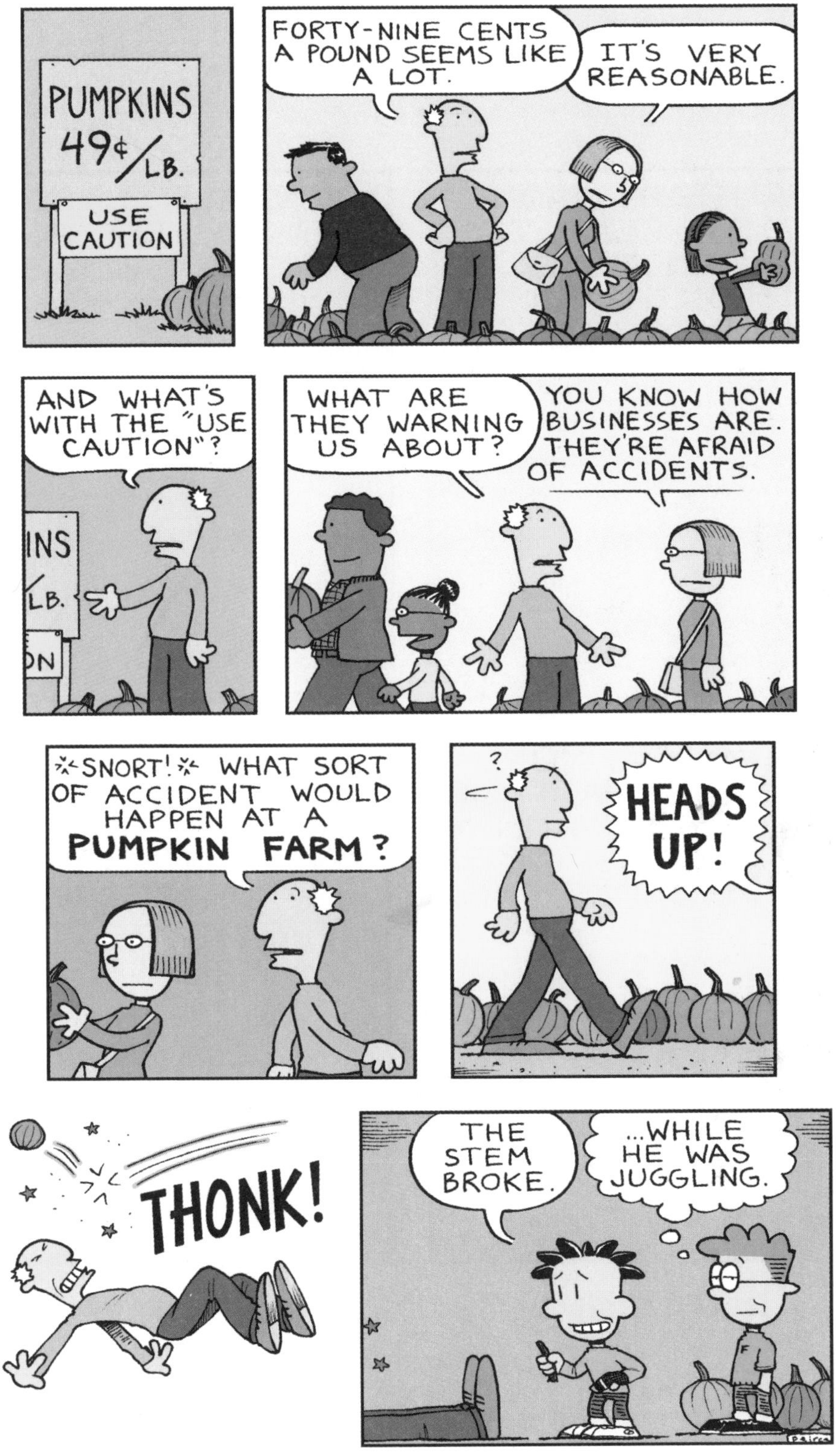
PUMPKINS 49¢/LB.
USE CAUTION
FORTY-NINE CENTS A POUND SEEMS LIKE A LOT.
IT'S VERY REASONABLE.
AND WHAT'S WITH THE "USE CAUTION"?
INS
LB.
ON
WHAT ARE THEY WARNING US ABOUT?
YOU KNOW HOW BUSINESSES ARE. THEY'RE AFRAID OF ACCIDENTS.
SNORT! WHAT SORT OF ACCIDENT WOULD HAPPEN AT A **PUMPKIN FARM**?
?
HEADS UP!
THONK!
THE STEM BROKE.
...WHILE HE WAS JUGGLING.

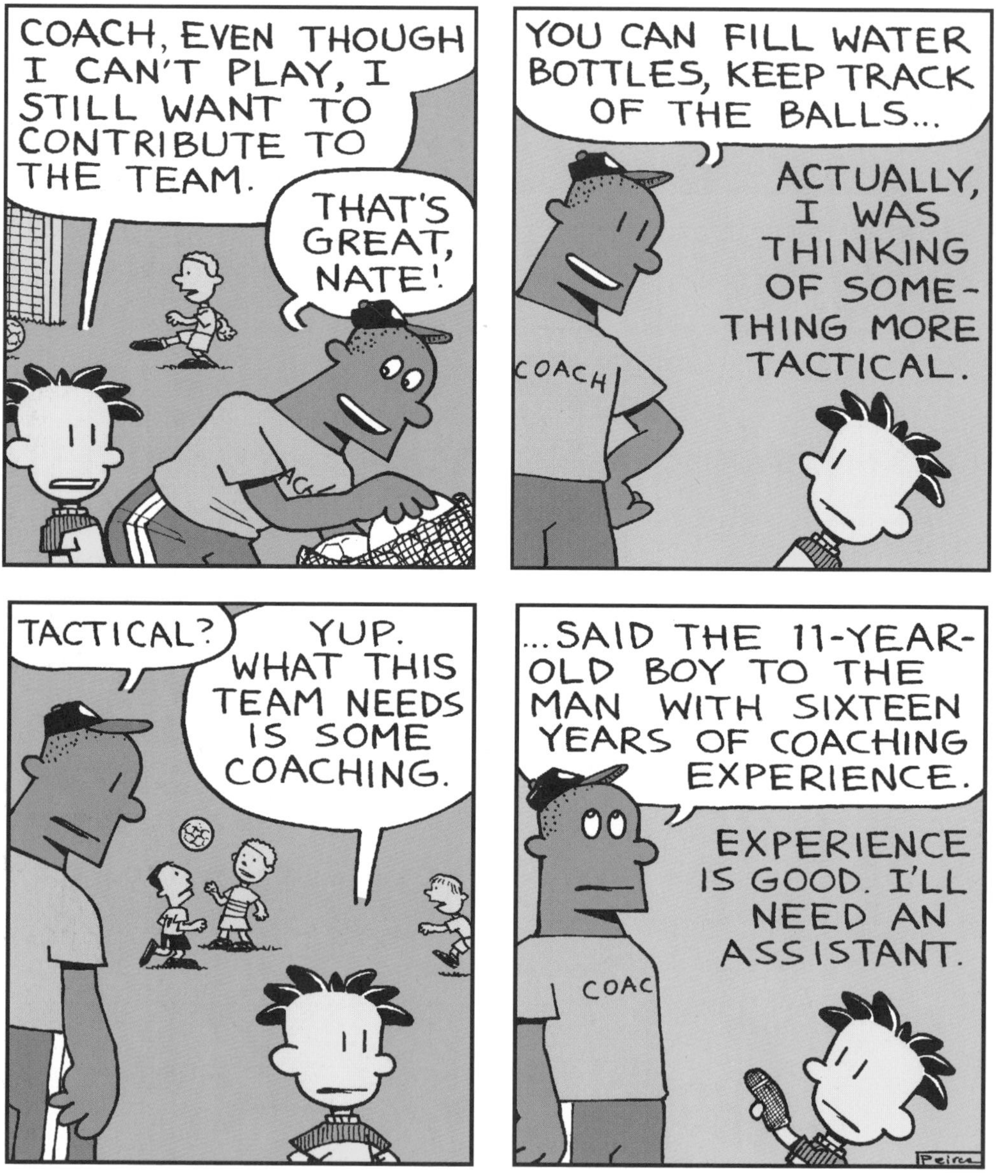
COACH, EVEN THOUGH I CAN'T PLAY, I STILL WANT TO CONTRIBUTE TO THE TEAM.
THAT'S GREAT, NATE!
YOU CAN FILL WATER BOTTLES, KEEP TRACK OF THE BALLS...
ACTUALLY, I WAS THINKING OF SOMETHING MORE TACTICAL.
COACH
TACTICAL?
YUP. WHAT THIS TEAM NEEDS IS SOME COACHING.
...SAID THE 11-YEAR-OLD BOY TO THE MAN WITH SIXTEEN YEARS OF COACHING EXPERIENCE.
EXPERIENCE IS GOOD. I'LL NEED AN ASSISTANT.
COAC
Peirce

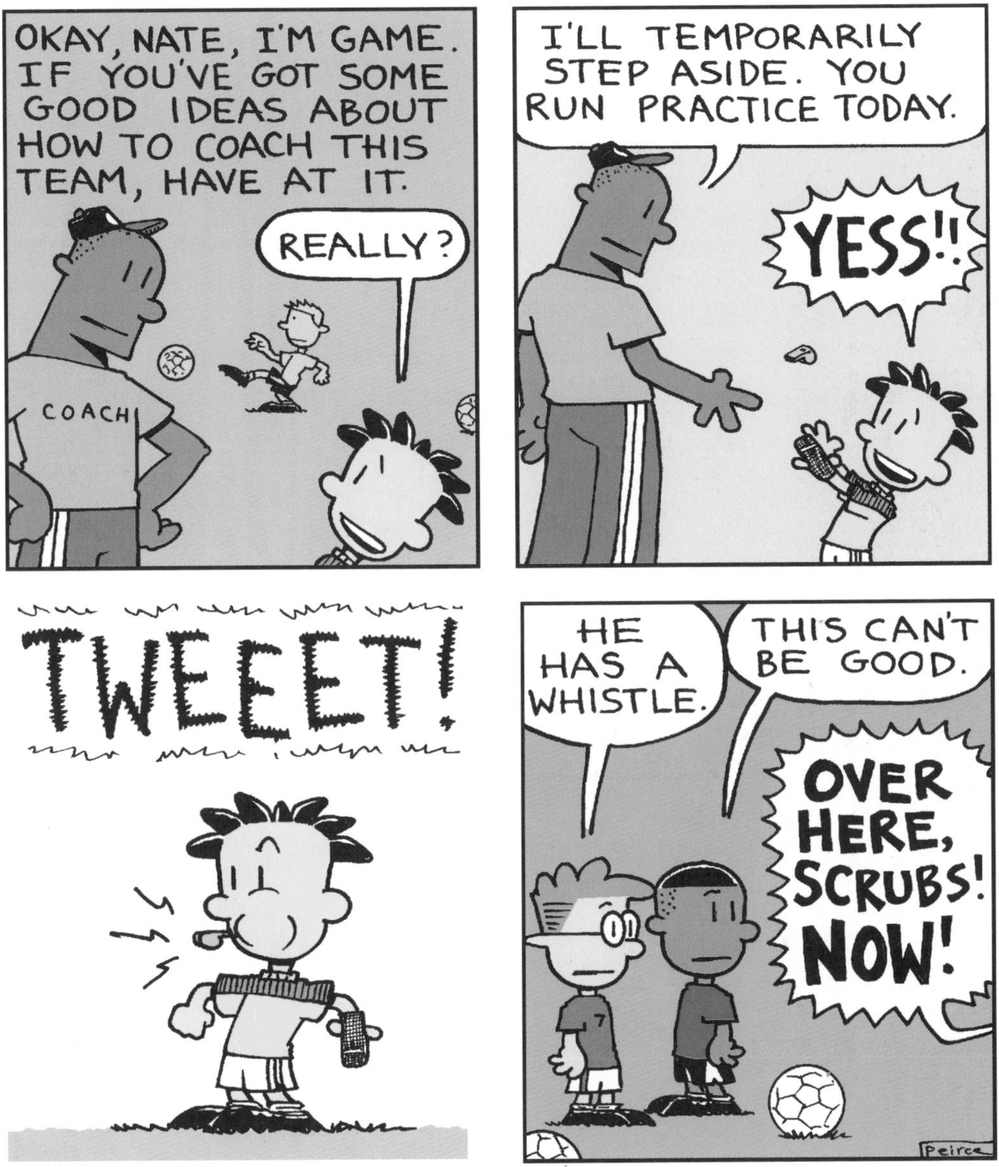
OKAY, NATE, I'M GAME. IF YOU'VE GOT SOME GOOD IDEAS ABOUT HOW TO COACH THIS TEAM, HAVE AT IT.
COACH
REALLY?
I'LL TEMPORARILY STEP ASIDE. YOU RUN PRACTICE TODAY.
YESS!!
TWEEET!
HE HAS A WHISTLE.
THIS CAN'T BE GOOD.
OVER HERE, SCRUBS! NOW!
Peirce

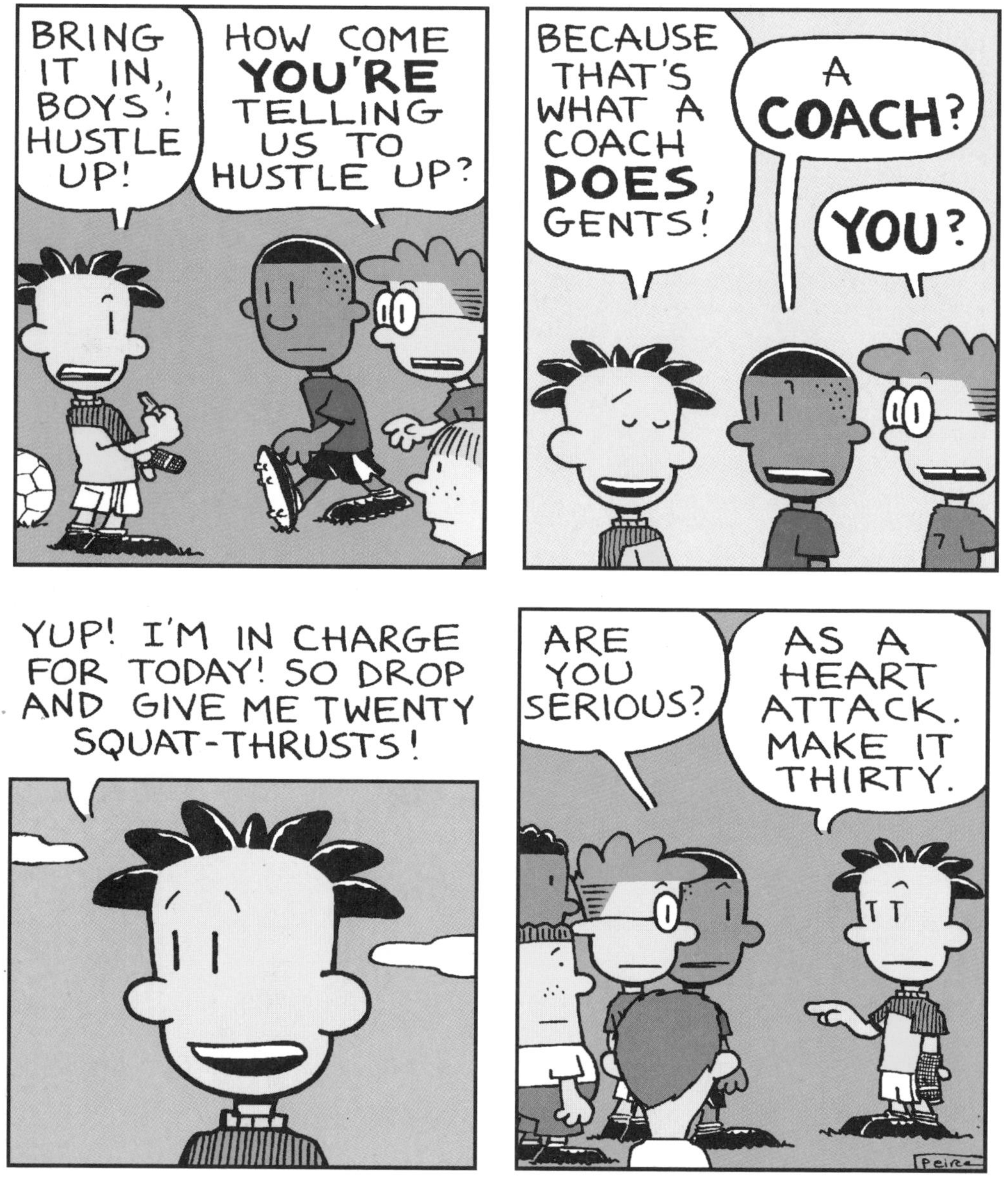
BRING IT IN, BOYS! HUSTLE UP!
HOW COME **YOU'RE** TELLING US TO HUSTLE UP?
BECAUSE THAT'S WHAT A COACH **DOES**, GENTS!
A **COACH**?
YOU?
YUP! I'M IN CHARGE FOR TODAY! SO DROP AND GIVE ME TWENTY SQUAT-THRUSTS!
ARE YOU SERIOUS?
AS A HEART ATTACK. MAKE IT THIRTY.
PEIRCE

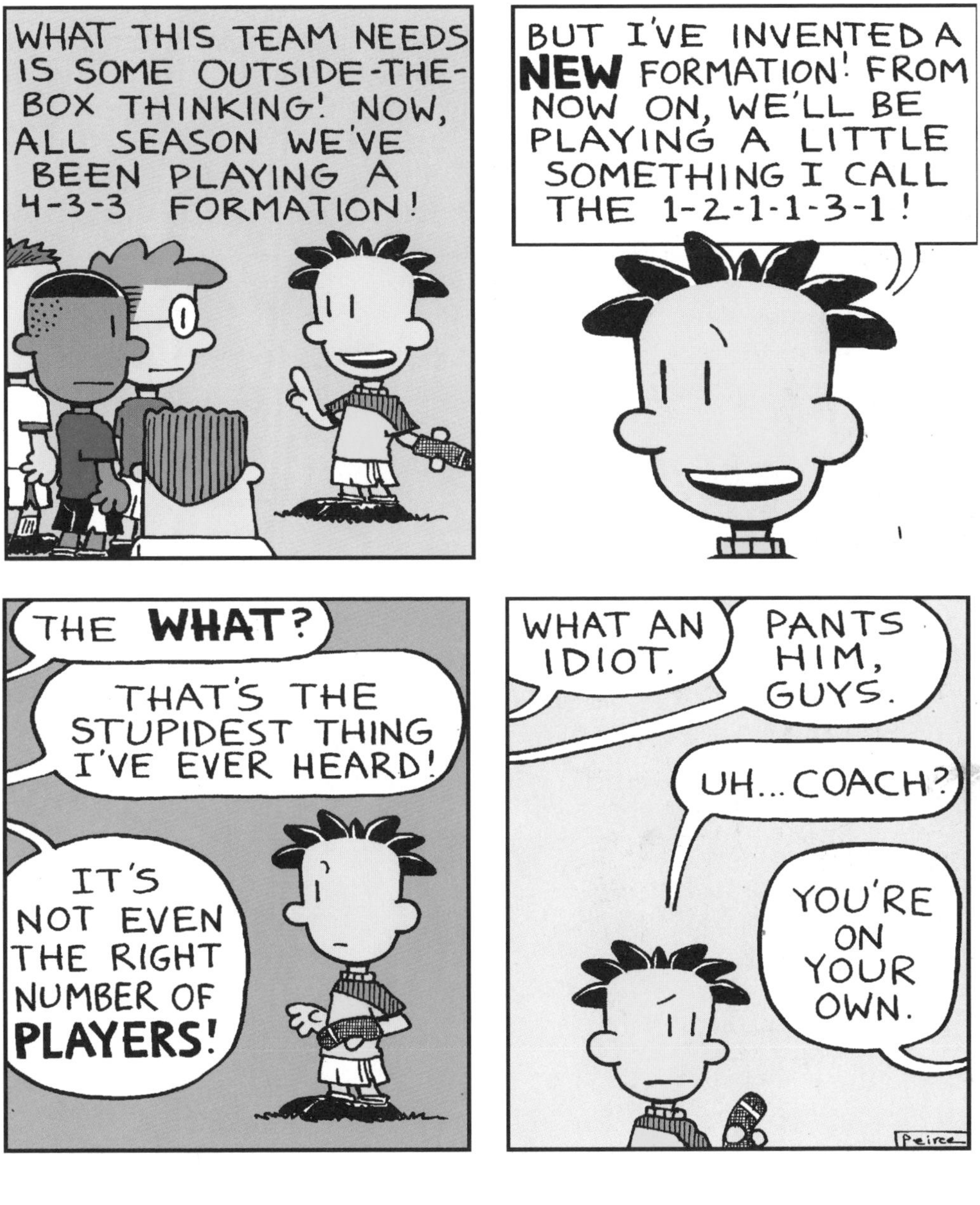
WHAT THIS TEAM NEEDS IS SOME OUTSIDE-THE-BOX THINKING! NOW, ALL SEASON WE'VE BEEN PLAYING A 4-3-3 FORMATION!
BUT I'VE INVENTED A **NEW** FORMATION! FROM NOW ON, WE'LL BE PLAYING A LITTLE SOMETHING I CALL THE 1-2-1-1-3-1!
THE **WHAT**?
THAT'S THE STUPIDEST THING I'VE EVER HEARD!
IT'S NOT EVEN THE RIGHT NUMBER OF **PLAYERS**!
WHAT AN IDIOT.
PANTS HIM, GUYS.
UH... COACH?
YOU'RE ON YOUR OWN.
Peirce

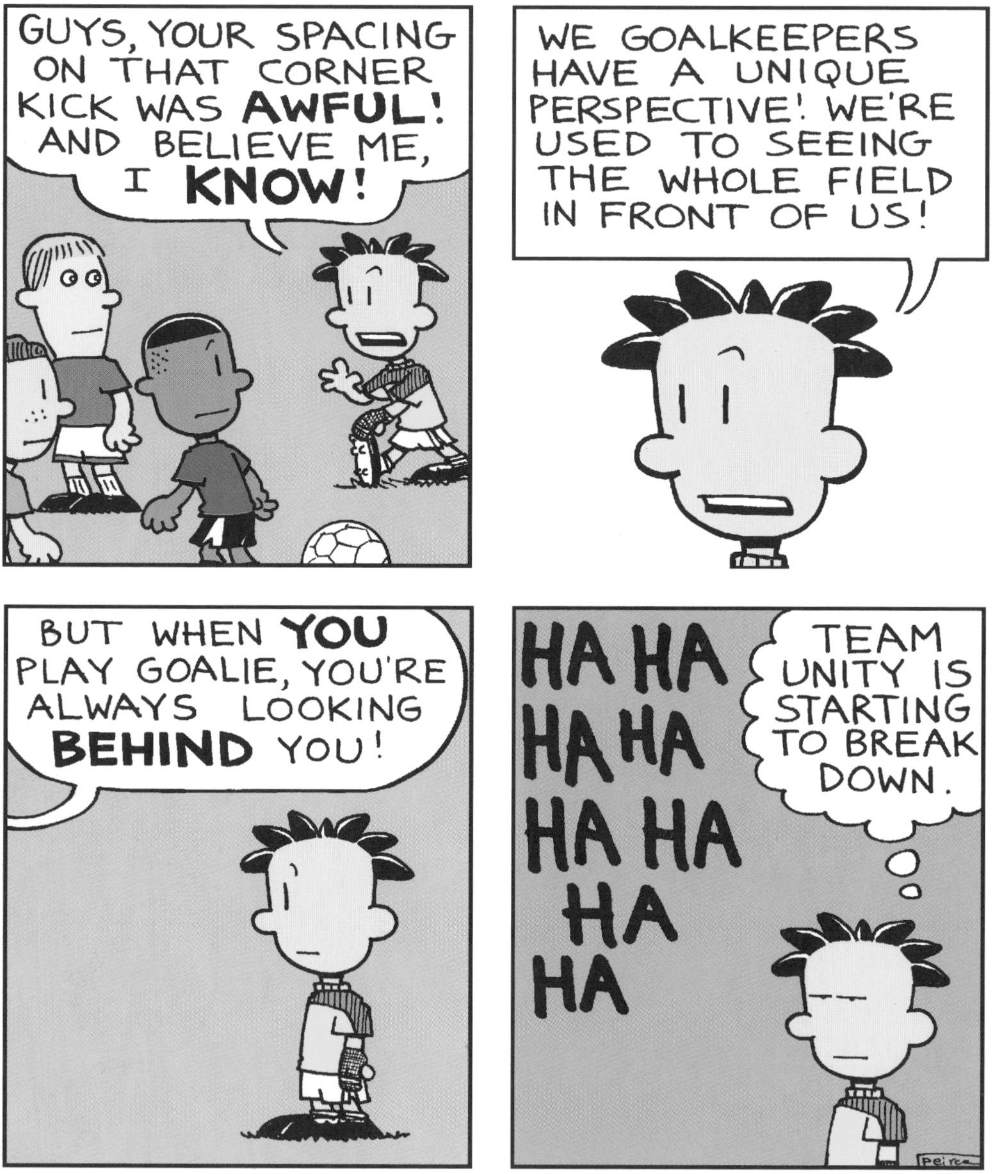
GUYS, YOUR SPACING ON THAT CORNER KICK WAS **AWFUL**! AND BELIEVE ME, I **KNOW**!
WE GOALKEEPERS HAVE A UNIQUE PERSPECTIVE! WE'RE USED TO SEEING THE WHOLE FIELD IN FRONT OF US!
BUT WHEN **YOU** PLAY GOALIE, YOU'RE ALWAYS LOOKING **BEHIND** YOU!
HA HA HA HA HA HA HA HA HA HA
TEAM UNITY IS STARTING TO BREAK DOWN.
PEIRCE

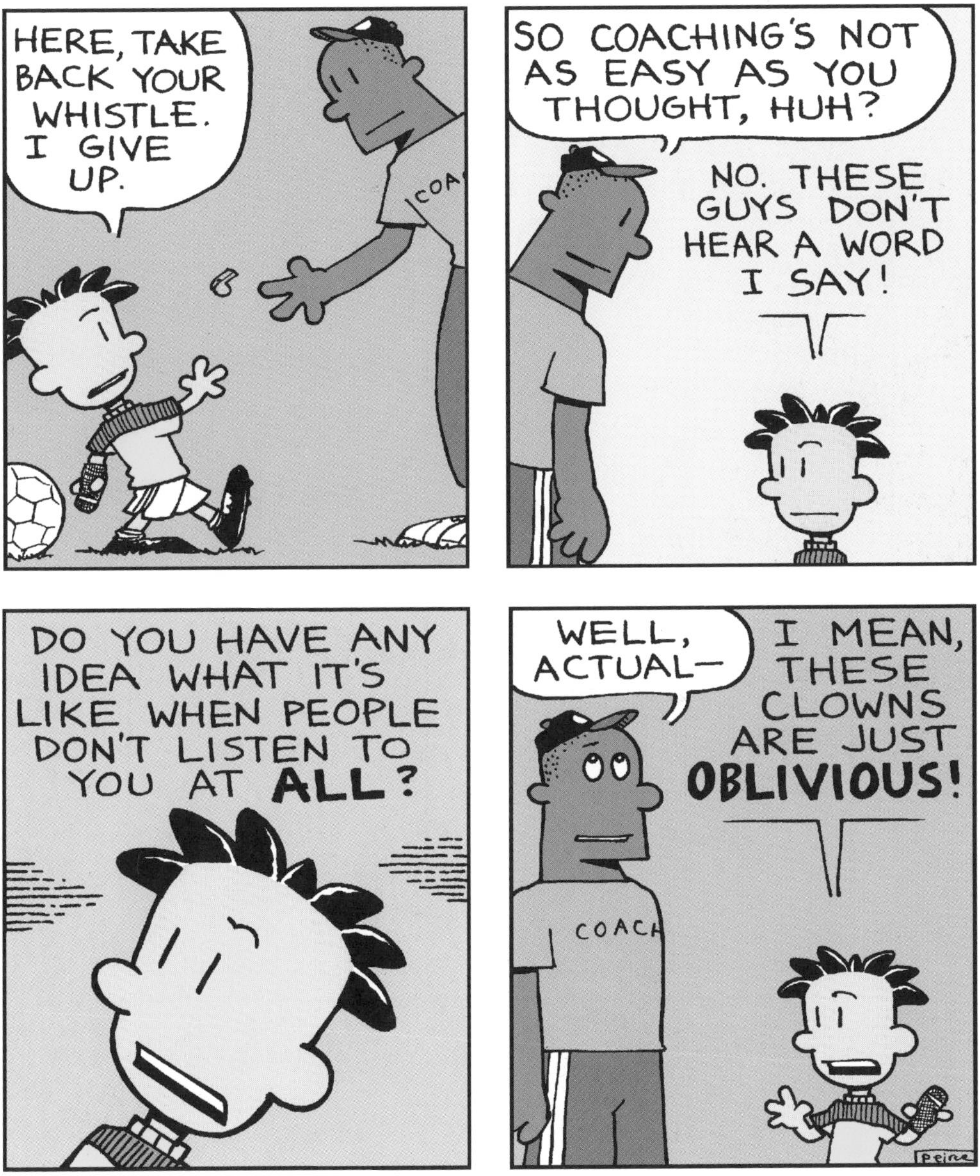
HERE, TAKE BACK YOUR WHISTLE. I GIVE UP.
COA
SO COACHING'S NOT AS EASY AS YOU THOUGHT, HUH?
NO. THESE GUYS DON'T HEAR A WORD I SAY!
DO YOU HAVE ANY IDEA WHAT IT'S LIKE WHEN PEOPLE DON'T LISTEN TO YOU AT **ALL**?
WELL, ACTUAL—
I MEAN, THESE CLOWNS ARE JUST **OBLIVIOUS**!
COACH
Peirce

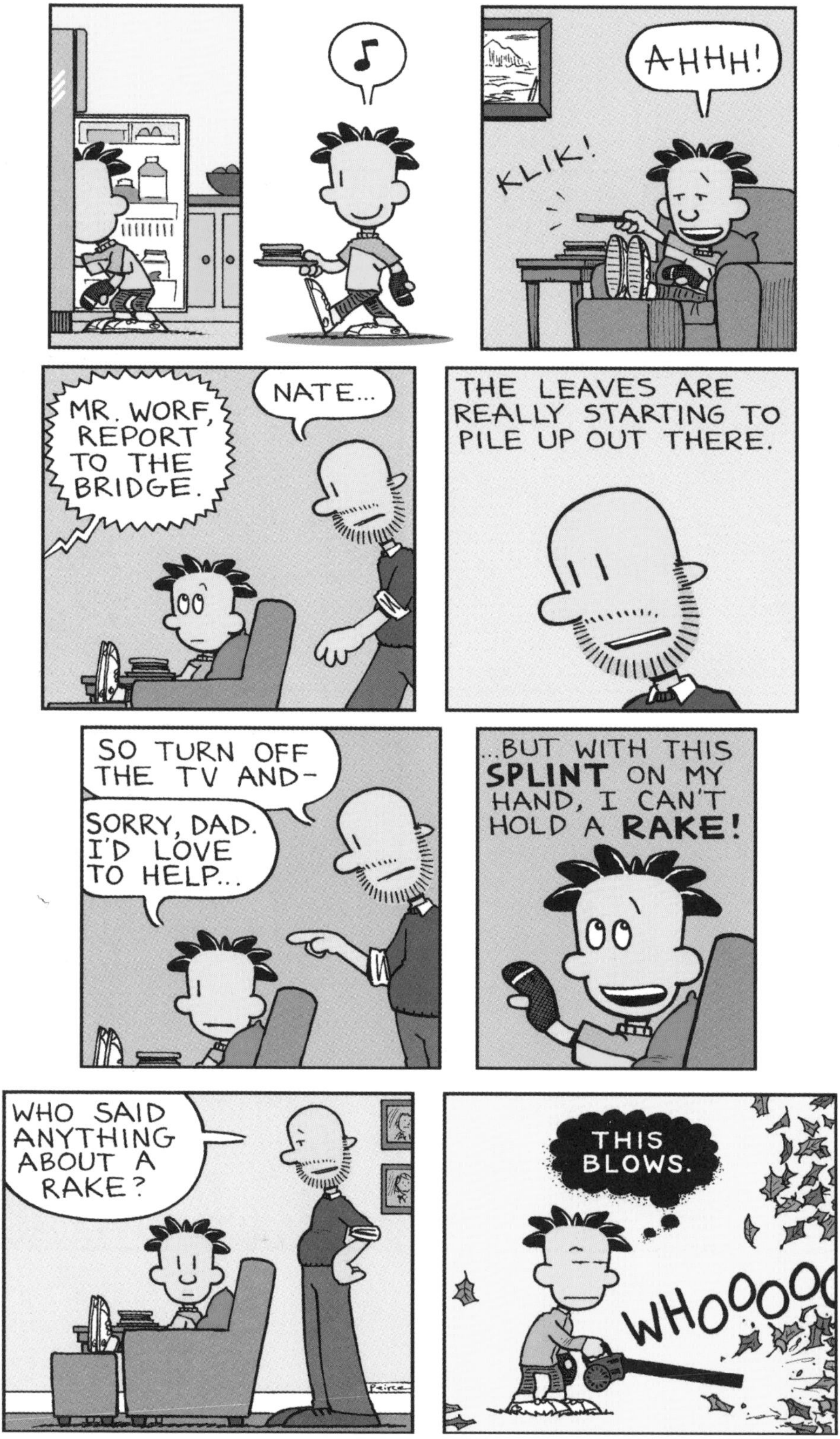
♪
AHHH!
KLIK!
MR. WORF, REPORT TO THE BRIDGE.
NATE...
THE LEAVES ARE REALLY STARTING TO PILE UP OUT THERE.
SO TURN OFF THE TV AND-
SORRY, DAD. I'D LOVE TO HELP...
...BUT WITH THIS **SPLINT** ON MY HAND, I CAN'T HOLD A **RAKE!**
WHO SAID ANYTHING ABOUT A RAKE?
Peirce
THIS BLOWS.
WHOOOOO

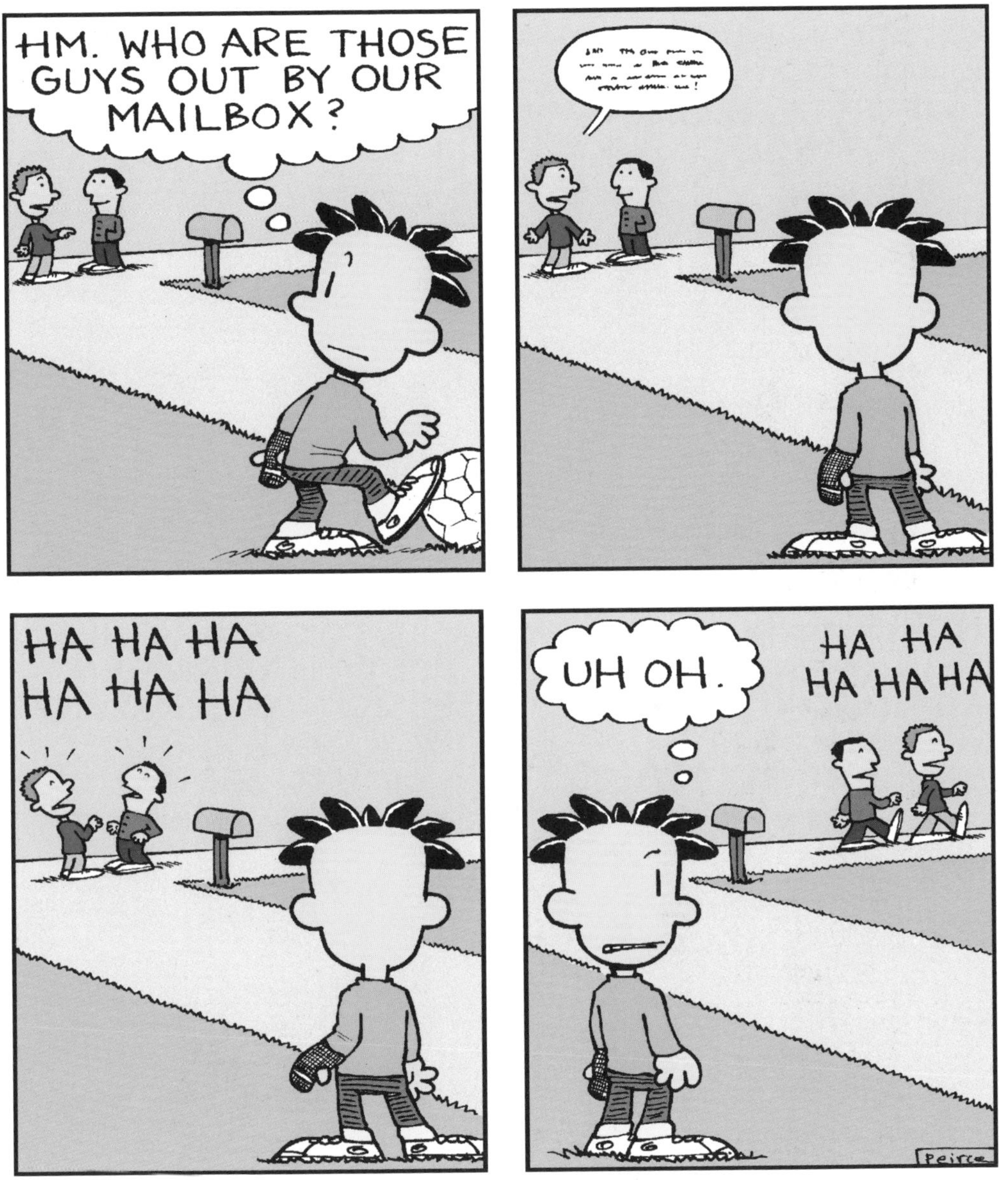
HM. WHO ARE THOSE GUYS OUT BY OUR MAILBOX?
HA HA HA HA HA HA
UH OH.
HA HA HA HA HA
peirce

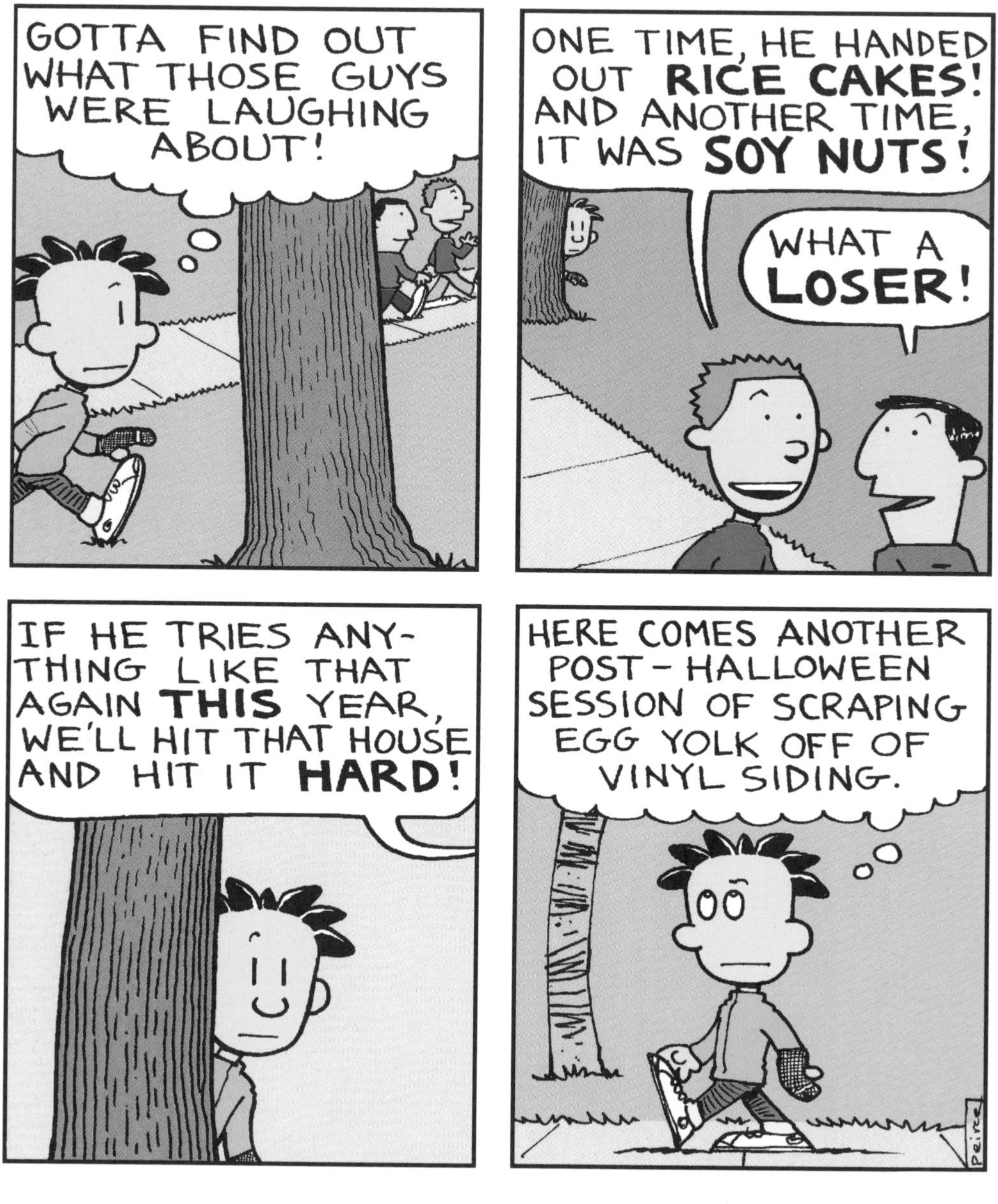
GOTTA FIND OUT WHAT THOSE GUYS WERE LAUGHING ABOUT!
ONE TIME, HE HANDED OUT RICE CAKES! AND ANOTHER TIME, IT WAS SOY NUTS!
WHAT A LOSER!
IF HE TRIES ANYTHING LIKE THAT AGAIN THIS YEAR, WE'LL HIT THAT HOUSE AND HIT IT HARD!
HERE COMES ANOTHER POST-HALLOWEEN SESSION OF SCRAPING EGG YOLK OFF OF VINYL SIDING.
Peirce

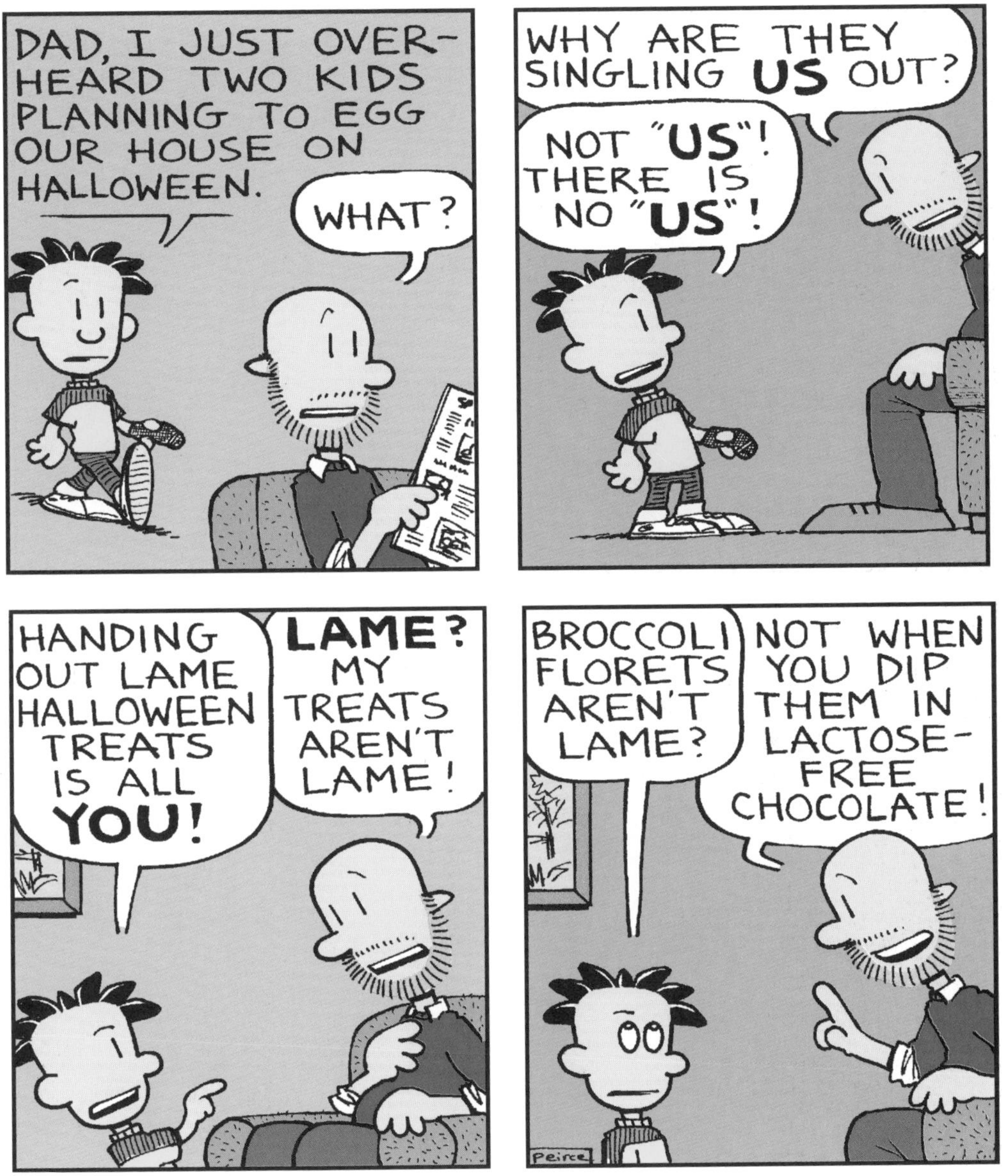
DAD, I JUST OVER-HEARD TWO KIDS PLANNING TO EGG OUR HOUSE ON HALLOWEEN.
WHAT?
WHY ARE THEY SINGLING US OUT?
NOT "US"! THERE IS NO "US"!
HANDING OUT LAME HALLOWEEN TREATS IS ALL YOU!
LAME? MY TREATS AREN'T LAME!
BROCCOLI FLORETS AREN'T LAME?
NOT WHEN YOU DIP THEM IN LACTOSE-FREE CHOCOLATE!
Peirce

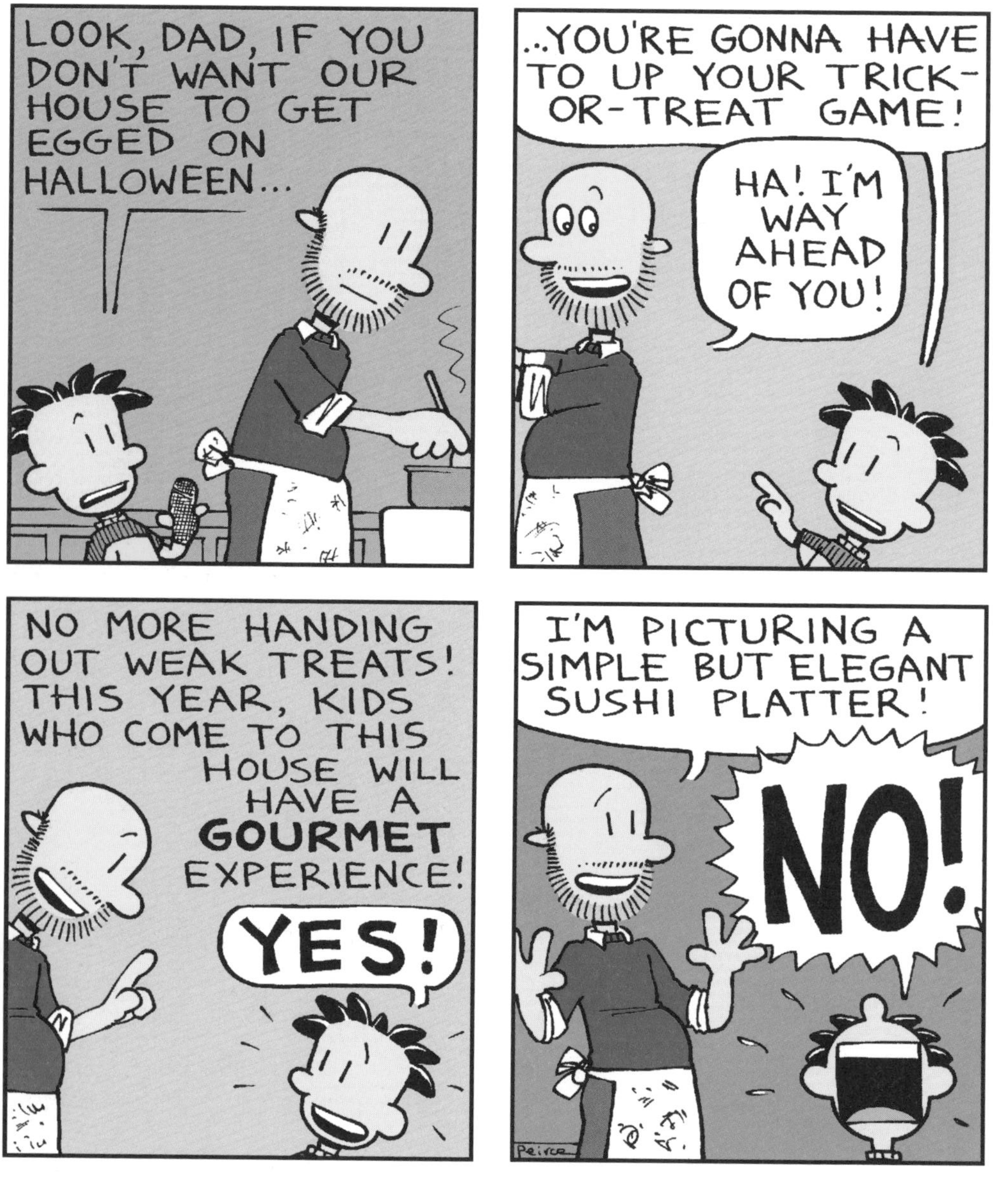
LOOK, DAD, IF YOU DON'T WANT OUR HOUSE TO GET EGGED ON HALLOWEEN...
..YOU'RE GONNA HAVE TO UP YOUR TRICK-OR-TREAT GAME!
HA! I'M WAY AHEAD OF YOU!
NO MORE HANDING OUT WEAK TREATS! THIS YEAR, KIDS WHO COME TO THIS HOUSE WILL HAVE A **GOURMET** EXPERIENCE!
YES!
I'M PICTURING A SIMPLE BUT ELEGANT SUSHI PLATTER!
NO!
Peirce

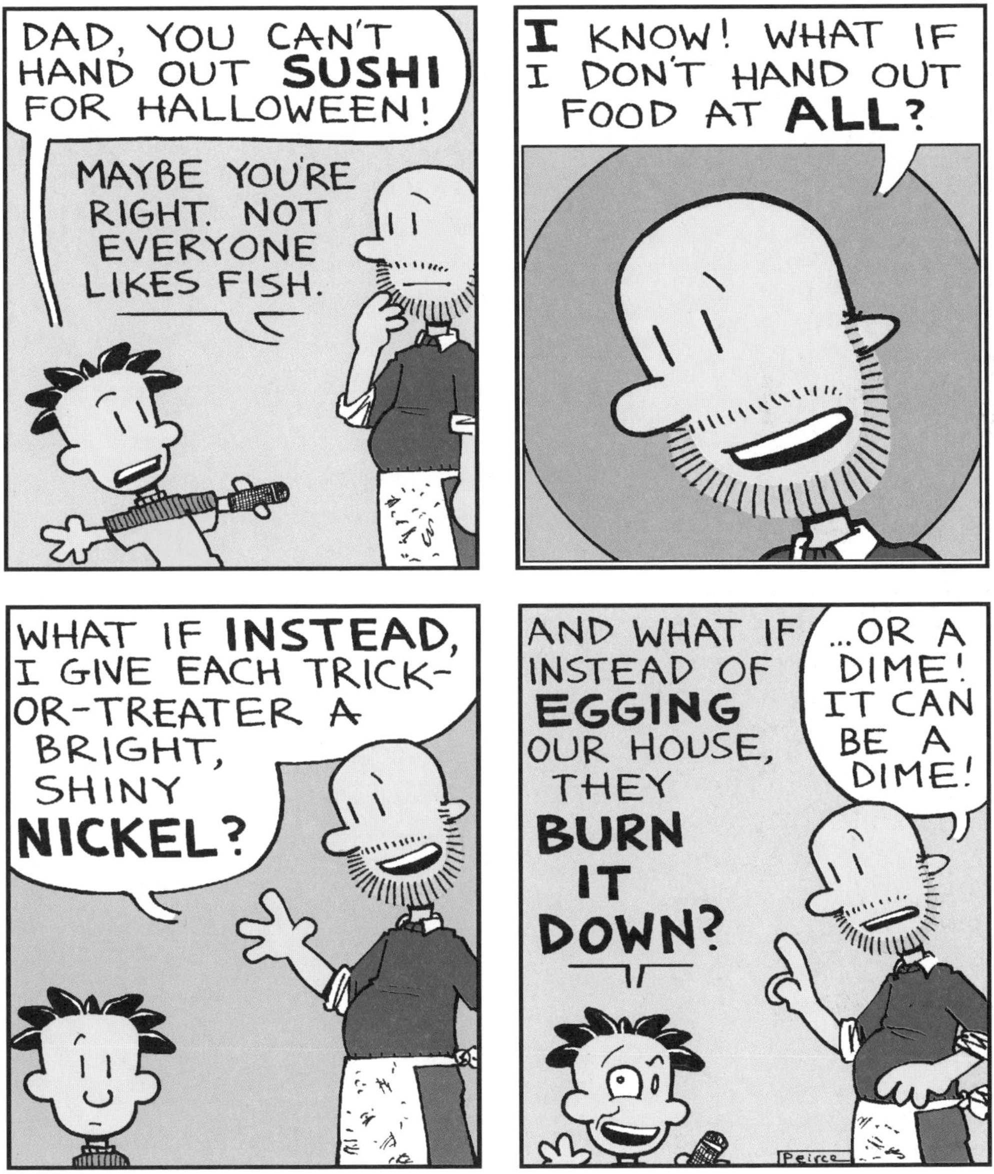
DAD, YOU CAN'T HAND OUT **SUSHI** FOR HALLOWEEN!
MAYBE YOU'RE RIGHT. NOT EVERYONE LIKES FISH.
I KNOW! WHAT IF I DON'T HAND OUT FOOD AT **ALL**?
WHAT IF **INSTEAD**, I GIVE EACH TRICK-OR-TREATER A BRIGHT, SHINY **NICKEL**?
AND WHAT IF INSTEAD OF **EGGING** OUR HOUSE, THEY **BURN IT DOWN**?
...OR A DIME! IT CAN BE A DIME!
Peirce

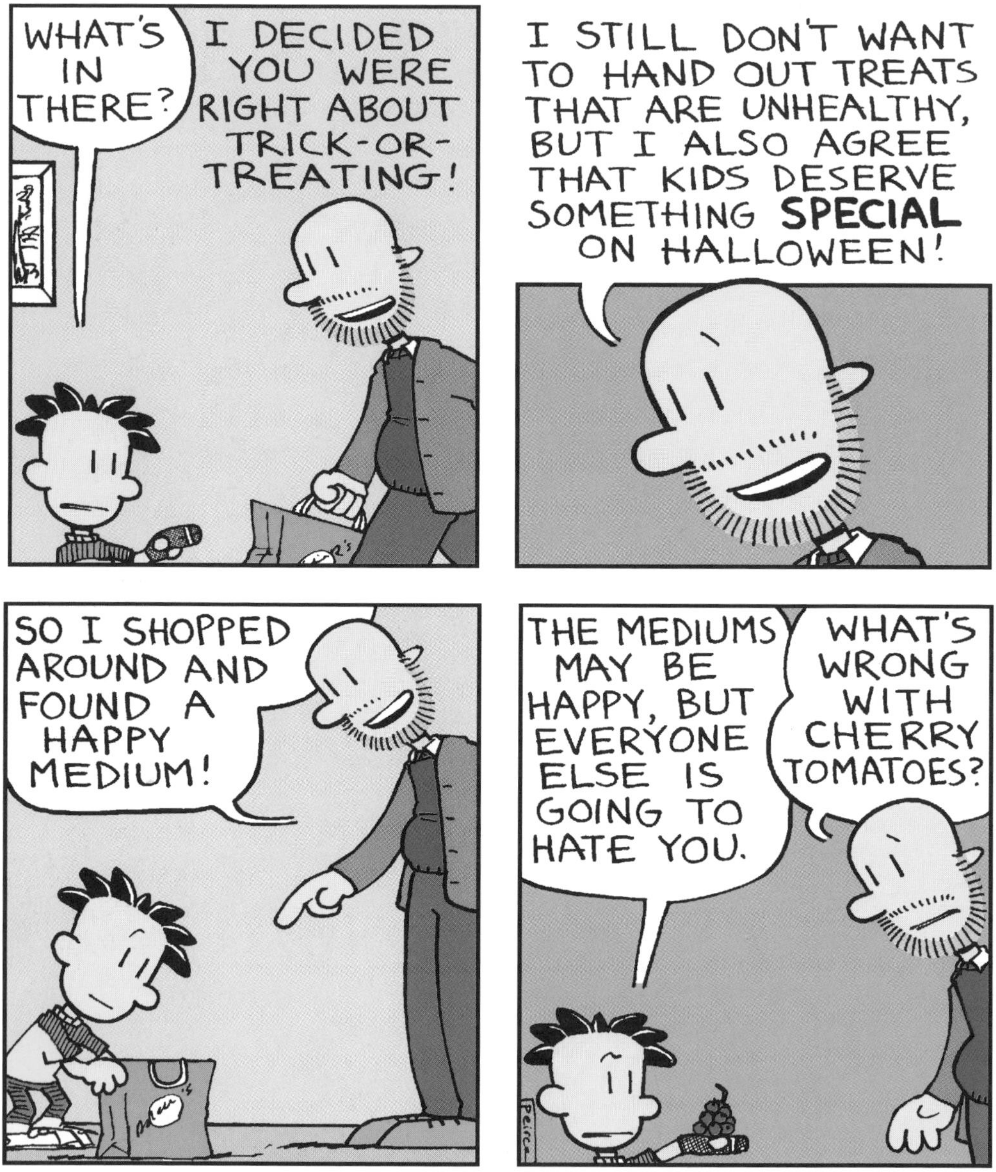
WHAT'S IN THERE?
I DECIDED YOU WERE RIGHT ABOUT TRICK-OR-TREATING!
I STILL DON'T WANT TO HAND OUT TREATS THAT ARE UNHEALTHY, BUT I ALSO AGREE THAT KIDS DESERVE SOMETHING SPECIAL ON HALLOWEEN!
SO I SHOPPED AROUND AND FOUND A HAPPY MEDIUM!
THE MEDIUMS MAY BE HAPPY, BUT EVERYONE ELSE IS GOING TO HATE YOU.
WHAT'S WRONG WITH CHERRY TOMATOES?
Peirce

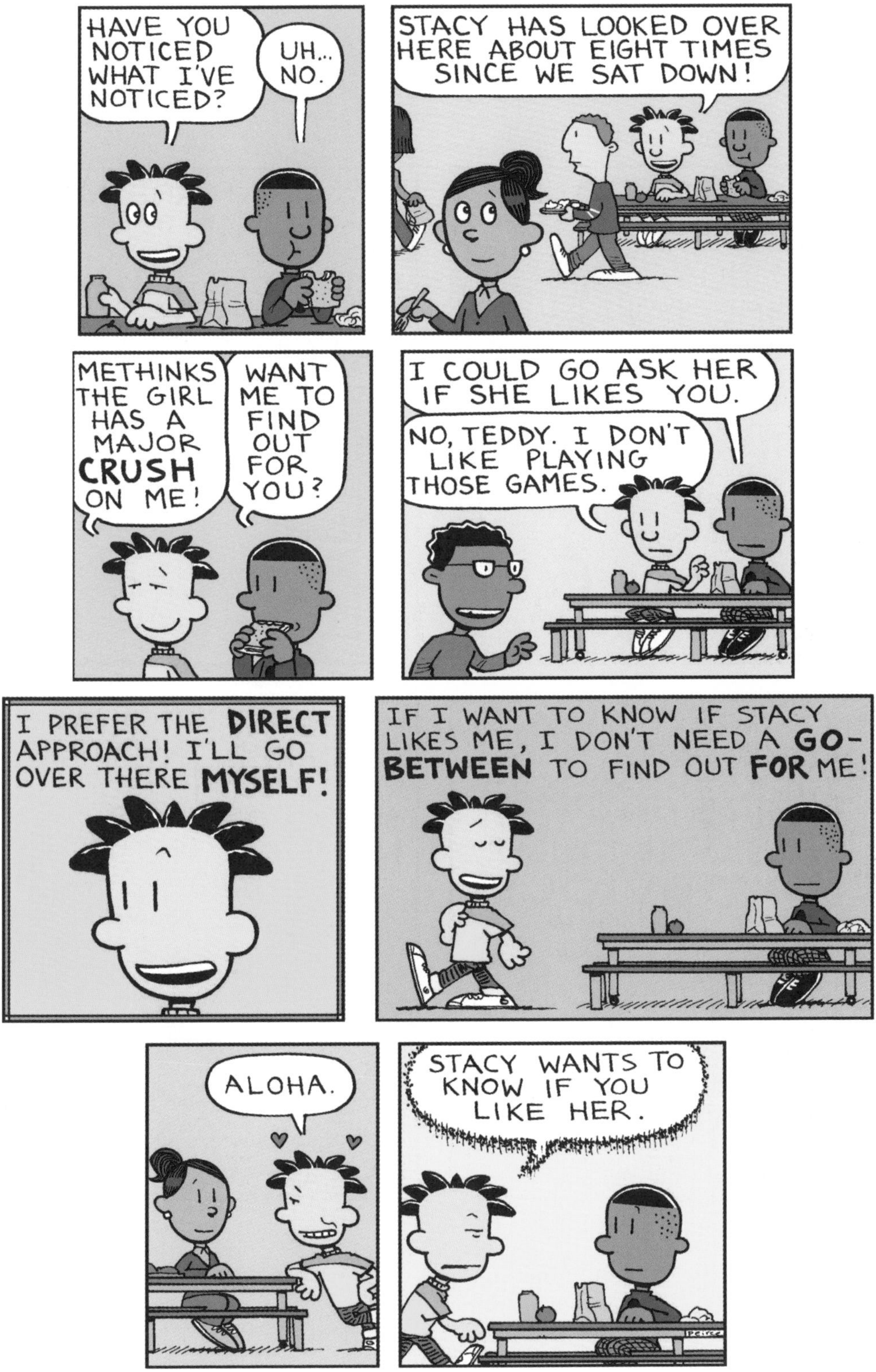
HAVE YOU NOTICED WHAT I'VE NOTICED?
UH... NO.
STACY HAS LOOKED OVER HERE ABOUT EIGHT TIMES SINCE WE SAT DOWN!
METHINKS THE GIRL HAS A MAJOR CRUSH ON ME!
WANT ME TO FIND OUT FOR YOU?
I COULD GO ASK HER IF SHE LIKES YOU.
NO, TEDDY. I DON'T LIKE PLAYING THOSE GAMES.
I PREFER THE DIRECT APPROACH! I'LL GO OVER THERE MYSELF!
IF I WANT TO KNOW IF STACY LIKES ME, I DON'T NEED A GO-BETWEEN TO FIND OUT FOR ME!
ALOHA.
STACY WANTS TO KNOW IF YOU LIKE HER.
PEIRCE

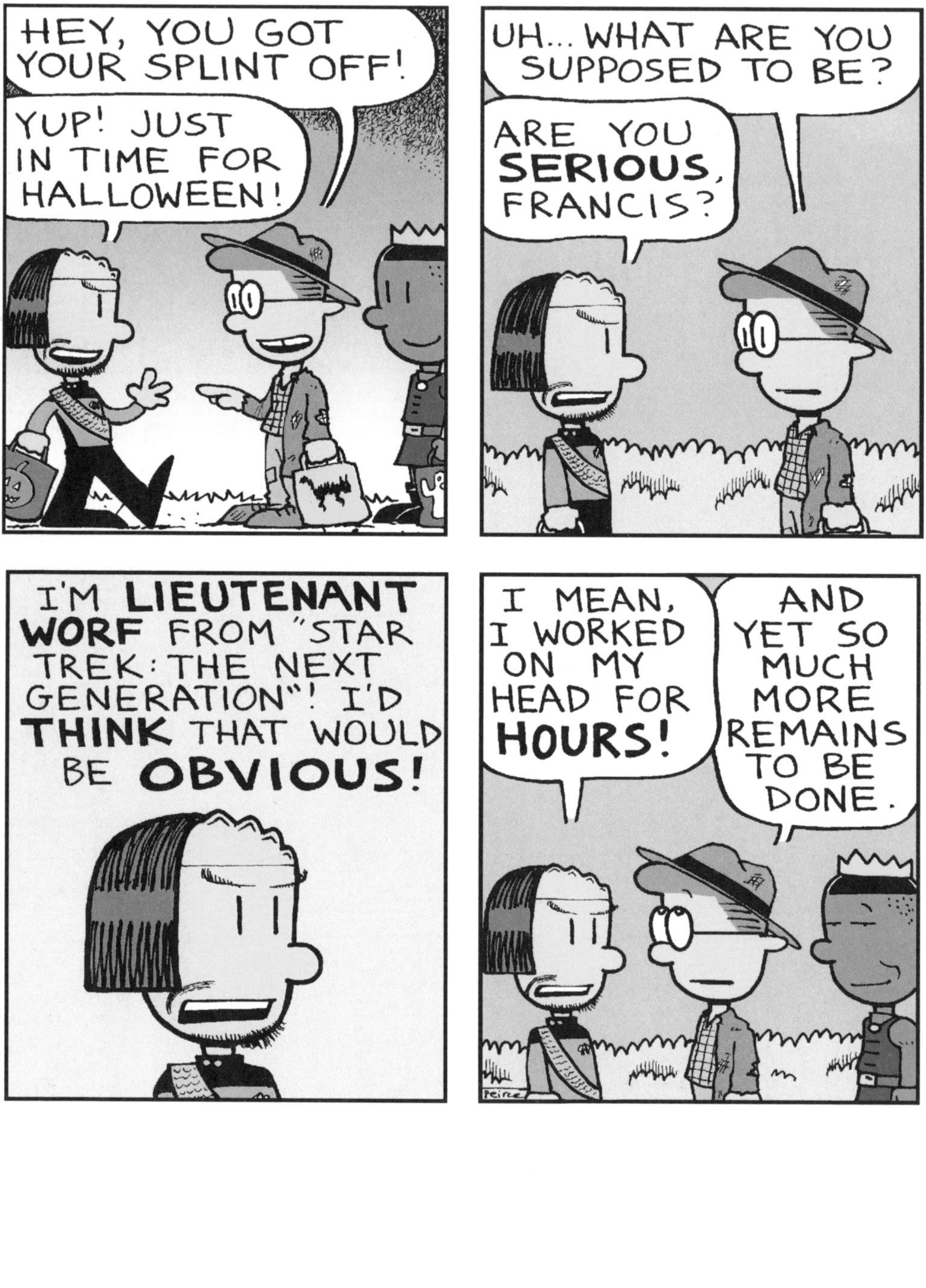
HEY, YOU GOT YOUR SPLINT OFF!
YUP! JUST IN TIME FOR HALLOWEEN!
UH... WHAT ARE YOU SUPPOSED TO BE?
ARE YOU SERIOUS, FRANCIS?
I'M LIEUTENANT WORF FROM "STAR TREK: THE NEXT GENERATION"! I'D THINK THAT WOULD BE OBVIOUS!
I MEAN, I WORKED ON MY HEAD FOR HOURS!
AND YET SO MUCH MORE REMAINS TO BE DONE.
Peirce

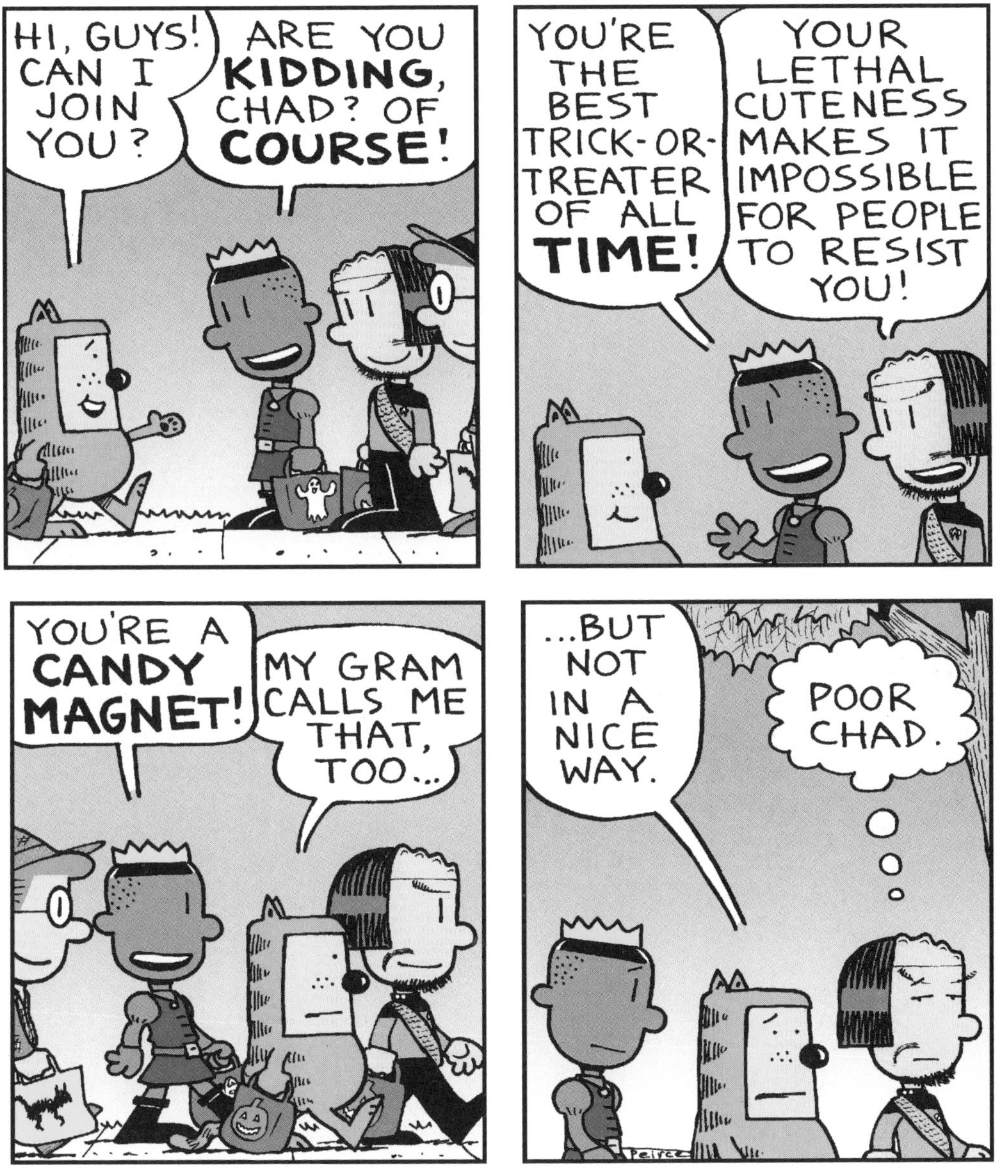
HI, GUYS! CAN I JOIN YOU?
ARE YOU **KIDDING**, CHAD? OF **COURSE**!
YOU'RE THE BEST TRICK-OR-TREATER OF ALL **TIME**!
YOUR LETHAL CUTENESS MAKES IT IMPOSSIBLE FOR PEOPLE TO RESIST YOU!
YOU'RE A **CANDY MAGNET**!
MY GRAM CALLS ME THAT, TOO...
...BUT NOT IN A NICE WAY.
POOR CHAD.
Peirce

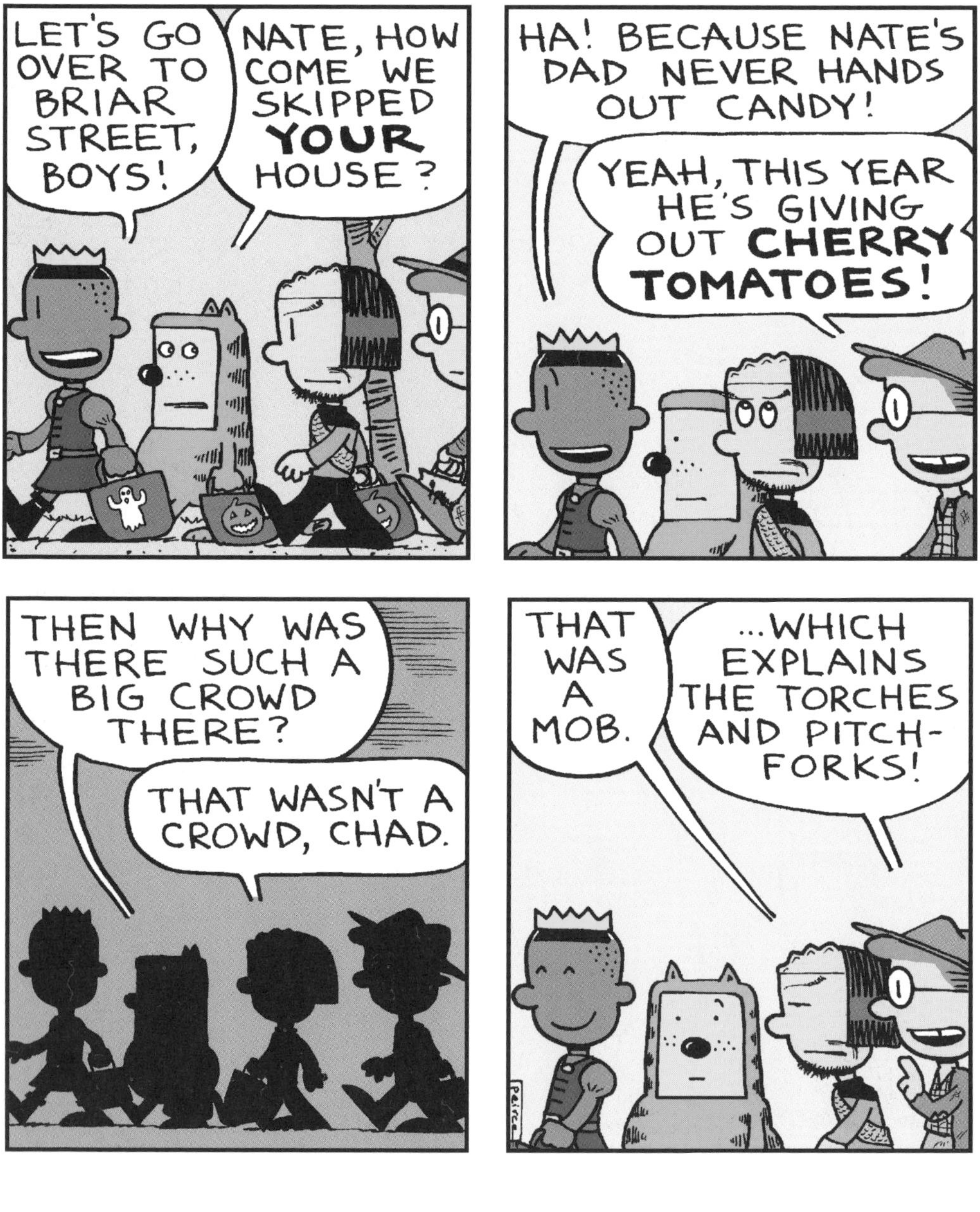
LET'S GO OVER TO BRIAR STREET, BOYS!
NATE, HOW COME WE SKIPPED **YOUR** HOUSE?
HA! BECAUSE NATE'S DAD NEVER HANDS OUT CANDY!
YEAH, THIS YEAR HE'S GIVING OUT **CHERRY TOMATOES!**
THEN WHY WAS THERE SUCH A BIG CROWD THERE?
THAT WASN'T A CROWD, CHAD.
THAT WAS A MOB.
...WHICH EXPLAINS THE TORCHES AND PITCH-FORKS!
PEIRCE

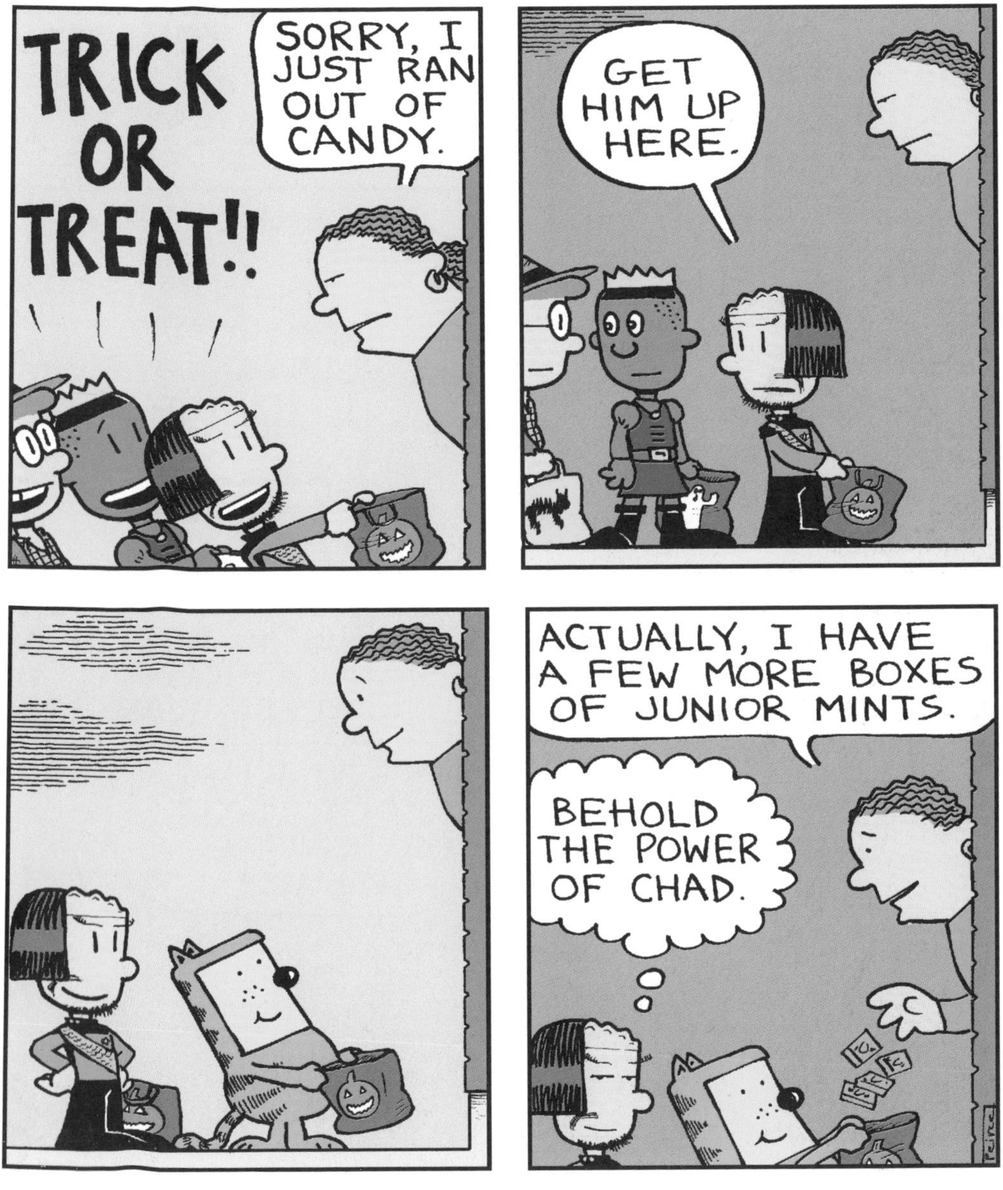
TRICK OR TREAT!!
SORRY, I JUST RAN OUT OF CANDY.
GET HIM UP HERE.
ACTUALLY, I HAVE A FEW MORE BOXES OF JUNIOR MINTS.
BEHOLD THE POWER OF CHAD.
Peirce

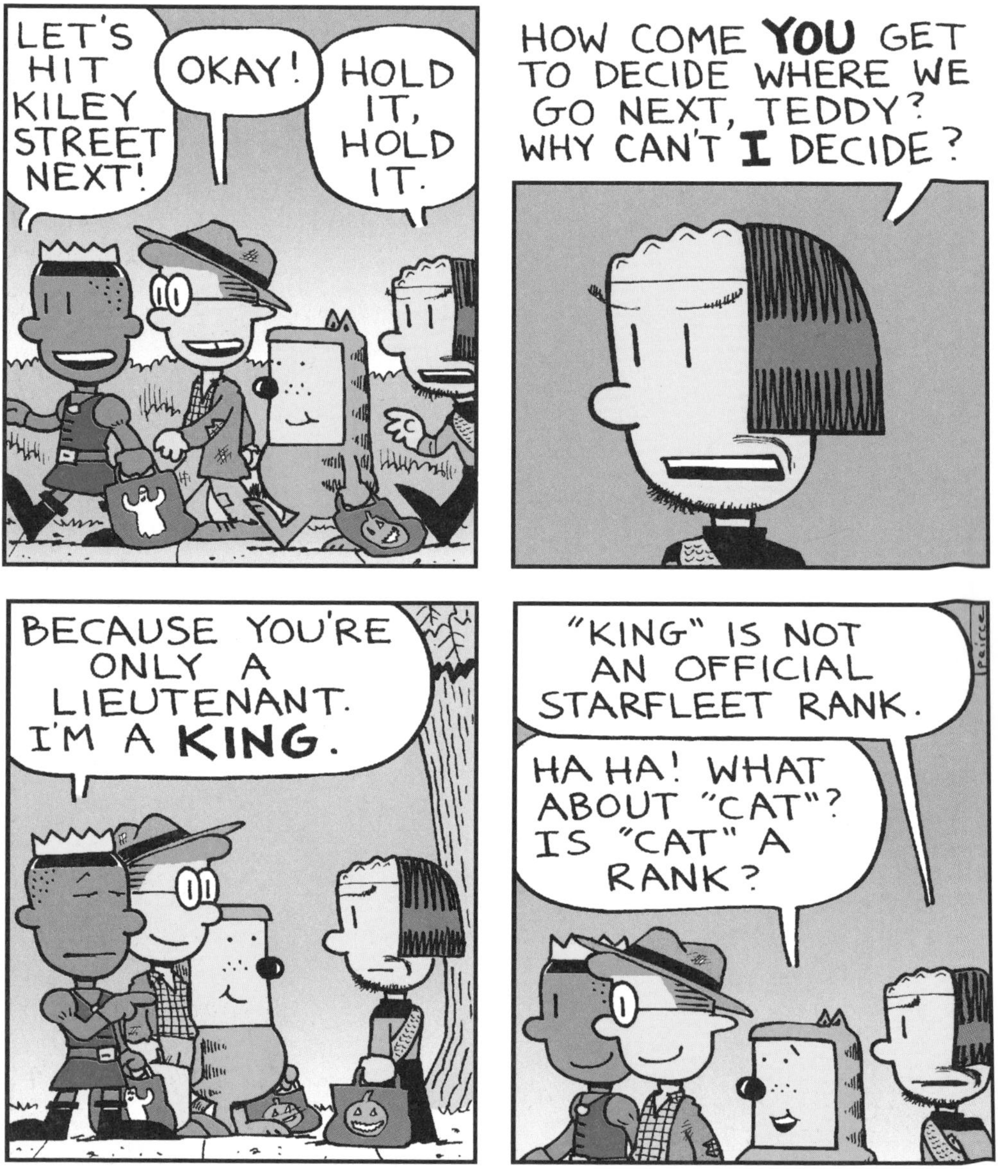
LET'S HIT KILEY STREET NEXT!
OKAY!
HOLD IT, HOLD IT.
HOW COME **YOU** GET TO DECIDE WHERE WE GO NEXT, TEDDY? WHY CAN'T **I** DECIDE?
BECAUSE YOU'RE ONLY A LIEUTENANT. I'M A **KING**.
"KING" IS NOT AN OFFICIAL STARFLEET RANK.
HA HA! WHAT ABOUT "CAT"? IS "CAT" A RANK?

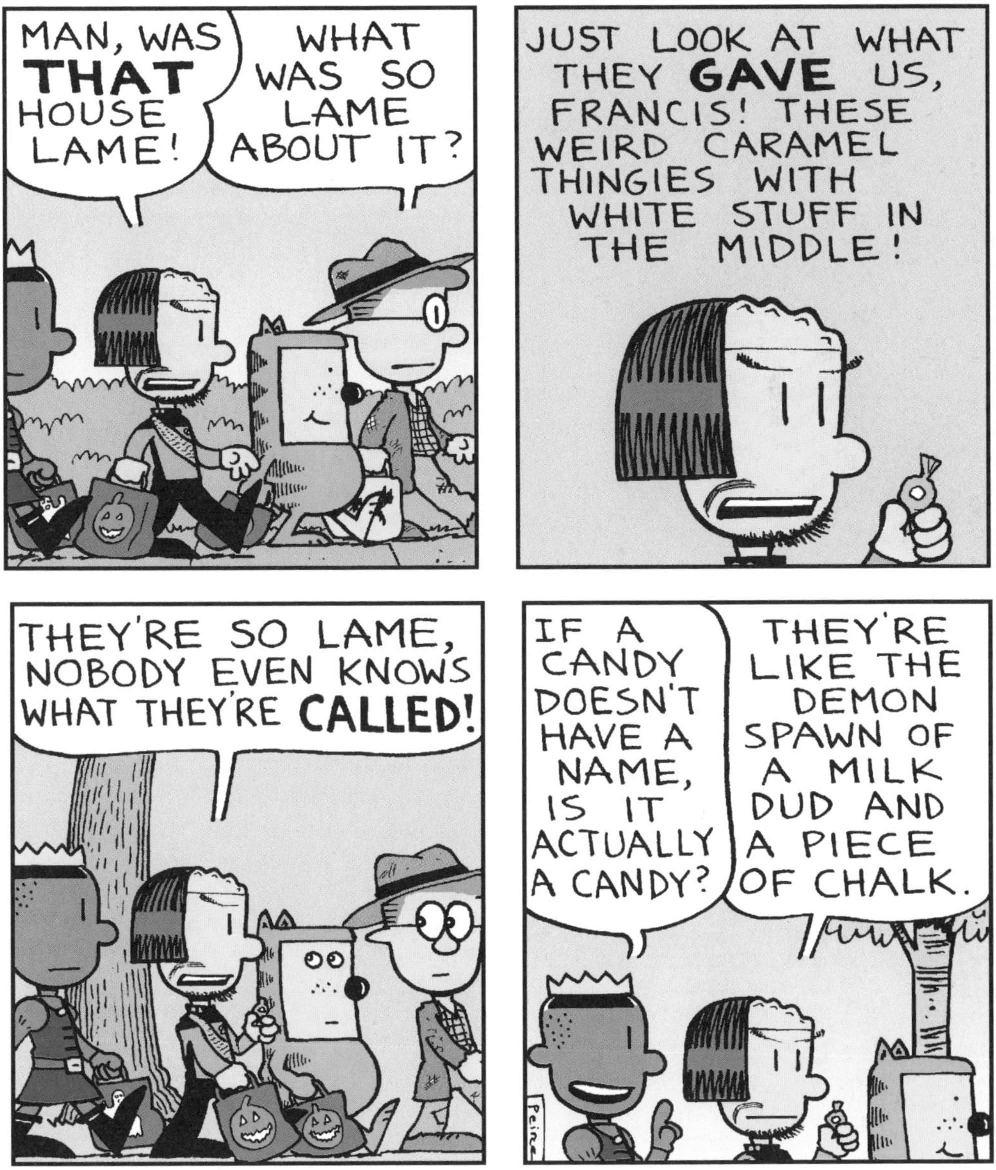
MAN, WAS **THAT** HOUSE LAME!
WHAT WAS SO LAME ABOUT IT?
JUST LOOK AT WHAT THEY **GAVE** US, FRANCIS! THESE WEIRD CARAMEL THINGIES WITH WHITE STUFF IN THE MIDDLE!
THEY'RE SO LAME, NOBODY EVEN KNOWS WHAT THEY'RE **CALLED**!
IF A CANDY DOESN'T HAVE A NAME, IS IT ACTUALLY A CANDY?
THEY'RE LIKE THE DEMON SPAWN OF A MILK DUD AND A PIECE OF CHALK.
Peirce

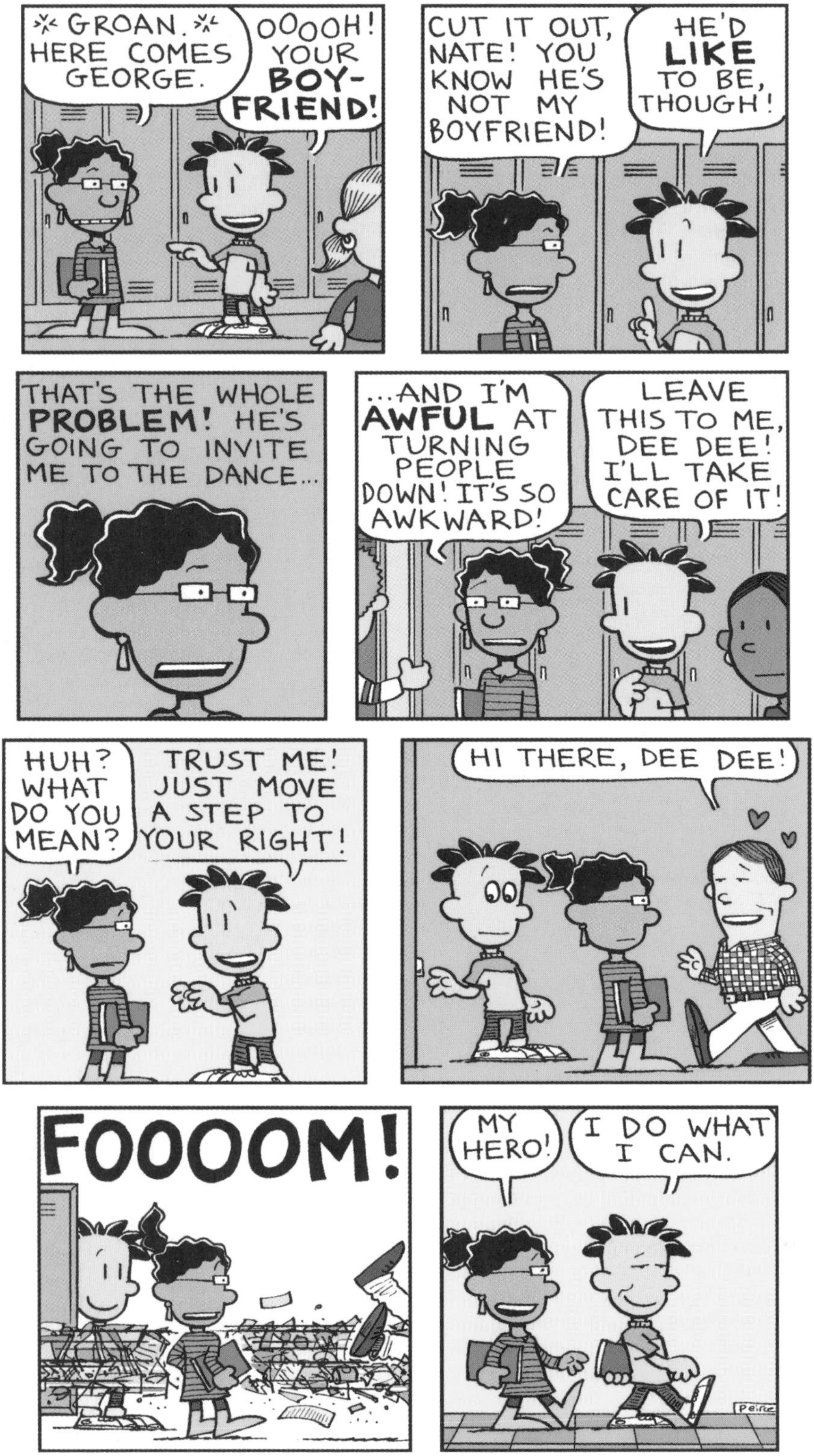
GROAN. HERE COMES GEORGE.
OOOOH! YOUR BOY-FRIEND!
CUT IT OUT, NATE! YOU KNOW HE'S NOT MY BOYFRIEND!
HE'D LIKE TO BE, THOUGH!
THAT'S THE WHOLE PROBLEM! HE'S GOING TO INVITE ME TO THE DANCE...
...AND I'M AWFUL AT TURNING PEOPLE DOWN! IT'S SO AWKWARD!
LEAVE THIS TO ME, DEE DEE! I'LL TAKE CARE OF IT!
HUH? WHAT DO YOU MEAN?
TRUST ME! JUST MOVE A STEP TO YOUR RIGHT!
HI THERE, DEE DEE!
FOOOOM!
MY HERO!
I DO WHAT I CAN.
PEIRCE

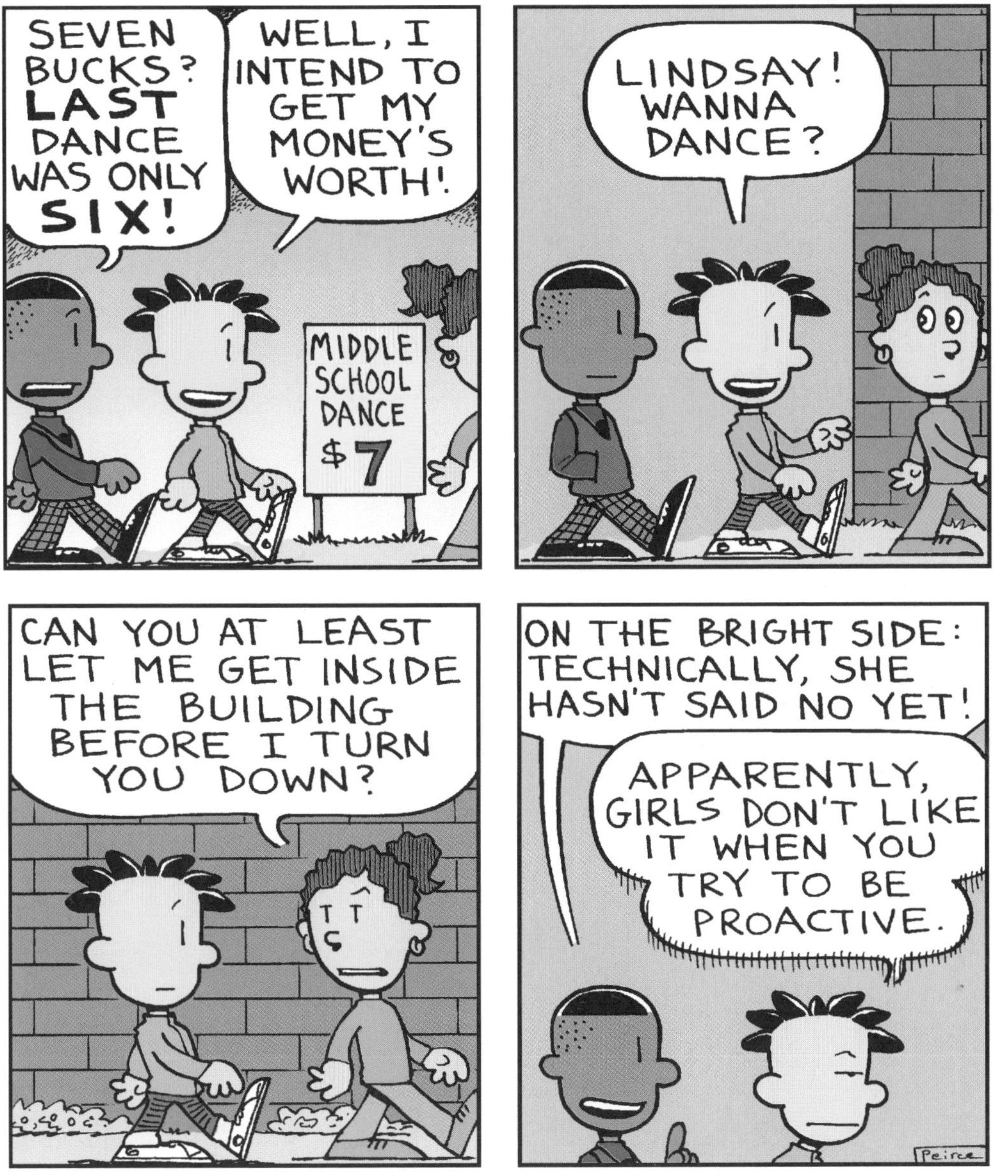
SEVEN BUCKS? **LAST** DANCE WAS ONLY **SIX!**
WELL, I INTEND TO GET MY MONEY'S WORTH!
MIDDLE SCHOOL DANCE $7
LINDSAY! WANNA DANCE?
CAN YOU AT LEAST LET ME GET INSIDE THE BUILDING BEFORE I TURN YOU DOWN?
ON THE BRIGHT SIDE: TECHNICALLY, SHE HASN'T SAID NO YET!
APPARENTLY, GIRLS DON'T LIKE IT WHEN YOU TRY TO BE PROACTIVE.
Peirce

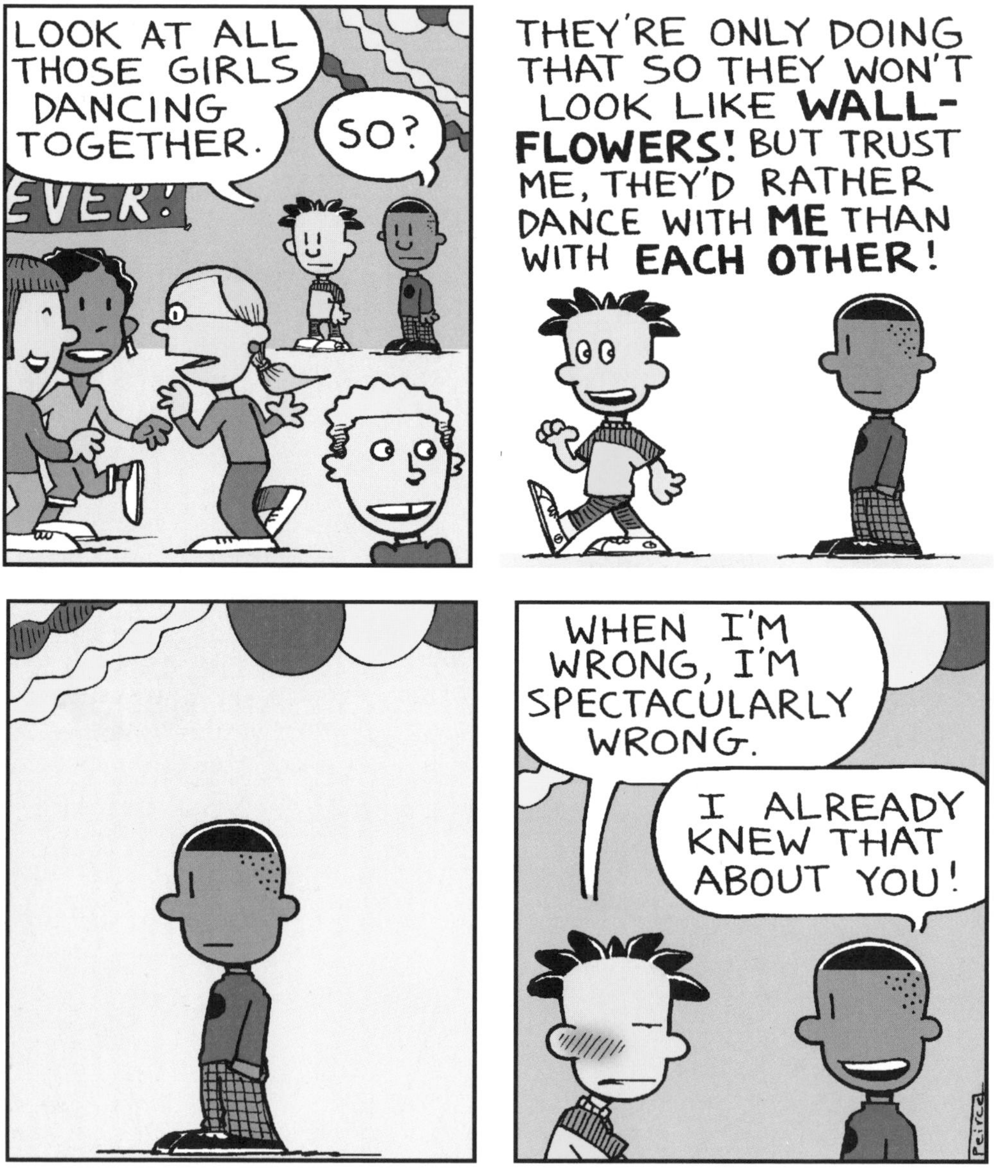
LOOK AT ALL THOSE GIRLS DANCING TOGETHER.
SO?
EVER!
THEY'RE ONLY DOING THAT SO THEY WON'T LOOK LIKE **WALL-FLOWERS!** BUT TRUST ME, THEY'D RATHER DANCE WITH **ME** THAN WITH **EACH OTHER**!
WHEN I'M WRONG, I'M SPECTACULARLY WRONG.
I ALREADY KNEW THAT ABOUT YOU!
Peirce

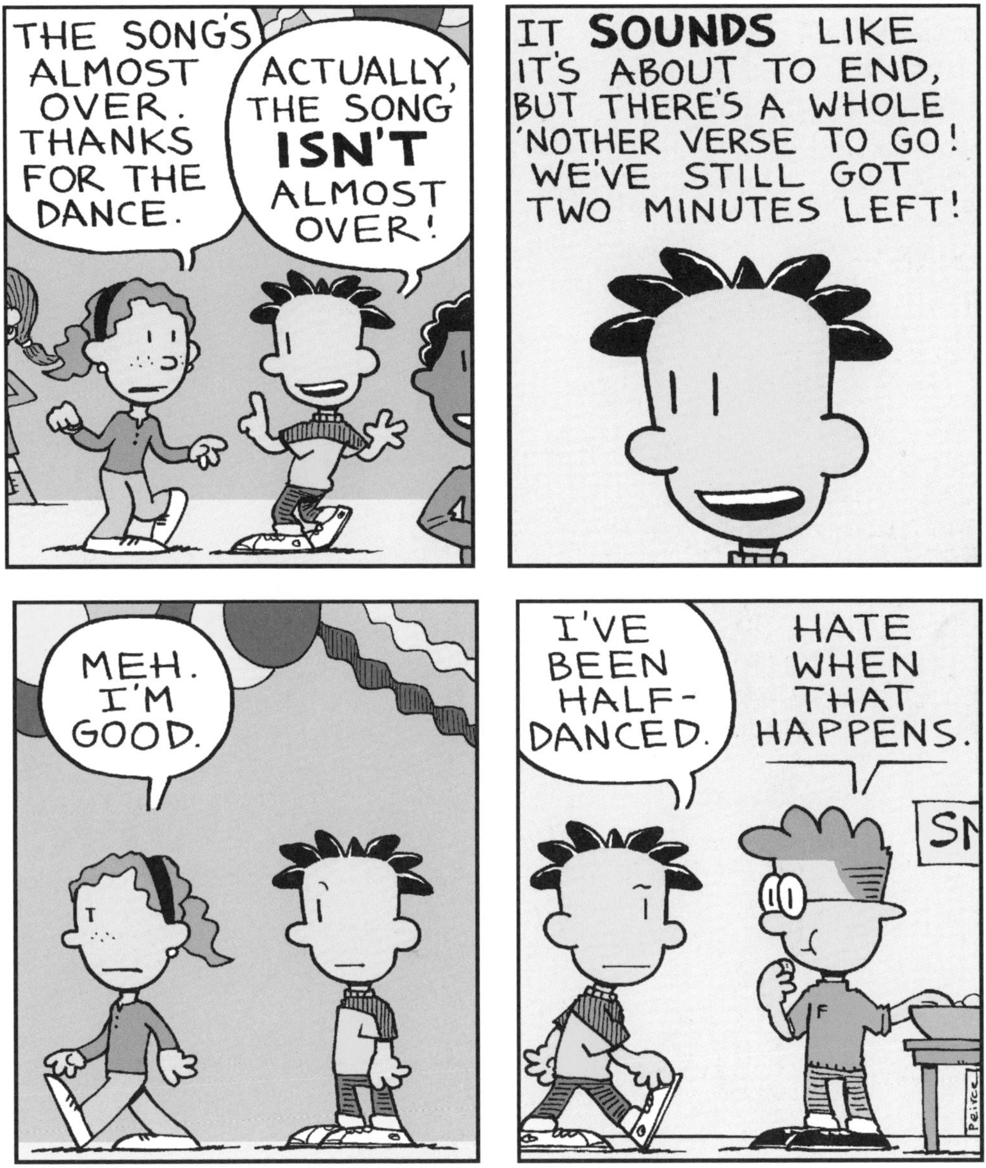
THE SONG'S ALMOST OVER. THANKS FOR THE DANCE.
ACTUALLY, THE SONG **ISN'T** ALMOST OVER!
IT **SOUNDS** LIKE IT'S ABOUT TO END, BUT THERE'S A WHOLE 'NOTHER VERSE TO GO! WE'VE STILL GOT TWO MINUTES LEFT!
MEH. I'M GOOD.
I'VE BEEN HALF-DANCED.
HATE WHEN THAT HAPPENS.
Peirce

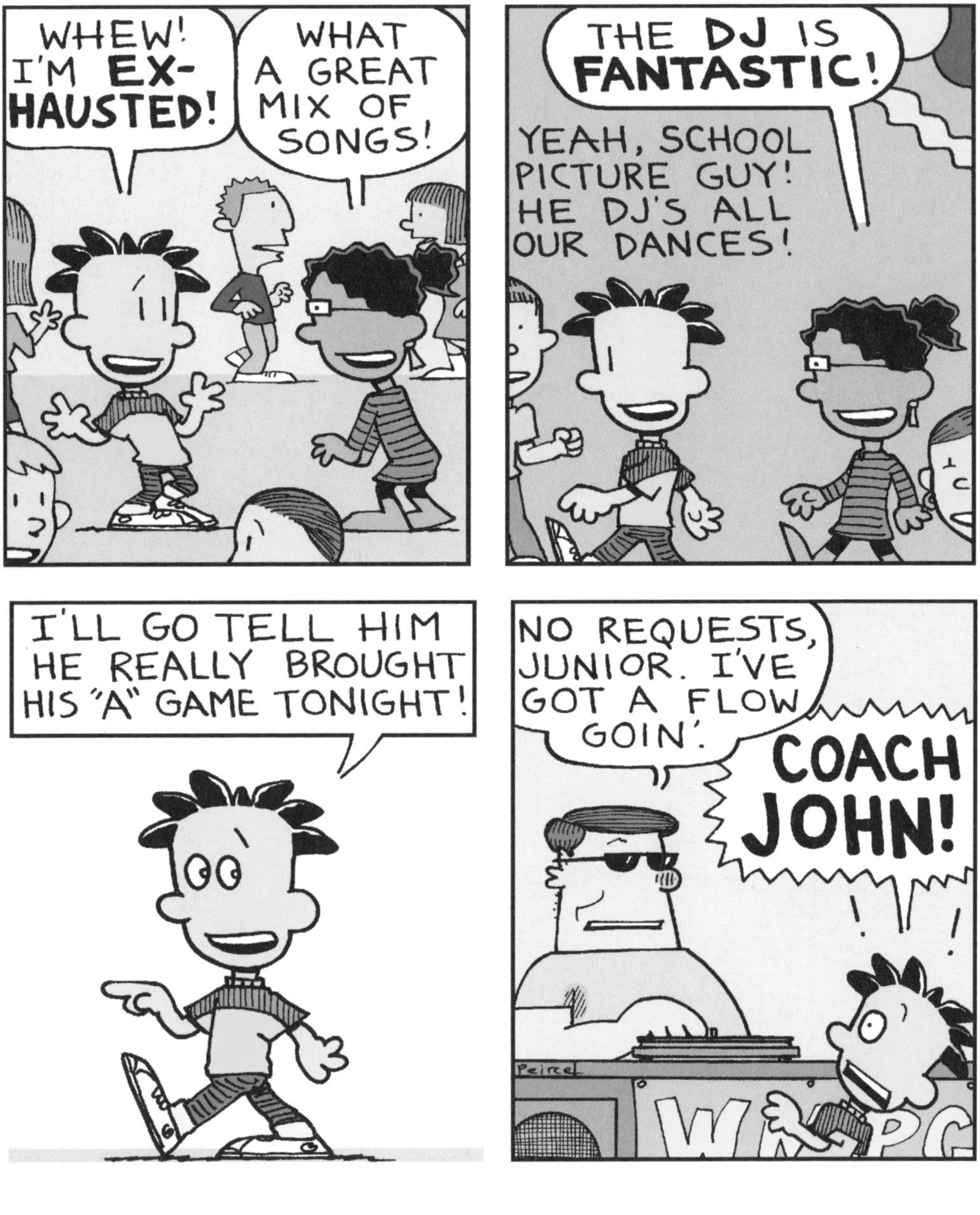
WHEW! I'M **EX-HAUSTED!**
WHAT A GREAT MIX OF SONGS!
THE **DJ** IS **FANTASTIC!**
YEAH, SCHOOL PICTURE GUY! HE DJ'S ALL OUR DANCES!
I'LL GO TELL HIM HE REALLY BROUGHT HIS "A" GAME TONIGHT!
NO REQUESTS, JUNIOR. I'VE GOT A FLOW GOIN'.
COACH JOHN!
! !
Peirce

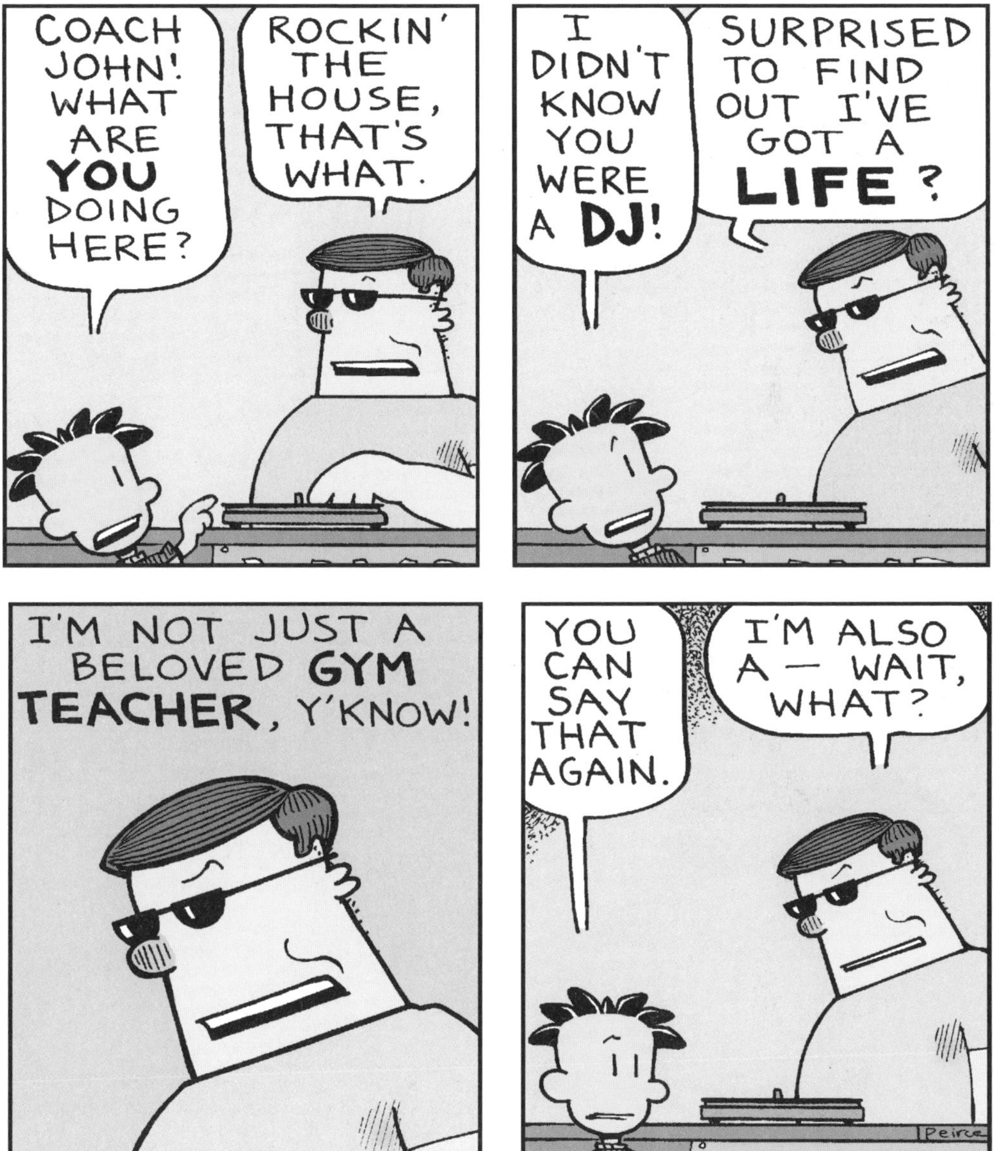
COACH JOHN! WHAT ARE **YOU** DOING HERE?
ROCKIN' THE HOUSE, THAT'S WHAT.
I DIDN'T KNOW YOU WERE A **DJ**!
SURPRISED TO FIND OUT I'VE GOT A **LIFE**?
I'M NOT JUST A BELOVED **GYM TEACHER**, Y'KNOW!
YOU CAN SAY THAT AGAIN.
I'M ALSO A — WAIT, WHAT?
Peirce

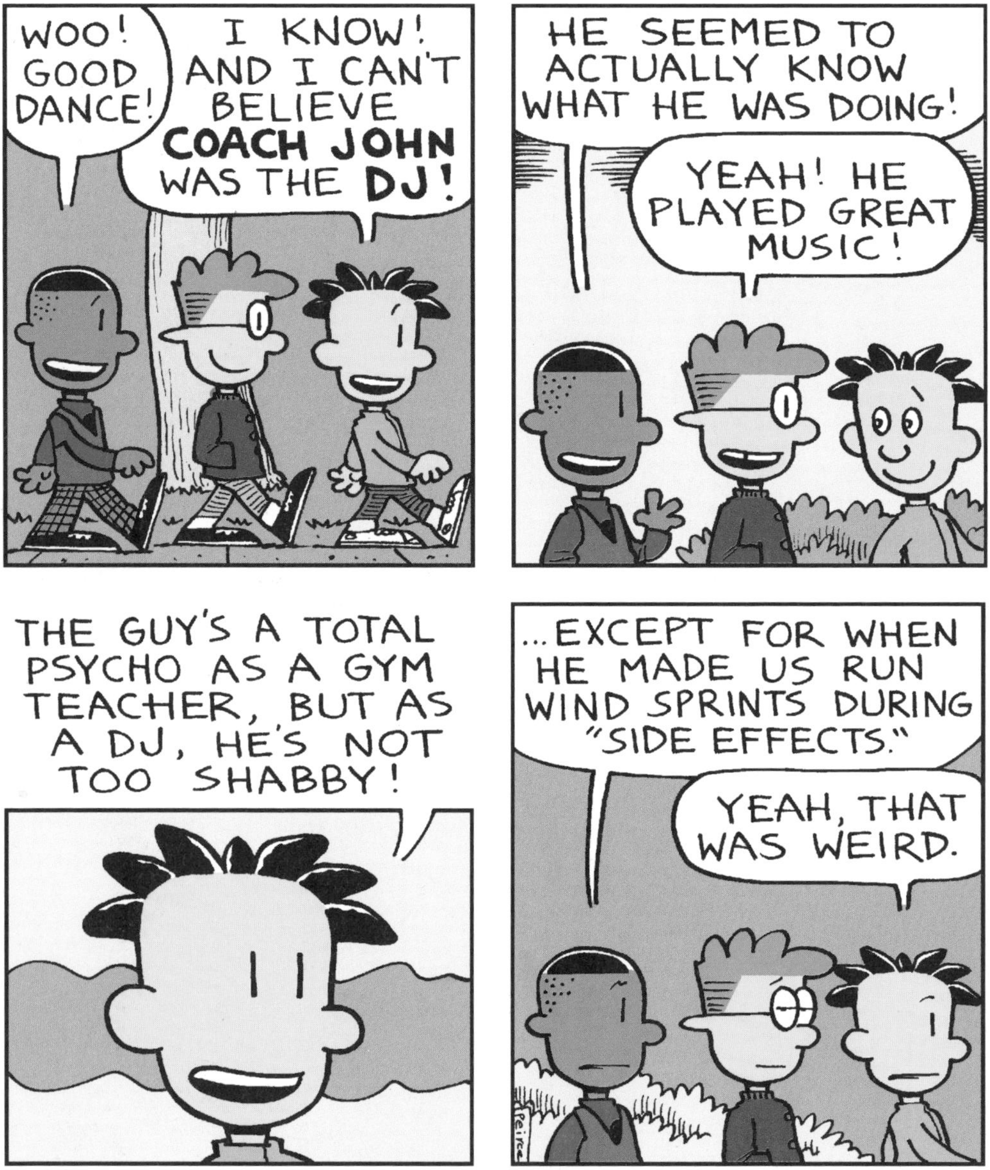
WOO! GOOD DANCE!
I KNOW! AND I CAN'T BELIEVE **COACH JOHN** WAS THE **DJ**!
HE SEEMED TO ACTUALLY KNOW WHAT HE WAS DOING!
YEAH! HE PLAYED GREAT MUSIC!
THE GUY'S A TOTAL PSYCHO AS A GYM TEACHER, BUT AS A DJ, HE'S NOT TOO SHABBY!
...EXCEPT FOR WHEN HE MADE US RUN WIND SPRINTS DURING "SIDE EFFECTS."
YEAH, THAT WAS WEIRD.
Peirce

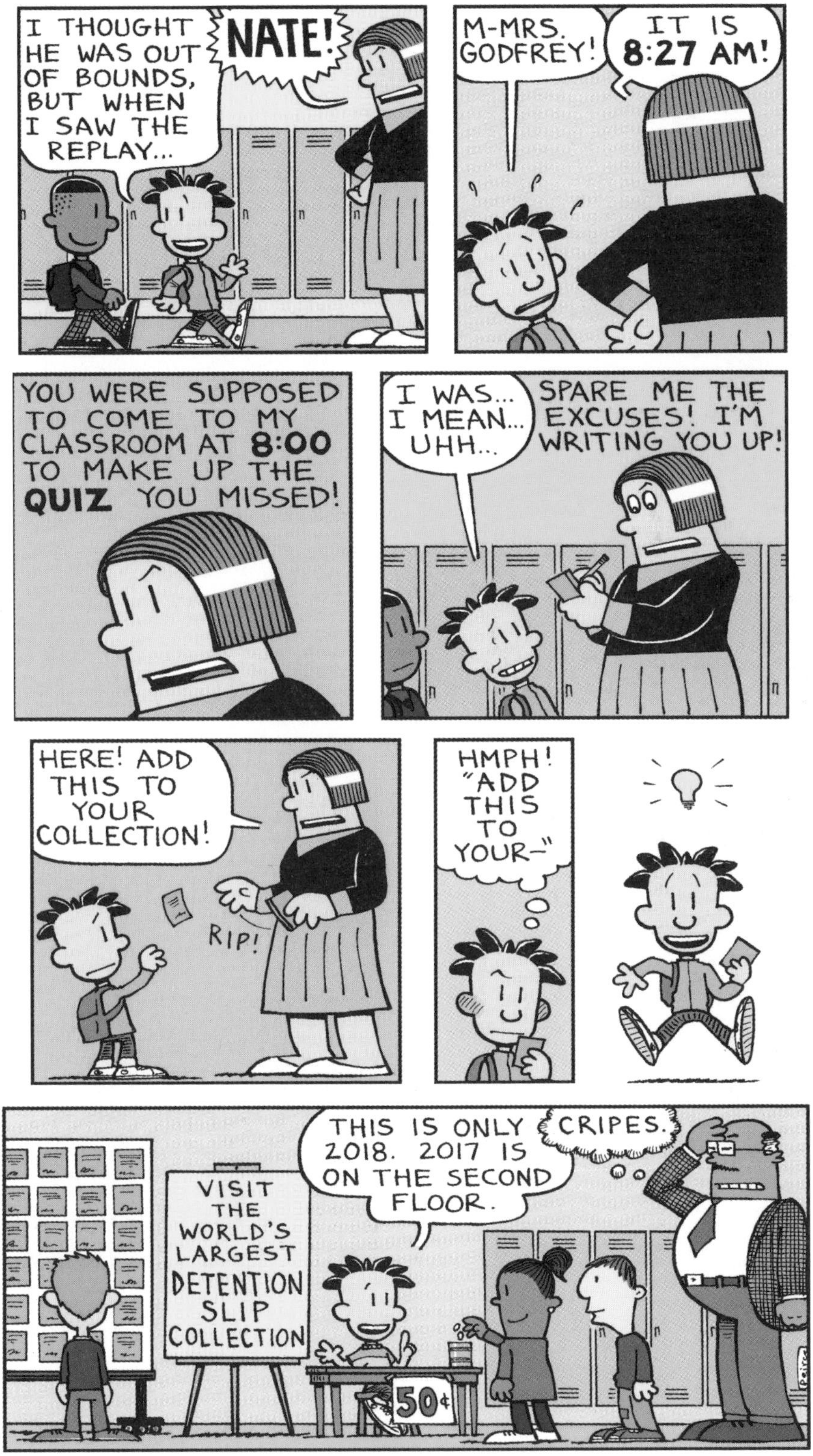

I THOUGHT HE WAS OUT OF BOUNDS, BUT WHEN I SAW THE REPLAY...
NATE!
M-MRS. GODFREY!
IT IS 8:27 AM!
YOU WERE SUPPOSED TO COME TO MY CLASSROOM AT 8:00 TO MAKE UP THE QUIZ YOU MISSED!
I WAS... I MEAN... UHH...
SPARE ME THE EXCUSES! I'M WRITING YOU UP!
HERE! ADD THIS TO YOUR COLLECTION!
RIP!
HMPH! "ADD THIS TO YOUR—"
VISIT THE WORLD'S LARGEST DETENTION SLIP COLLECTION
THIS IS ONLY 2018. 2017 IS ON THE SECOND FLOOR.
CRIPES.
50¢

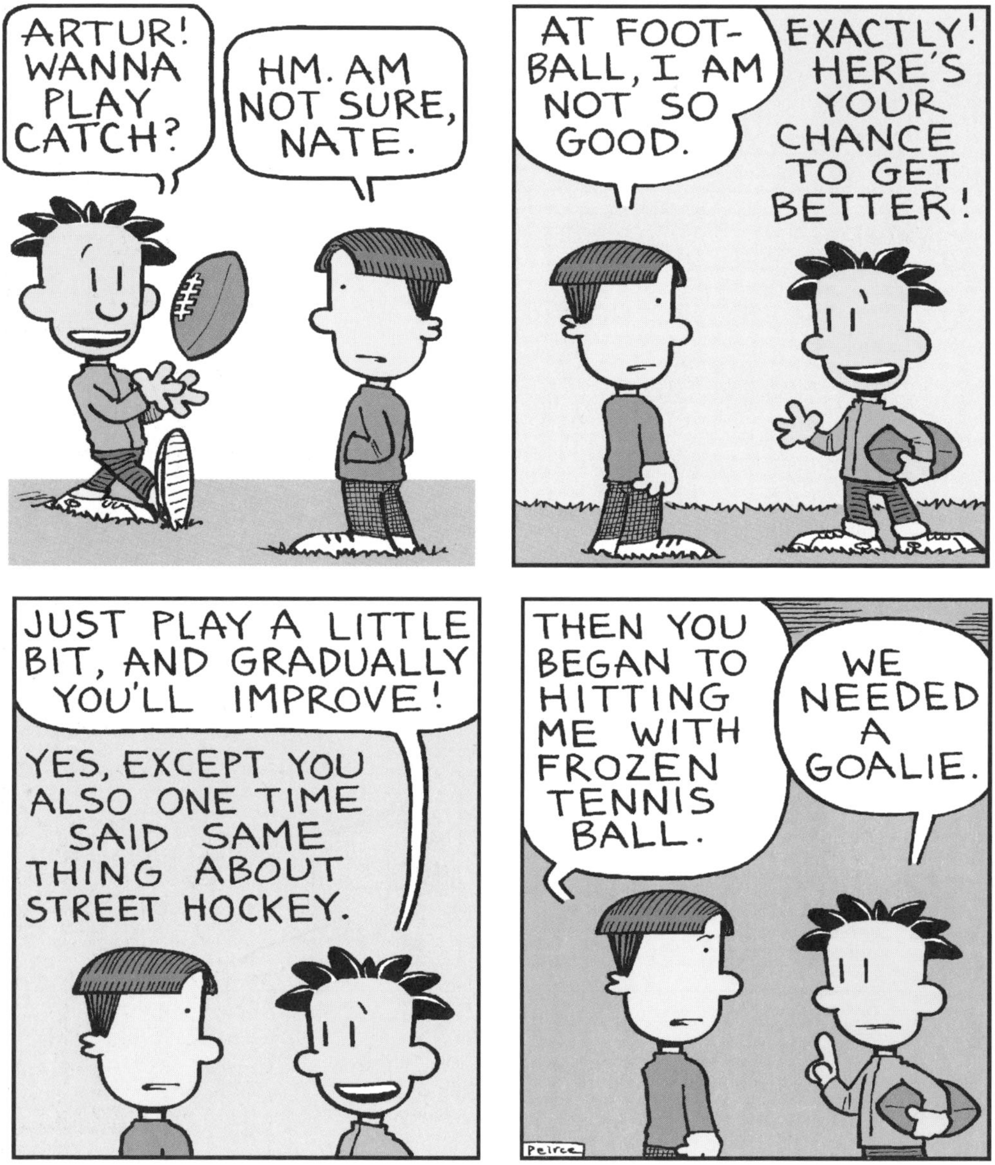
ARTUR! WANNA PLAY CATCH?
HM. AM NOT SURE, NATE.
AT FOOT-BALL, I AM NOT SO GOOD.
EXACTLY! HERE'S YOUR CHANCE TO GET BETTER!
JUST PLAY A LITTLE BIT, AND GRADUALLY YOU'LL IMPROVE!
YES, EXCEPT YOU ALSO ONE TIME SAID SAME THING ABOUT STREET HOCKEY.
THEN YOU BEGAN TO HITTING ME WITH FROZEN TENNIS BALL.
WE NEEDED A GOALIE.
Peirce

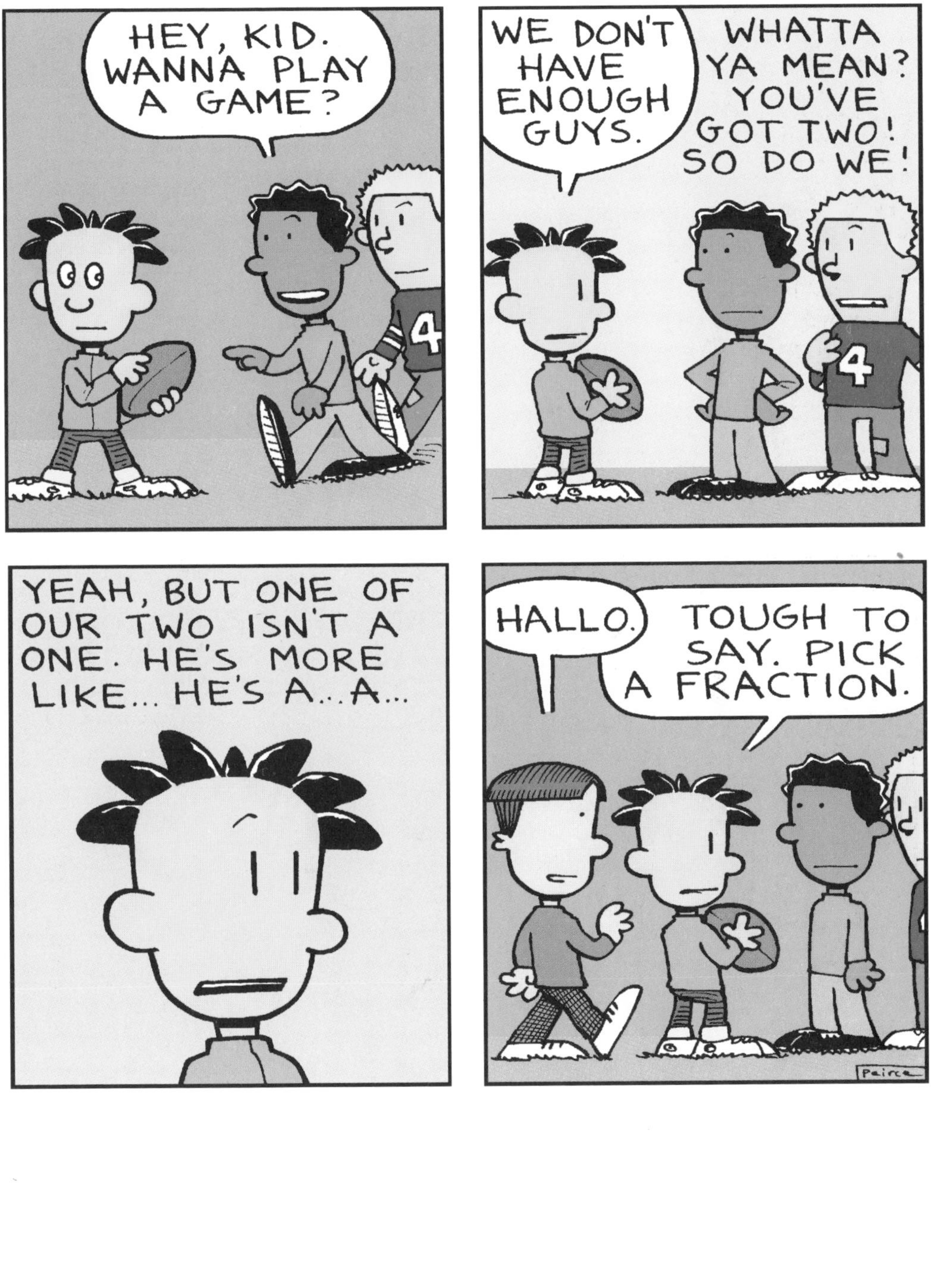
HEY, KID. WANNA PLAY A GAME?
WE DON'T HAVE ENOUGH GUYS.
WHATTA YA MEAN? YOU'VE GOT TWO! SO DO WE!
YEAH, BUT ONE OF OUR TWO ISN'T A ONE. HE'S MORE LIKE... HE'S A... A...
HALLO.
TOUGH TO SAY. PICK A FRACTION.
Peirce

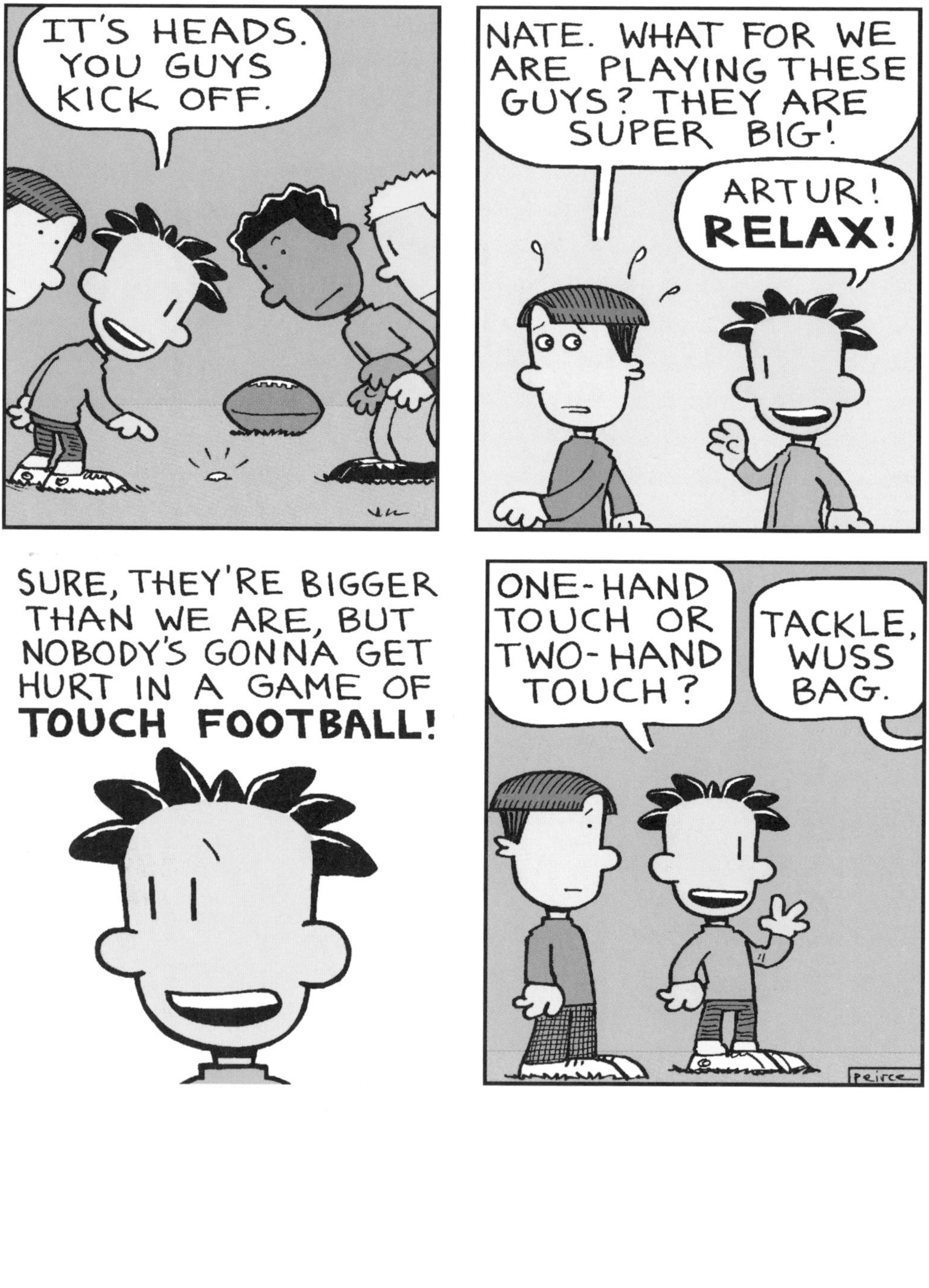
IT'S HEADS. YOU GUYS KICK OFF.
NATE. WHAT FOR WE ARE PLAYING THESE GUYS? THEY ARE SUPER BIG!
ARTUR! **RELAX!**
SURE, THEY'RE BIGGER THAN WE ARE, BUT NOBODY'S GONNA GET HURT IN A GAME OF **TOUCH FOOTBALL!**
ONE-HAND TOUCH OR TWO-HAND TOUCH?
TACKLE, WUSS BAG.
peirce

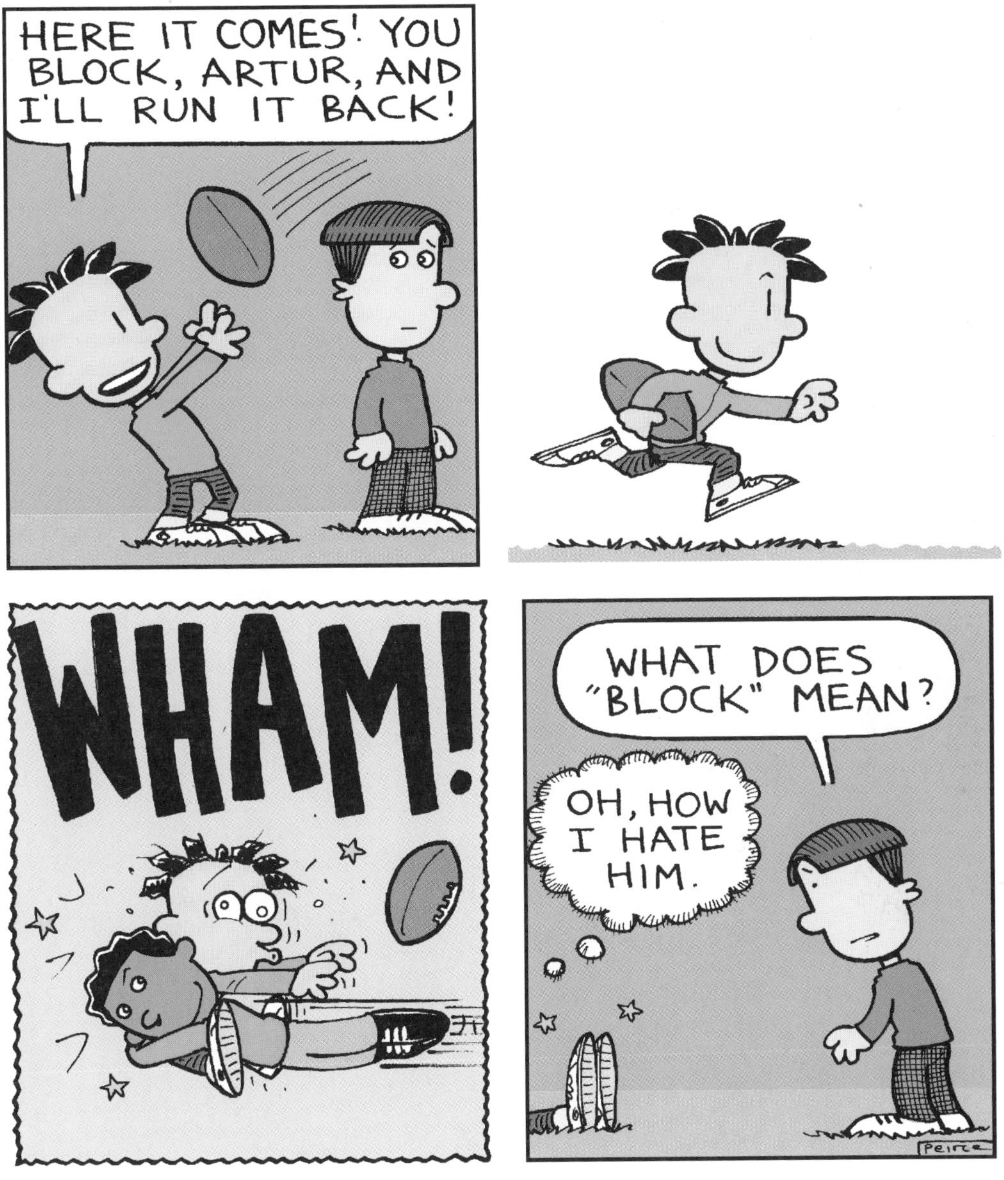
HERE IT COMES! YOU BLOCK, ARTUR, AND I'LL RUN IT BACK!
WHAM!
WHAT DOES "BLOCK" MEAN?
OH, HOW I HATE HIM.
Peirce

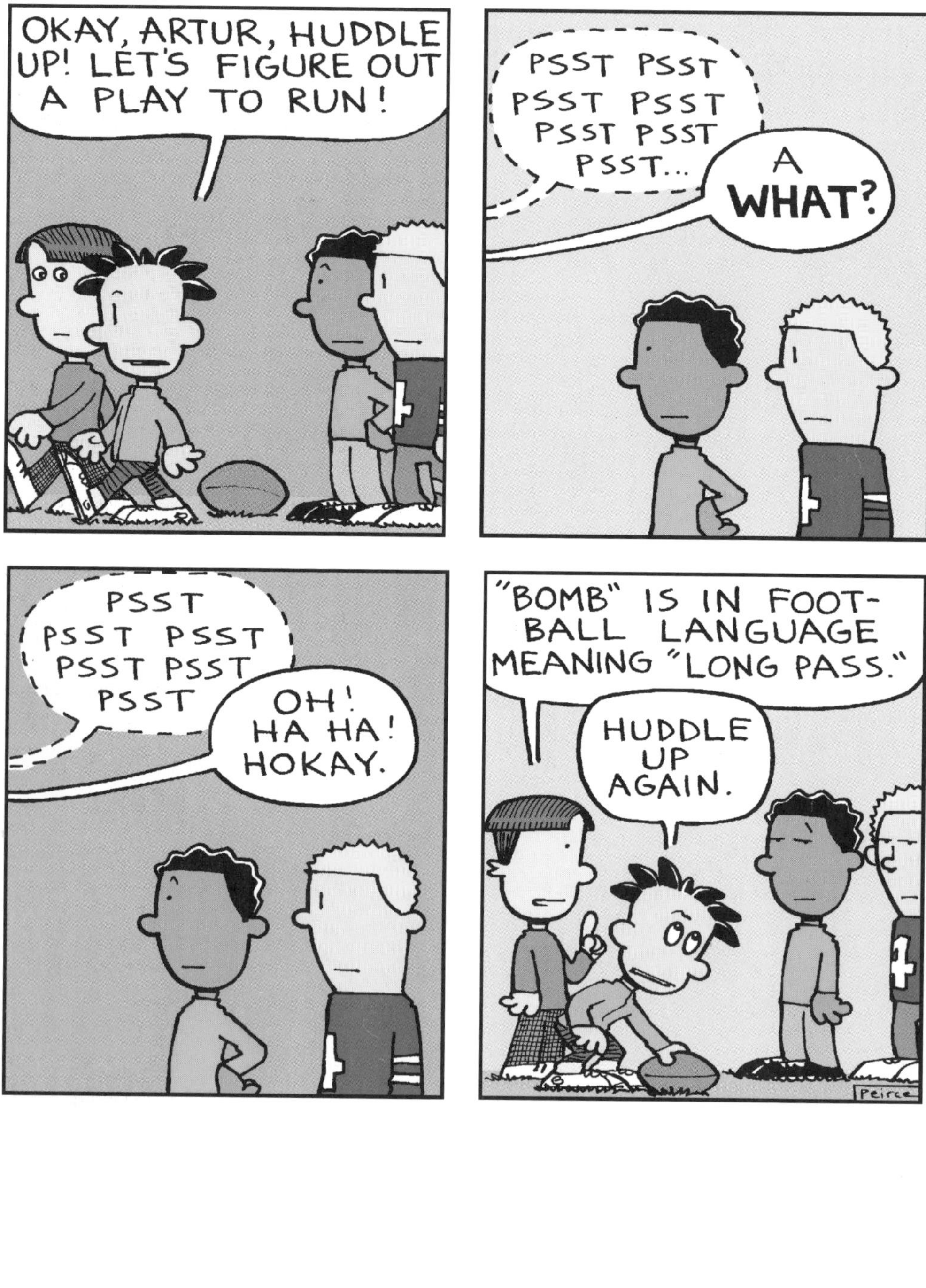
OKAY, ARTUR, HUDDLE UP! LET'S FIGURE OUT A PLAY TO RUN!
PSST PSST PSST PSST PSST PSST PSST...
A WHAT?
PSST PSST PSST PSST PSST PSST
OH! HA HA! HOKAY.
"BOMB" IS IN FOOT-BALL LANGUAGE MEANING "LONG PASS."
HUDDLE UP AGAIN.
Peirce

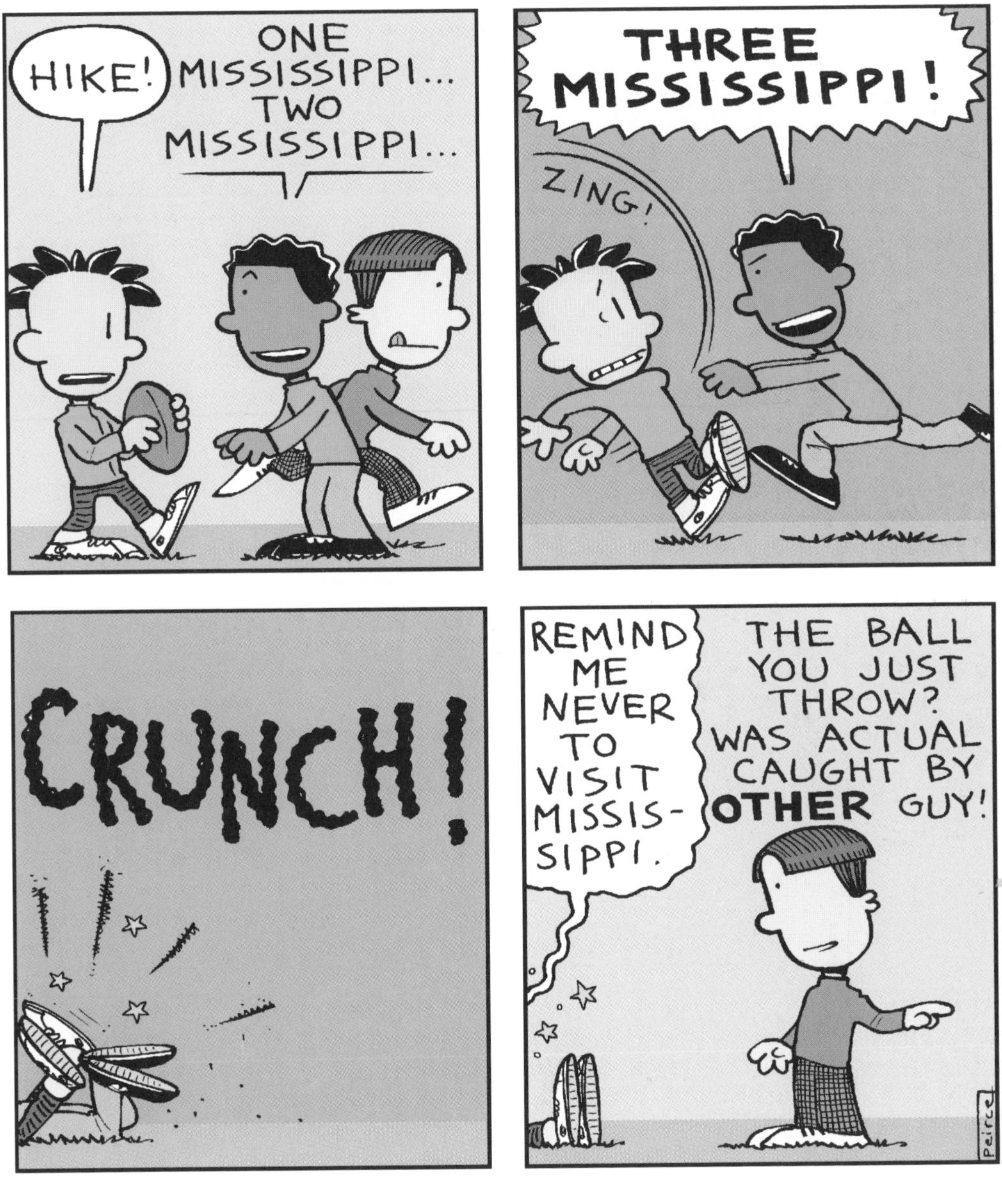
HIKE!
ONE MISSISSIPPI... TWO MISSISSIPPI...
THREE MISSISSIPPI!
ZING!
CRUNCH!
REMIND ME NEVER TO VISIT MISSIS-SIPPI.
THE BALL YOU JUST THROW? WAS ACTUAL CAUGHT BY OTHER GUY!
peirce

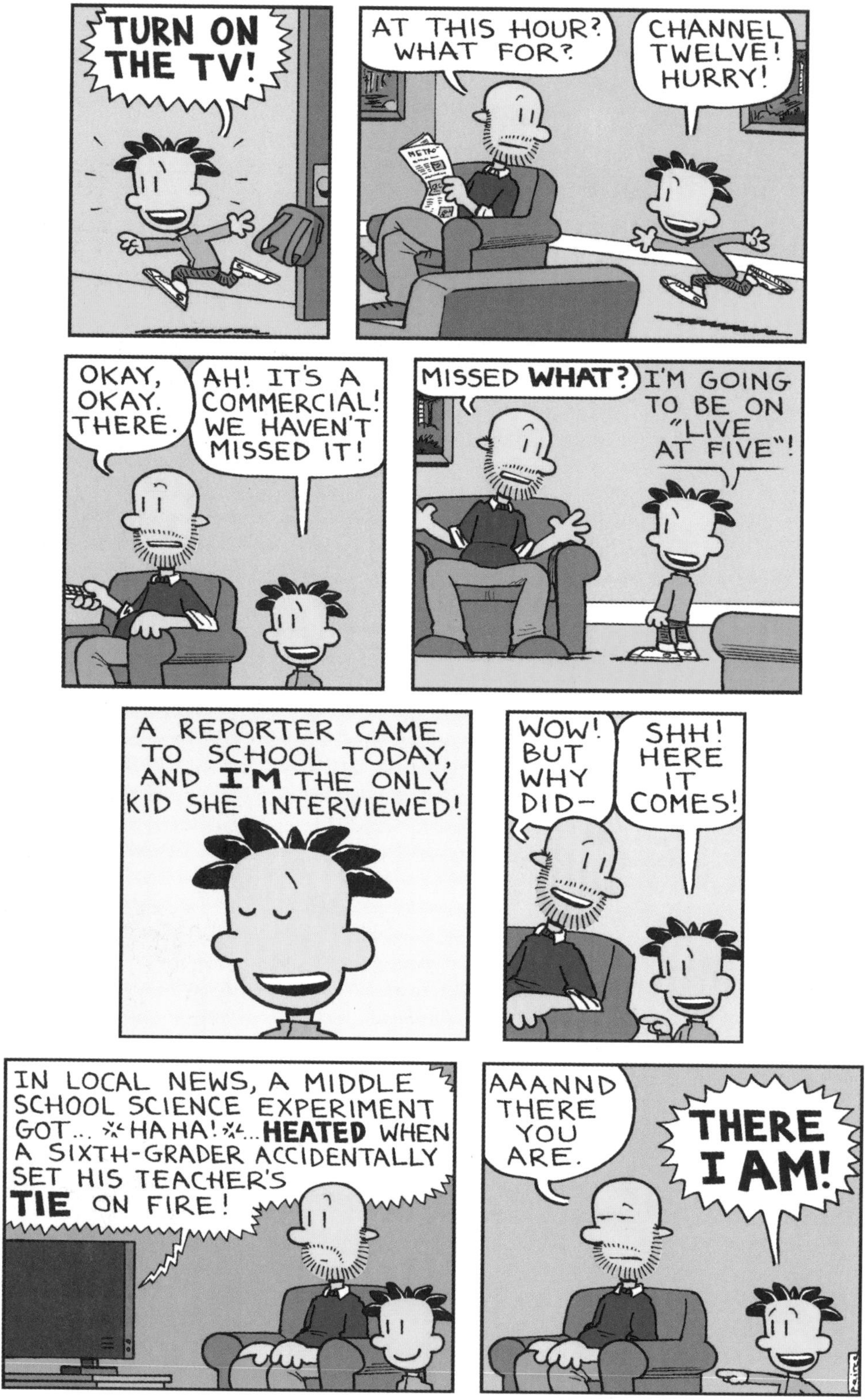
TURN ON THE TV!
AT THIS HOUR? WHAT FOR?
CHANNEL TWELVE! HURRY!
OKAY, OKAY. THERE.
AH! IT'S A COMMERCIAL! WE HAVEN'T MISSED IT!
MISSED WHAT?
I'M GOING TO BE ON "LIVE AT FIVE"!
A REPORTER CAME TO SCHOOL TODAY, AND I'M THE ONLY KID SHE INTERVIEWED!
WOW! BUT WHY DID-
SHH! HERE IT COMES!
IN LOCAL NEWS, A MIDDLE SCHOOL SCIENCE EXPERIMENT GOT... HA HA! ...HEATED WHEN A SIXTH-GRADER ACCIDENTALLY SET HIS TEACHER'S TIE ON FIRE!
AAANND THERE YOU ARE.
THERE I AM!

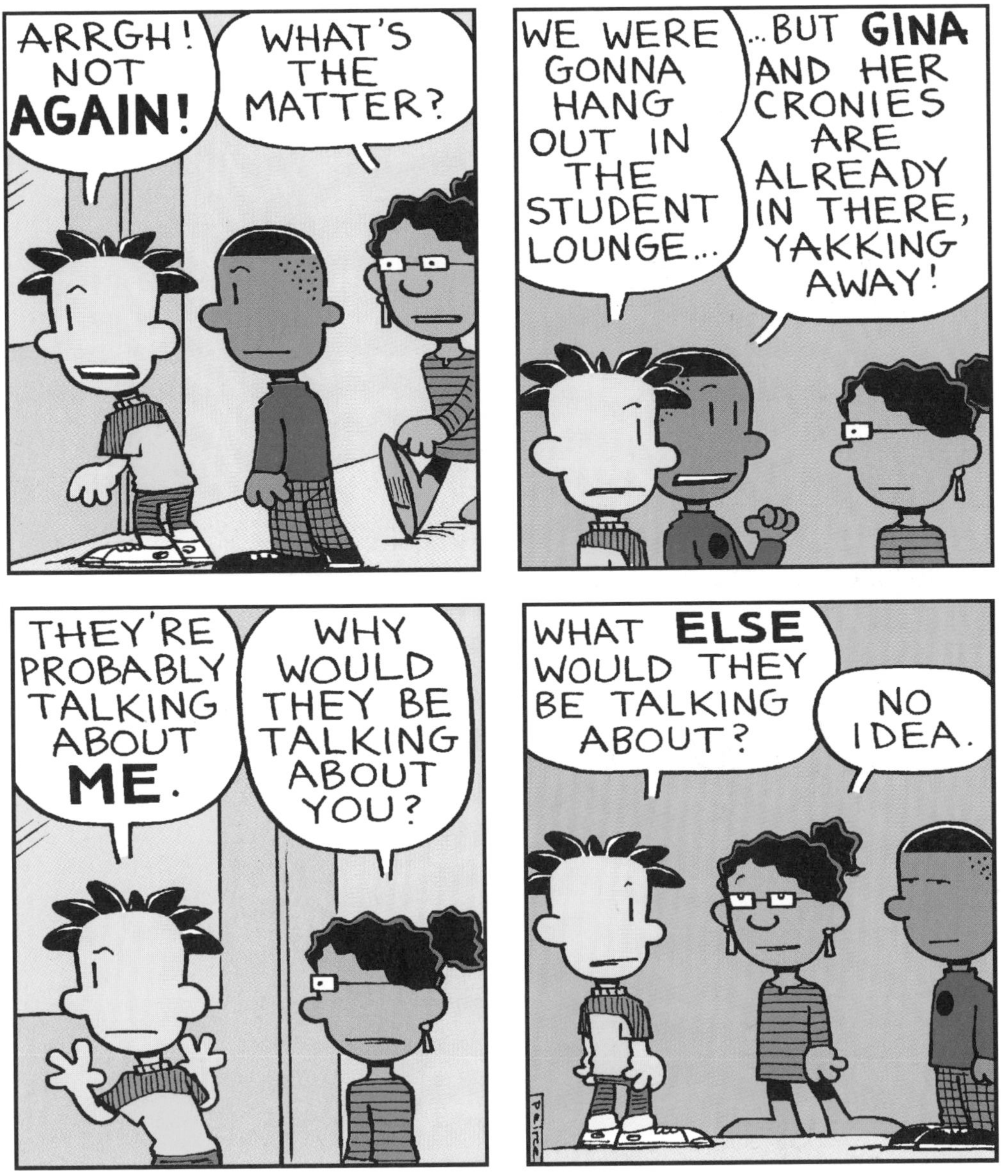
ARRGH! NOT AGAIN!
WHAT'S THE MATTER?
WE WERE GONNA HANG OUT IN THE STUDENT LOUNGE...
...BUT GINA AND HER CRONIES ARE ALREADY IN THERE, YAKKING AWAY!
THEY'RE PROBABLY TALKING ABOUT ME.
WHY WOULD THEY BE TALKING ABOUT YOU?
WHAT ELSE WOULD THEY BE TALKING ABOUT?
NO IDEA.
PEIRCE

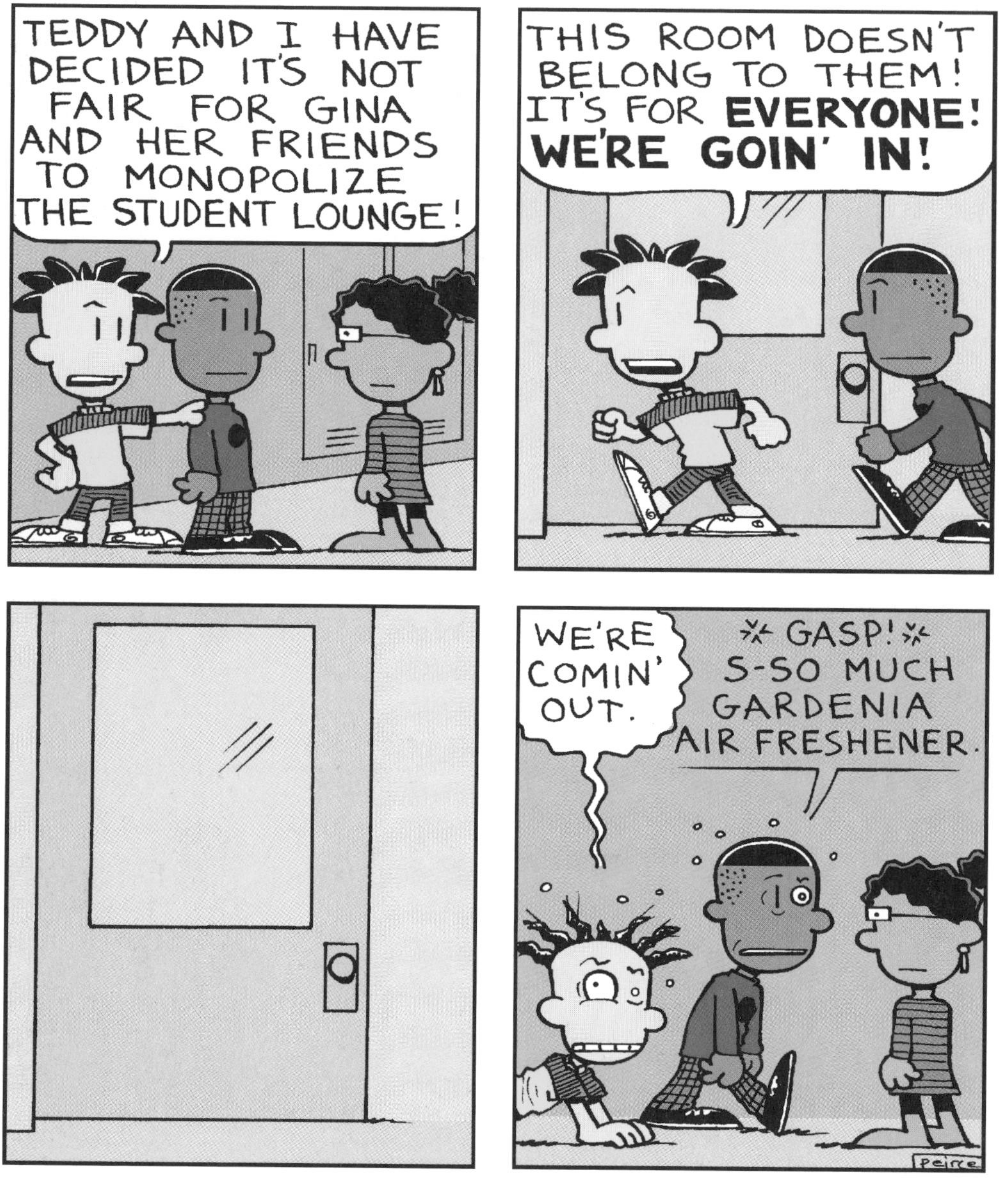
TEDDY AND I HAVE DECIDED IT'S NOT FAIR FOR GINA AND HER FRIENDS TO MONOPOLIZE THE STUDENT LOUNGE!
THIS ROOM DOESN'T BELONG TO THEM! IT'S FOR EVERYONE! WE'RE GOIN' IN!
WE'RE COMIN' OUT.
GASP! S-SO MUCH GARDENIA AIR FRESHENER.
Peirce

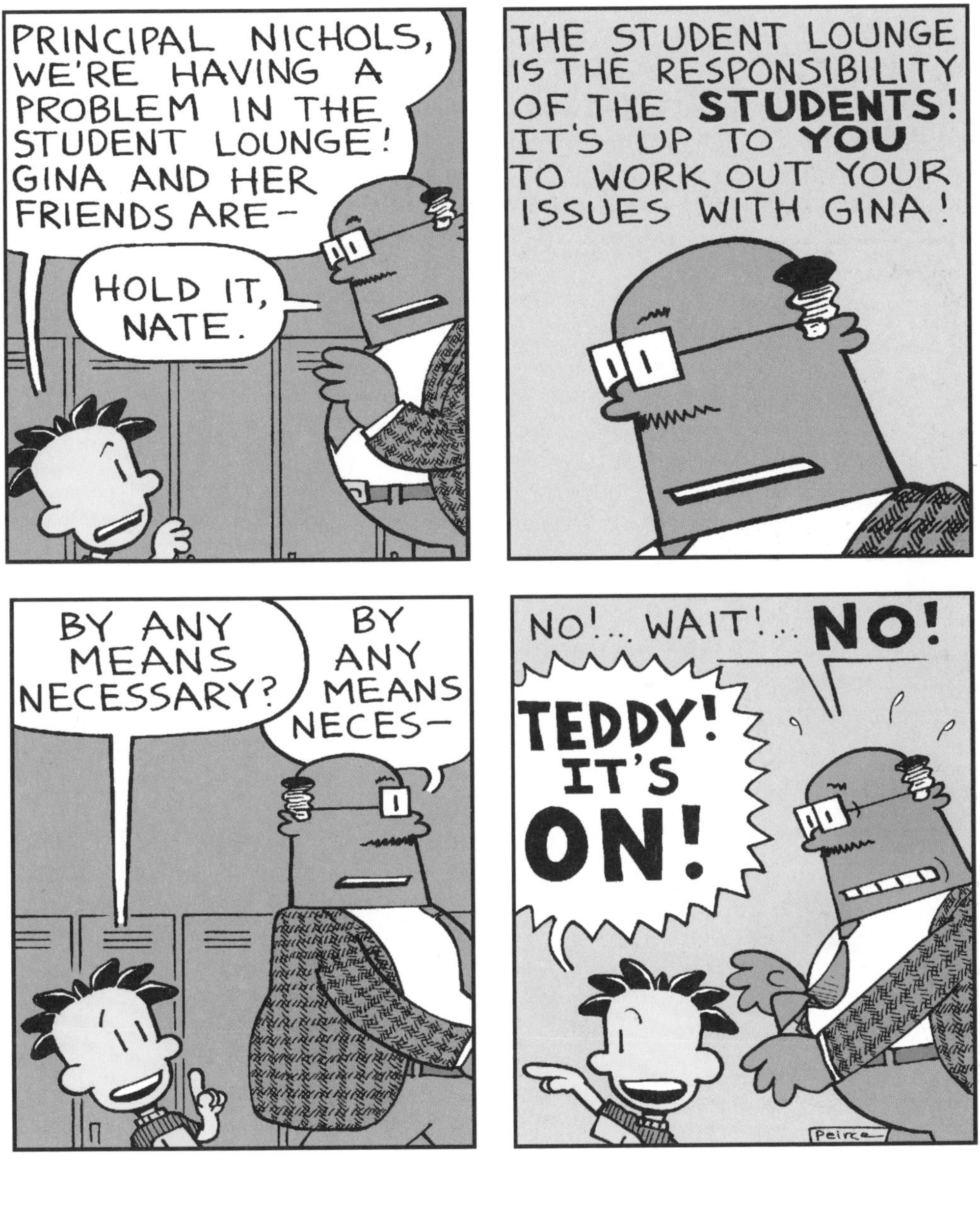
PRINCIPAL NICHOLS, WE'RE HAVING A PROBLEM IN THE STUDENT LOUNGE! GINA AND HER FRIENDS ARE-
HOLD IT, NATE.
THE STUDENT LOUNGE IS THE RESPONSIBILITY OF THE **STUDENTS**! IT'S UP TO **YOU** TO WORK OUT YOUR ISSUES WITH GINA!
BY ANY MEANS NECESSARY?
BY ANY MEANS NECES-
TEDDY! IT'S ON!
NO!... WAIT!... **NO!**
Peirce

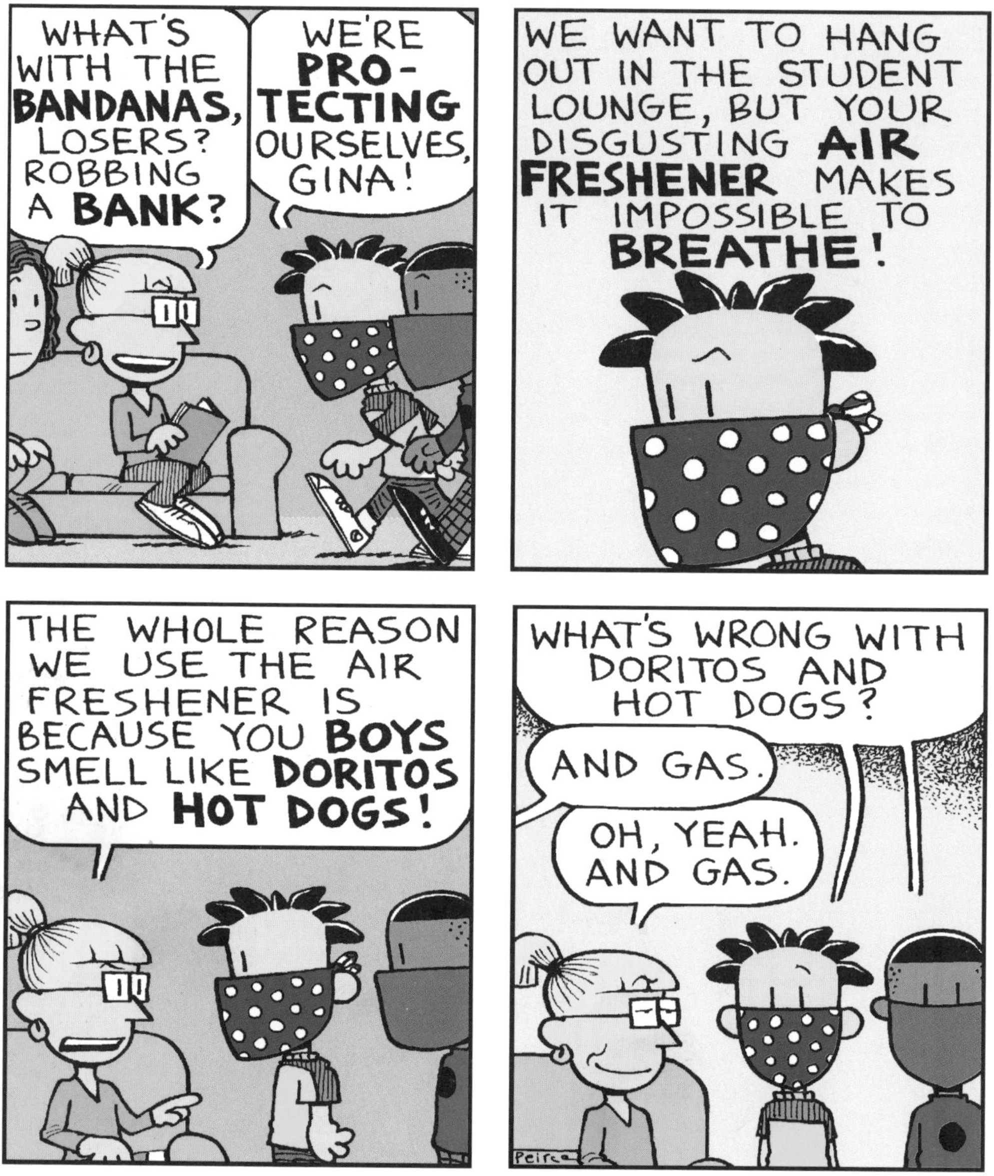
WHAT'S WITH THE BANDANAS, LOSERS? ROBBING A BANK?
WE'RE PRO-TECTING OURSELVES, GINA!
WE WANT TO HANG OUT IN THE STUDENT LOUNGE, BUT YOUR DISGUSTING AIR FRESHENER MAKES IT IMPOSSIBLE TO BREATHE!
THE WHOLE REASON WE USE THE AIR FRESHENER IS BECAUSE YOU BOYS SMELL LIKE DORITOS AND HOT DOGS!
WHAT'S WRONG WITH DORITOS AND HOT DOGS?
AND GAS.
OH, YEAH. AND GAS.
Peirce

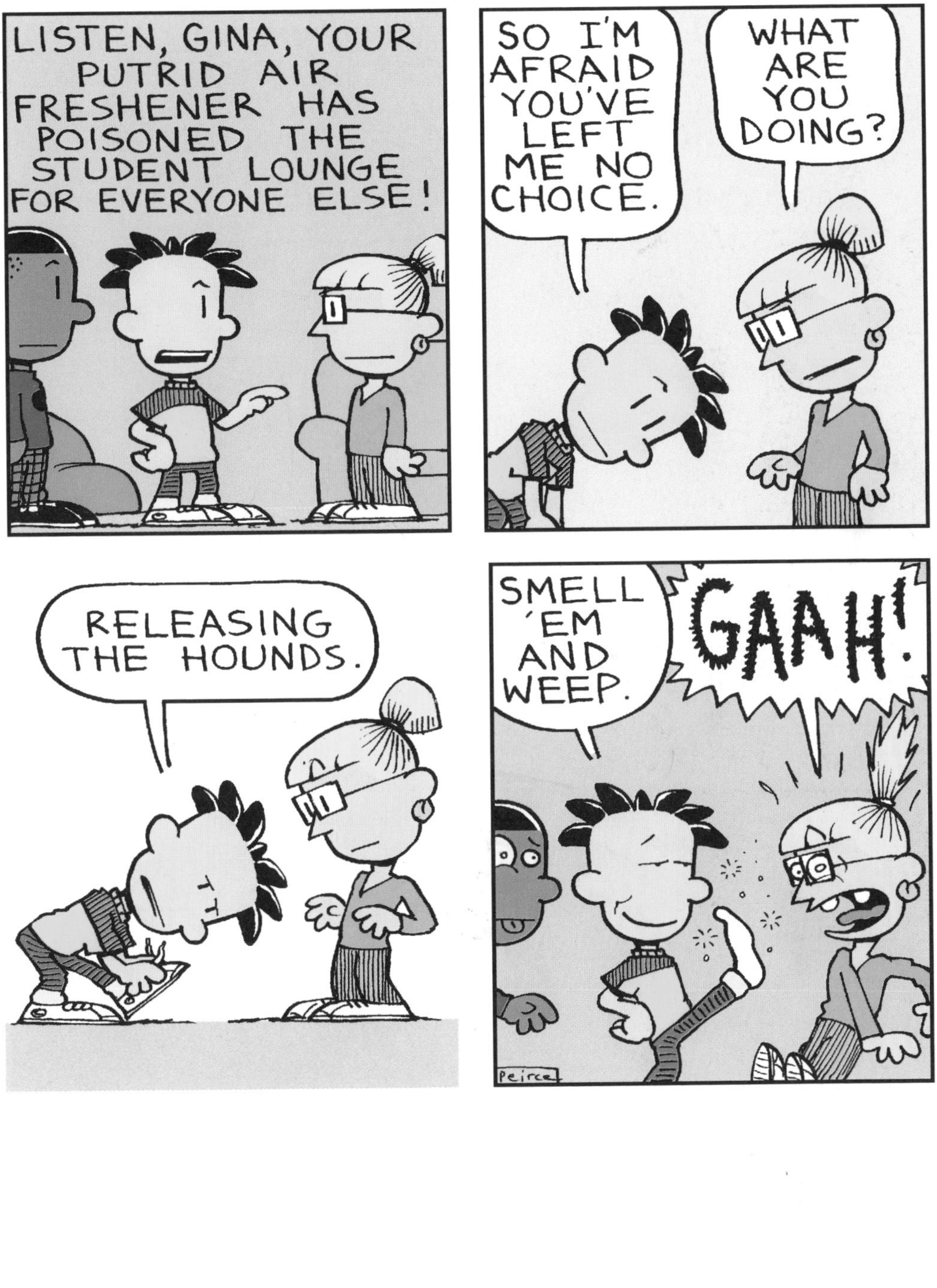
LISTEN, GINA, YOUR PUTRID AIR FRESHENER HAS POISONED THE STUDENT LOUNGE FOR EVERYONE ELSE!
SO I'M AFRAID YOU'VE LEFT ME NO CHOICE.
WHAT ARE YOU DOING?
RELEASING THE HOUNDS.
SMELL 'EM AND WEEP.
GAAH!
Peirce

HA! DID YOU SEE HOW FAST THOSE GIRLS CLEARED OUT OF HERE? THE STUDENT LOUNGE IS **OURS**!
UH-HUH.
THE SMELL OF MY **FEET** TOTALLY OVERPOWERED GINA'S AIR FRESHENER!
Y-YEAH.
AHHHHHHHH! FIGHT FIRE WITH FIRE, I ALWAYS SAY!
TEDDY?
I NEEDED TO LIE DOWN.
peirce

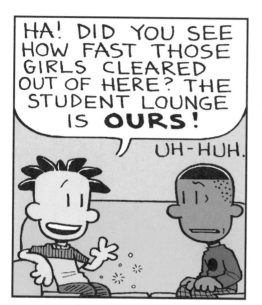

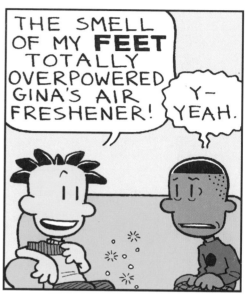

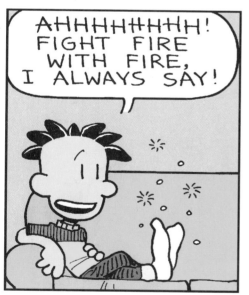

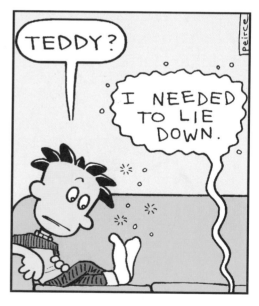

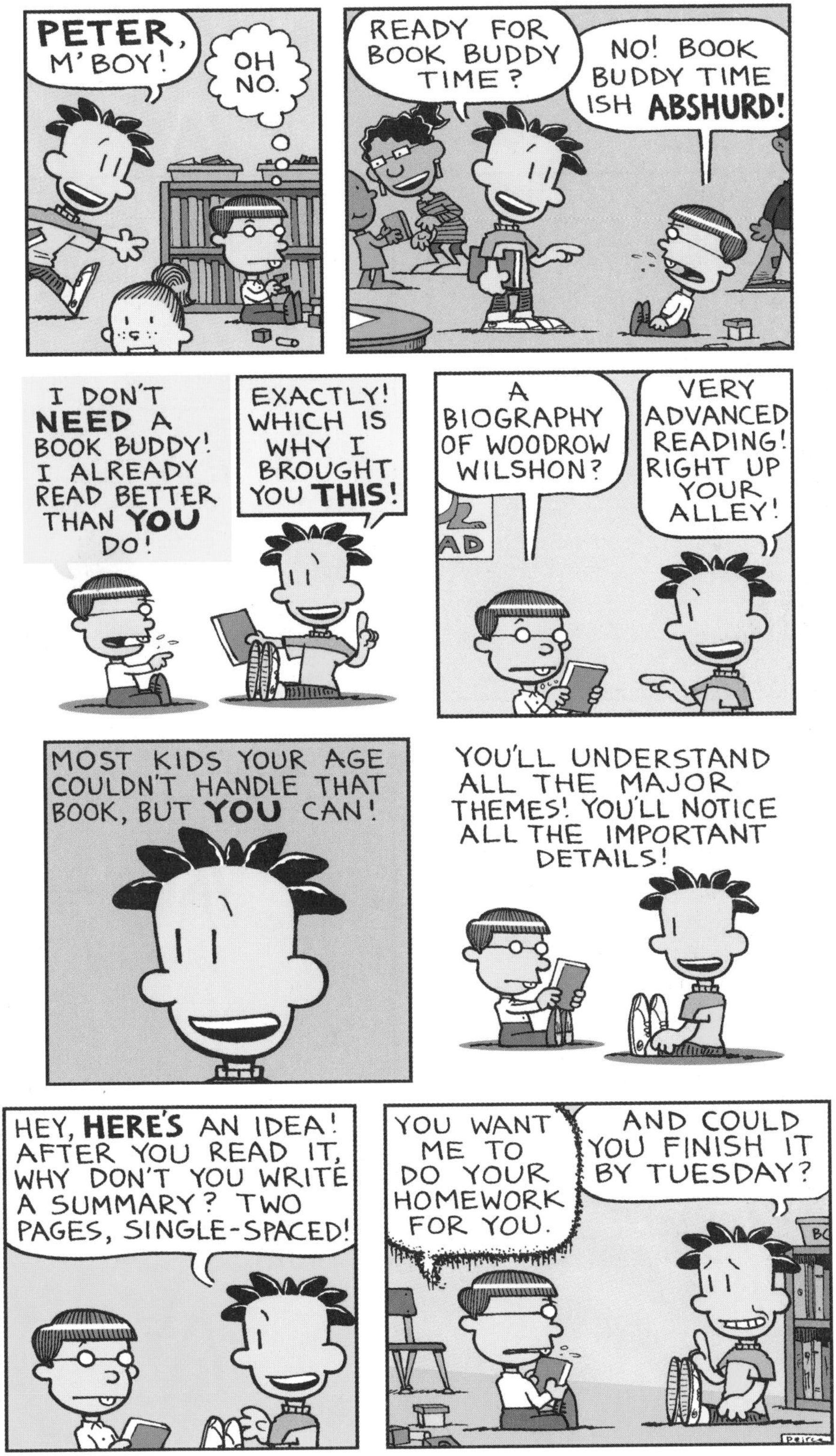
PETER, M'BOY!
OH NO.
READY FOR BOOK BUDDY TIME?
NO! BOOK BUDDY TIME ISH ABSHURD!
I DON'T NEED A BOOK BUDDY! I ALREADY READ BETTER THAN YOU DO!
EXACTLY! WHICH IS WHY I BROUGHT YOU THIS!
A BIOGRAPHY OF WOODROW WILSHON?
VERY ADVANCED READING! RIGHT UP YOUR ALLEY!
MOST KIDS YOUR AGE COULDN'T HANDLE THAT BOOK, BUT YOU CAN!
YOU'LL UNDERSTAND ALL THE MAJOR THEMES! YOU'LL NOTICE ALL THE IMPORTANT DETAILS!
HEY, HERE'S AN IDEA! AFTER YOU READ IT, WHY DON'T YOU WRITE A SUMMARY? TWO PAGES, SINGLE-SPACED!
YOU WANT ME TO DO YOUR HOMEWORK FOR YOU.
AND COULD YOU FINISH IT BY TUESDAY?
PEIRCE

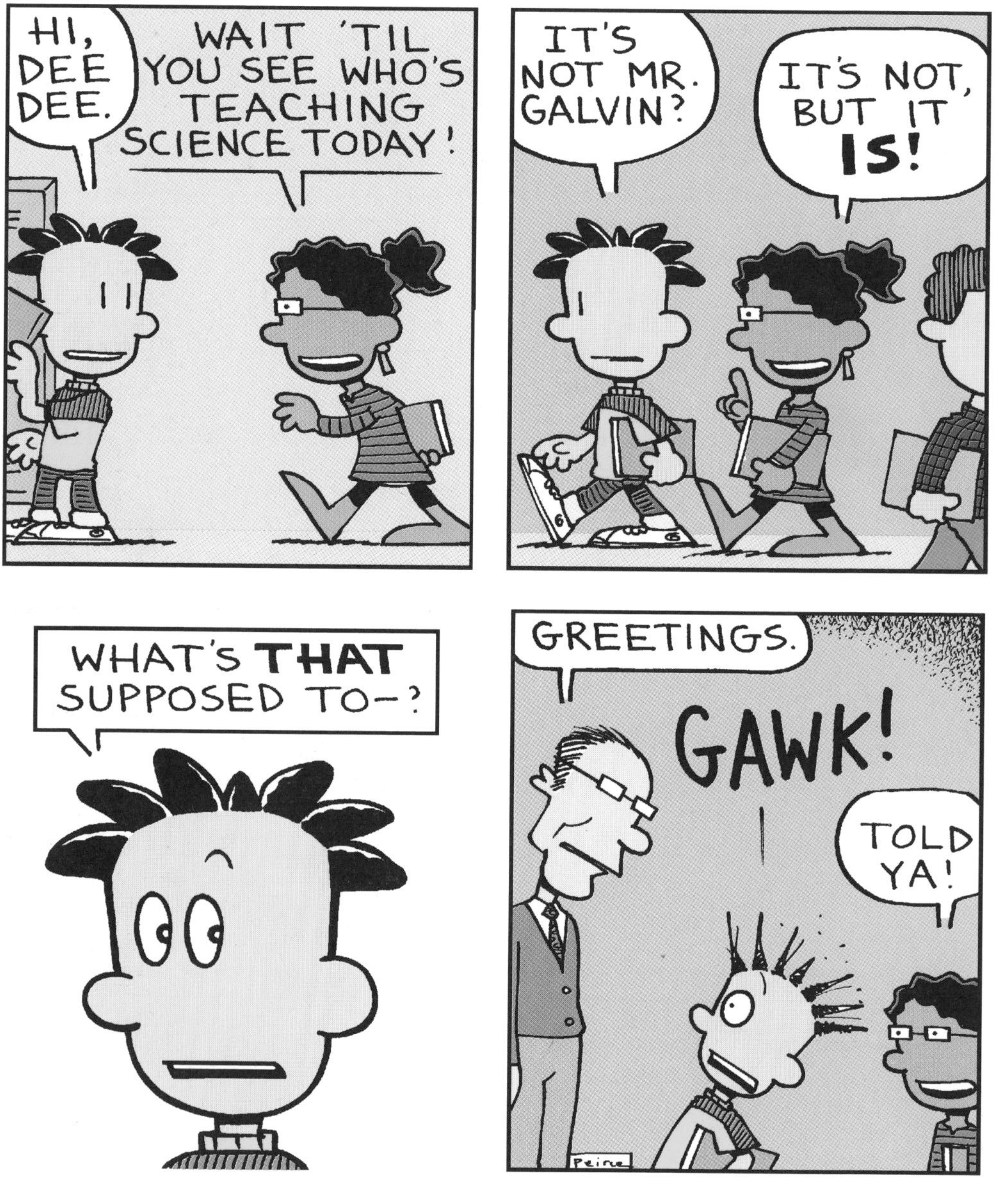
HI, DEE DEE.
WAIT 'TIL YOU SEE WHO'S TEACHING SCIENCE TODAY!
IT'S NOT MR. GALVIN?
IT'S NOT, BUT IT IS!
WHAT'S THAT SUPPOSED TO-?
GREETINGS.
GAWK!
TOLD YA!
Peirce

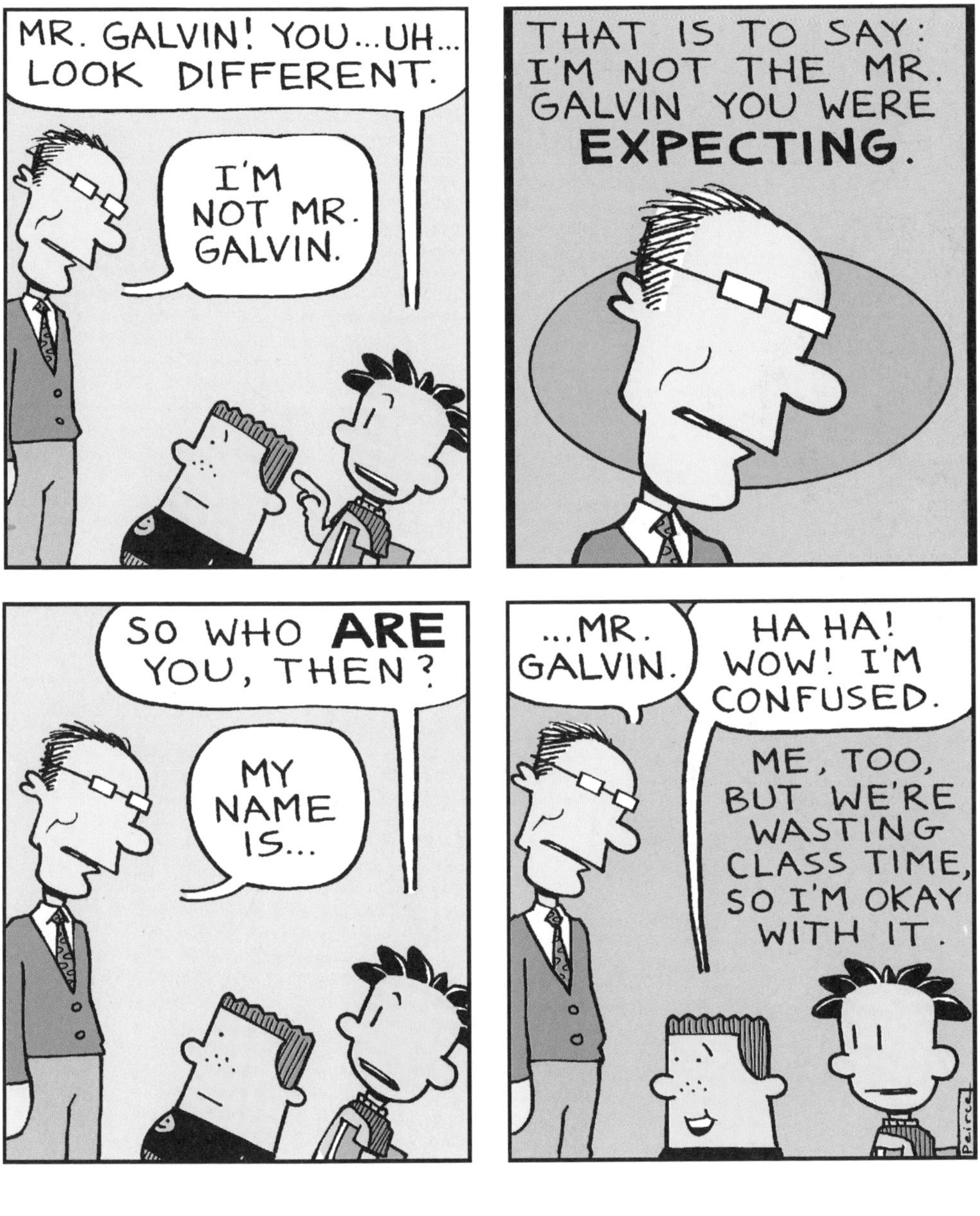

MR. GALVIN! YOU...UH... LOOK DIFFERENT.
I'M NOT MR. GALVIN.
THAT IS TO SAY: I'M NOT THE MR. GALVIN YOU WERE **EXPECTING**.
SO WHO **ARE** YOU, THEN?
MY NAME IS...
...MR. GALVIN.
HA HA! WOW! I'M CONFUSED.
ME, TOO, BUT WE'RE WASTING CLASS TIME, SO I'M OKAY WITH IT.
Peirce

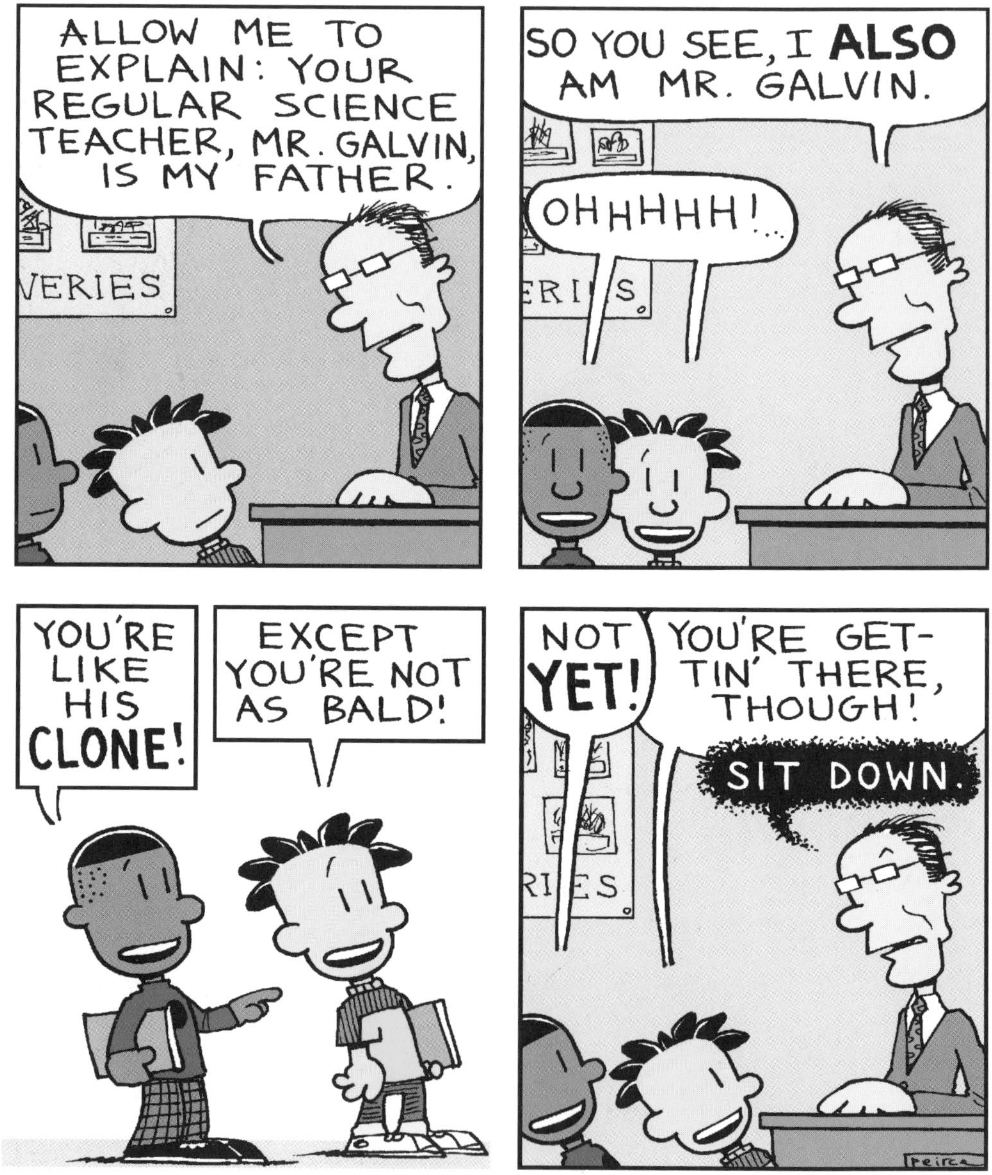
ALLOW ME TO EXPLAIN: YOUR REGULAR SCIENCE TEACHER, MR. GALVIN, IS MY FATHER.
VERIES
SO YOU SEE, I **ALSO** AM MR. GALVIN.
OHHHHH!...
YOU'RE LIKE HIS **CLONE!**
EXCEPT YOU'RE NOT AS BALD!
NOT **YET!**
YOU'RE GET-TIN' THERE, THOUGH!
SIT DOWN.
RIES
peirce

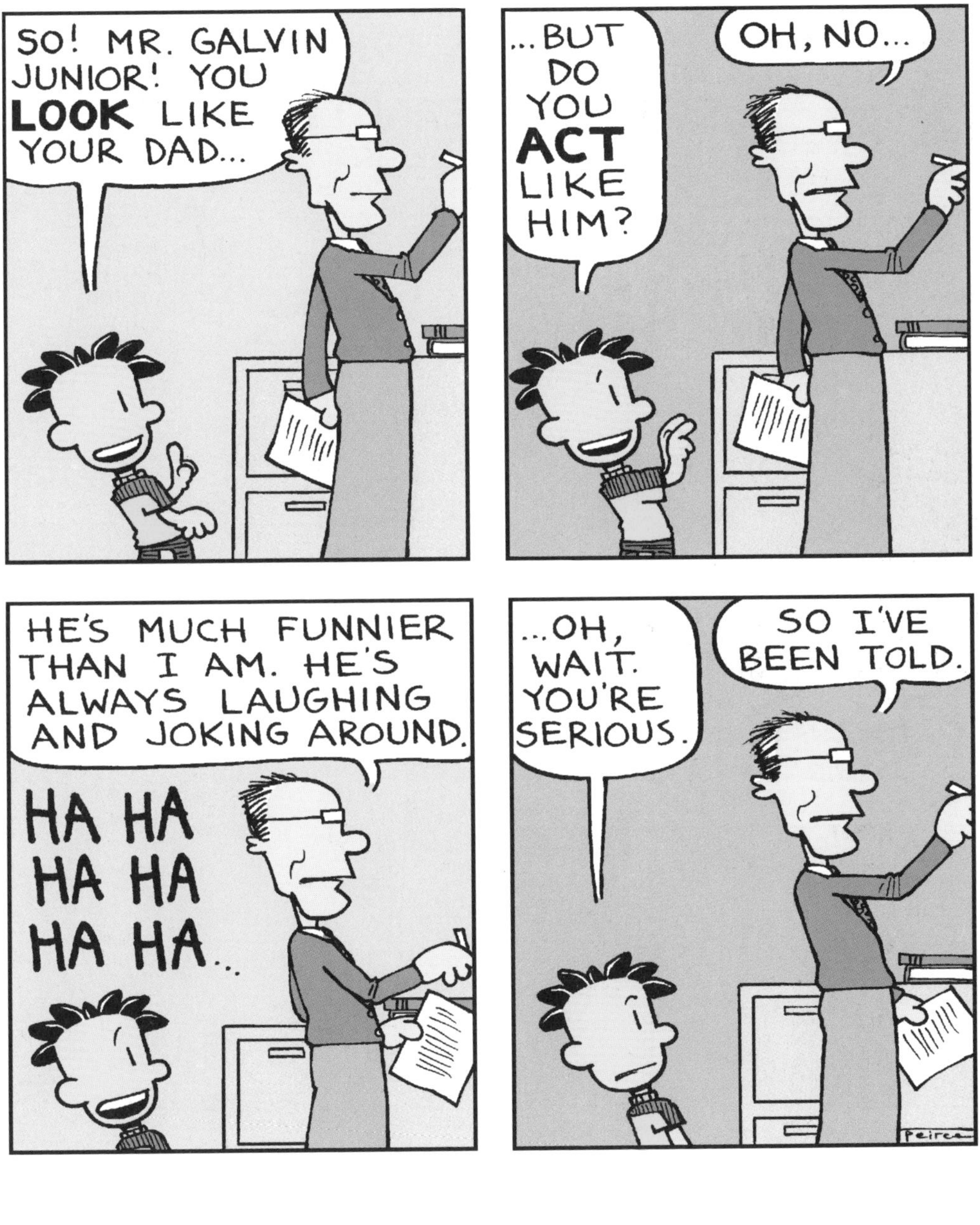
SO! MR. GALVIN JUNIOR! YOU **LOOK** LIKE YOUR DAD...
...BUT DO YOU **ACT** LIKE HIM?
OH, NO...
HE'S MUCH FUNNIER THAN I AM. HE'S ALWAYS LAUGHING AND JOKING AROUND.
HA HA HA HA HA HA...
...OH, WAIT. YOU'RE SERIOUS.
SO I'VE BEEN TOLD.
Peirce

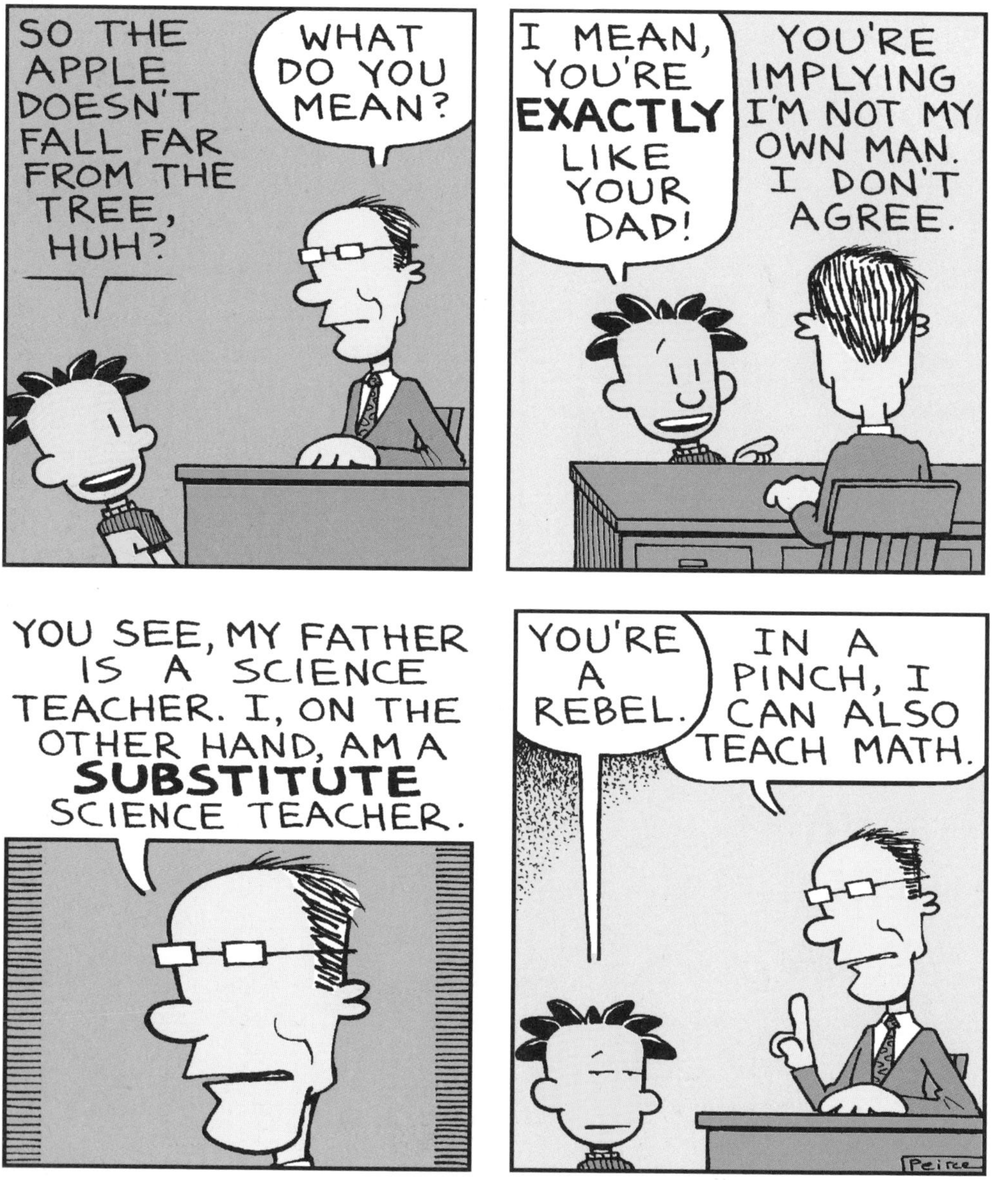
SO THE APPLE DOESN'T FALL FAR FROM THE TREE, HUH?
WHAT DO YOU MEAN?
I MEAN, YOU'RE **EXACTLY** LIKE YOUR DAD!
YOU'RE IMPLYING I'M NOT MY OWN MAN. I DON'T AGREE.
YOU SEE, MY FATHER IS A SCIENCE TEACHER. I, ON THE OTHER HAND, AM A **SUBSTITUTE** SCIENCE TEACHER.
YOU'RE A REBEL.
IN A PINCH, I CAN ALSO TEACH MATH.
Peirce

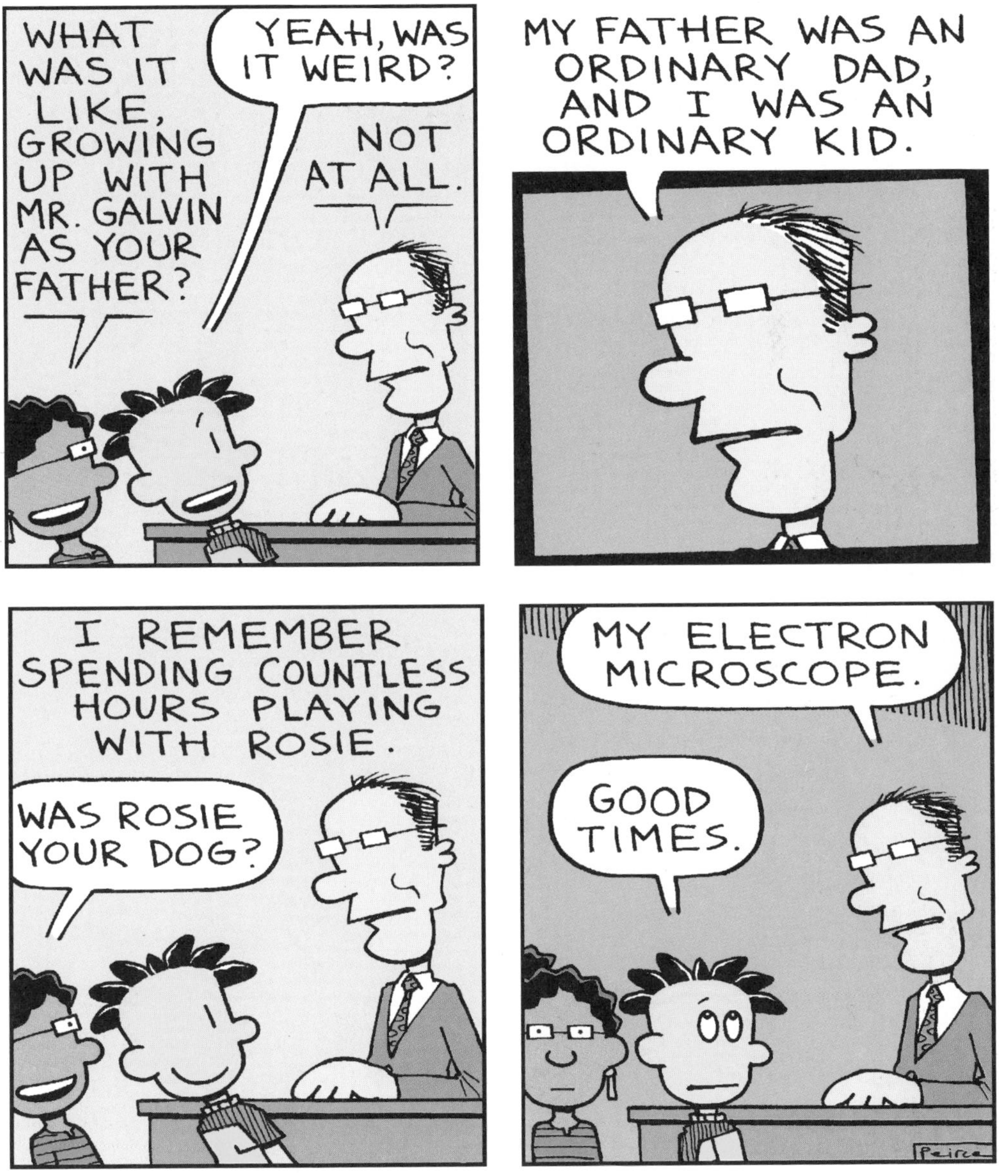
WHAT WAS IT LIKE, GROWING UP WITH MR. GALVIN AS YOUR FATHER?
YEAH, WAS IT WEIRD?
NOT AT ALL.
MY FATHER WAS AN ORDINARY DAD, AND I WAS AN ORDINARY KID.
I REMEMBER SPENDING COUNTLESS HOURS PLAYING WITH ROSIE.
WAS ROSIE YOUR DOG?
MY ELECTRON MICROSCOPE.
GOOD TIMES.
Peirce

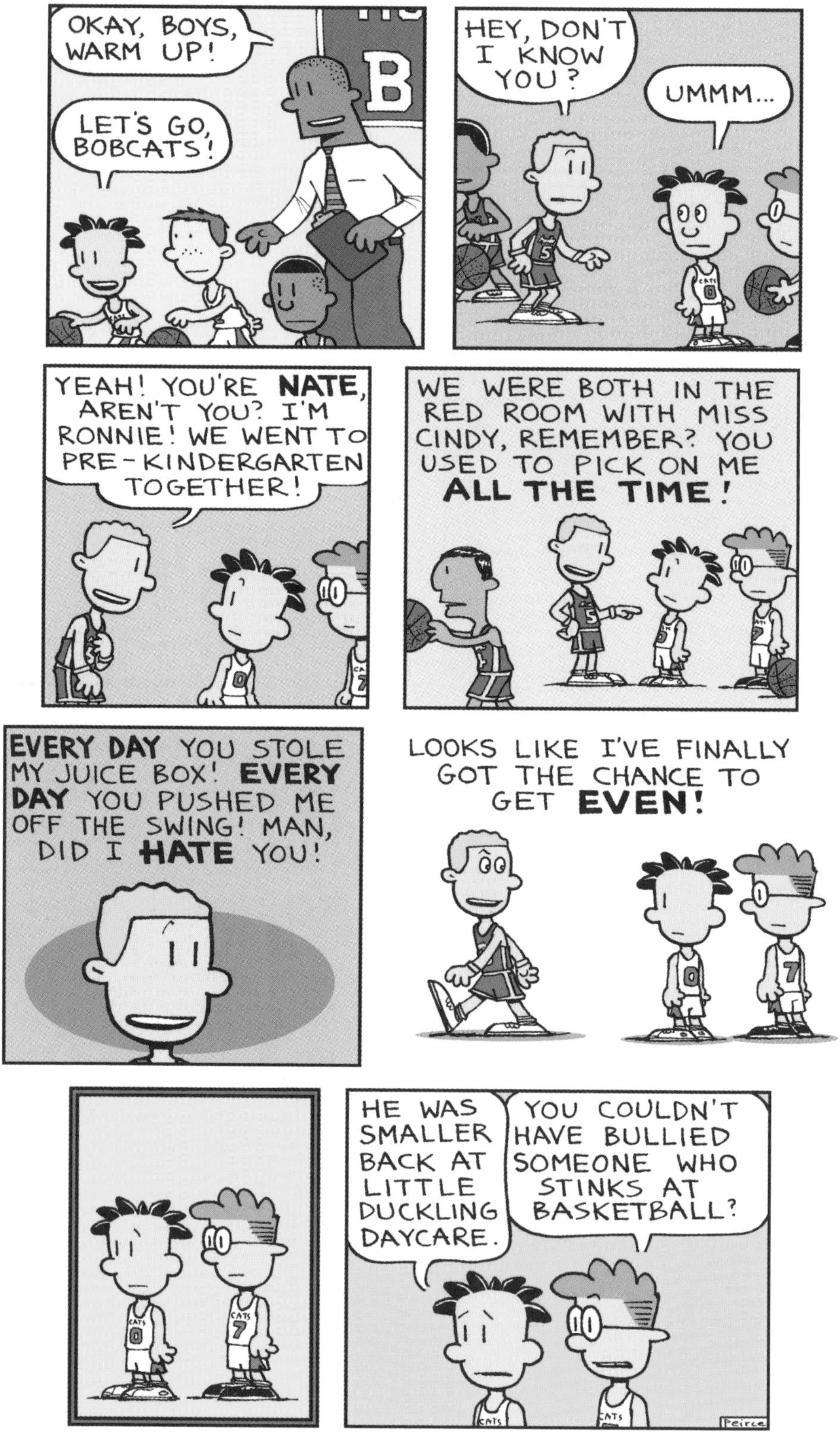

OKAY, BOYS, WARM UP!
LET'S GO, BOBCATS!
HEY, DON'T I KNOW YOU?
UMMM...
YEAH! YOU'RE NATE, AREN'T YOU? I'M RONNIE! WE WENT TO PRE-KINDERGARTEN TOGETHER!
WE WERE BOTH IN THE RED ROOM WITH MISS CINDY, REMEMBER? YOU USED TO PICK ON ME ALL THE TIME!
EVERY DAY YOU STOLE MY JUICE BOX! EVERY DAY YOU PUSHED ME OFF THE SWING! MAN, DID I HATE YOU!
LOOKS LIKE I'VE FINALLY GOT THE CHANCE TO GET EVEN!
HE WAS SMALLER BACK AT LITTLE DUCKLING DAYCARE.
YOU COULDN'T HAVE BULLIED SOMEONE WHO STINKS AT BASKETBALL?
Peirce

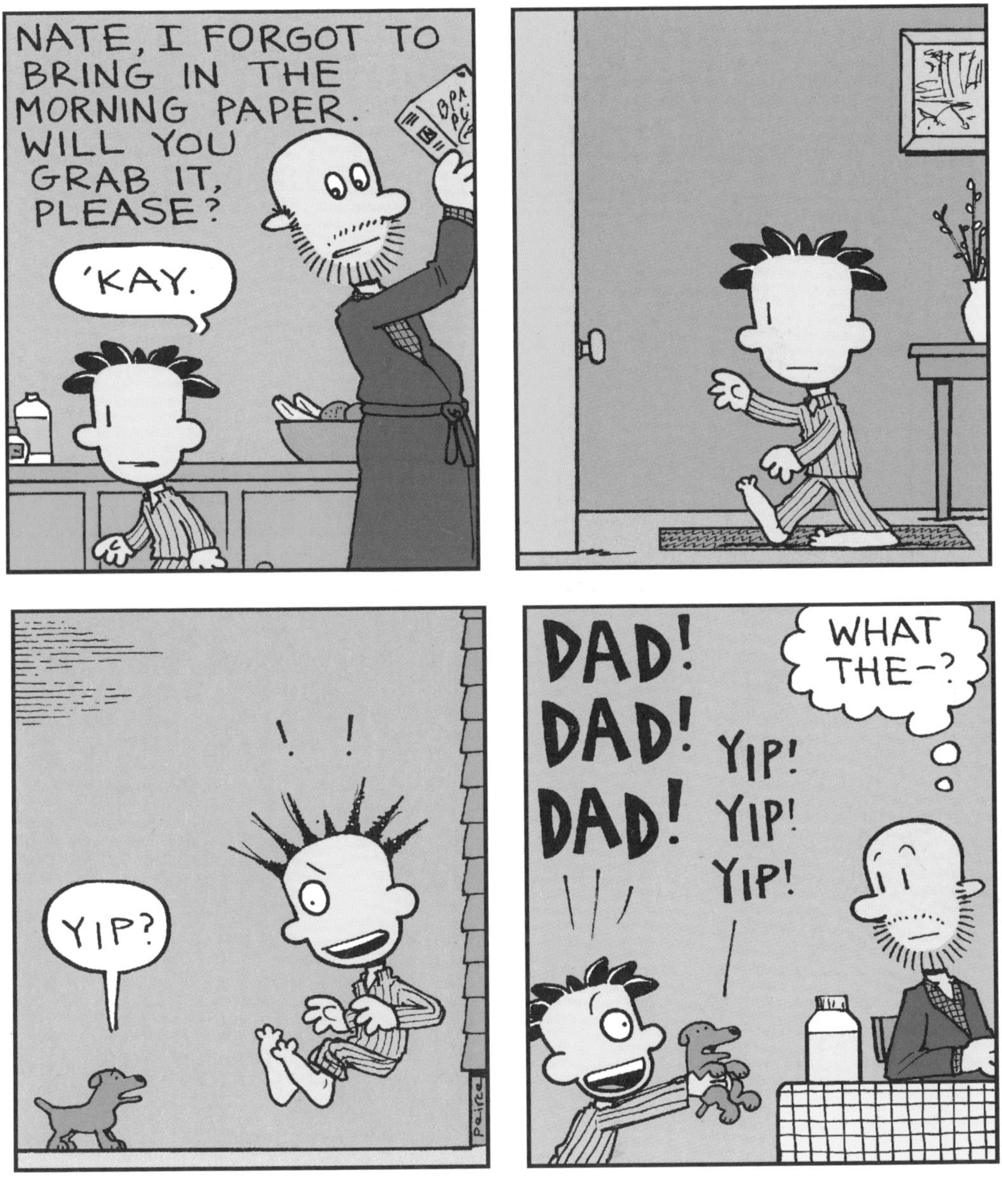
NATE, I FORGOT TO BRING IN THE MORNING PAPER. WILL YOU GRAB IT, PLEASE?
'KAY.
! !
YIP?
DAD! DAD! DAD!
YIP! YIP! YIP!
WHAT THE-?

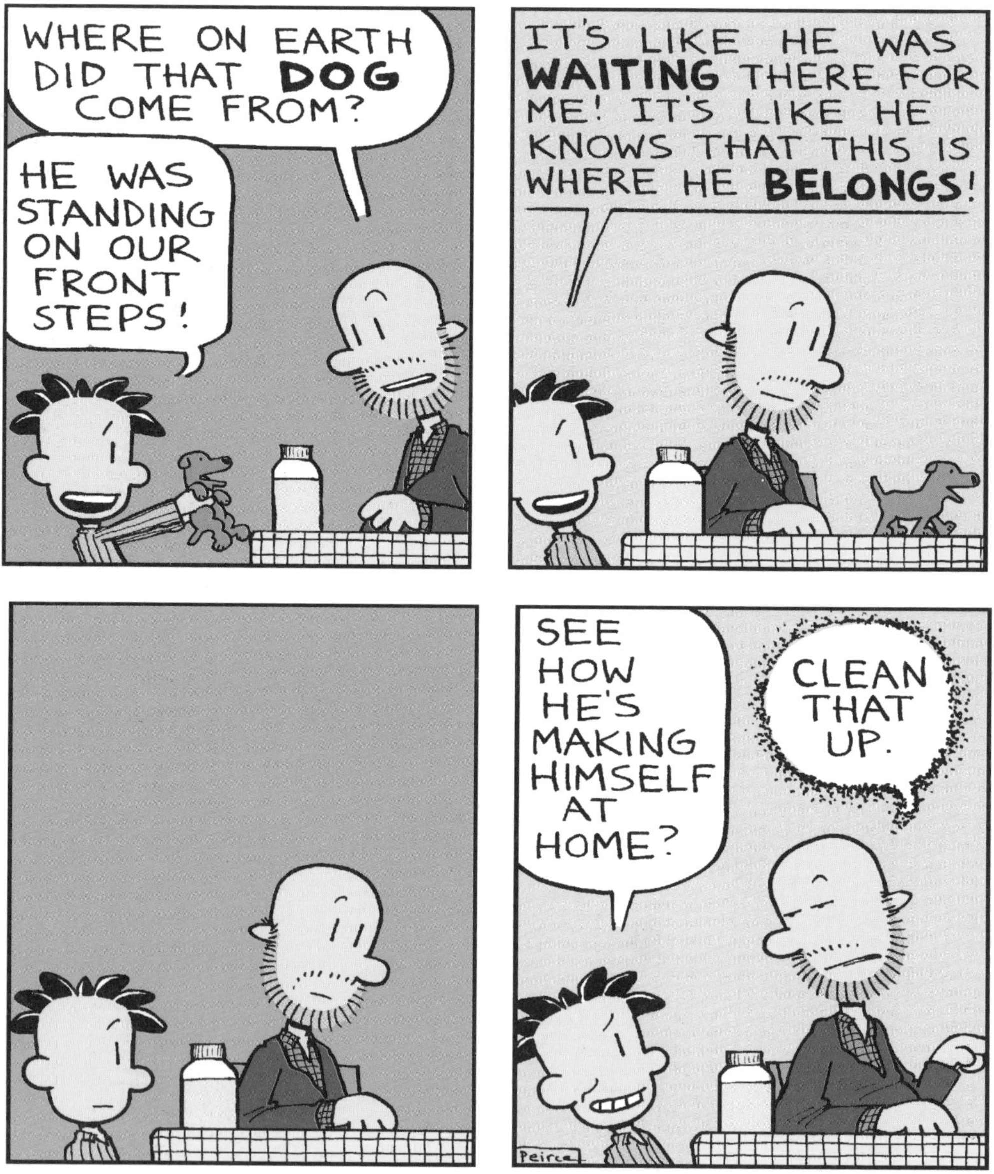
WHERE ON EARTH DID THAT DOG COME FROM?
HE WAS STANDING ON OUR FRONT STEPS!
IT'S LIKE HE WAS WAITING THERE FOR ME! IT'S LIKE HE KNOWS THAT THIS IS WHERE HE BELONGS!
SEE HOW HE'S MAKING HIMSELF AT HOME?
CLEAN THAT UP.
Peirce

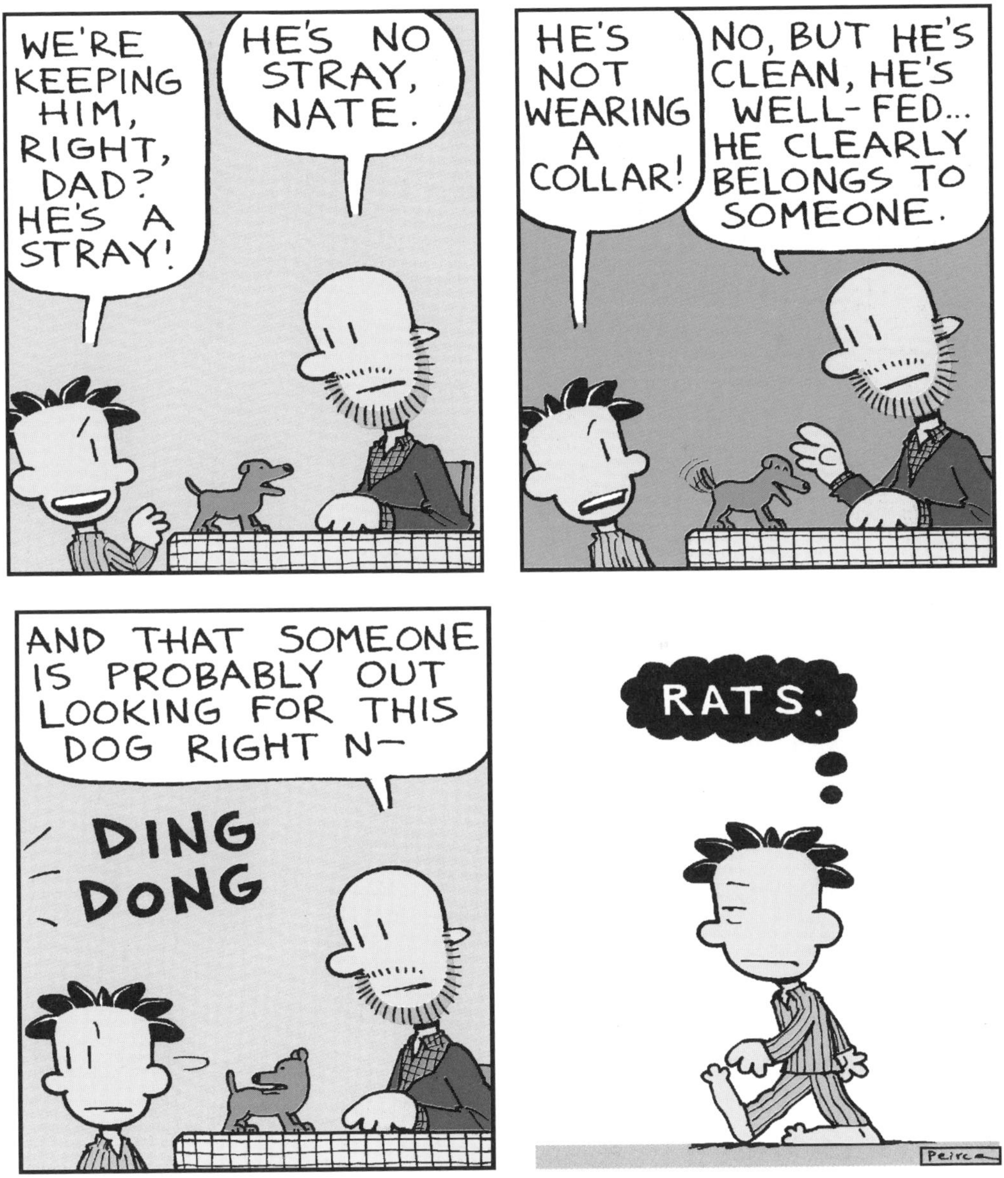

WE'RE KEEPING HIM, RIGHT, DAD? HE'S A STRAY!
HE'S NO STRAY, NATE.
HE'S NOT WEARING A COLLAR!
NO, BUT HE'S CLEAN, HE'S WELL-FED... HE CLEARLY BELONGS TO SOMEONE.
AND THAT SOMEONE IS PROBABLY OUT LOOKING FOR THIS DOG RIGHT N—
DING DONG
RATS.
Peirce

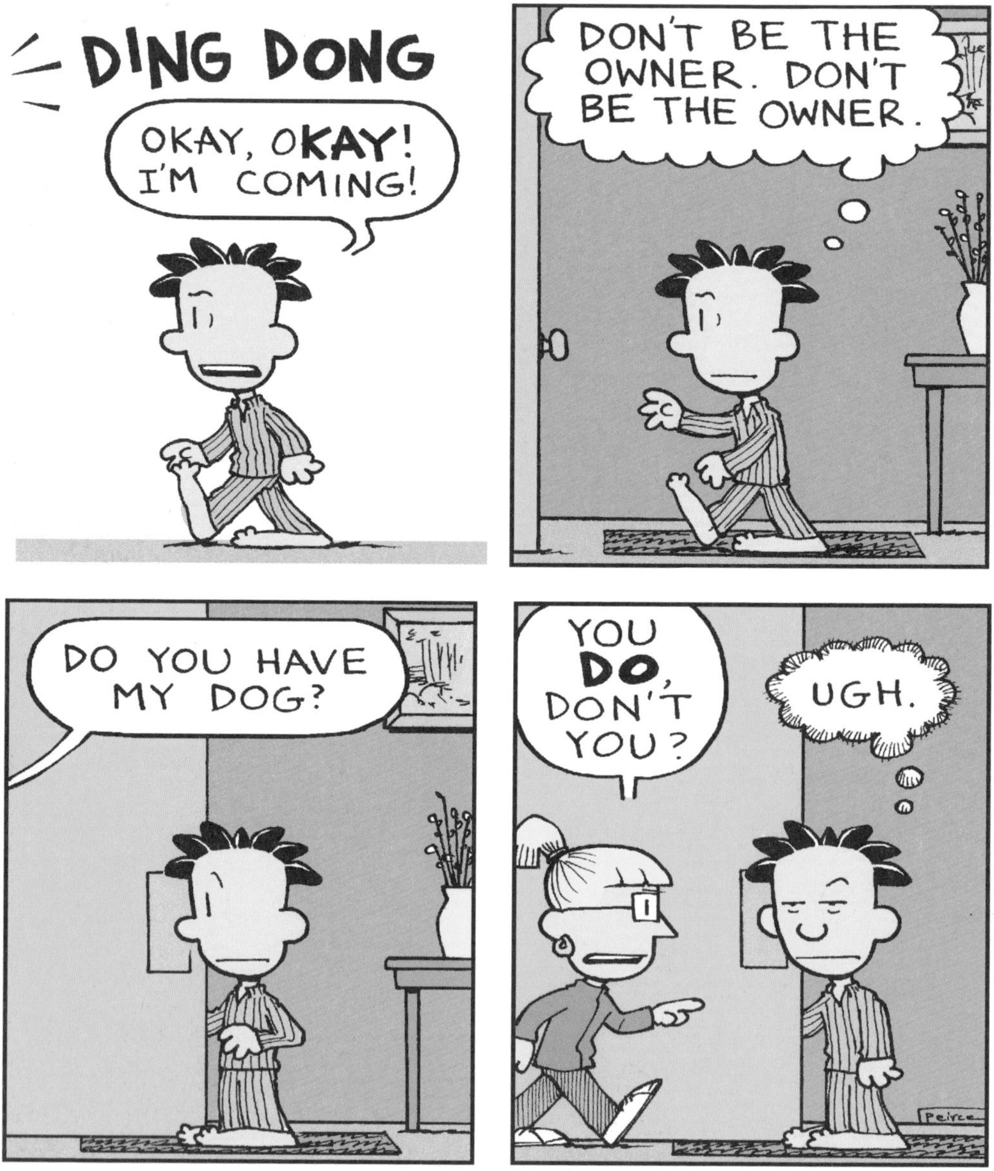
DING DONG
OKAY, OKAY! I'M COMING!
DON'T BE THE OWNER. DON'T BE THE OWNER.
DO YOU HAVE MY DOG?
YOU DO, DON'T YOU?
UGH.
Peirce

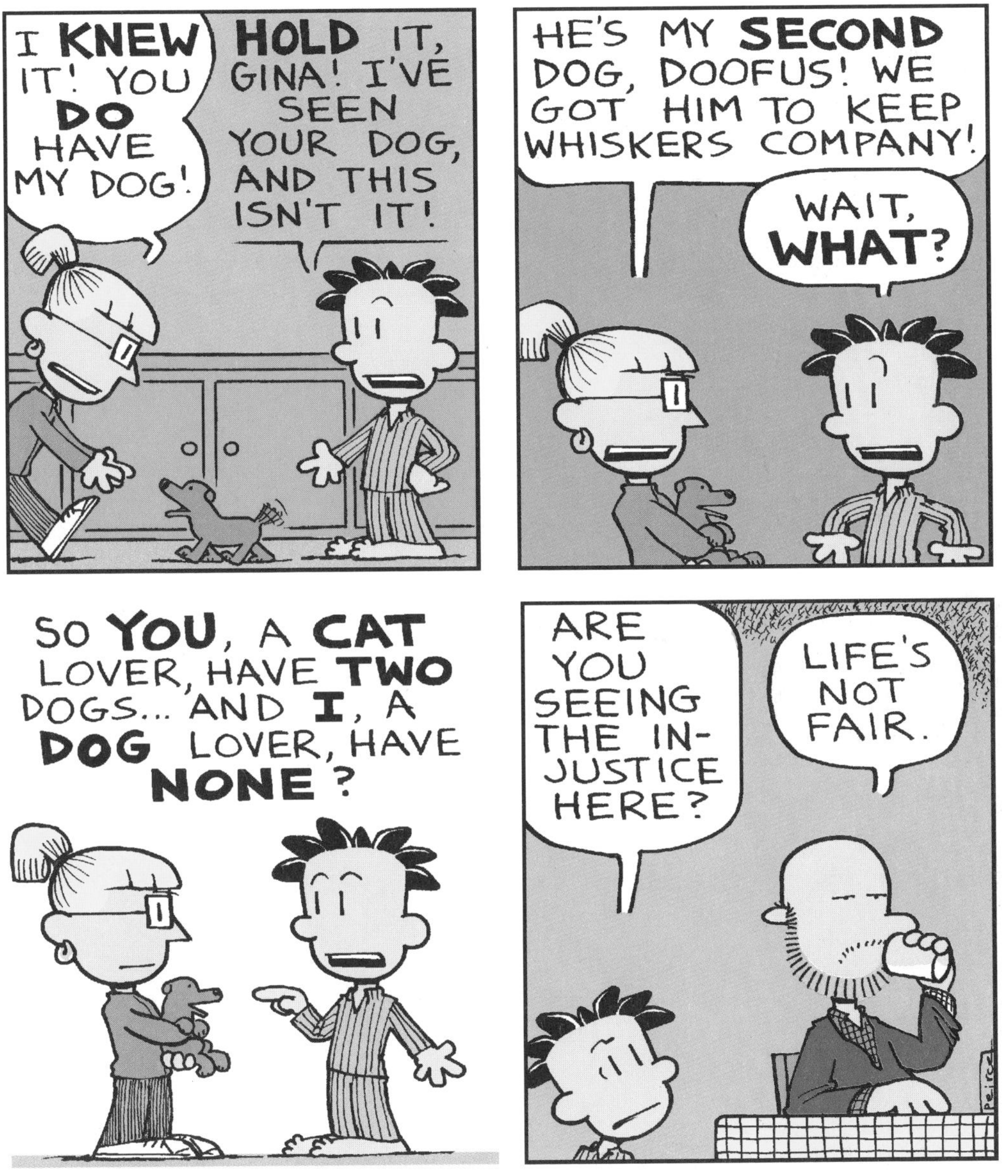
I KNEW IT! YOU DO HAVE MY DOG!
HOLD IT, GINA! I'VE SEEN YOUR DOG, AND THIS ISN'T IT!
HE'S MY SECOND DOG, DOOFUS! WE GOT HIM TO KEEP WHISKERS COMPANY!
WAIT, WHAT?
SO YOU, A CAT LOVER, HAVE TWO DOGS... AND I, A DOG LOVER, HAVE NONE?
ARE YOU SEEING THE IN-JUSTICE HERE?
LIFE'S NOT FAIR.
PEIRCE

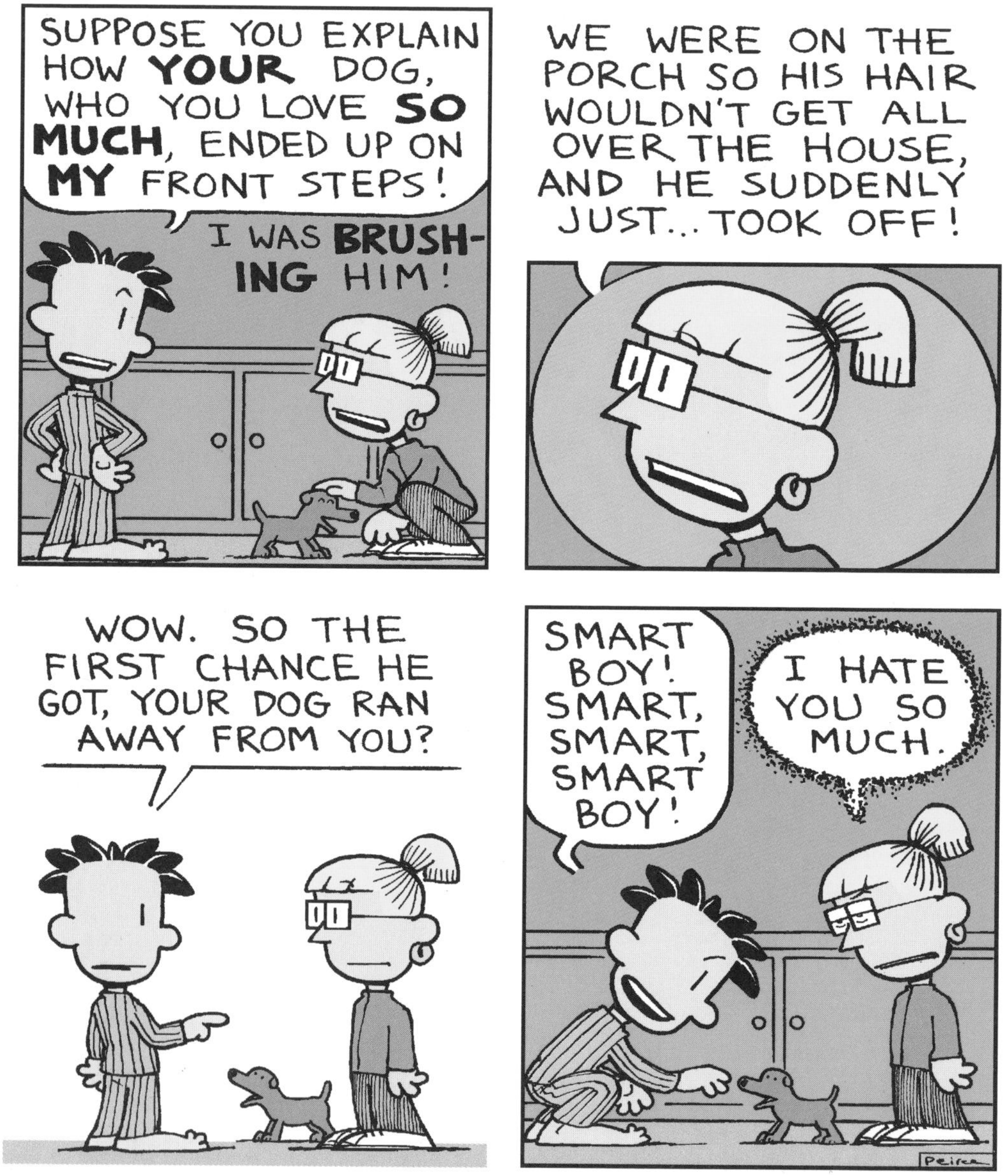
SUPPOSE YOU EXPLAIN HOW YOUR DOG, WHO YOU LOVE SO MUCH, ENDED UP ON MY FRONT STEPS!
I WAS BRUSHING HIM!
WE WERE ON THE PORCH SO HIS HAIR WOULDN'T GET ALL OVER THE HOUSE, AND HE SUDDENLY JUST... TOOK OFF!
WOW. SO THE FIRST CHANCE HE GOT, YOUR DOG RAN AWAY FROM YOU?
SMART BOY! SMART, SMART, SMART BOY!
I HATE YOU SO MUCH.
PEIRCE

YOU MAY BEGIN THE QUIZ... **NOW.**

HMM... I'LL SKIP THIS ONE.

AND I'LL SKIP THIS ONE... AND THIS ONE.

...AND **THIS** ONE! MAN, WHAT A SKIPPY QUIZ!

HEH. SKIPPY. LIKE SKIPPY PEANUT BUTTER.

I'LL BET DAD PACKED ME A PEANUT BUTTER SANDWICH FOR LUNCH... **AGAIN.**

I HOPE HE USED THE SMOOTH AND NOT THE CHUNKY. THE CHUNKY GETS ALL STUCK IN YOUR TEETH.

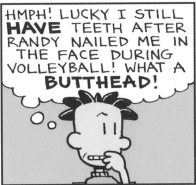

HMPH! LUCKY I STILL **HAVE** TEETH AFTER RANDY NAILED ME IN THE FACE DURING VOLLEYBALL! WHAT A **BUTTHEAD!**

HA! WHAT IF HE ACTUALLY HAD A BUTT FOR A HEAD? GOTTA DRAW A CARTOON ABOUT THAT!

I COULD DO A WHOLE GRAPHIC NOVEL ABOUT WHAT A **MORON** RANDY IS! AND I'LL CALL IT...

TIME! HAND 'EM IN, PEOPLE!

HOW ABOUT THAT SOCIAL STUDIES QUIZ?

SO EASY!

CHUNKY.

97

WHATCHA DOIN'?
WRITING A CHILDREN'S BOOK!
WHAT? YOU KNOW NOTHING ABOUT WRITING A CHILDREN'S BOOK!
SURE, I DO! IT'S A CINCH!
I'VE GOT A CURIOUS PUPPY, A MISCHIEVOUS MONKEY, A GAME OF LASER TAG, A GAPING HEAD WOUND, AND A FLESH-EATING VIRUS! WHAT MORE DO I NEED?
HOW ABOUT A GHOST-WRITER?
SNORT! YEAH, LIKE I'M GONNA WRITE A KIDS' BOOK ABOUT A GHOST! GREAT IDEA, EINSTEIN!
Peirce

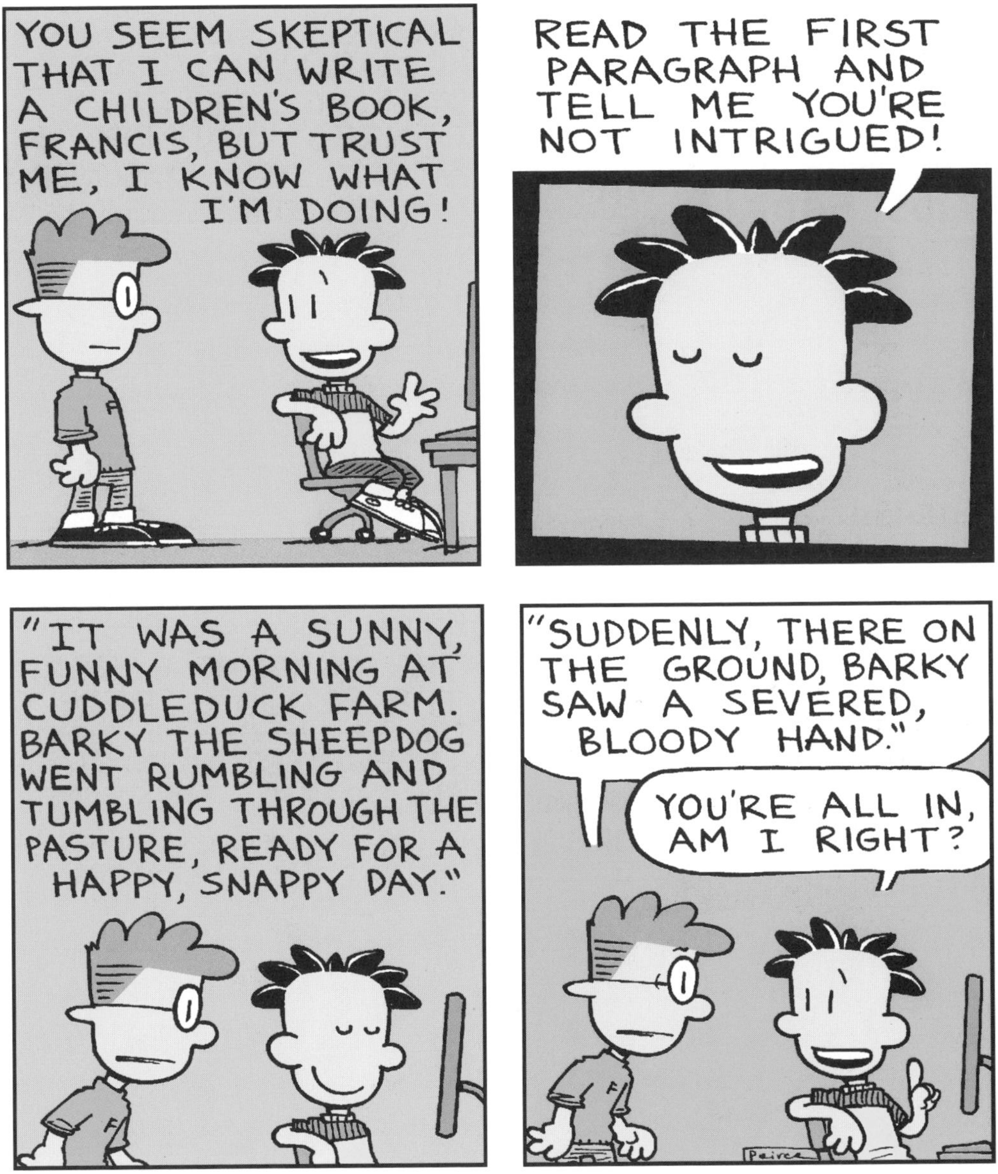
YOU SEEM SKEPTICAL THAT I CAN WRITE A CHILDREN'S BOOK, FRANCIS, BUT TRUST ME, I KNOW WHAT I'M DOING!
READ THE FIRST PARAGRAPH AND TELL ME YOU'RE NOT INTRIGUED!
"IT WAS A SUNNY, FUNNY MORNING AT CUDDLEDUCK FARM. BARKY THE SHEEPDOG WENT RUMBLING AND TUMBLING THROUGH THE PASTURE, READY FOR A HAPPY, SNAPPY DAY."
"SUDDENLY, THERE ON THE GROUND, BARKY SAW A SEVERED, BLOODY HAND."
YOU'RE ALL IN, AM I RIGHT?
Peirce

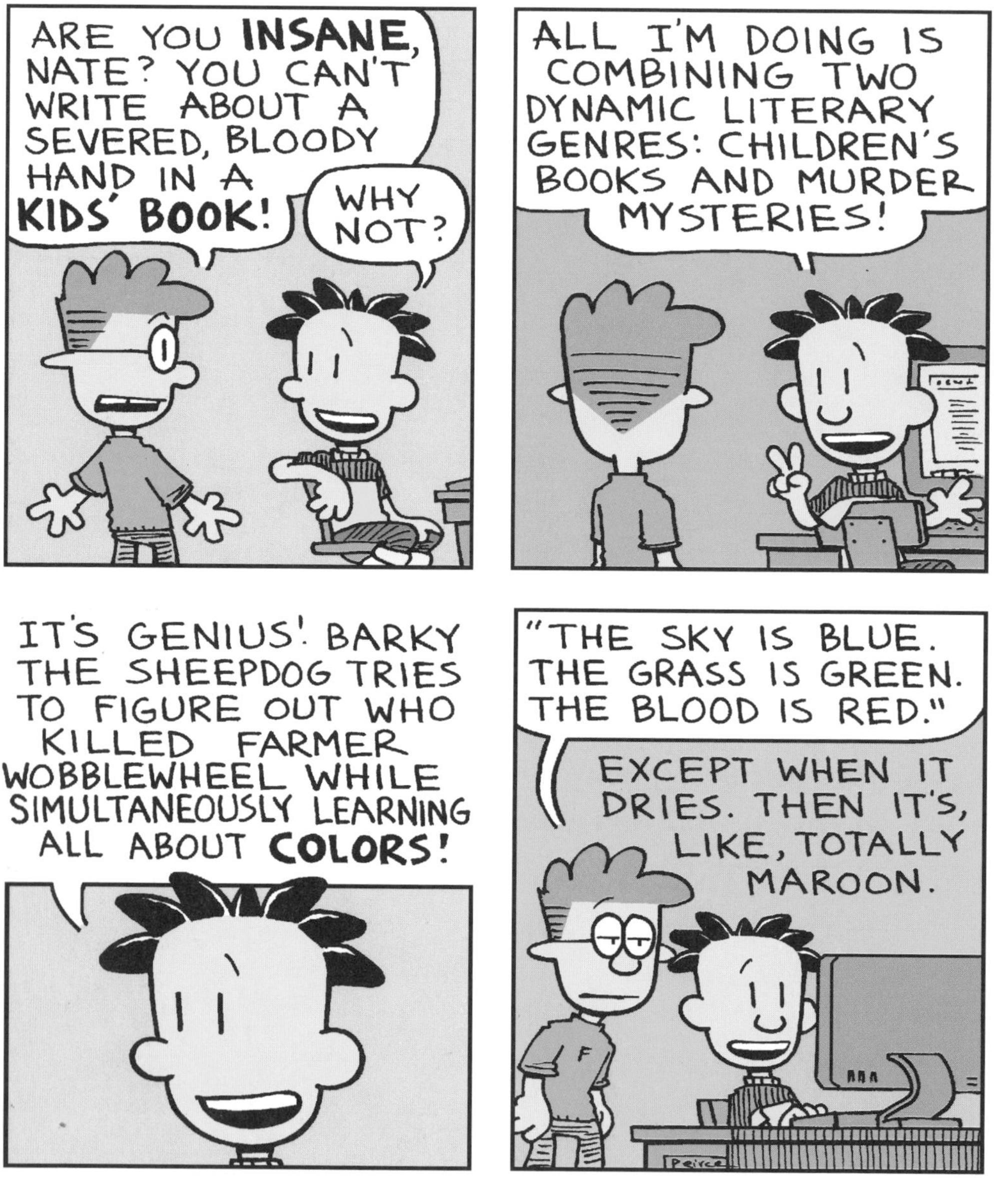
ARE YOU INSANE, NATE? YOU CAN'T WRITE ABOUT A SEVERED, BLOODY HAND IN A KIDS' BOOK!
WHY NOT?
ALL I'M DOING IS COMBINING TWO DYNAMIC LITERARY GENRES: CHILDREN'S BOOKS AND MURDER MYSTERIES!
IT'S GENIUS! BARKY THE SHEEPDOG TRIES TO FIGURE OUT WHO KILLED FARMER WOBBLEWHEEL WHILE SIMULTANEOUSLY LEARNING ALL ABOUT COLORS!
"THE SKY IS BLUE. THE GRASS IS GREEN. THE BLOOD IS RED."
EXCEPT WHEN IT DRIES. THEN IT'S, LIKE, TOTALLY MAROON.
F
Peirce

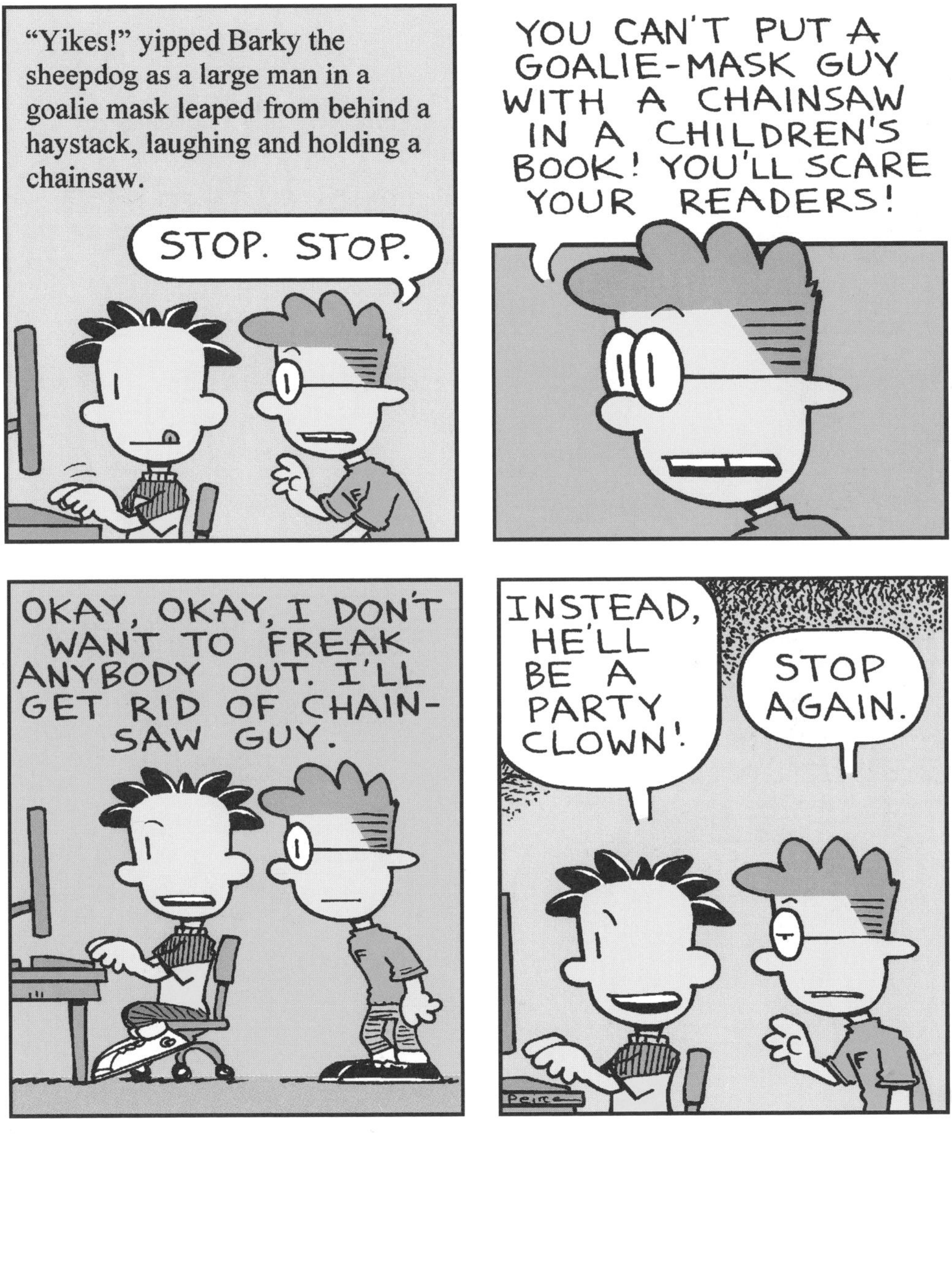
"Yikes!" yipped Barky the sheepdog as a large man in a goalie mask leaped from behind a haystack, laughing and holding a chainsaw.
STOP. STOP.
YOU CAN'T PUT A GOALIE-MASK GUY WITH A CHAINSAW IN A CHILDREN'S BOOK! YOU'LL SCARE YOUR READERS!
OKAY, OKAY, I DON'T WANT TO FREAK ANYBODY OUT. I'LL GET RID OF CHAIN-SAW GUY.
INSTEAD, HE'LL BE A PARTY CLOWN!
STOP AGAIN.

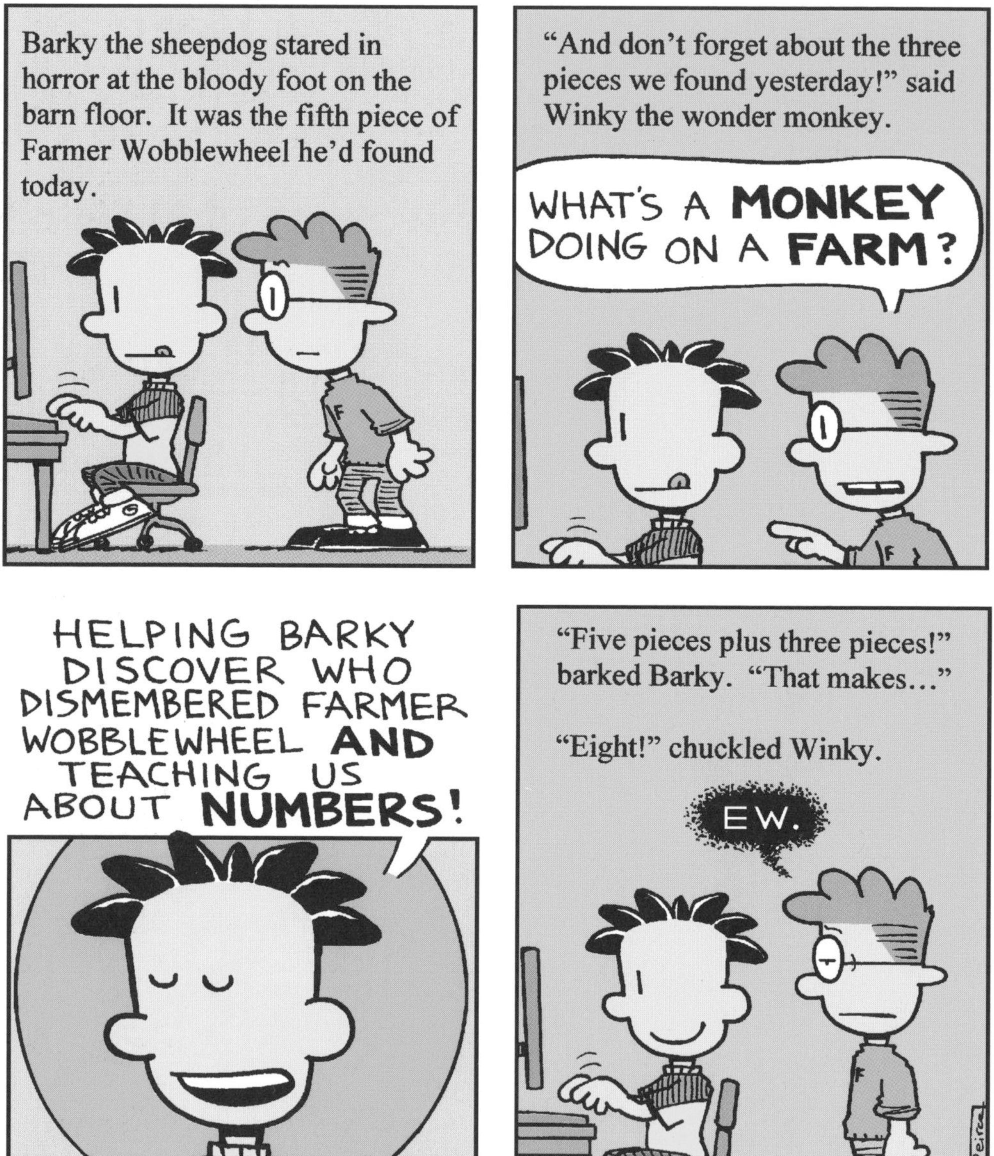
Barky the sheepdog stared in horror at the bloody foot on the barn floor. It was the fifth piece of Farmer Wobblewheel he'd found today.
"And don't forget about the three pieces we found yesterday!" said Winky the wonder monkey.
WHAT'S A MONKEY DOING ON A FARM?
HELPING BARKY DISCOVER WHO DISMEMBERED FARMER WOBBLEWHEEL AND TEACHING US ABOUT NUMBERS!
"Five pieces plus three pieces!" barked Barky. "That makes…"
"Eight!" chuckled Winky.
EW.
Peirce

STILL WORKING ON YOUR STUPID CHILDREN'S BOOK?
JUST FINISHED IT!
AND DID BARKY THE SHEEPDOG DISCOVER WHO KILLED FARMER WOBBLE-WHEEL?
NOBODY KILLED HIM! HE DIED OF A HEART ATTACK!
BUT HE WAS IN PIECES ALL OVER THE BARN-YARD!
RIGHT! BECAUSE HE WAS TORN APART BY HIS FLOCK OF PIGS!
FLOCK?
THE MORAL OF THE STORY IS: RESPECT ANIMALS... OR ELSE!
Peirce

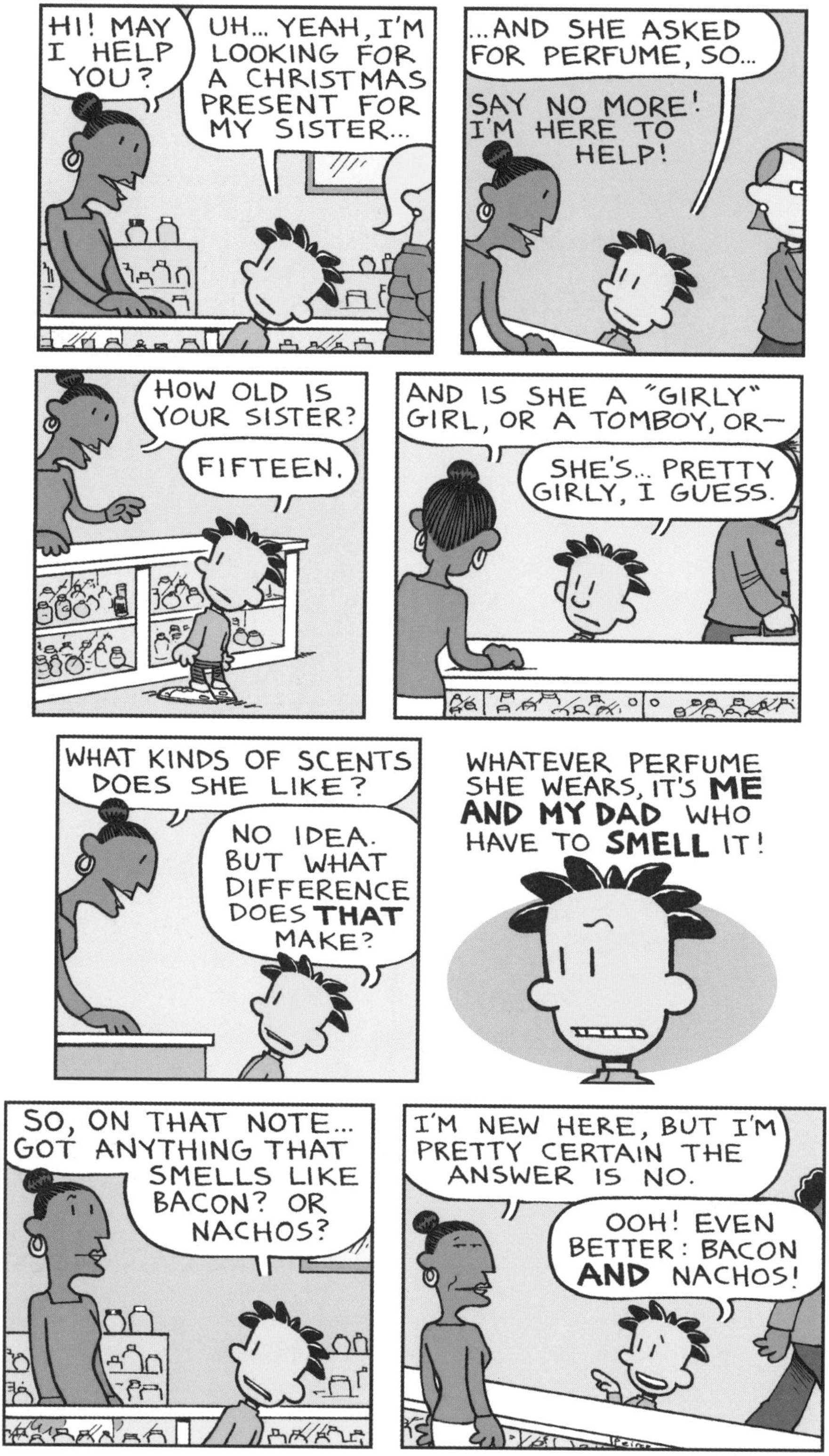
HI! MAY I HELP YOU?
UH... YEAH, I'M LOOKING FOR A CHRISTMAS PRESENT FOR MY SISTER...
...AND SHE ASKED FOR PERFUME, SO...
SAY NO MORE! I'M HERE TO HELP!
HOW OLD IS YOUR SISTER?
FIFTEEN.
AND IS SHE A "GIRLY" GIRL, OR A TOMBOY, OR—
SHE'S... PRETTY GIRLY, I GUESS.
WHAT KINDS OF SCENTS DOES SHE LIKE?
NO IDEA. BUT WHAT DIFFERENCE DOES THAT MAKE?
WHATEVER PERFUME SHE WEARS, IT'S ME AND MY DAD WHO HAVE TO SMELL IT!
SO, ON THAT NOTE... GOT ANYTHING THAT SMELLS LIKE BACON? OR NACHOS?
I'M NEW HERE, BUT I'M PRETTY CERTAIN THE ANSWER IS NO.
OOH! EVEN BETTER: BACON AND NACHOS!

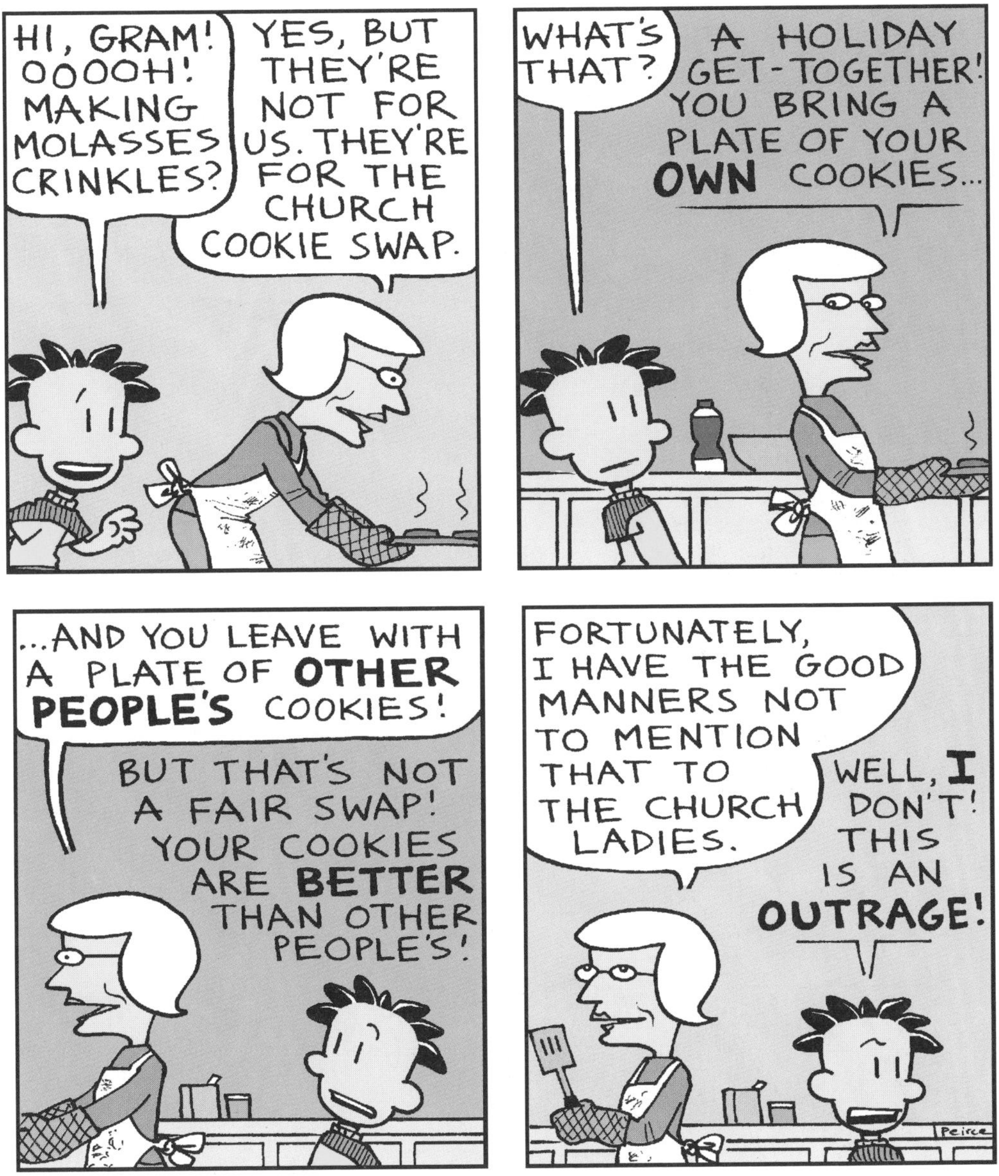

HI, GRAM! OOOOH! MAKING MOLASSES CRINKLES?
YES, BUT THEY'RE NOT FOR US. THEY'RE FOR THE CHURCH COOKIE SWAP.
WHAT'S THAT?
A HOLIDAY GET-TOGETHER! YOU BRING A PLATE OF YOUR **OWN** COOKIES...
...AND YOU LEAVE WITH A PLATE OF **OTHER PEOPLE'S** COOKIES!
BUT THAT'S NOT A FAIR SWAP! YOUR COOKIES ARE **BETTER** THAN OTHER PEOPLE'S!
FORTUNATELY, I HAVE THE GOOD MANNERS NOT TO MENTION THAT TO THE CHURCH LADIES.
WELL, **I** DON'T! THIS IS AN **OUTRAGE!**
Peirce

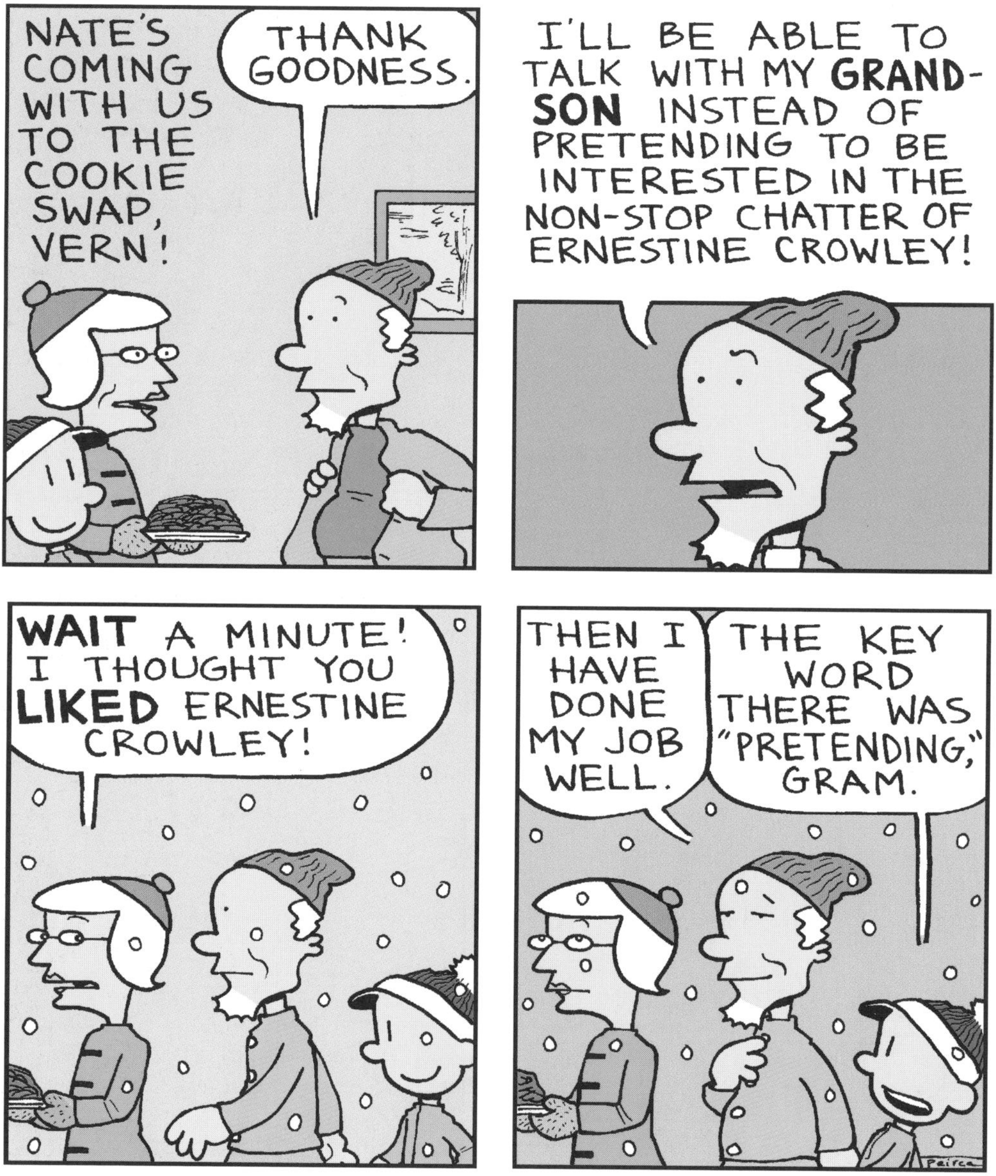
NATE'S COMING WITH US TO THE COOKIE SWAP, VERN!
THANK GOODNESS.
I'LL BE ABLE TO TALK WITH MY **GRANDSON** INSTEAD OF PRETENDING TO BE INTERESTED IN THE NON-STOP CHATTER OF ERNESTINE CROWLEY!
WAIT A MINUTE! I THOUGHT YOU **LIKED** ERNESTINE CROWLEY!
THEN I HAVE DONE MY JOB WELL.
THE KEY WORD THERE WAS "PRETENDING," GRAM.
Peirce

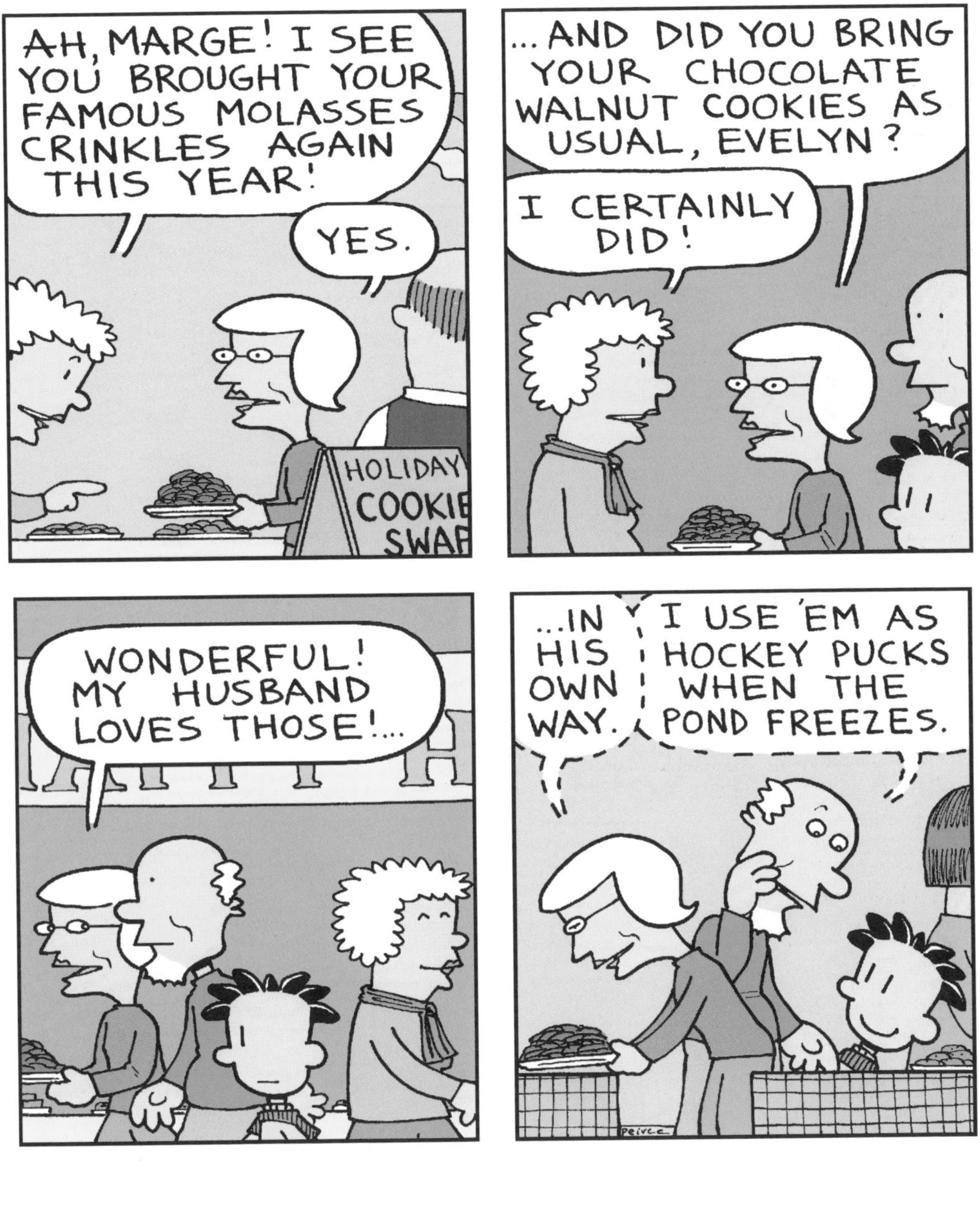

AH, MARGE! I SEE YOU BROUGHT YOUR FAMOUS MOLASSES CRINKLES AGAIN THIS YEAR!
YES.
HOLIDAY COOKIE SWAP
...AND DID YOU BRING YOUR CHOCOLATE WALNUT COOKIES AS USUAL, EVELYN?
I CERTAINLY DID!
WONDERFUL! MY HUSBAND LOVES THOSE!...
...IN HIS OWN WAY.
I USE 'EM AS HOCKEY PUCKS WHEN THE POND FREEZES.

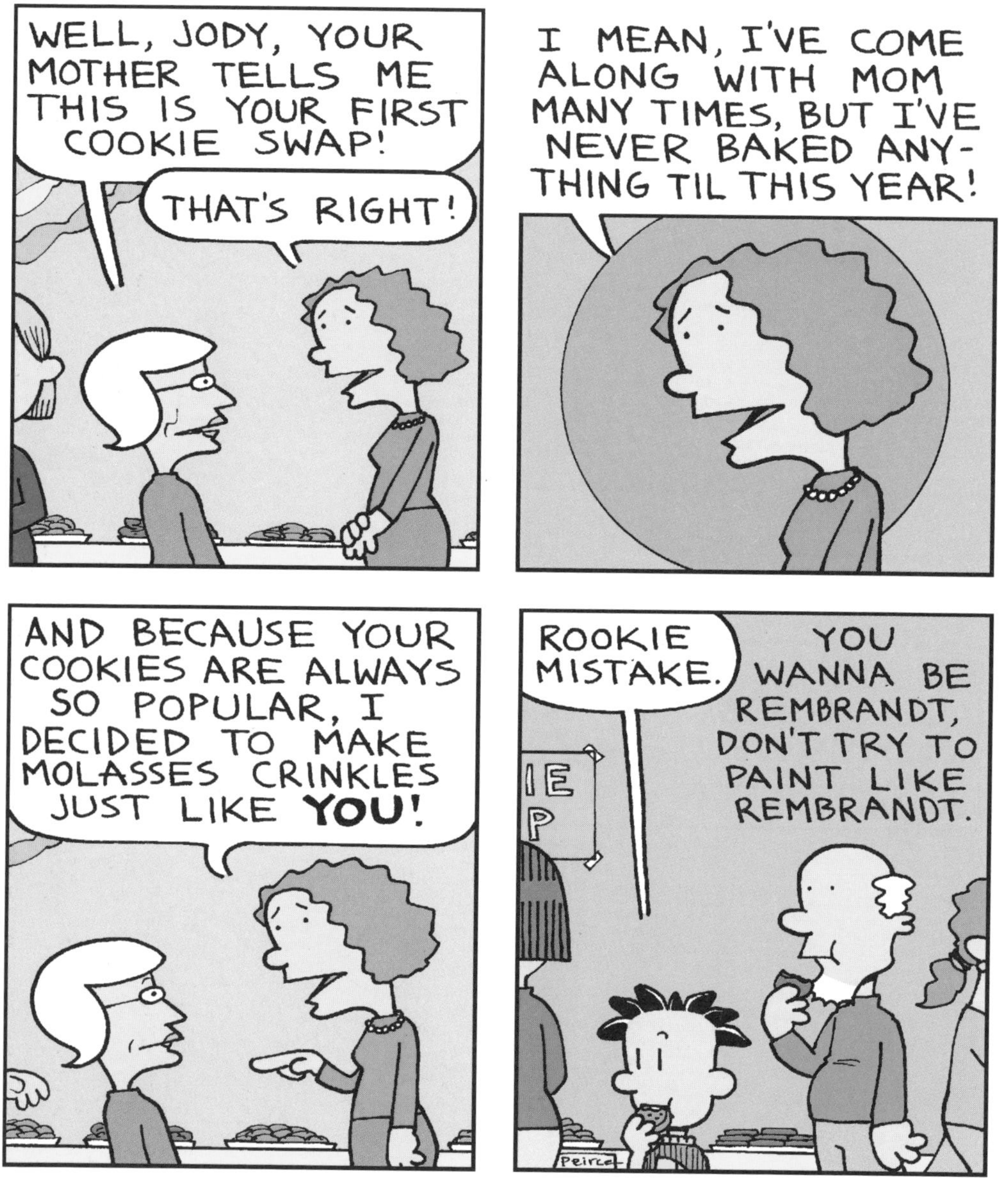
WELL, JODY, YOUR MOTHER TELLS ME THIS IS YOUR FIRST COOKIE SWAP!
THAT'S RIGHT!
I MEAN, I'VE COME ALONG WITH MOM MANY TIMES, BUT I'VE NEVER BAKED ANY-THING TIL THIS YEAR!
AND BECAUSE YOUR COOKIES ARE ALWAYS SO POPULAR, I DECIDED TO MAKE MOLASSES CRINKLES JUST LIKE **YOU**!
ROOKIE MISTAKE.
YOU WANNA BE REMBRANDT, DON'T TRY TO PAINT LIKE REMBRANDT.
Peirce

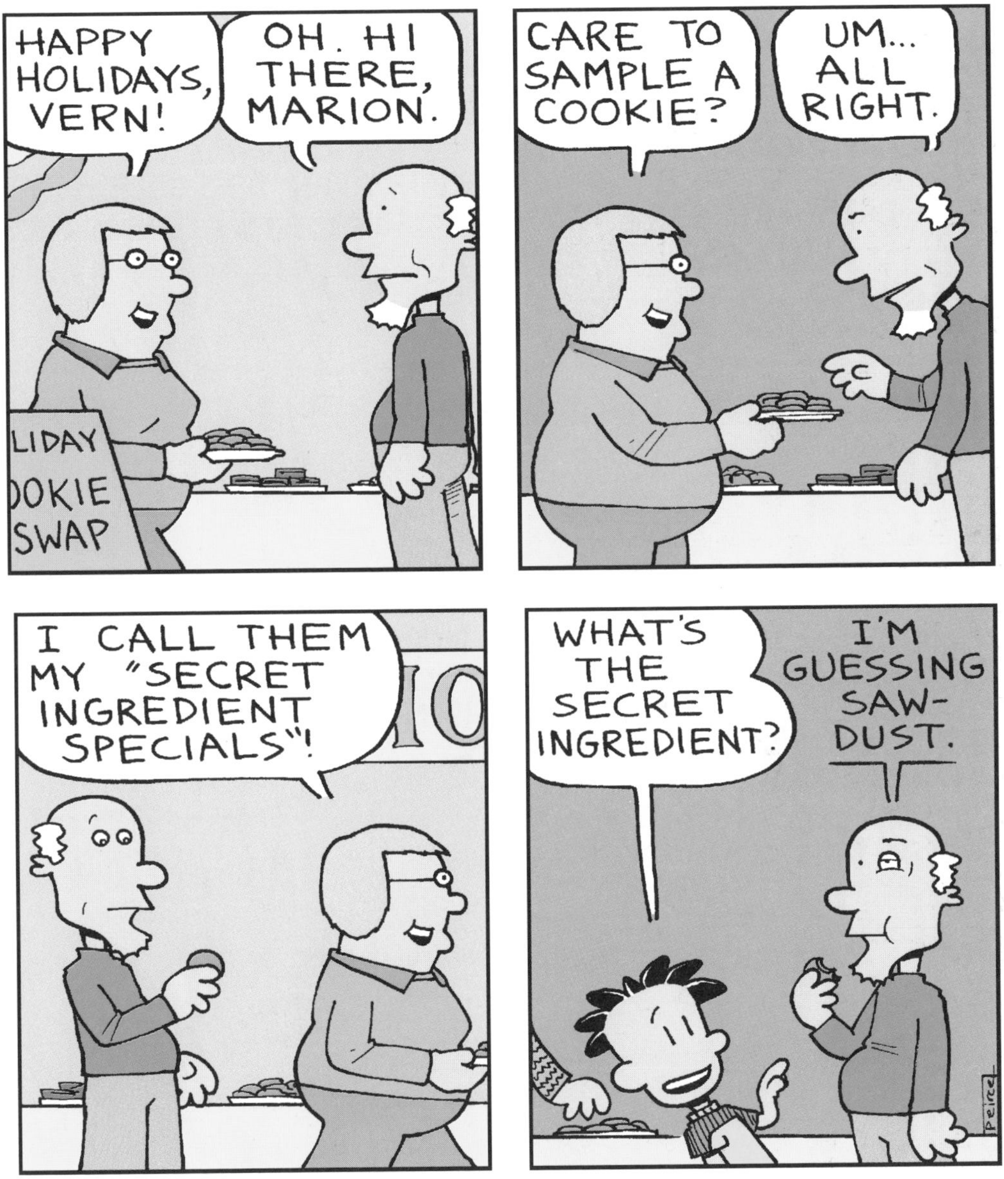
HAPPY HOLIDAYS, VERN!
OH. HI THERE, MARION.
LIDAY
OOKIE
SWAP
CARE TO SAMPLE A COOKIE?
UM... ALL RIGHT.
I CALL THEM MY "SECRET INGREDIENT SPECIALS"!
WHAT'S THE SECRET INGREDIENT?
I'M GUESSING SAW-DUST.
PEIRCE

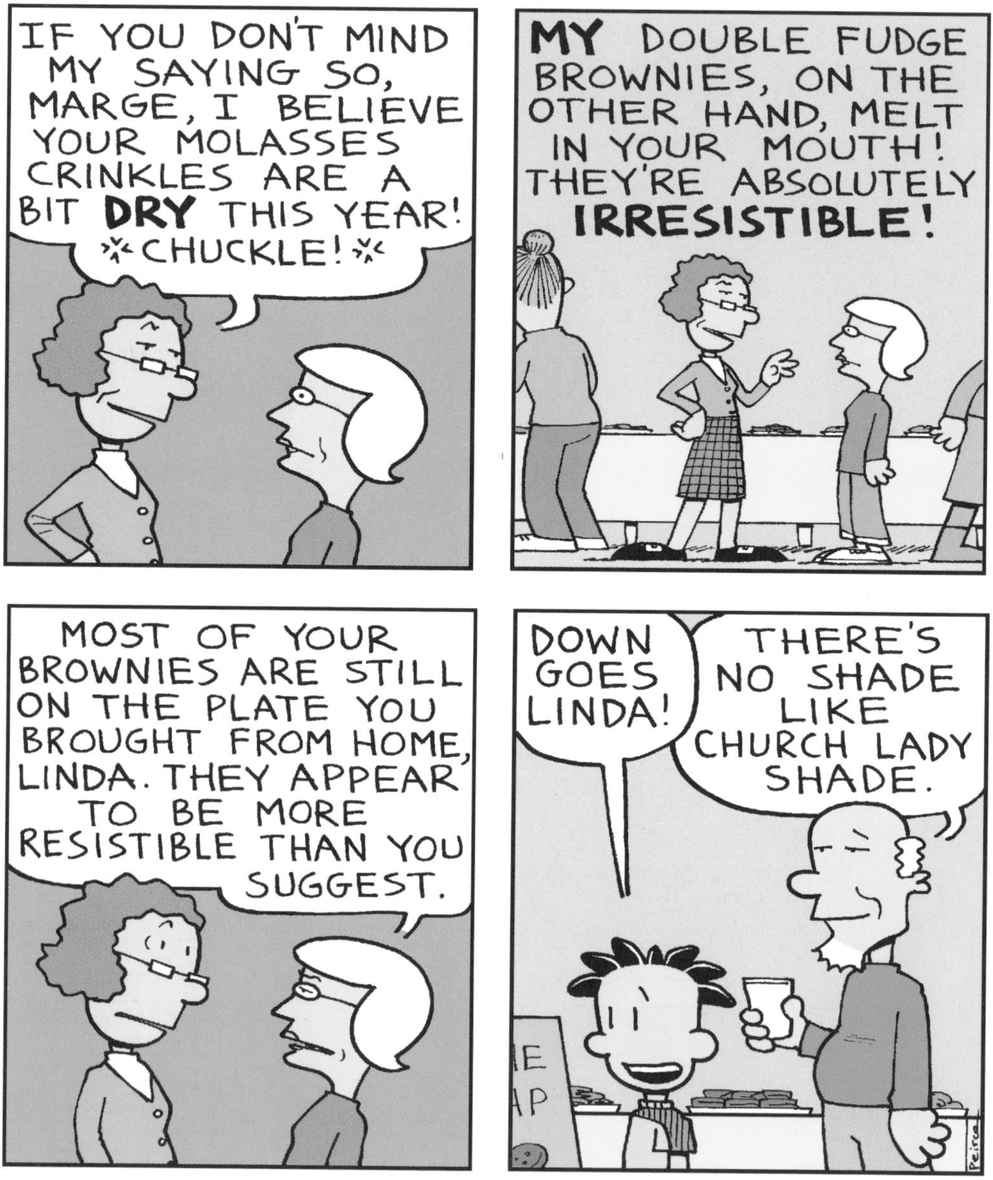
IF YOU DON'T MIND MY SAYING SO, MARGE, I BELIEVE YOUR MOLASSES CRINKLES ARE A BIT DRY THIS YEAR! *CHUCKLE!*
MY DOUBLE FUDGE BROWNIES, ON THE OTHER HAND, MELT IN YOUR MOUTH! THEY'RE ABSOLUTELY IRRESISTIBLE!
MOST OF YOUR BROWNIES ARE STILL ON THE PLATE YOU BROUGHT FROM HOME, LINDA. THEY APPEAR TO BE MORE RESISTIBLE THAN YOU SUGGEST.
DOWN GOES LINDA!
THERE'S NO SHADE LIKE CHURCH LADY SHADE.
Peirce

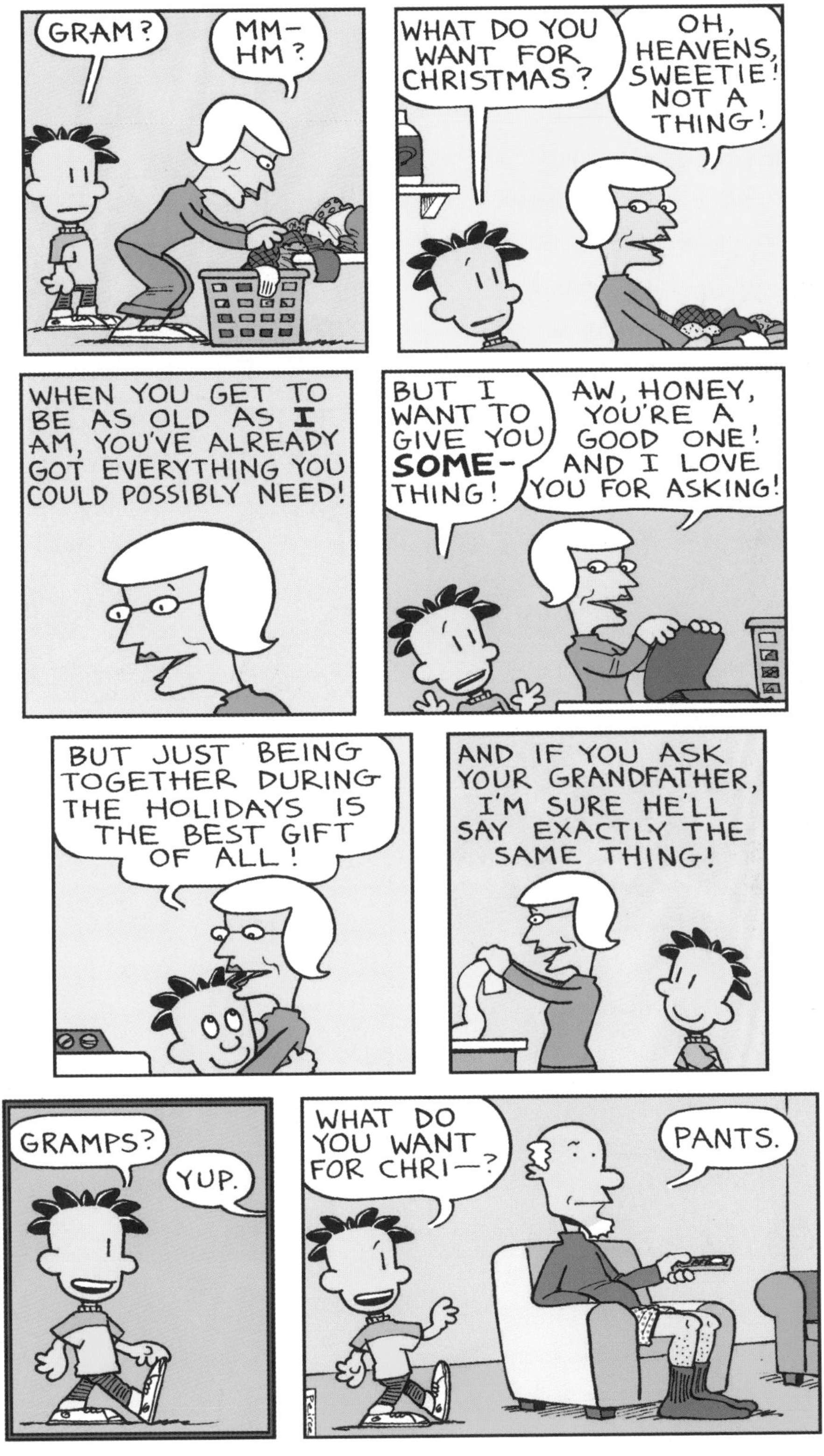
GRAM?
MM-HM?
WHAT DO YOU WANT FOR CHRISTMAS?
OH, HEAVENS, SWEETIE! NOT A THING!
WHEN YOU GET TO BE AS OLD AS **I** AM, YOU'VE ALREADY GOT EVERYTHING YOU COULD POSSIBLY NEED!
BUT I WANT TO GIVE YOU **SOME**-THING!
AW, HONEY, YOU'RE A GOOD ONE! AND I LOVE YOU FOR ASKING!
BUT JUST BEING TOGETHER DURING THE HOLIDAYS IS THE BEST GIFT OF ALL!
AND IF YOU ASK YOUR GRANDFATHER, I'M SURE HE'LL SAY EXACTLY THE SAME THING!
GRAMPS?
YUP.
WHAT DO YOU WANT FOR CHRI—?
PANTS.
Peirce

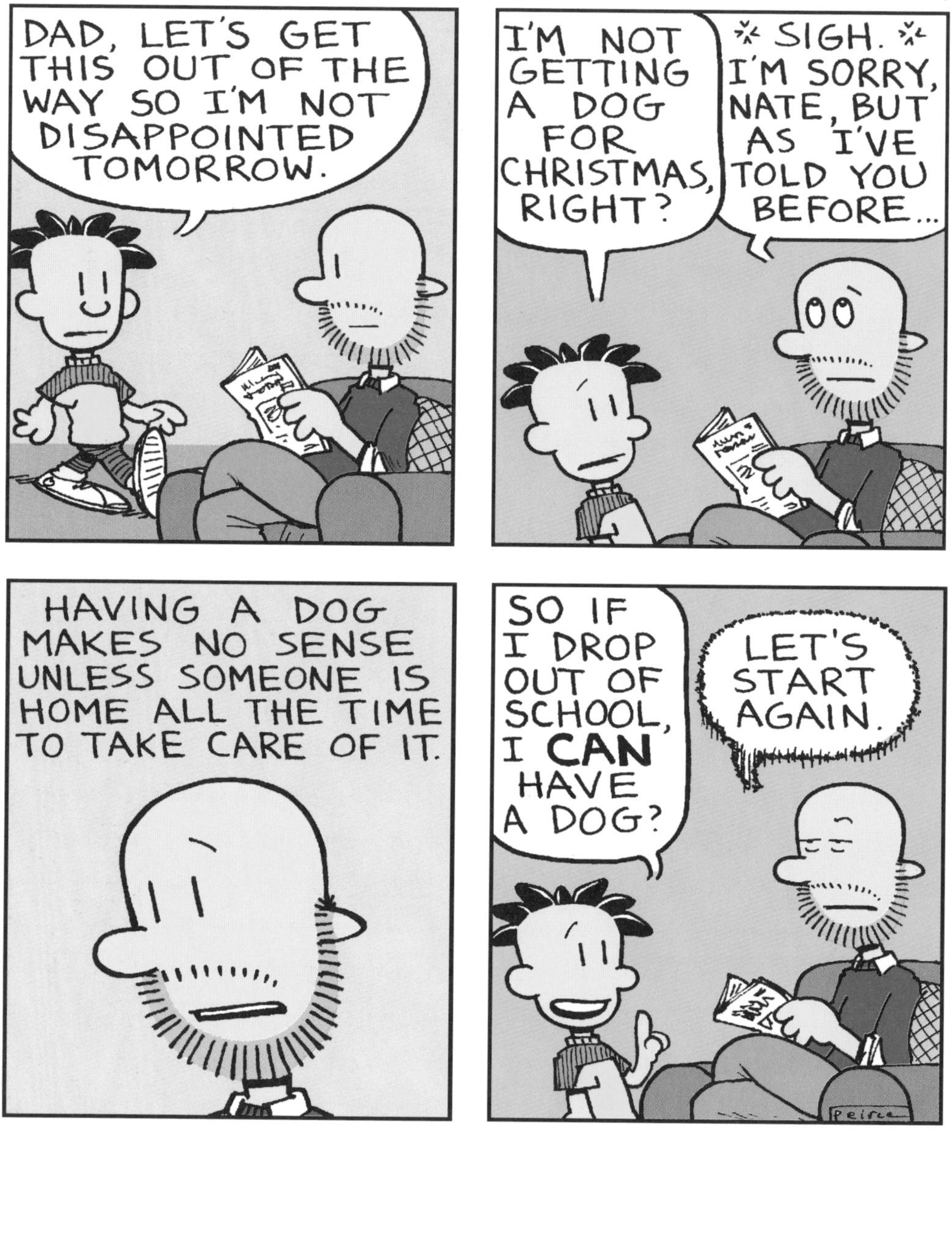
DAD, LET'S GET THIS OUT OF THE WAY SO I'M NOT DISAPPOINTED TOMORROW.
I'M NOT GETTING A DOG FOR CHRISTMAS, RIGHT?
SIGH. I'M SORRY, NATE, BUT AS I'VE TOLD YOU BEFORE...
HAVING A DOG MAKES NO SENSE UNLESS SOMEONE IS HOME ALL THE TIME TO TAKE CARE OF IT.
SO IF I DROP OUT OF SCHOOL, I **CAN** HAVE A DOG?
LET'S START AGAIN.
Peirce

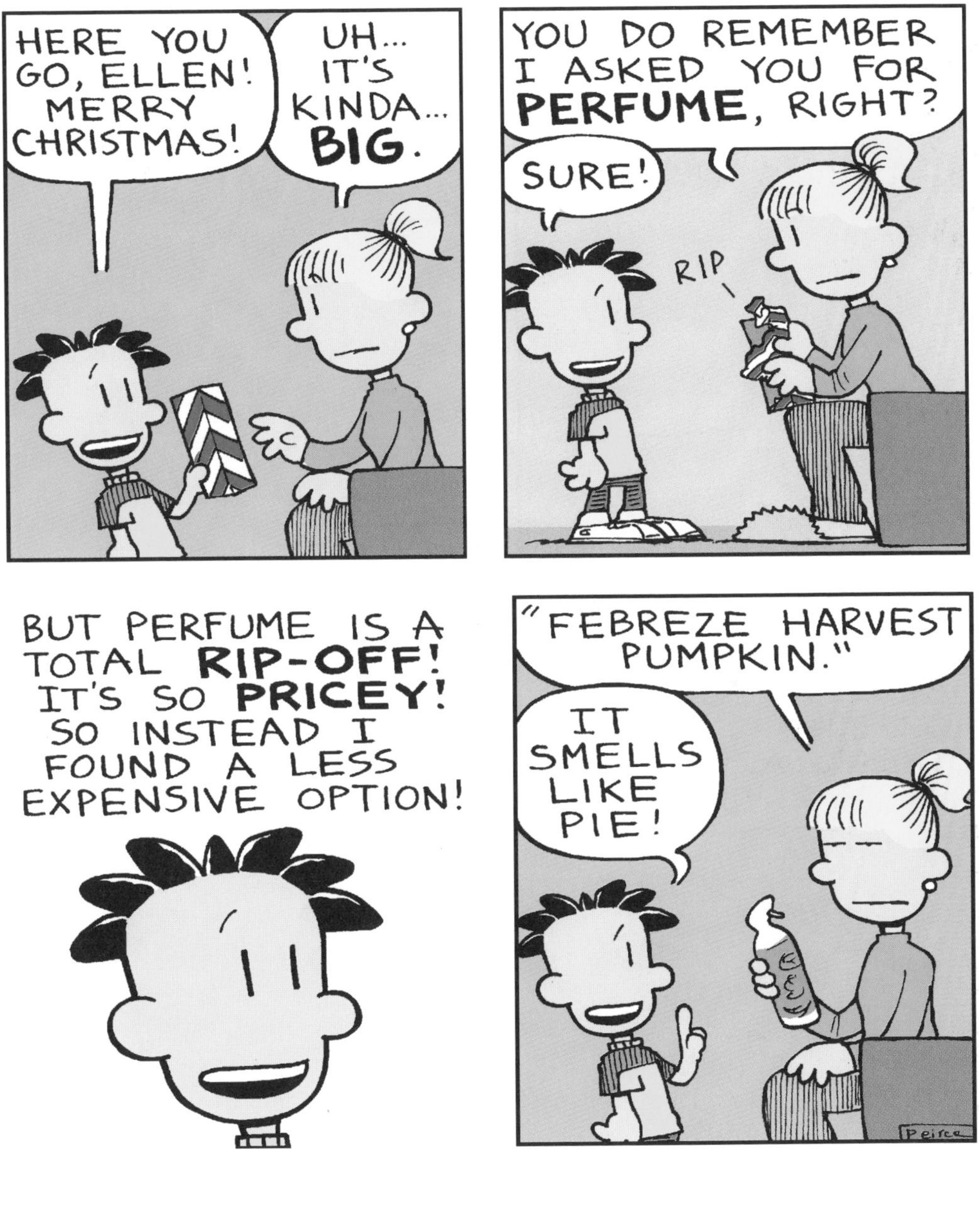
HERE YOU GO, ELLEN! MERRY CHRISTMAS!
UH... IT'S KINDA... **BIG**.
YOU DO REMEMBER I ASKED YOU FOR **PERFUME**, RIGHT?
SURE!
RIP
BUT PERFUME IS A TOTAL **RIP-OFF**! IT'S SO **PRICEY**! SO INSTEAD I FOUND A LESS EXPENSIVE OPTION!
"FEBREZE HARVEST PUMPKIN."
IT SMELLS LIKE PIE!
Peirce

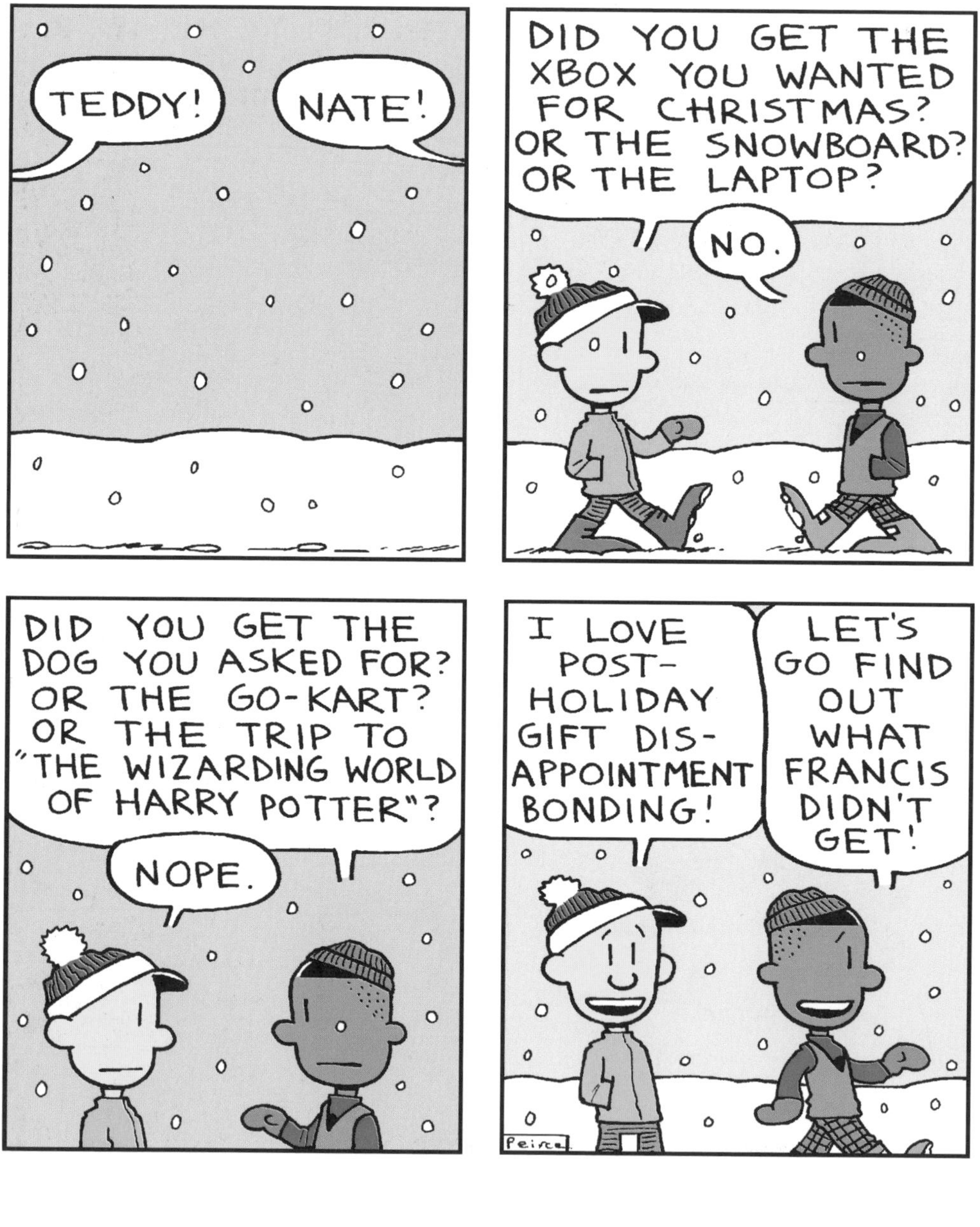
TEDDY!
NATE!
DID YOU GET THE XBOX YOU WANTED FOR CHRISTMAS? OR THE SNOWBOARD? OR THE LAPTOP?
NO.
DID YOU GET THE DOG YOU ASKED FOR? OR THE GO-KART? OR THE TRIP TO "THE WIZARDING WORLD OF HARRY POTTER"?
NOPE.
I LOVE POST-HOLIDAY GIFT DIS-APPOINTMENT BONDING!
LET'S GO FIND OUT WHAT FRANCIS DIDN'T GET!
Peirce

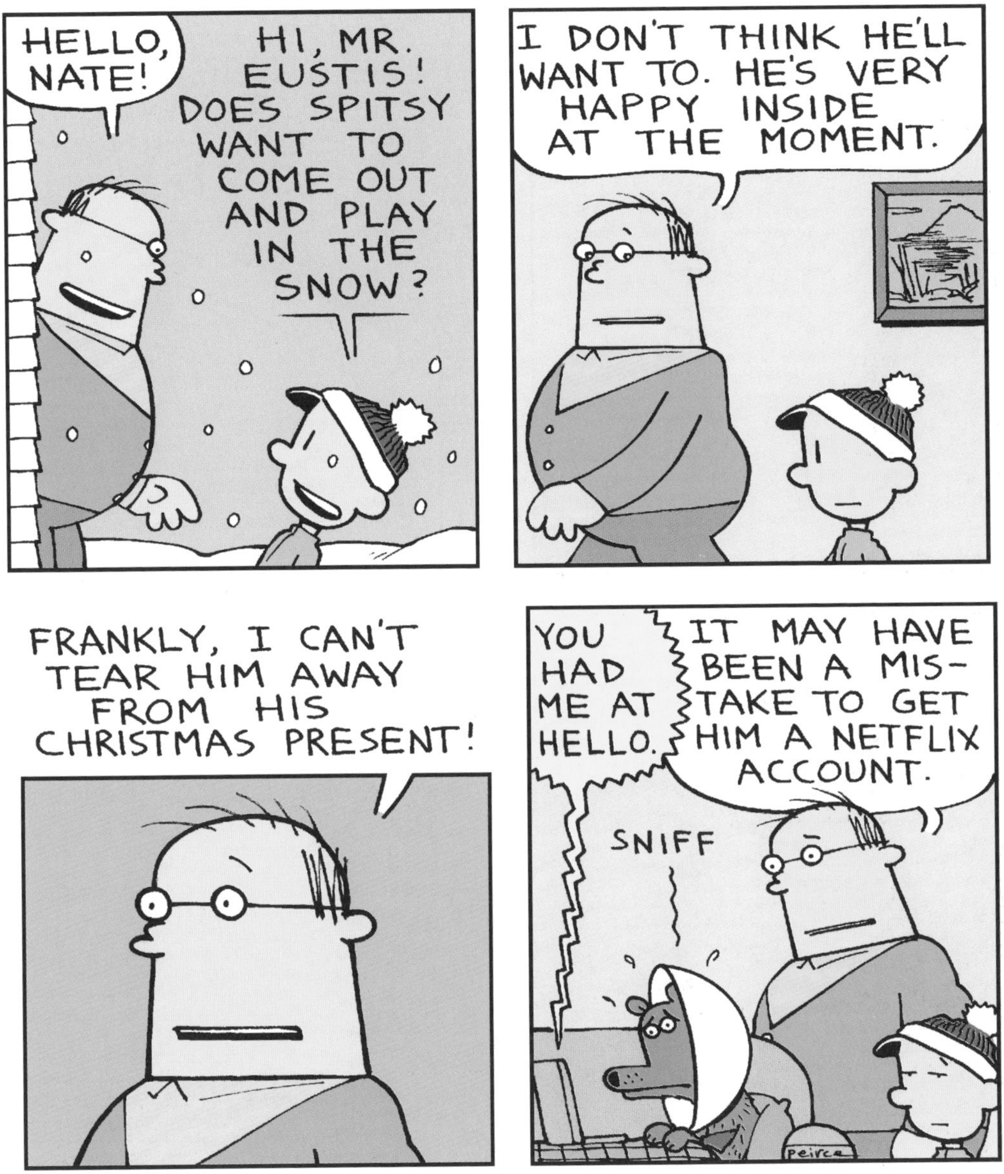
HELLO, NATE!
HI, MR. EUSTIS! DOES SPITSY WANT TO COME OUT AND PLAY IN THE SNOW?
I DON'T THINK HE'LL WANT TO. HE'S VERY HAPPY INSIDE AT THE MOMENT.
FRANKLY, I CAN'T TEAR HIM AWAY FROM HIS CHRISTMAS PRESENT!
IT MAY HAVE BEEN A MIS-TAKE TO GET HIM A NETFLIX ACCOUNT.
YOU HAD ME AT HELLO.
SNIFF
peirce

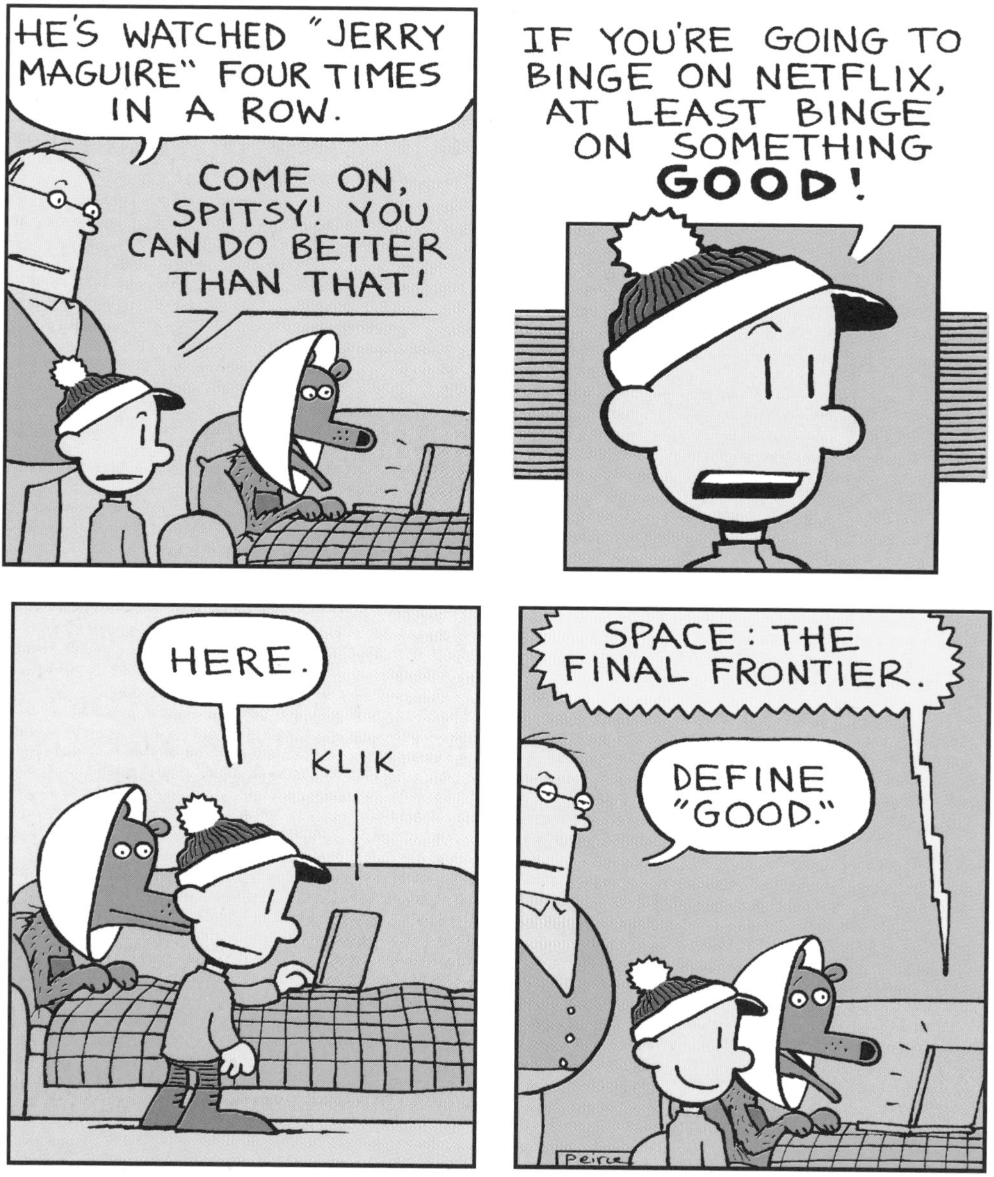
HE'S WATCHED "JERRY MAGUIRE" FOUR TIMES IN A ROW.
COME ON, SPITSY! YOU CAN DO BETTER THAN THAT!
IF YOU'RE GOING TO BINGE ON NETFLIX, AT LEAST BINGE ON SOMETHING GOOD!
HERE.
KLIK
SPACE: THE FINAL FRONTIER.
DEFINE "GOOD."
Peirce

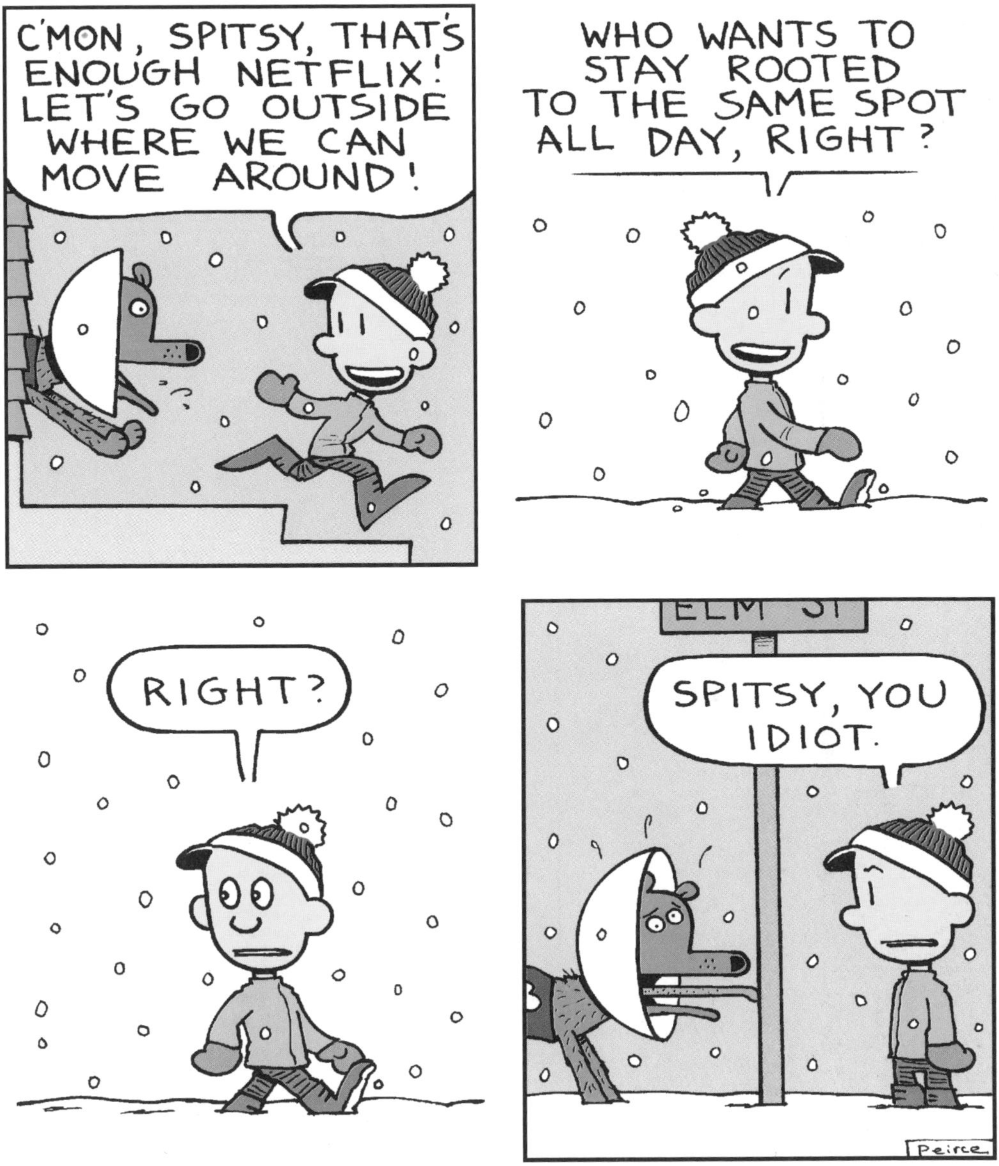
C'MON, SPITSY, THAT'S ENOUGH NETFLIX! LET'S GO OUTSIDE WHERE WE CAN MOVE AROUND!
WHO WANTS TO STAY ROOTED TO THE SAME SPOT ALL DAY, RIGHT?
RIGHT?
ELM ST
SPITSY, YOU IDIOT.
Peirce

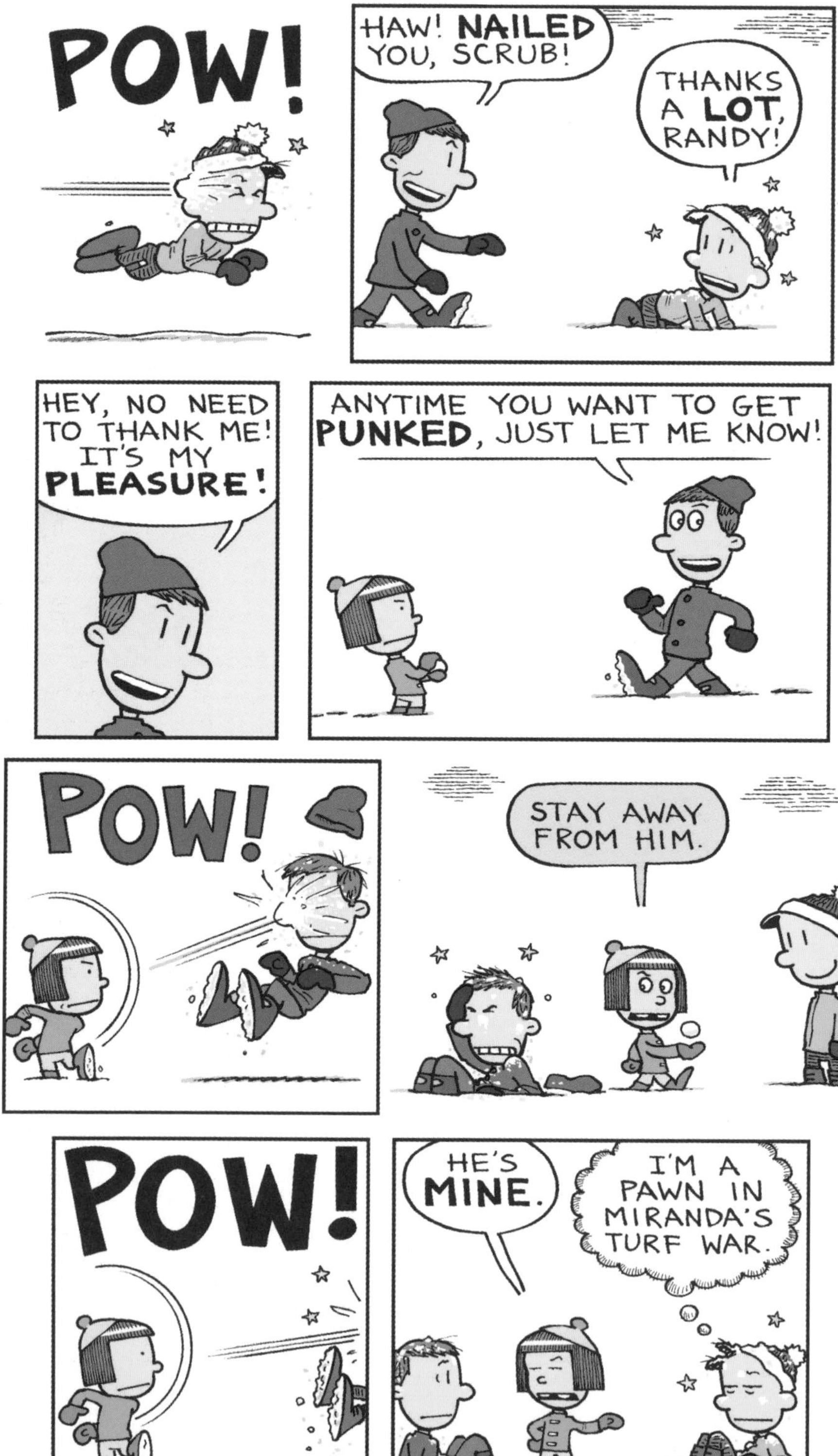
POW!
HAW! NAILED YOU, SCRUB!
THANKS A LOT, RANDY!
HEY, NO NEED TO THANK ME! IT'S MY PLEASURE!
ANYTIME YOU WANT TO GET PUNKED, JUST LET ME KNOW!
POW!
STAY AWAY FROM HIM.
POW!
HE'S MINE.
I'M A PAWN IN MIRANDA'S TURF WAR.
Peirce

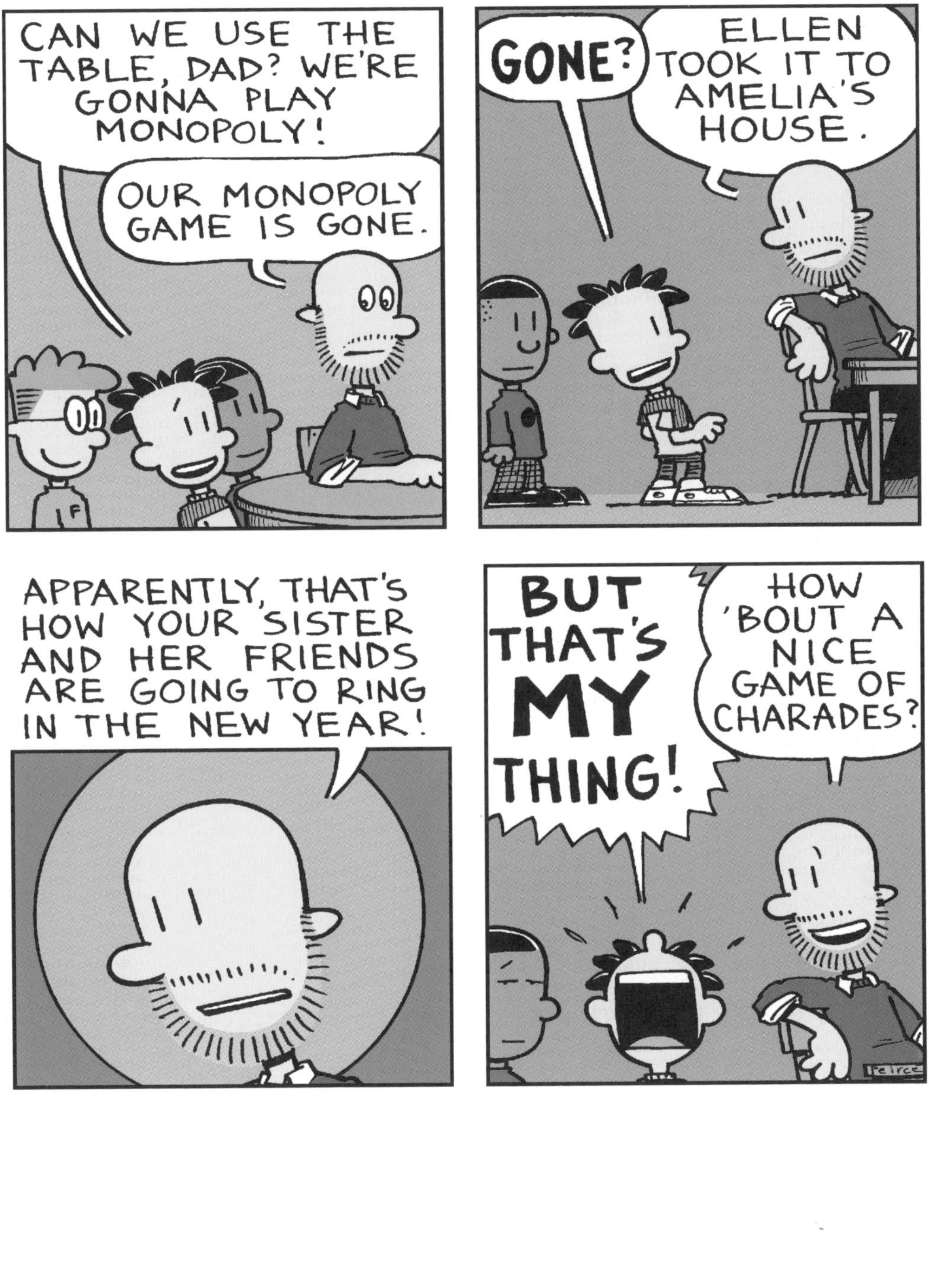
CAN WE USE THE TABLE, DAD? WE'RE GONNA PLAY MONOPOLY!
OUR MONOPOLY GAME IS GONE.
GONE?
ELLEN TOOK IT TO AMELIA'S HOUSE.
APPARENTLY, THAT'S HOW YOUR SISTER AND HER FRIENDS ARE GOING TO RING IN THE NEW YEAR!
BUT THAT'S MY THING!
HOW 'BOUT A NICE GAME OF CHARADES?
Peirce

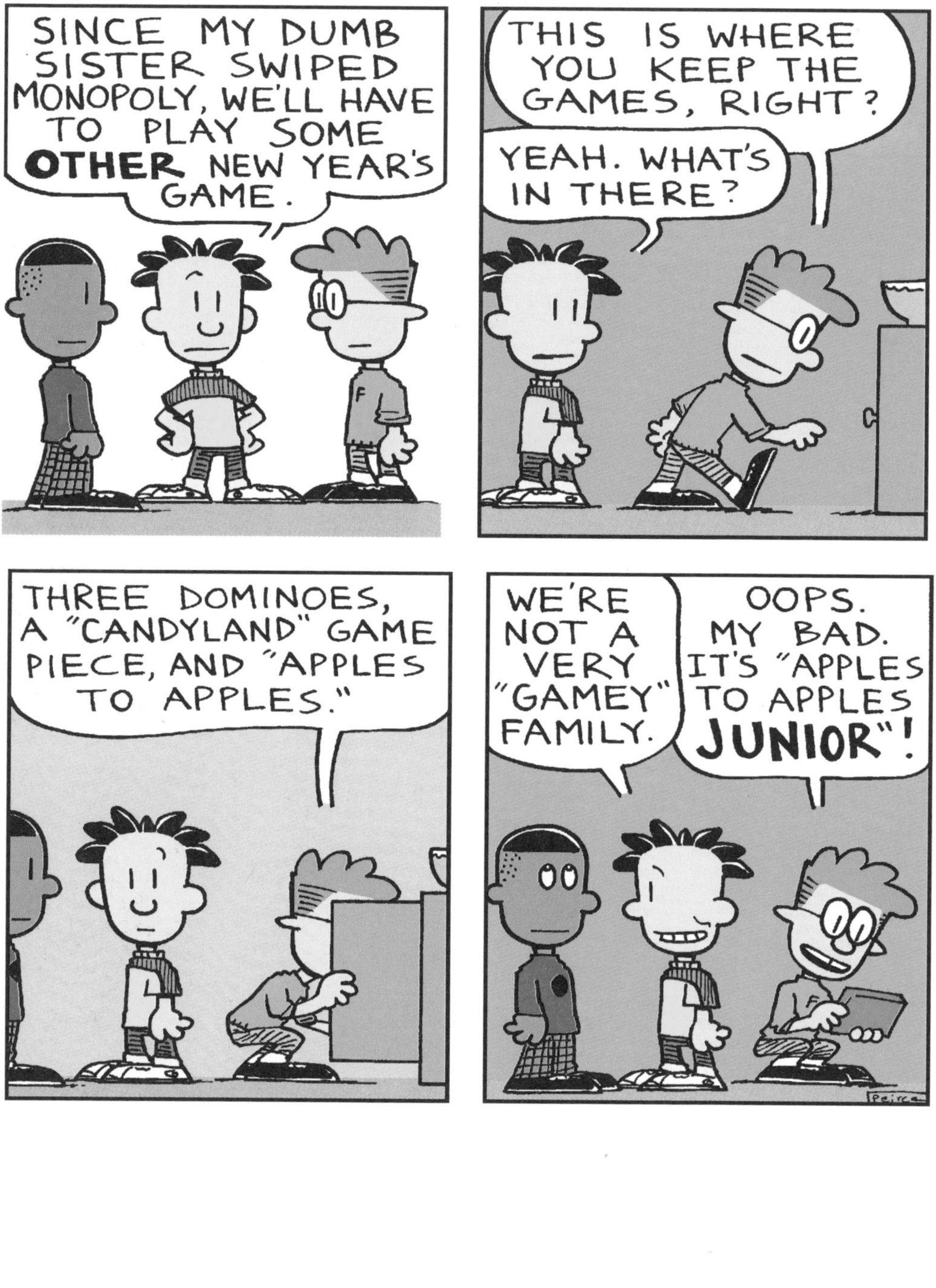
SINCE MY DUMB SISTER SWIPED MONOPOLY, WE'LL HAVE TO PLAY SOME **OTHER** NEW YEAR'S GAME.
THIS IS WHERE YOU KEEP THE GAMES, RIGHT?
YEAH. WHAT'S IN THERE?
THREE DOMINOES, A "CANDYLAND" GAME PIECE, AND "APPLES TO APPLES."
WE'RE NOT A VERY "GAMEY" FAMILY.
OOPS. MY BAD. IT'S "APPLES TO APPLES **JUNIOR**"!
Peirce

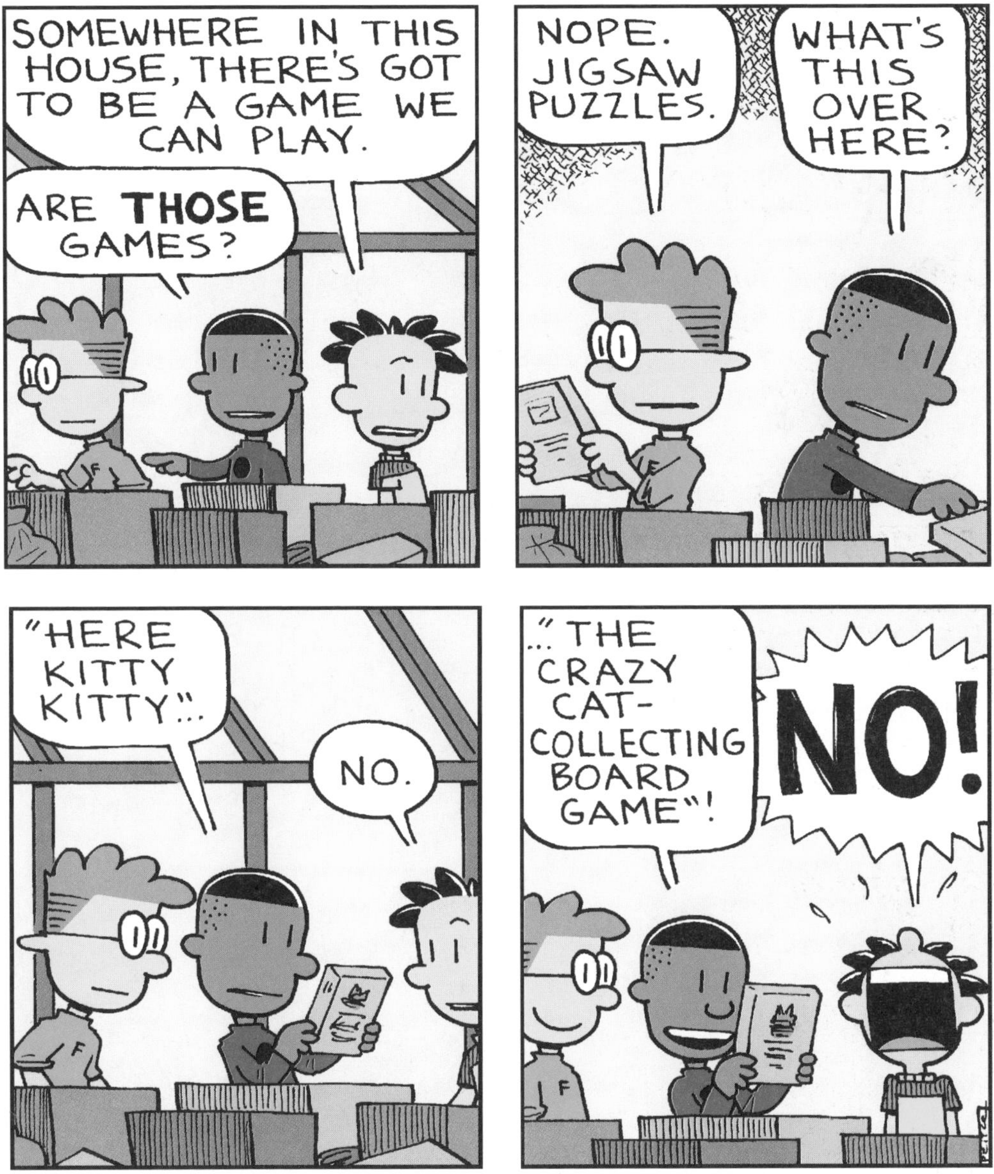
SOMEWHERE IN THIS HOUSE, THERE'S GOT TO BE A GAME WE CAN PLAY.
ARE **THOSE** GAMES?
NOPE. JIGSAW PUZZLES.
WHAT'S THIS OVER HERE?
"HERE KITTY KITTY"...
NO.
..."THE CRAZY CAT-COLLECTING BOARD GAME"!
NO!

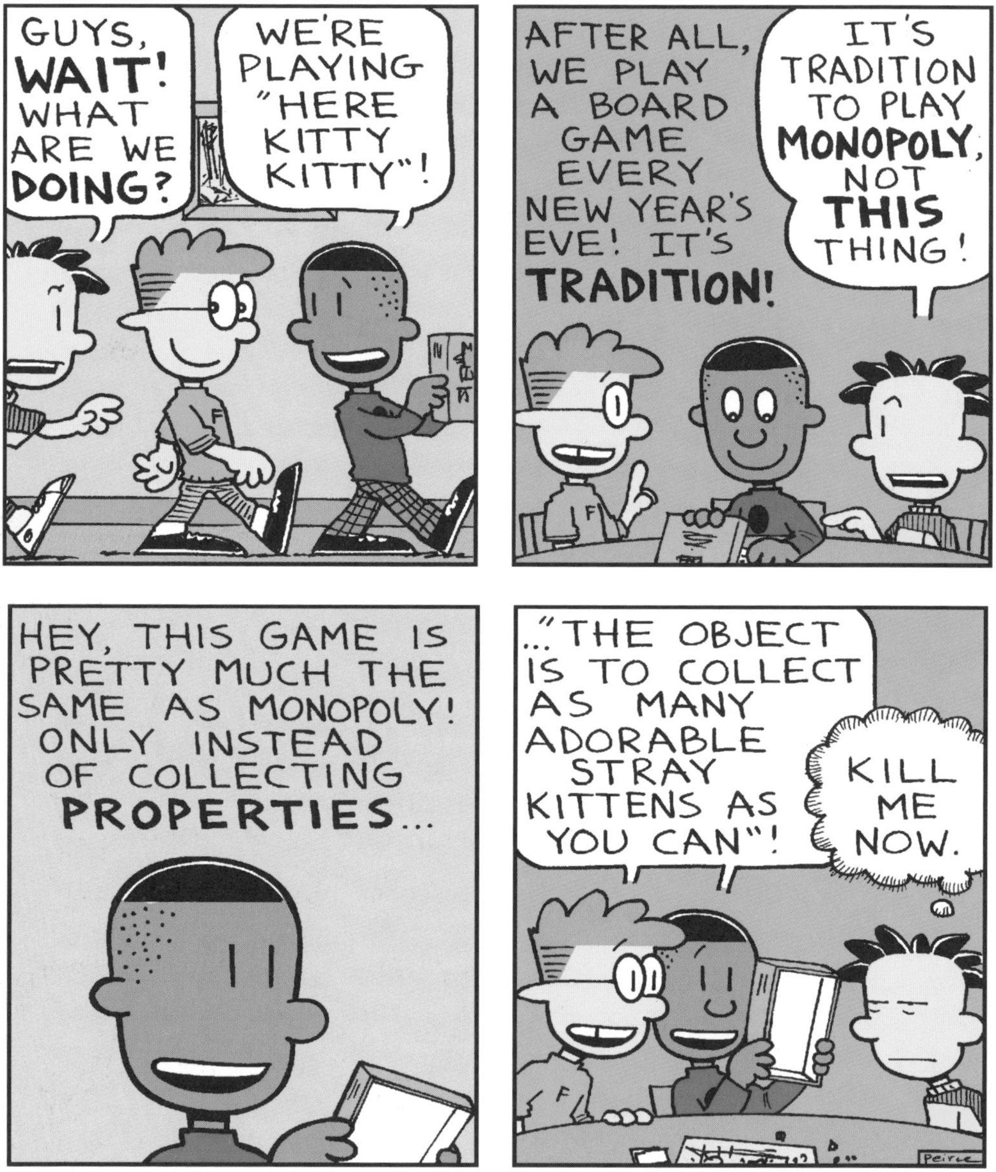
GUYS, **WAIT!** WHAT ARE WE **DOING?**
WE'RE PLAYING "HERE KITTY KITTY"!
AFTER ALL, WE PLAY A BOARD GAME EVERY NEW YEAR'S EVE! IT'S **TRADITION!**
IT'S TRADITION TO PLAY **MONOPOLY**, NOT **THIS** THING!
HEY, THIS GAME IS PRETTY MUCH THE SAME AS MONOPOLY! ONLY INSTEAD OF COLLECTING **PROPERTIES**...
..."THE OBJECT IS TO COLLECT AS MANY ADORABLE STRAY KITTENS AS YOU CAN"!
KILL ME NOW.
Peirce

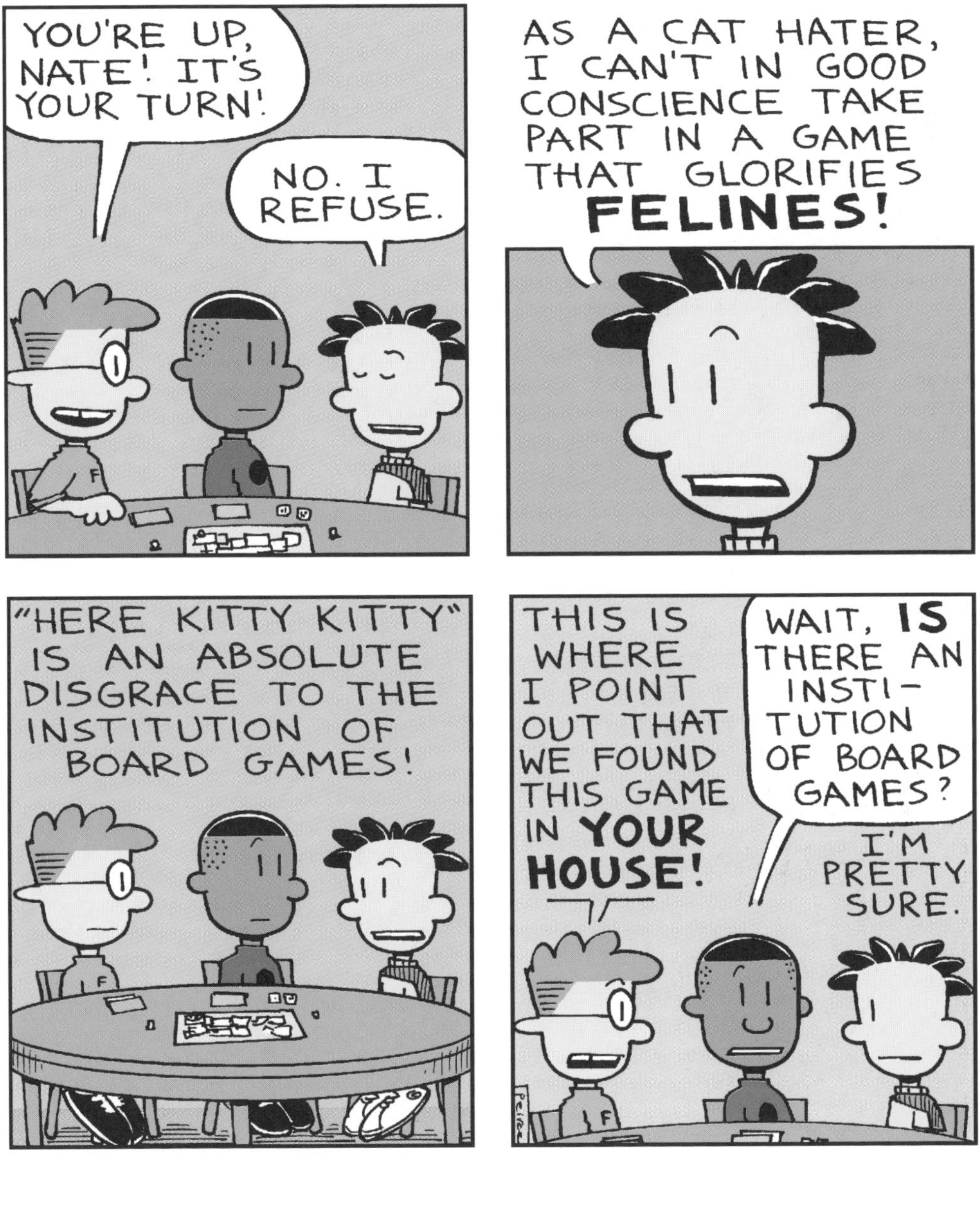
YOU'RE UP, NATE! IT'S YOUR TURN!
NO. I REFUSE.
AS A CAT HATER, I CAN'T IN GOOD CONSCIENCE TAKE PART IN A GAME THAT GLORIFIES **FELINES!**
"HERE KITTY KITTY" IS AN ABSOLUTE DISGRACE TO THE INSTITUTION OF BOARD GAMES!
THIS IS WHERE I POINT OUT THAT WE FOUND THIS GAME IN **YOUR HOUSE!**
WAIT, **IS** THERE AN INSTI- TUTION OF BOARD GAMES?
I'M PRETTY SURE.
PEIRCE

FRANCIS HAS A POINT, NATE: WHAT'S "HERE KITTY KITTY" DOING IN **YOUR HOUSE**?
HOW SHOULD **I** KNOW?
MAYBE IT'S MY SISTER'S! MAYBE WE GOT IT AS A GIFT FROM SOME CRAZY, CAT-LOVING GREAT AUNT!
A PERSON CAN'T BE HELD RESPONSIBLE FOR EVERY LITTLE THING IN HIS ATTIC!
REMEMBER THAT TIME IN **YOUR** ATTIC WE FOUND–
WE AGREED NEVER TO SPEAK OF THAT AGAIN.
Peirce

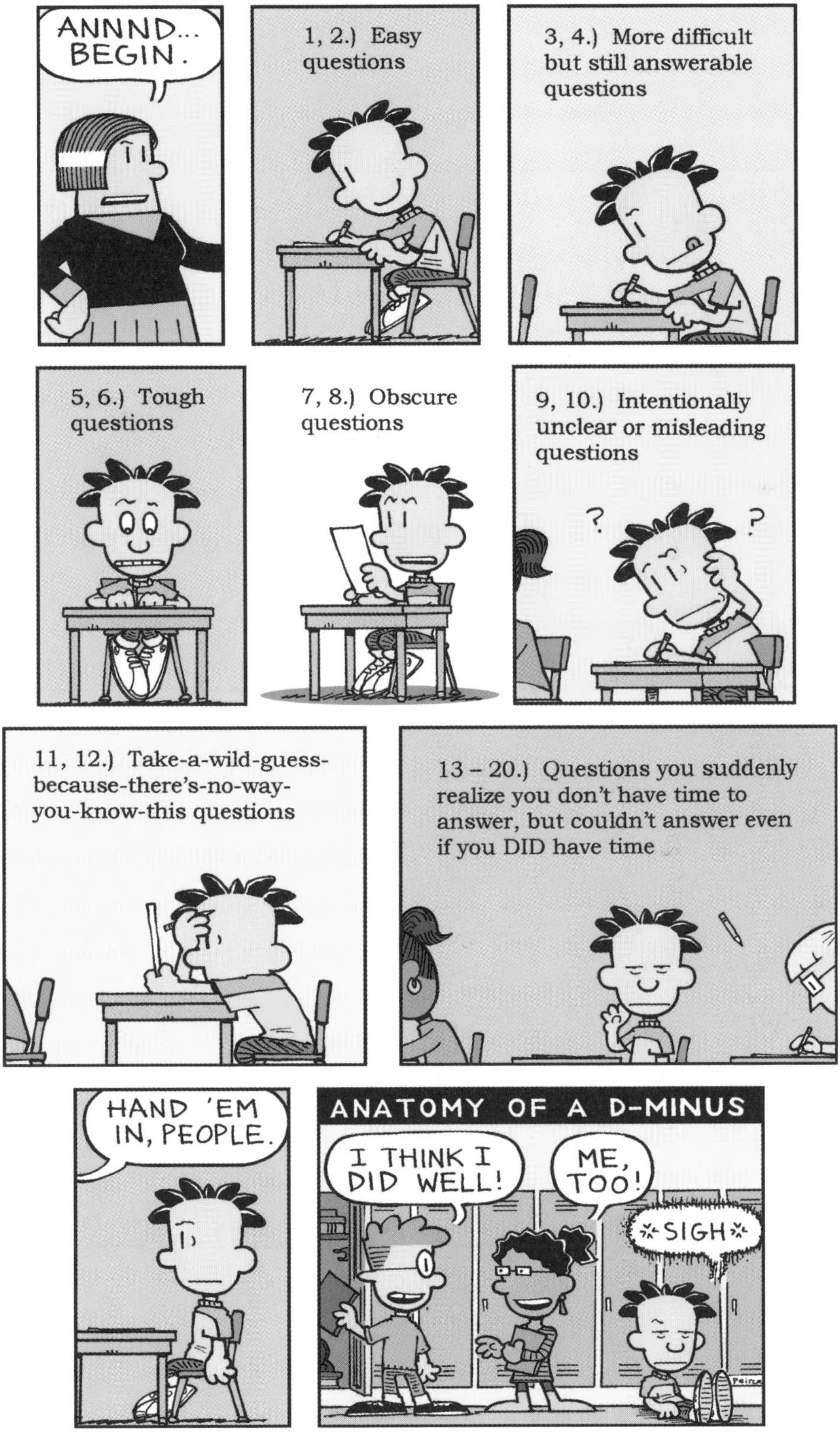
ANNND... BEGIN.
1, 2.) Easy questions
3, 4.) More difficult but still answerable questions
5, 6.) Tough questions
7, 8.) Obscure questions
?
?
9, 10.) Intentionally unclear or misleading questions
11, 12.) Take-a-wild-guess-because-there's-no-way-you-know-this questions
13 – 20.) Questions you suddenly realize you don't have time to answer, but couldn't answer even if you DID have time
HAND 'EM IN, PEOPLE.
ANATOMY OF A D-MINUS
I THINK I DID WELL!
ME, TOO!
SIGH
Peirce

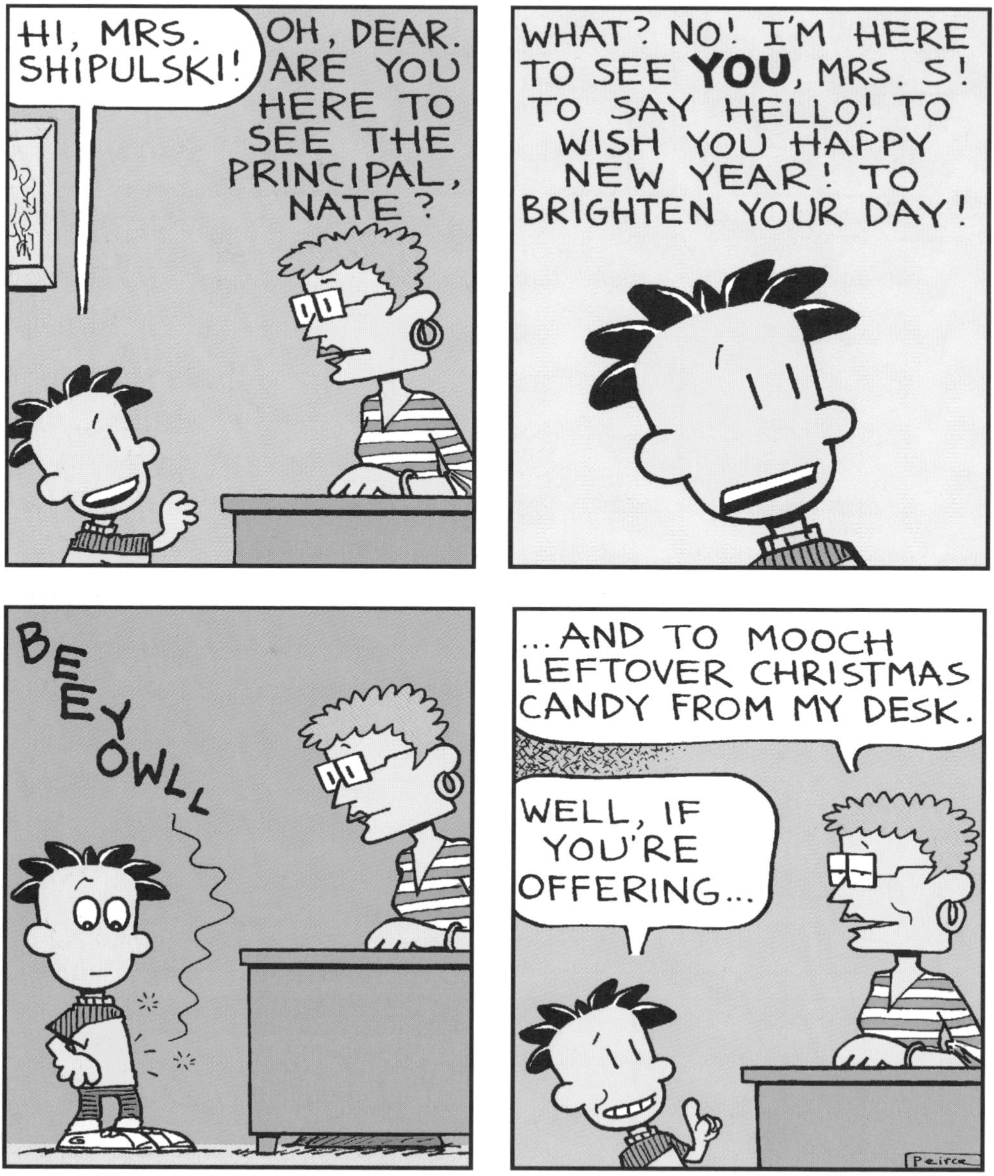
HI, MRS. SHIPULSKI!
OH, DEAR. ARE YOU HERE TO SEE THE PRINCIPAL, NATE?
WHAT? NO! I'M HERE TO SEE YOU, MRS. S! TO SAY HELLO! TO WISH YOU HAPPY NEW YEAR! TO BRIGHTEN YOUR DAY!
BEEYOWLL
...AND TO MOOCH LEFTOVER CHRISTMAS CANDY FROM MY DESK.
WELL, IF YOU'RE OFFERING...
Peirce

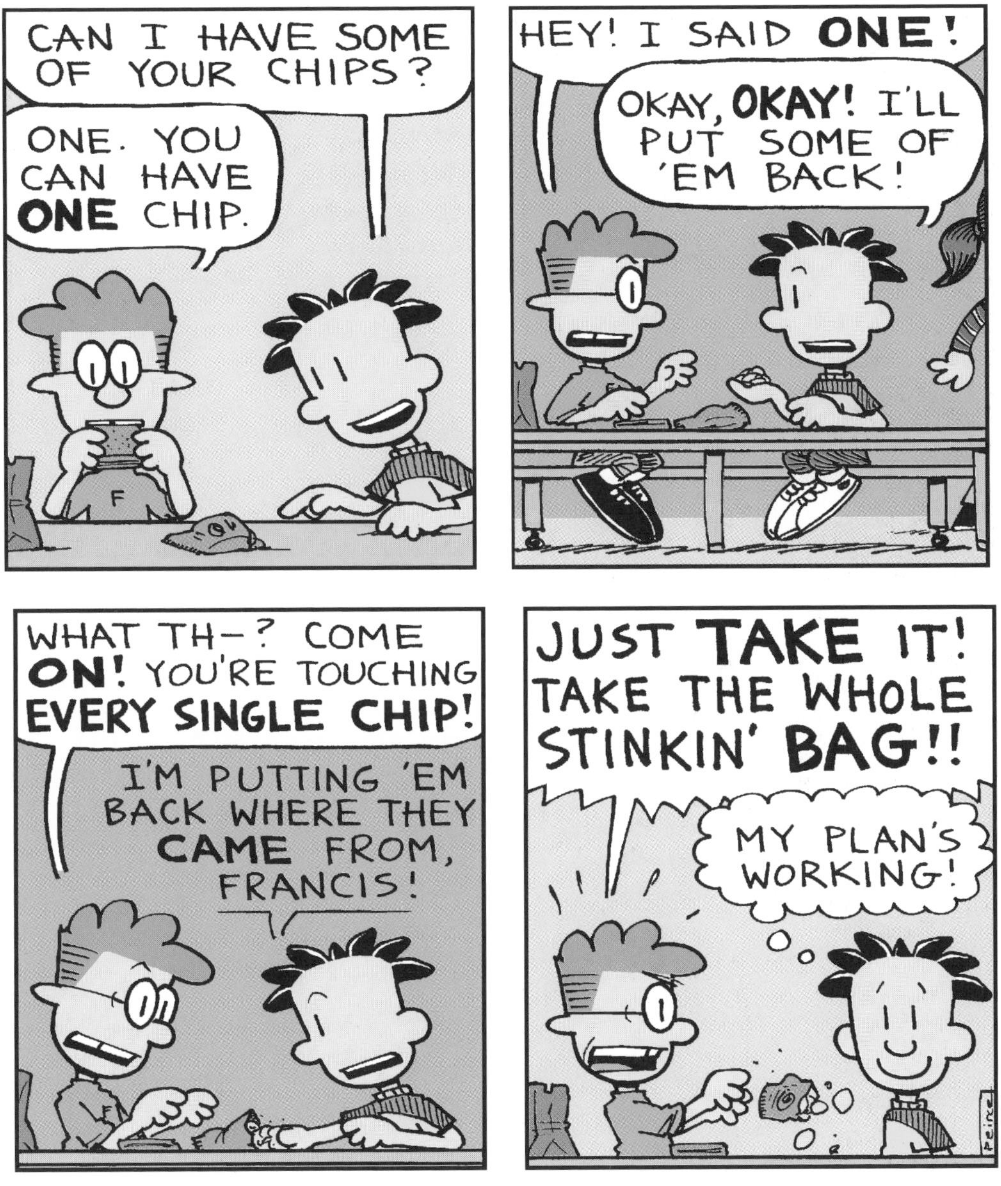
CAN I HAVE SOME OF YOUR CHIPS?
ONE. YOU CAN HAVE ONE CHIP.
HEY! I SAID ONE!
OKAY, OKAY! I'LL PUT SOME OF 'EM BACK!
WHAT TH—? COME ON! YOU'RE TOUCHING EVERY SINGLE CHIP!
I'M PUTTING 'EM BACK WHERE THEY CAME FROM, FRANCIS!
JUST TAKE IT! TAKE THE WHOLE STINKIN' BAG!!
MY PLAN'S WORKING!
Peirce

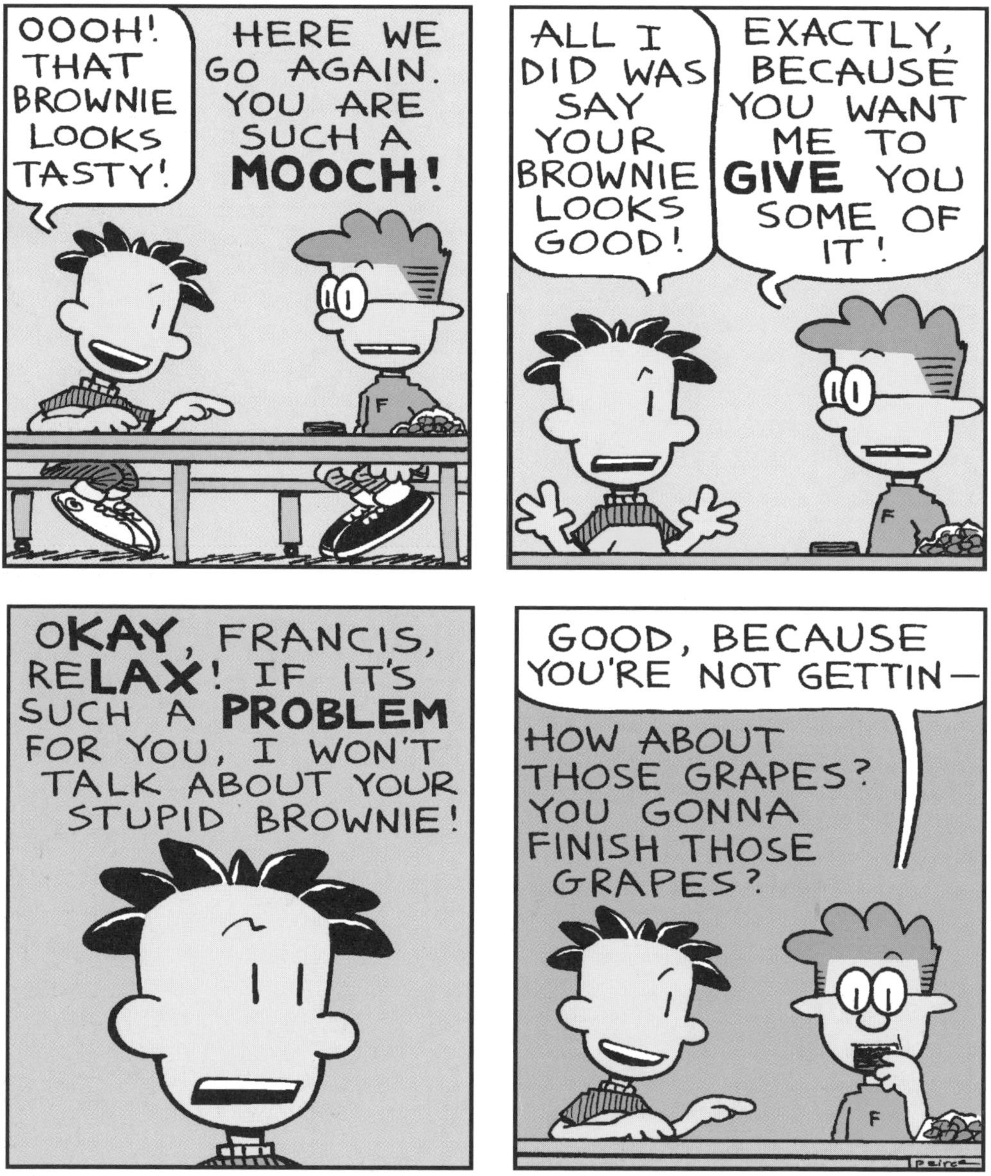
OOOH! THAT BROWNIE LOOKS TASTY!
HERE WE GO AGAIN. YOU ARE SUCH A MOOCH!
ALL I DID WAS SAY YOUR BROWNIE LOOKS GOOD!
EXACTLY, BECAUSE YOU WANT ME TO GIVE YOU SOME OF IT!
OKAY, FRANCIS, RELAX! IF IT'S SUCH A PROBLEM FOR YOU, I WON'T TALK ABOUT YOUR STUPID BROWNIE!
GOOD, BECAUSE YOU'RE NOT GETTIN—
HOW ABOUT THOSE GRAPES? YOU GONNA FINISH THOSE GRAPES?

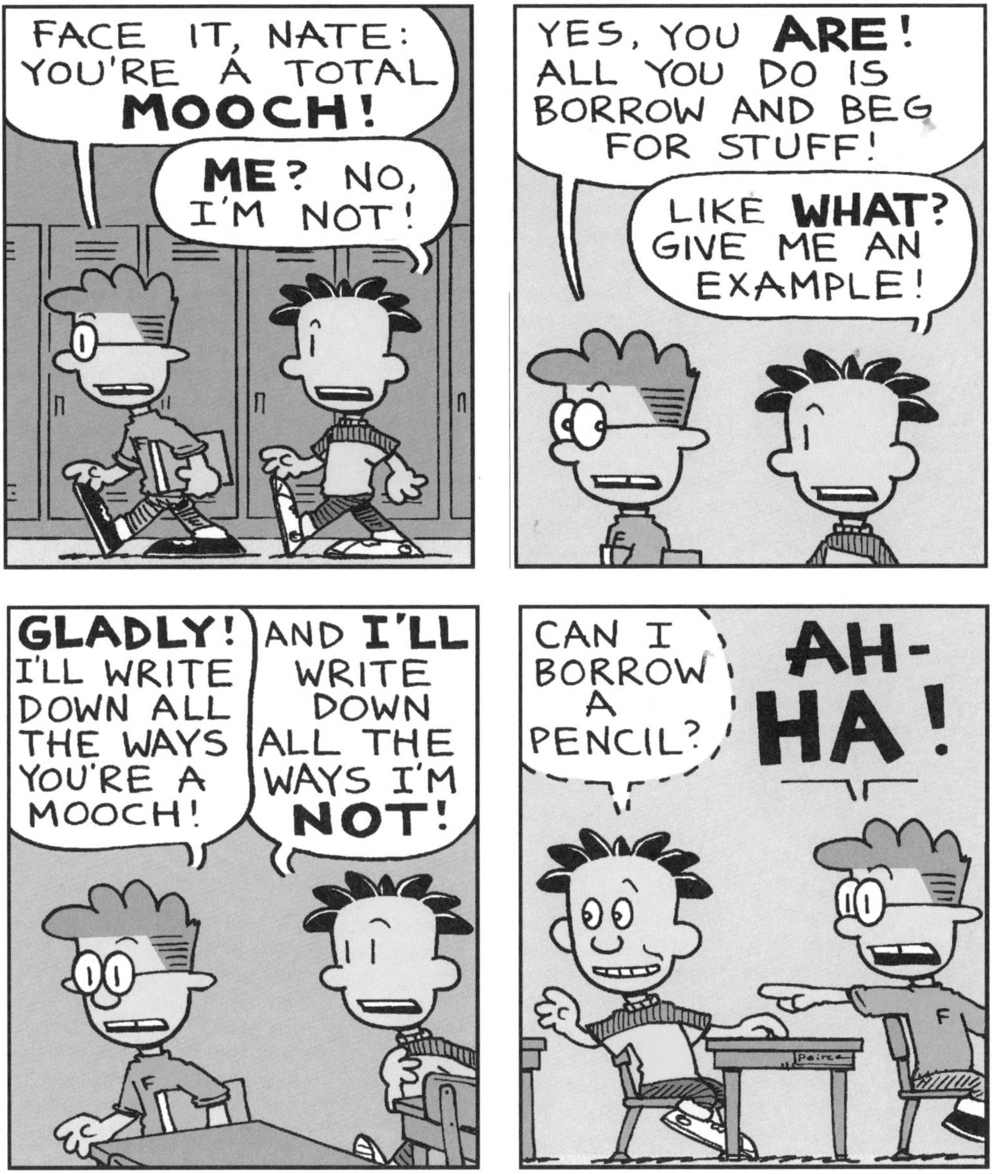
FACE IT, NATE: YOU'RE A TOTAL **MOOCH**!
ME? NO, I'M NOT!
YES, YOU **ARE**! ALL YOU DO IS BORROW AND BEG FOR STUFF!
LIKE **WHAT**? GIVE ME AN EXAMPLE!
GLADLY! I'LL WRITE DOWN ALL THE WAYS YOU'RE A MOOCH!
AND **I'LL** WRITE DOWN ALL THE WAYS I'M **NOT**!
CAN I BORROW A PENCIL?
AH-HA!

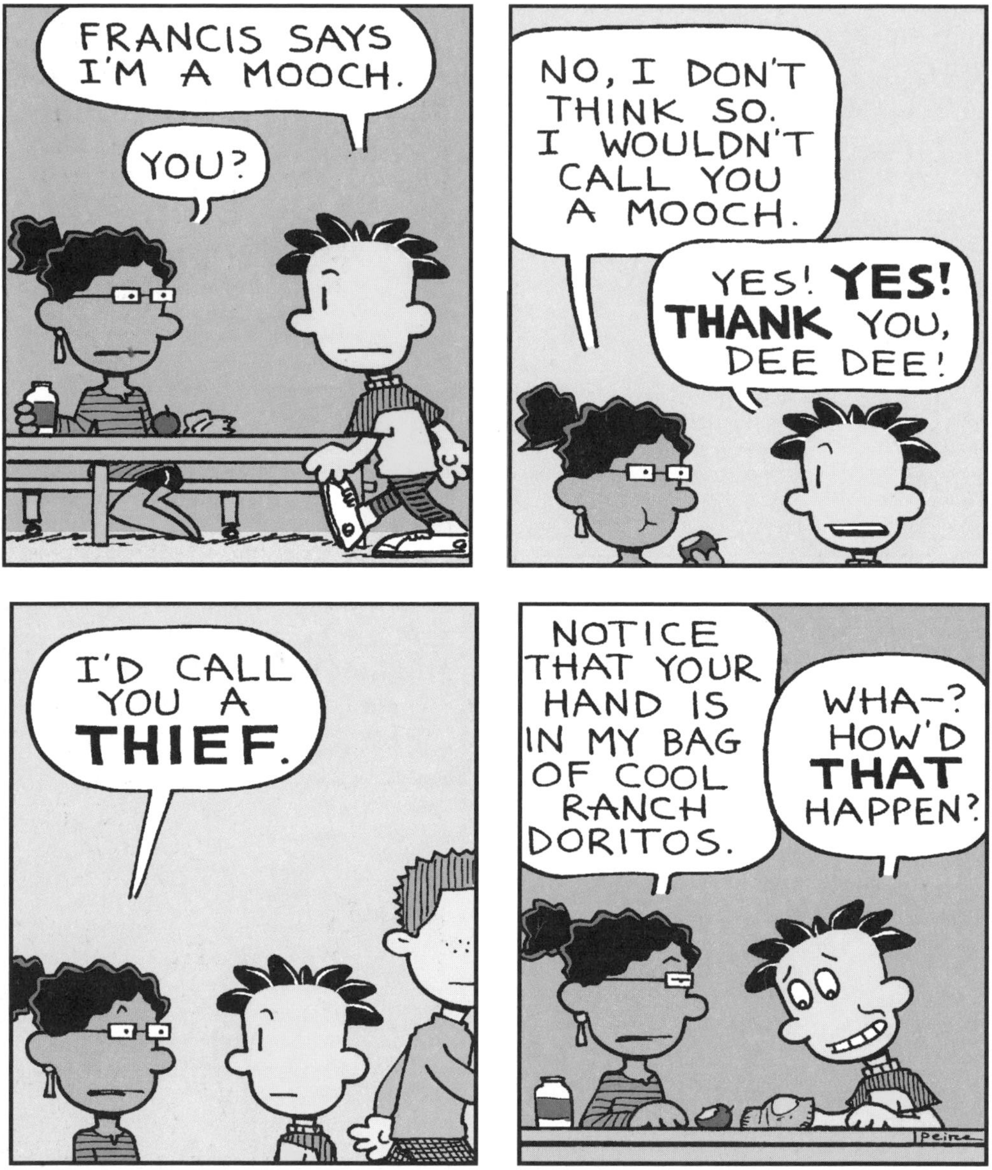
FRANCIS SAYS I'M A MOOCH.
YOU?
NO, I DON'T THINK SO. I WOULDN'T CALL YOU A MOOCH.
YES! YES! THANK YOU, DEE DEE!
I'D CALL YOU A THIEF.
NOTICE THAT YOUR HAND IS IN MY BAG OF COOL RANCH DORITOS.
WHA–? HOW'D THAT HAPPEN?
Peirce

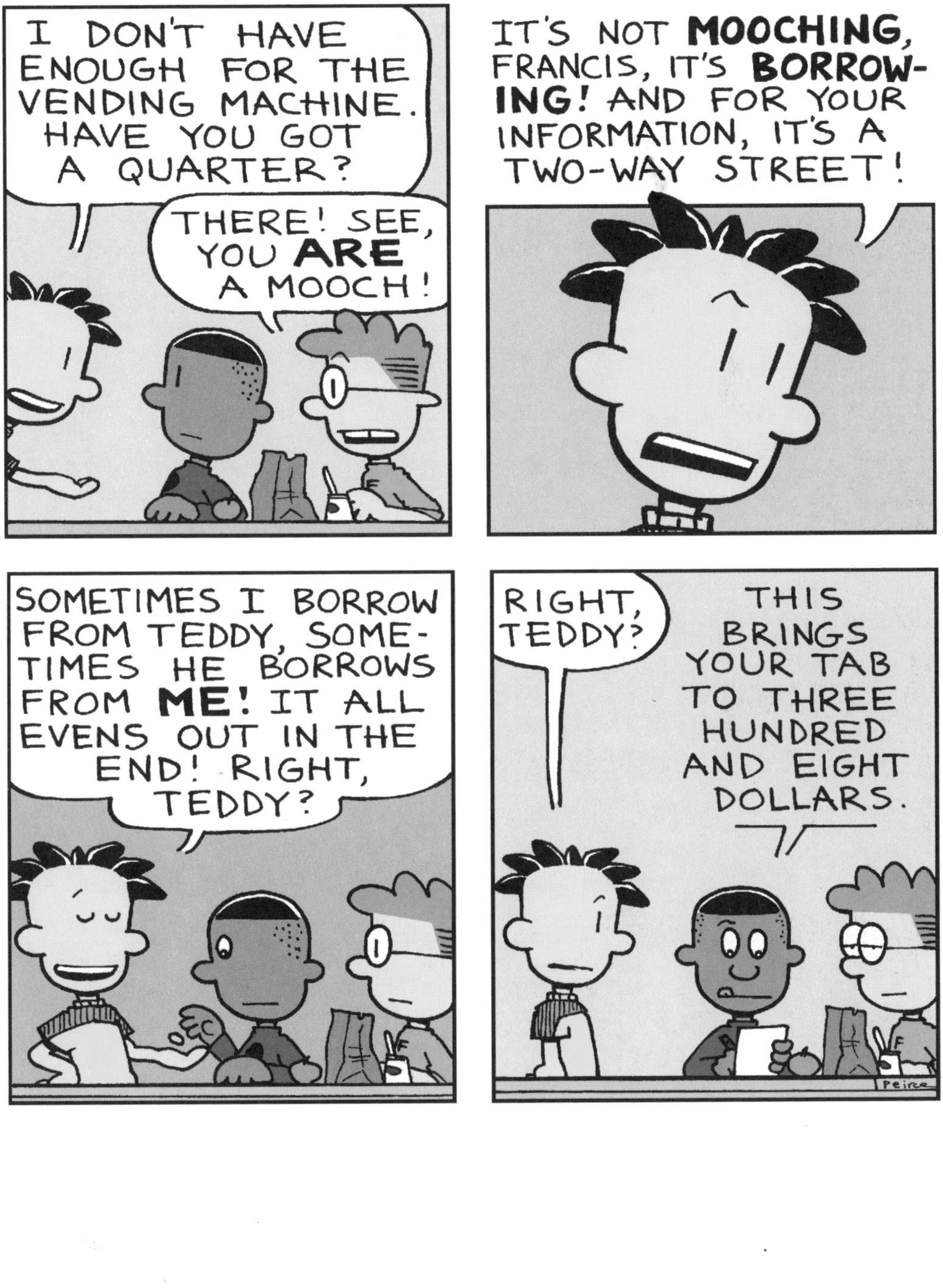
I DON'T HAVE ENOUGH FOR THE VENDING MACHINE. HAVE YOU GOT A QUARTER?
THERE! SEE, YOU **ARE** A MOOCH!
IT'S NOT **MOOCHING**, FRANCIS, IT'S **BORROWING!** AND FOR YOUR INFORMATION, IT'S A TWO-WAY STREET!
SOMETIMES I BORROW FROM TEDDY, SOMETIMES HE BORROWS FROM **ME!** IT ALL EVENS OUT IN THE END! RIGHT, TEDDY?
RIGHT, TEDDY?
THIS BRINGS YOUR TAB TO THREE HUNDRED AND EIGHT DOLLARS.
Peirce

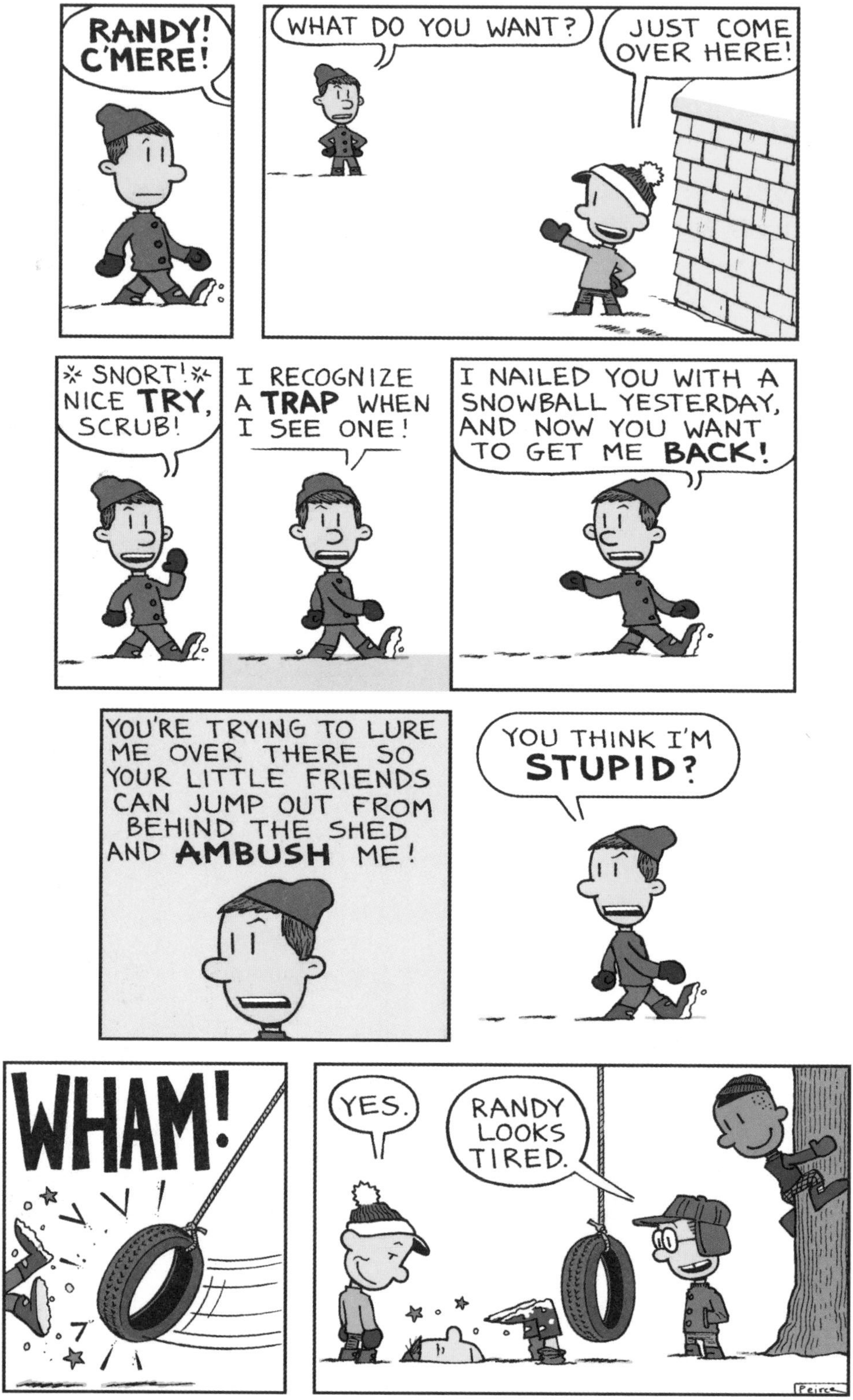
RANDY! C'MERE!
WHAT DO YOU WANT?
JUST COME OVER HERE!
SNORT! NICE TRY, SCRUB!
I RECOGNIZE A TRAP WHEN I SEE ONE!
I NAILED YOU WITH A SNOWBALL YESTERDAY, AND NOW YOU WANT TO GET ME BACK!
YOU'RE TRYING TO LURE ME OVER THERE SO YOUR LITTLE FRIENDS CAN JUMP OUT FROM BEHIND THE SHED AND AMBUSH ME!
YOU THINK I'M STUPID?
WHAM!
YES.
RANDY LOOKS TIRED.
Peirce

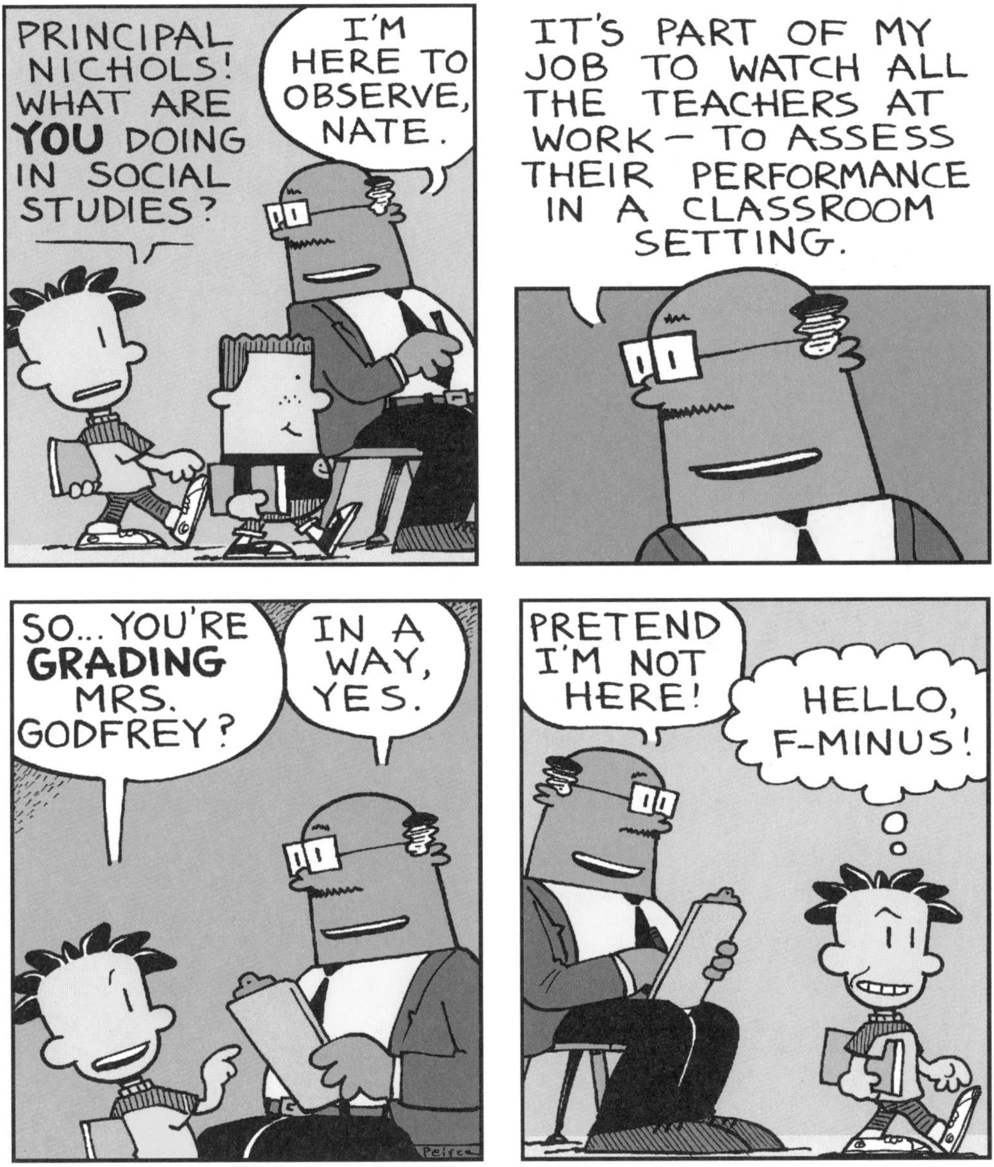
PRINCIPAL NICHOLS! WHAT ARE **YOU** DOING IN SOCIAL STUDIES?
I'M HERE TO OBSERVE, NATE.
IT'S PART OF MY JOB TO WATCH ALL THE TEACHERS AT WORK – TO ASSESS THEIR PERFORMANCE IN A CLASSROOM SETTING.
SO... YOU'RE **GRADING** MRS. GODFREY?
IN A WAY, YES.
PRETEND I'M NOT HERE!
HELLO, F-MINUS!

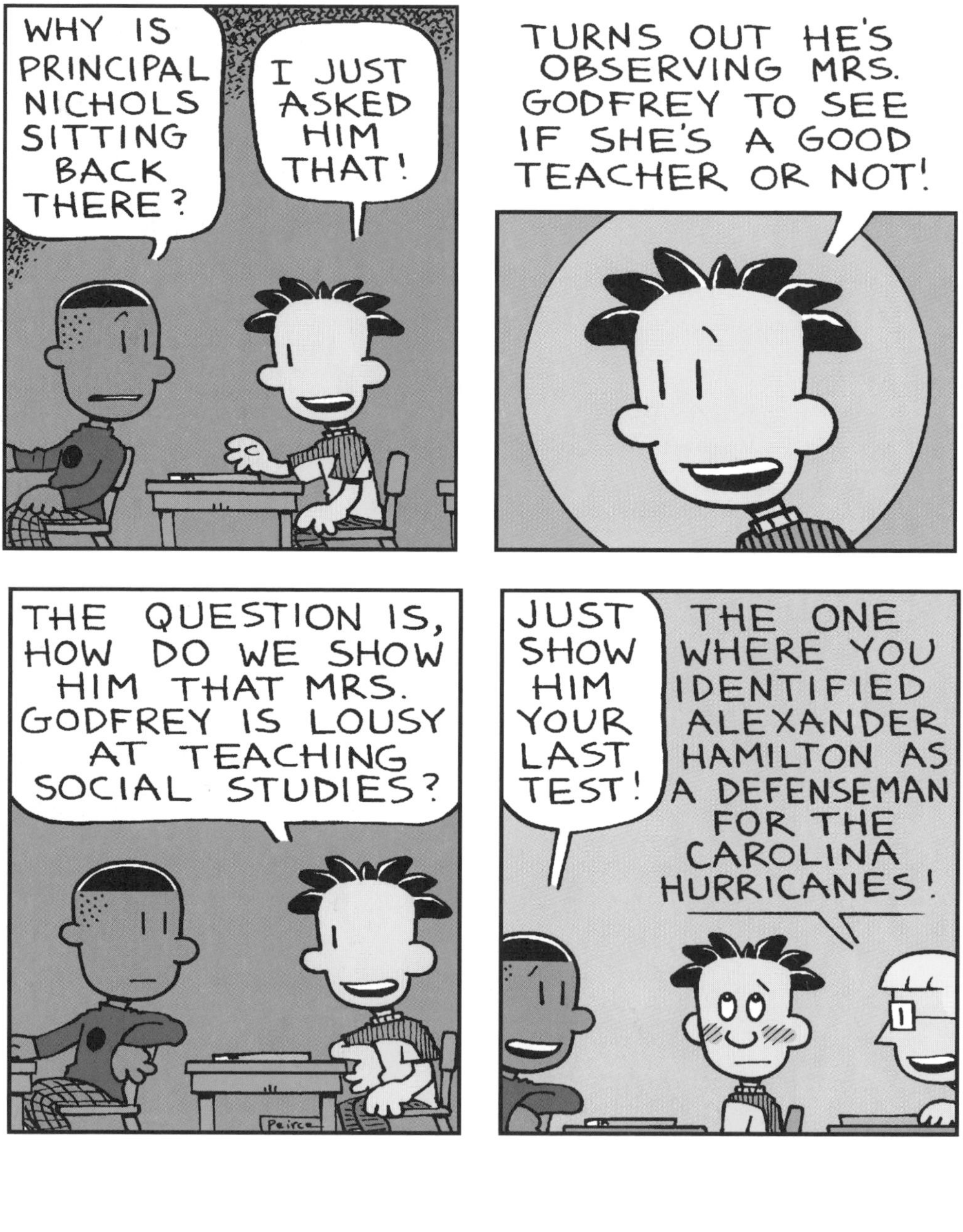

WHY IS PRINCIPAL NICHOLS SITTING BACK THERE?
I JUST ASKED HIM THAT!
TURNS OUT HE'S OBSERVING MRS. GODFREY TO SEE IF SHE'S A GOOD TEACHER OR NOT!
THE QUESTION IS, HOW DO WE SHOW HIM THAT MRS. GODFREY IS LOUSY AT TEACHING SOCIAL STUDIES?
JUST SHOW HIM YOUR LAST TEST!
THE ONE WHERE YOU IDENTIFIED ALEXANDER HAMILTON AS A DEFENSEMAN FOR THE CAROLINA HURRICANES!
Peirce

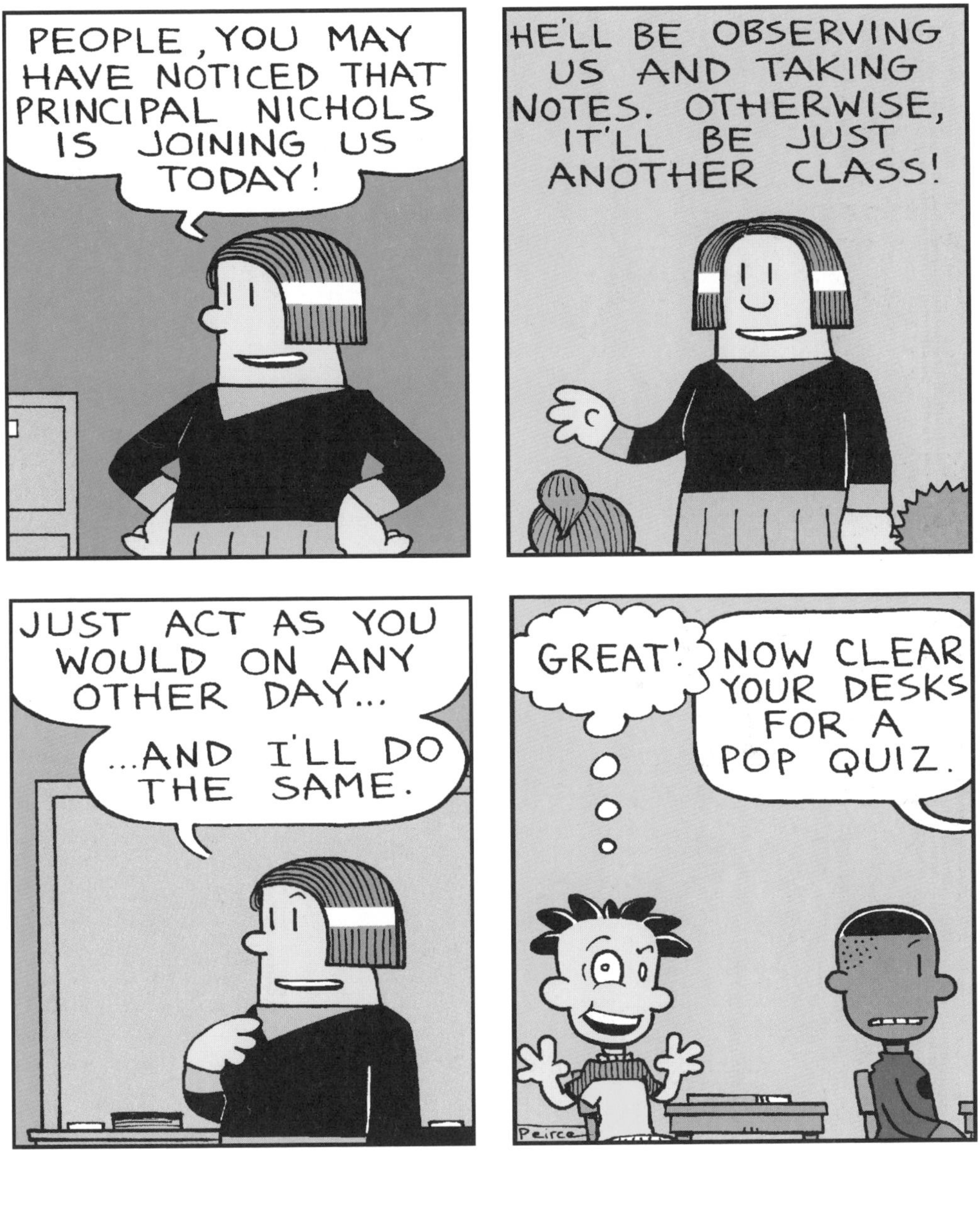
PEOPLE, YOU MAY HAVE NOTICED THAT PRINCIPAL NICHOLS IS JOINING US TODAY!
HE'LL BE OBSERVING US AND TAKING NOTES. OTHERWISE, IT'LL BE JUST ANOTHER CLASS!
JUST ACT AS YOU WOULD ON ANY OTHER DAY...
...AND I'LL DO THE SAME.
GREAT!
NOW CLEAR YOUR DESKS FOR A POP QUIZ.
Peirce

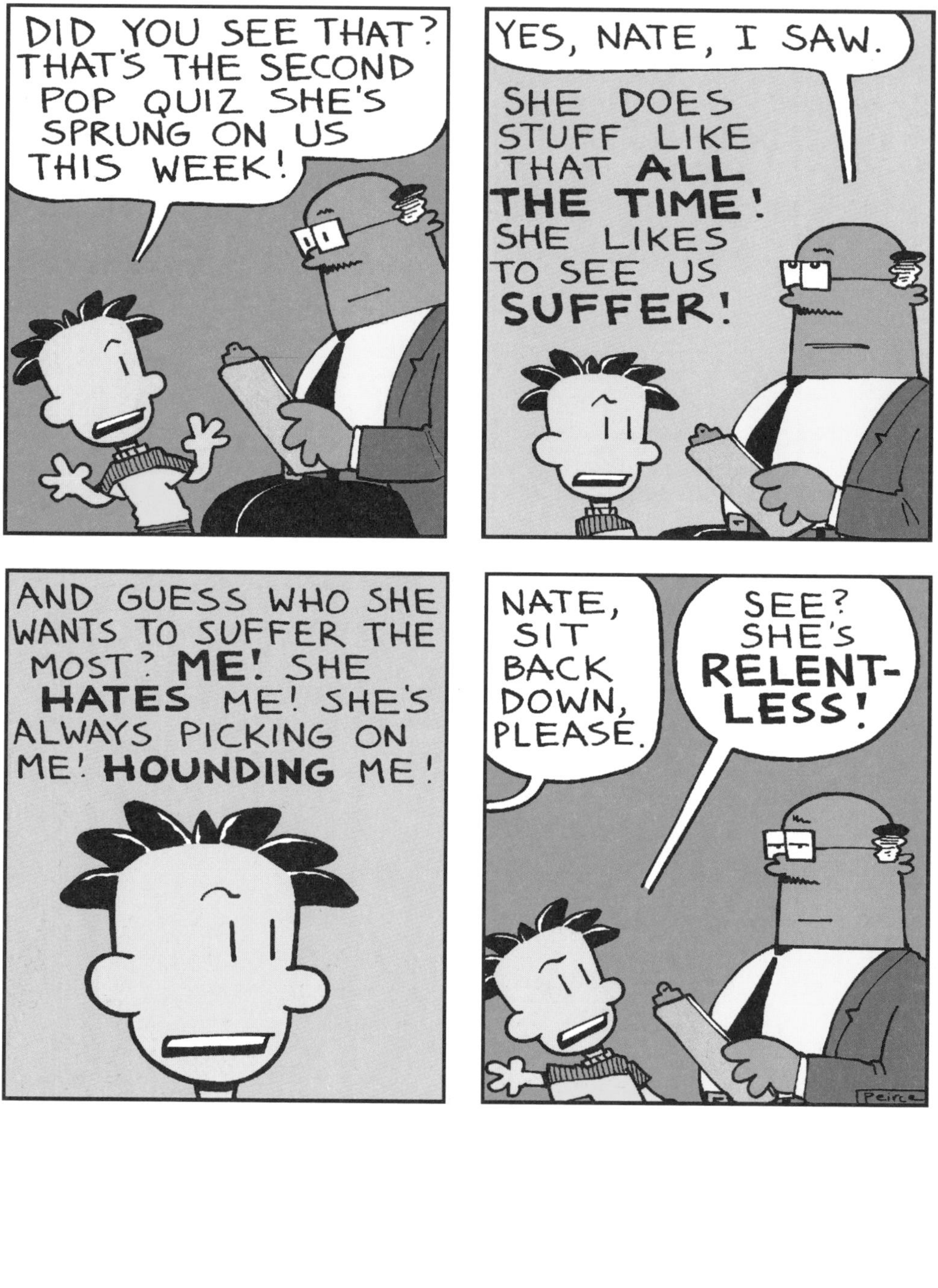
DID YOU SEE THAT? THAT'S THE SECOND POP QUIZ SHE'S SPRUNG ON US THIS WEEK!
YES, NATE, I SAW.
SHE DOES STUFF LIKE THAT ALL THE TIME! SHE LIKES TO SEE US SUFFER!
AND GUESS WHO SHE WANTS TO SUFFER THE MOST? ME! SHE HATES ME! SHE'S ALWAYS PICKING ON ME! HOUNDING ME!
NATE, SIT BACK DOWN, PLEASE.
SEE? SHE'S RELENT-LESS!
Peirce

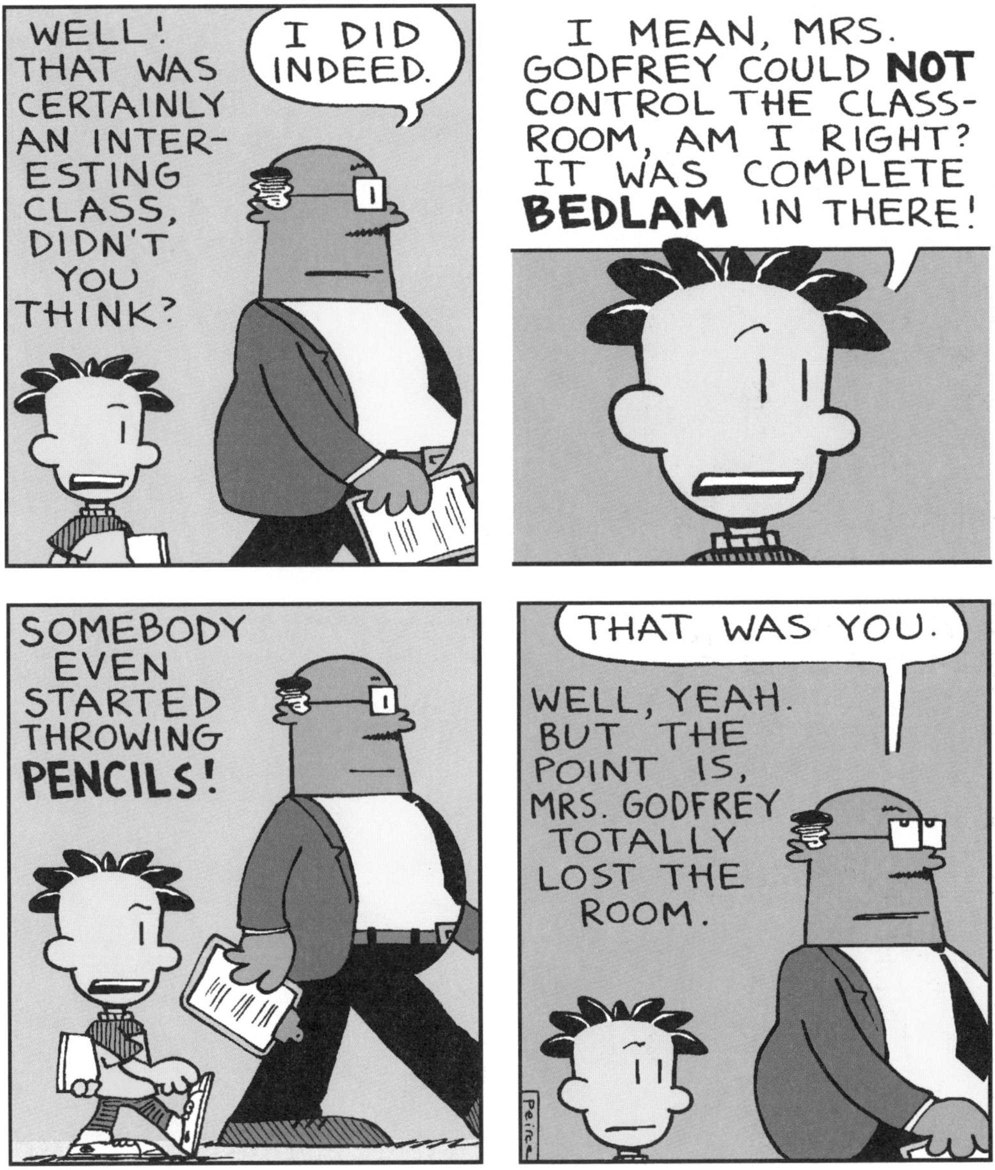
WELL! THAT WAS CERTAINLY AN INTERESTING CLASS, DIDN'T YOU THINK?
I DID INDEED.
I MEAN, MRS. GODFREY COULD **NOT** CONTROL THE CLASSROOM, AM I RIGHT? IT WAS COMPLETE **BEDLAM** IN THERE!
SOMEBODY EVEN STARTED THROWING **PENCILS**!
THAT WAS YOU.
WELL, YEAH. BUT THE POINT IS, MRS. GODFREY TOTALLY LOST THE ROOM.
Peirce

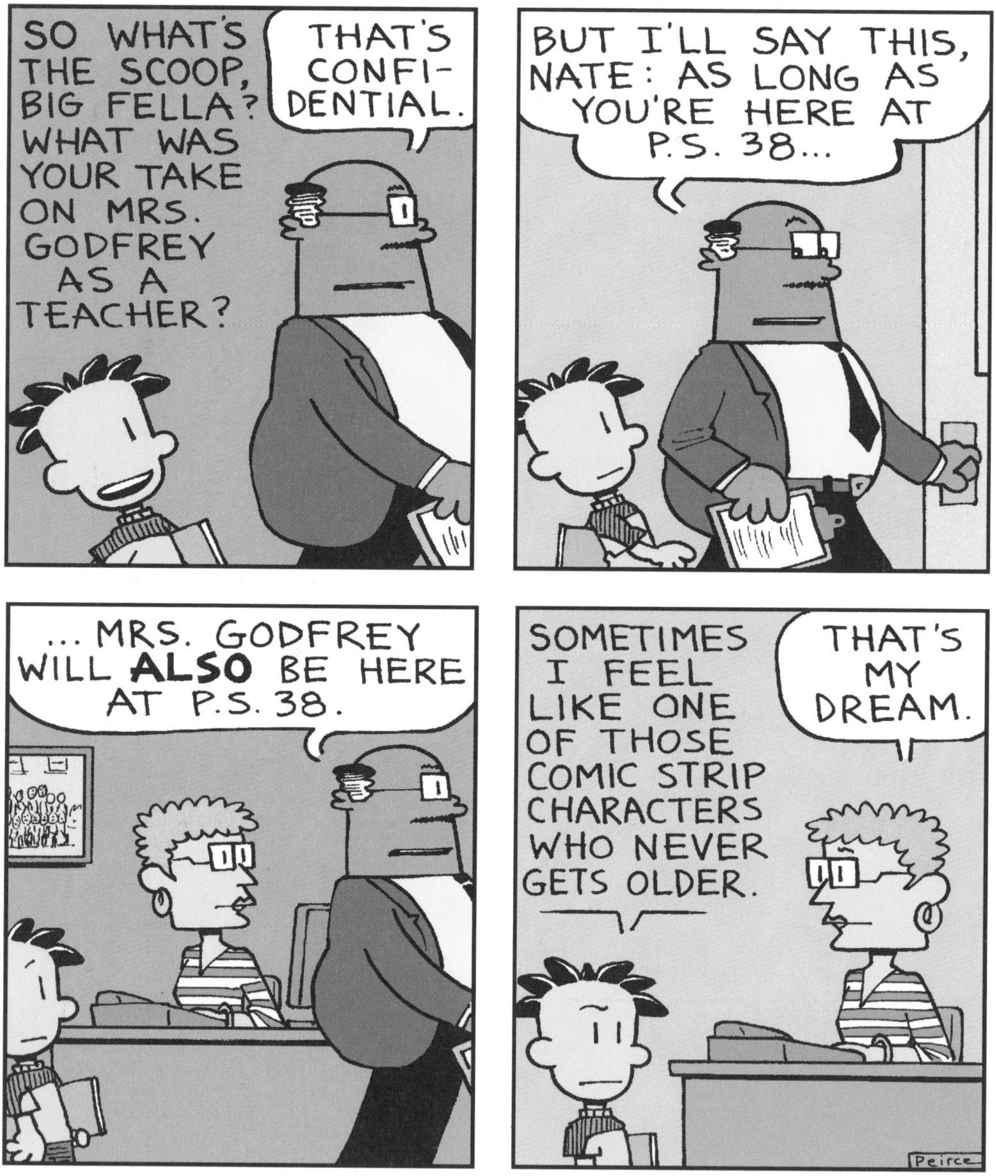
SO WHAT'S THE SCOOP, BIG FELLA? WHAT WAS YOUR TAKE ON MRS. GODFREY AS A TEACHER?
THAT'S CONFI-DENTIAL.
BUT I'LL SAY THIS, NATE: AS LONG AS YOU'RE HERE AT P.S. 38...
...MRS. GODFREY WILL **ALSO** BE HERE AT P.S. 38.
SOMETIMES I FEEL LIKE ONE OF THOSE COMIC STRIP CHARACTERS WHO NEVER GETS OLDER.
THAT'S MY DREAM.
Peirce

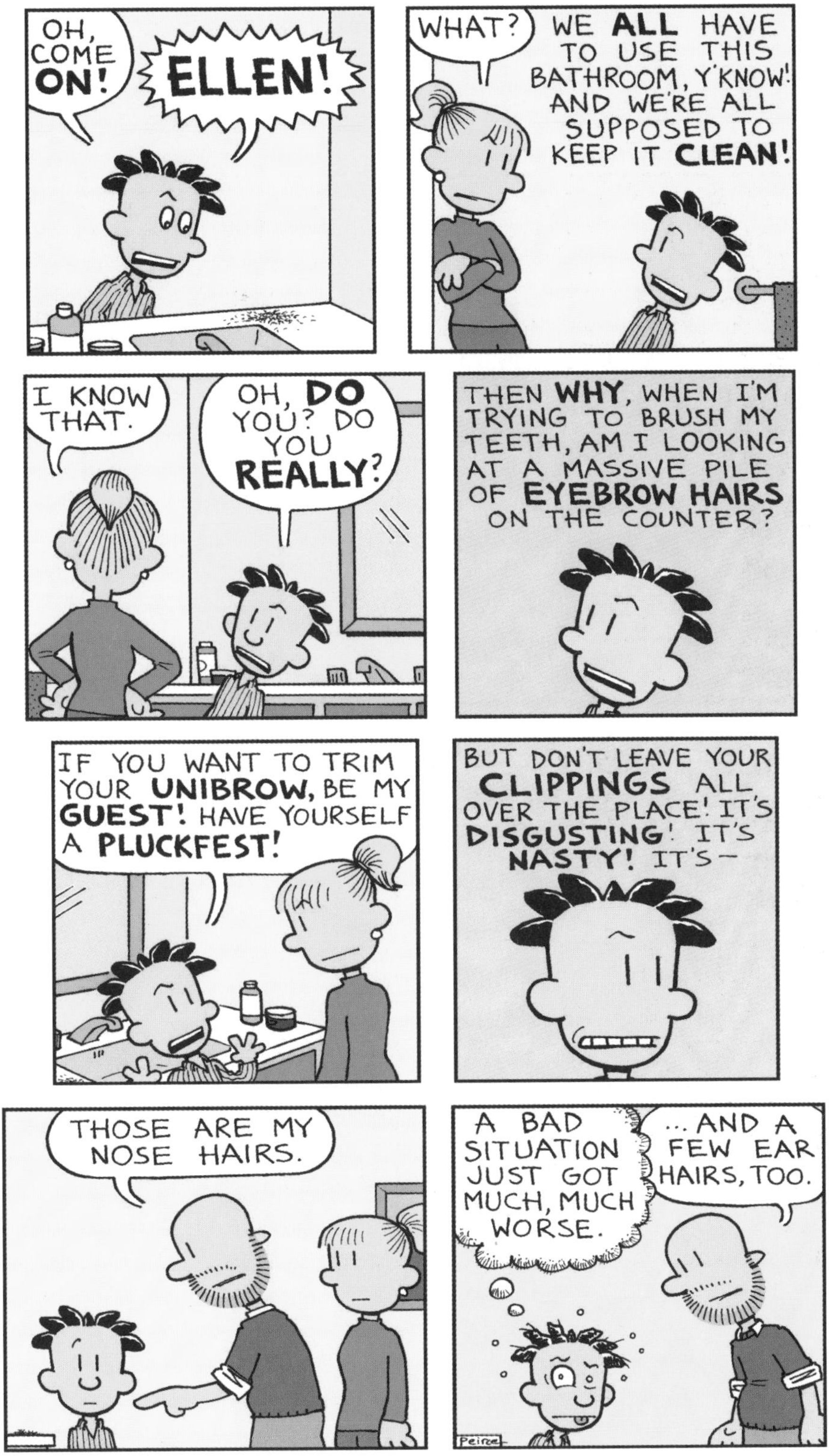
OH, COME ON!
ELLEN!
WHAT?
WE ALL HAVE TO USE THIS BATHROOM, Y'KNOW! AND WE'RE ALL SUPPOSED TO KEEP IT CLEAN!
I KNOW THAT.
OH, DO YOU? DO YOU REALLY?
THEN WHY, WHEN I'M TRYING TO BRUSH MY TEETH, AM I LOOKING AT A MASSIVE PILE OF EYEBROW HAIRS ON THE COUNTER?
IF YOU WANT TO TRIM YOUR UNIBROW, BE MY GUEST! HAVE YOURSELF A PLUCKFEST!
BUT DON'T LEAVE YOUR CLIPPINGS ALL OVER THE PLACE! IT'S DISGUSTING! IT'S NASTY! IT'S—
THOSE ARE MY NOSE HAIRS.
A BAD SITUATION JUST GOT MUCH, MUCH WORSE.
...AND A FEW EAR HAIRS, TOO.
Peirce

SIGH
WHAT'S WRONG, CHAD?
SOME 7TH GRADERS GAVE ME A NICKNAME I DON'T LIKE.
BECAUSE MY LAST NAME'S APPLEWHITE, THEY STARTED CALLING ME "APPLE CHEEKS." THEN THEY SHORTENED IT TO—
HEY, CHEEKS.
HEH HEH.
POOR CHAD.
Peirce

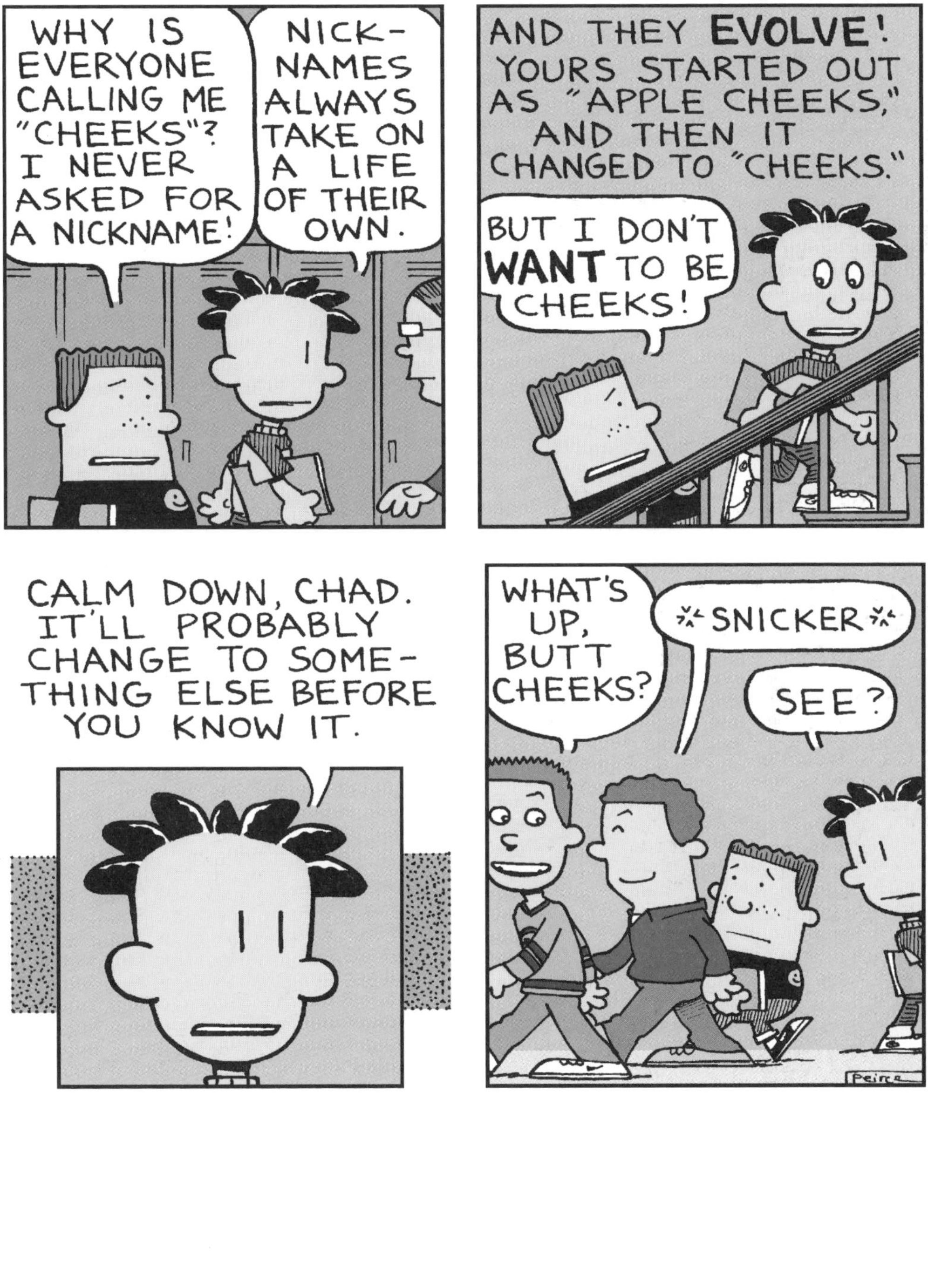
WHY IS EVERYONE CALLING ME "CHEEKS"? I NEVER ASKED FOR A NICKNAME!
NICK-NAMES ALWAYS TAKE ON A LIFE OF THEIR OWN.
AND THEY **EVOLVE**! YOURS STARTED OUT AS "APPLE CHEEKS," AND THEN IT CHANGED TO "CHEEKS."
BUT I DON'T **WANT** TO BE CHEEKS!
CALM DOWN, CHAD. IT'LL PROBABLY CHANGE TO SOME-THING ELSE BEFORE YOU KNOW IT.
WHAT'S UP, BUTT CHEEKS?
SNICKER
SEE?

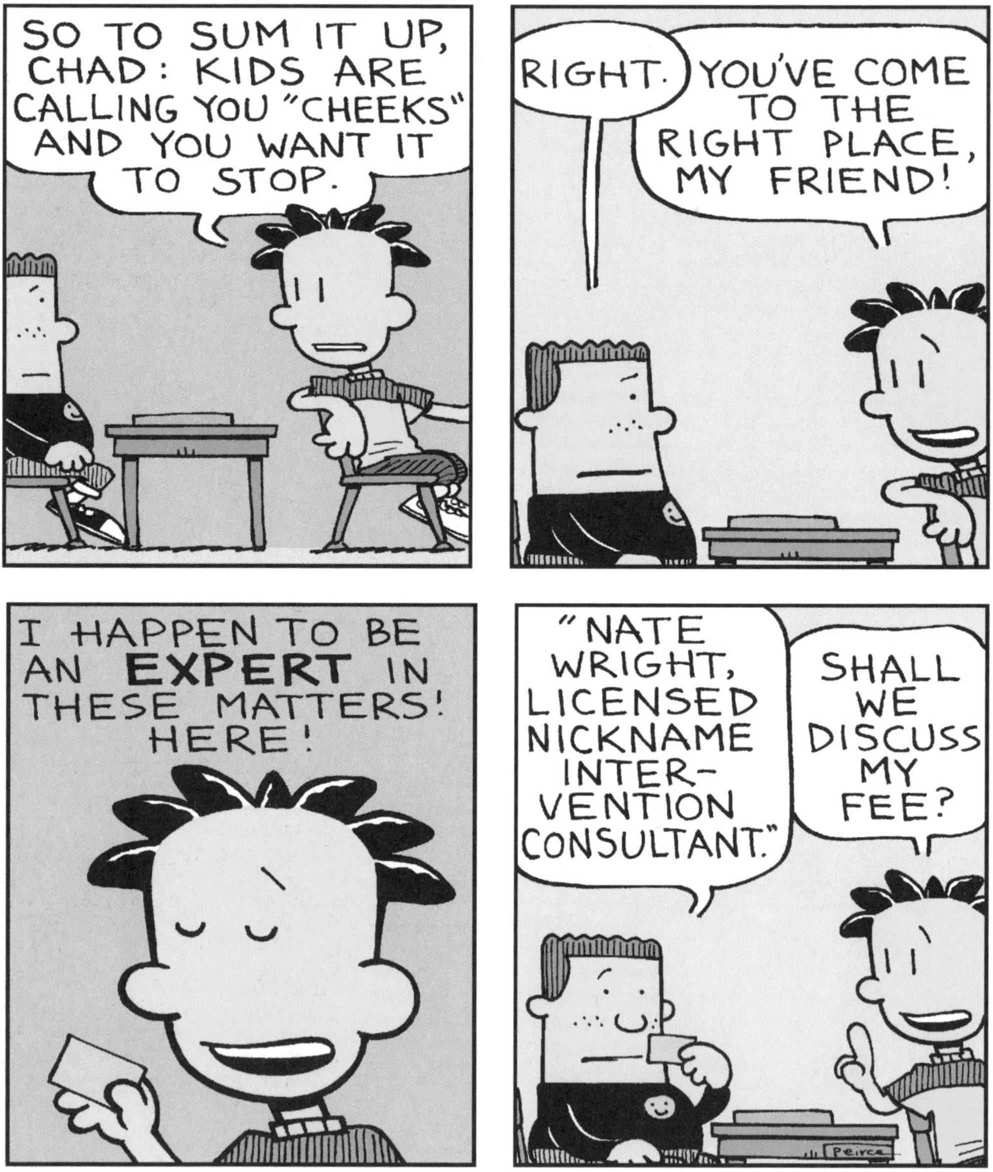
SO TO SUM IT UP, CHAD: KIDS ARE CALLING YOU "CHEEKS" AND YOU WANT IT TO STOP.
RIGHT.
YOU'VE COME TO THE RIGHT PLACE, MY FRIEND!
I HAPPEN TO BE AN **EXPERT** IN THESE MATTERS! HERE!
"NATE WRIGHT, LICENSED NICKNAME INTER-VENTION CONSULTANT."
SHALL WE DISCUSS MY FEE?
Peirce

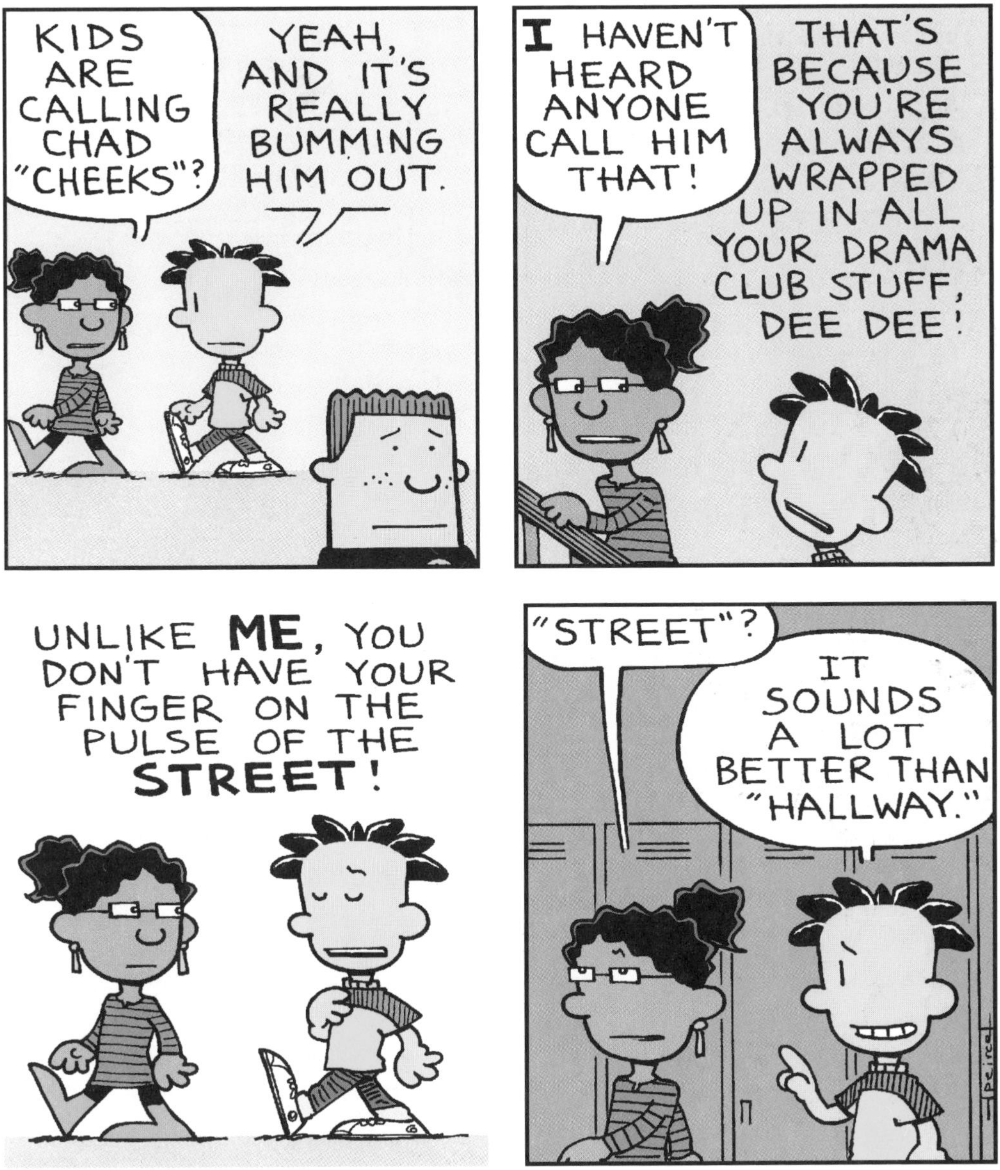
KIDS ARE CALLING CHAD "CHEEKS"?
YEAH, AND IT'S REALLY BUMMING HIM OUT.
I HAVEN'T HEARD ANYONE CALL HIM THAT!
THAT'S BECAUSE YOU'RE ALWAYS WRAPPED UP IN ALL YOUR DRAMA CLUB STUFF, DEE DEE!
UNLIKE **ME**, YOU DON'T HAVE YOUR FINGER ON THE PULSE OF THE **STREET**!
"STREET"?
IT SOUNDS A LOT BETTER THAN "HALLWAY."
peirce

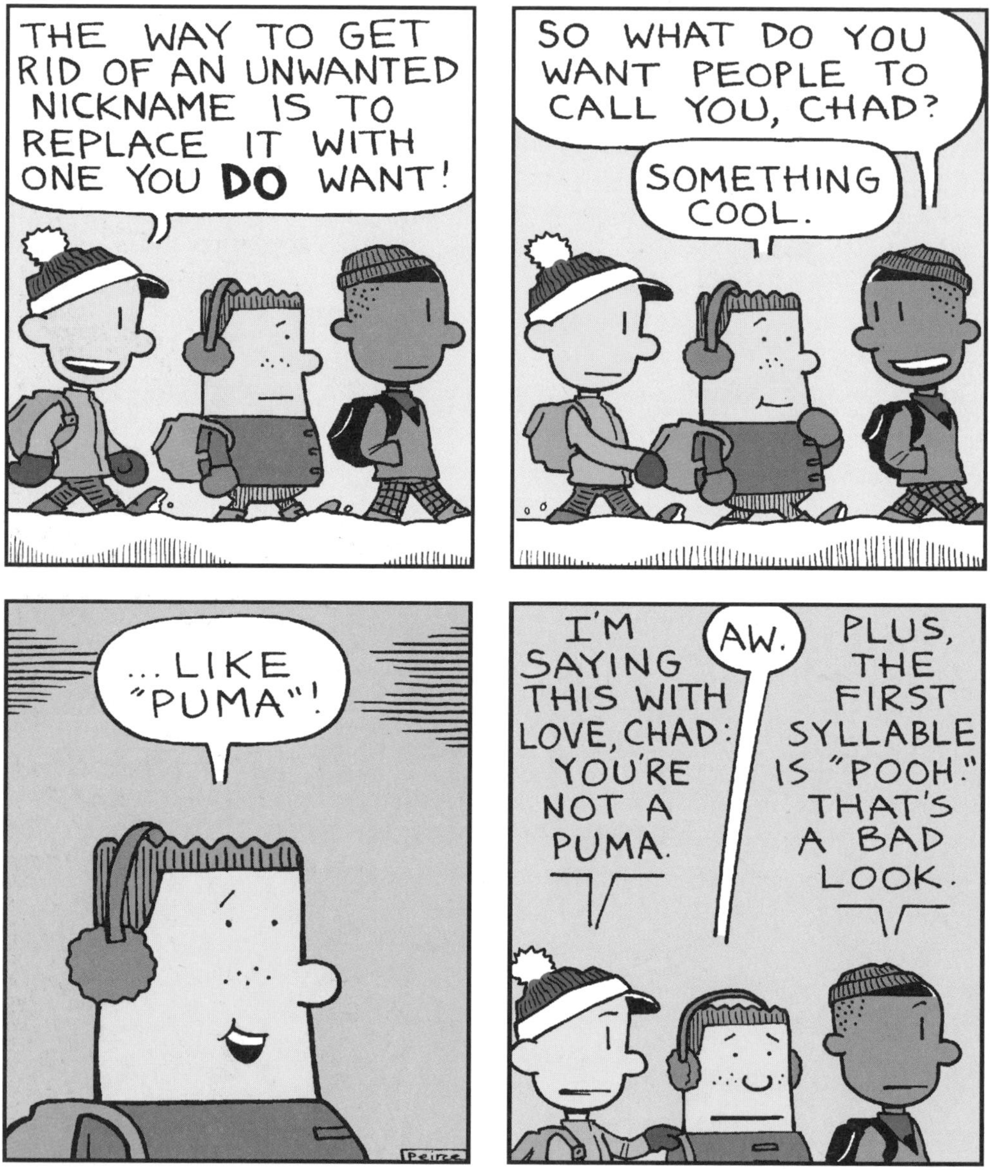
THE WAY TO GET RID OF AN UNWANTED NICKNAME IS TO REPLACE IT WITH ONE YOU **DO** WANT!
SO WHAT DO YOU WANT PEOPLE TO CALL YOU, CHAD?
SOMETHING COOL.
...LIKE "PUMA"!
Peirce
I'M SAYING THIS WITH LOVE, CHAD: YOU'RE NOT A PUMA.
AW.
PLUS, THE FIRST SYLLABLE IS "POOH." THAT'S A BAD LOOK.

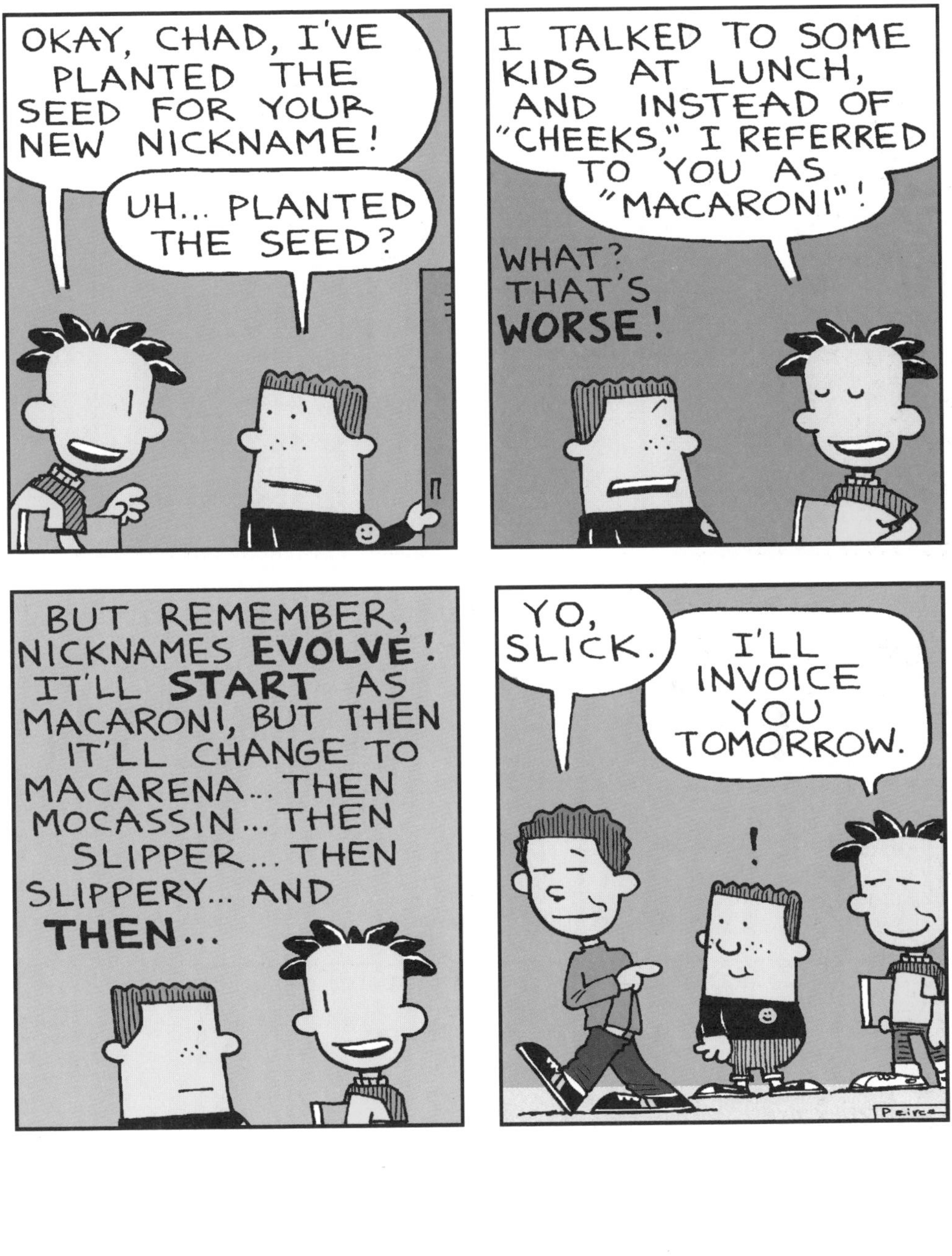
OKAY, CHAD, I'VE PLANTED THE SEED FOR YOUR NEW NICKNAME!
UH... PLANTED THE SEED?
I TALKED TO SOME KIDS AT LUNCH, AND INSTEAD OF "CHEEKS," I REFERRED TO YOU AS "MACARONI"!
WHAT? THAT'S **WORSE**!
BUT REMEMBER, NICKNAMES **EVOLVE**! IT'LL **START** AS MACARONI, BUT THEN IT'LL CHANGE TO MACARENA... THEN MOCASSIN... THEN SLIPPER... THEN SLIPPERY... AND **THEN**...
YO, SLICK.
I'LL INVOICE YOU TOMORROW.
!
Peirce

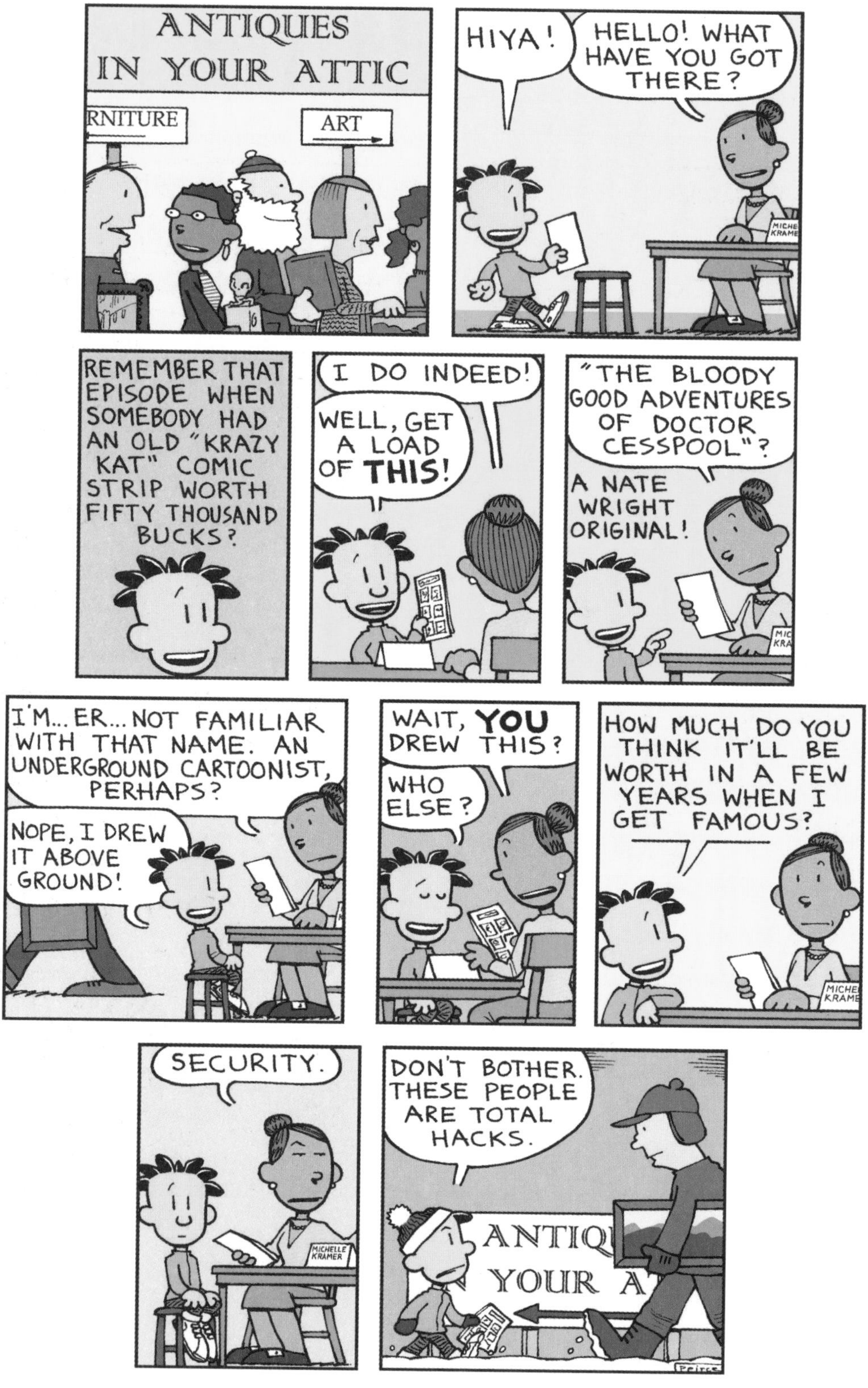
ANTIQUES IN YOUR ATTIC
RNITURE
ART
16
HIYA!
HELLO! WHAT HAVE YOU GOT THERE?
MICHE KRAME
REMEMBER THAT EPISODE WHEN SOMEBODY HAD AN OLD "KRAZY KAT" COMIC STRIP WORTH FIFTY THOUSAND BUCKS?
I DO INDEED!
WELL, GET A LOAD OF **THIS**!
"THE BLOODY GOOD ADVENTURES OF DOCTOR CESSPOOL"?
A NATE WRIGHT ORIGINAL!
I'M... ER... NOT FAMILIAR WITH THAT NAME. AN UNDERGROUND CARTOONIST, PERHAPS?
NOPE, I DREW IT ABOVE GROUND!
WAIT, **YOU** DREW THIS?
WHO ELSE?
HOW MUCH DO YOU THINK IT'LL BE WORTH IN A FEW YEARS WHEN I GET FAMOUS?
MICHE KRAME
SECURITY.
MICHELLE KRAMER
DON'T BOTHER. THESE PEOPLE ARE TOTAL HACKS.
ANTIQ YOUR A
Peirce

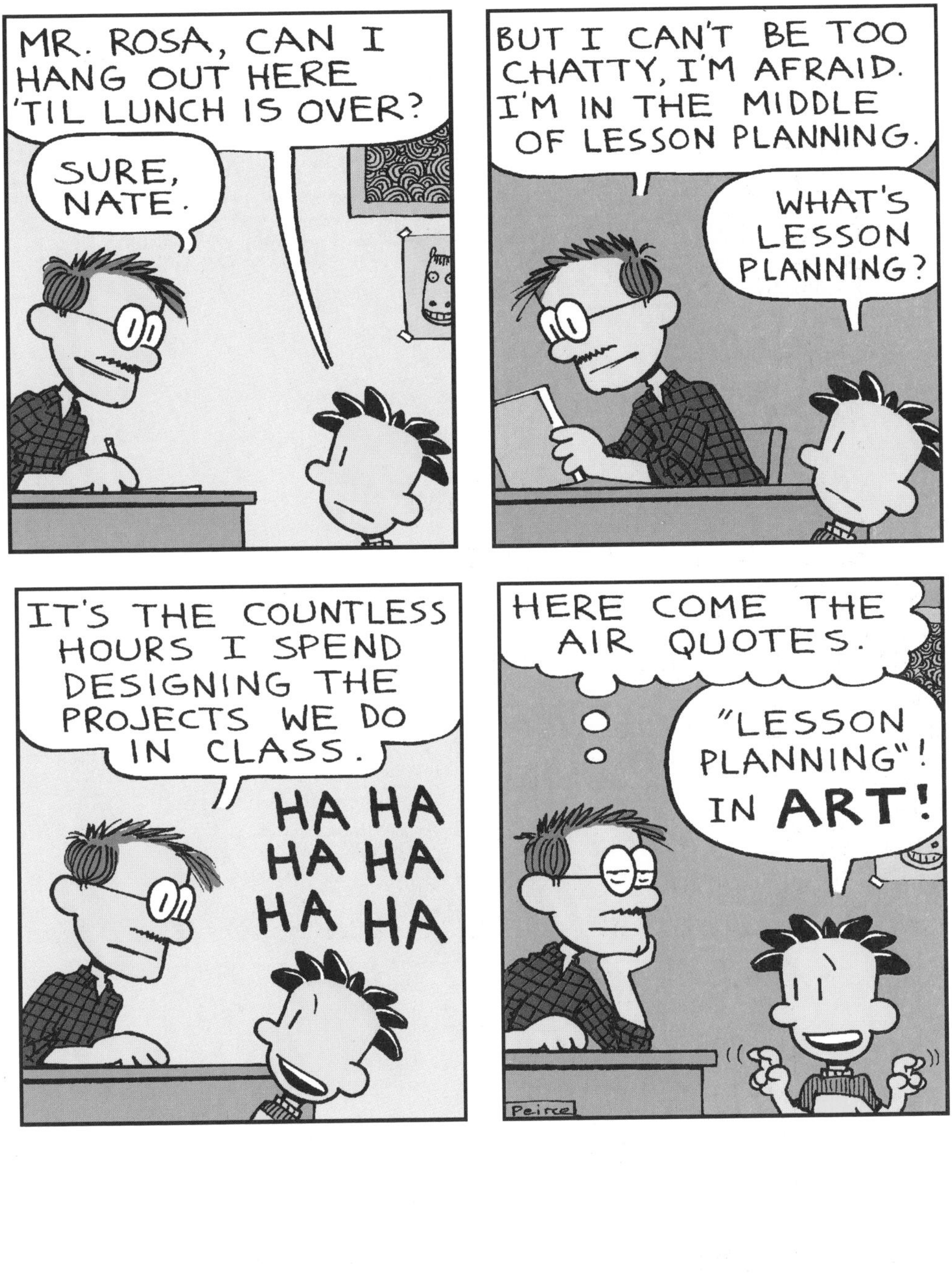
MR. ROSA, CAN I HANG OUT HERE 'TIL LUNCH IS OVER?
SURE, NATE.
BUT I CAN'T BE TOO CHATTY, I'M AFRAID. I'M IN THE MIDDLE OF LESSON PLANNING.
WHAT'S LESSON PLANNING?
IT'S THE COUNTLESS HOURS I SPEND DESIGNING THE PROJECTS WE DO IN CLASS.
HA HA HA HA HA HA
HERE COME THE AIR QUOTES.
"LESSON PLANNING"! IN ART!
Peirce

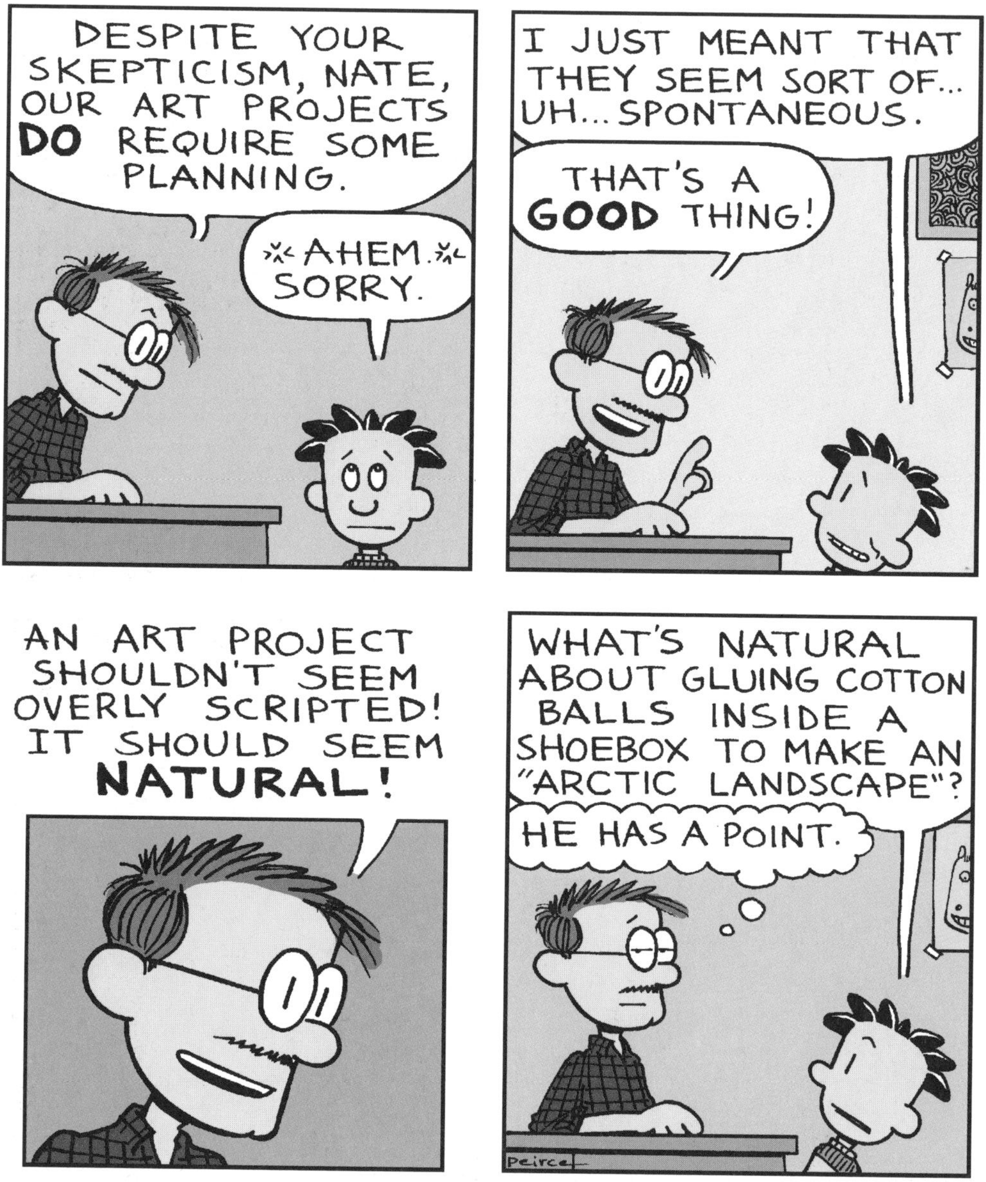
DESPITE YOUR SKEPTICISM, NATE, OUR ART PROJECTS DO REQUIRE SOME PLANNING.
AHEM. SORRY.
I JUST MEANT THAT THEY SEEM SORT OF... UH... SPONTANEOUS.
THAT'S A GOOD THING!
AN ART PROJECT SHOULDN'T SEEM OVERLY SCRIPTED! IT SHOULD SEEM NATURAL!
WHAT'S NATURAL ABOUT GLUING COTTON BALLS INSIDE A SHOEBOX TO MAKE AN "ARCTIC LANDSCAPE"?
HE HAS A POINT.
peirce

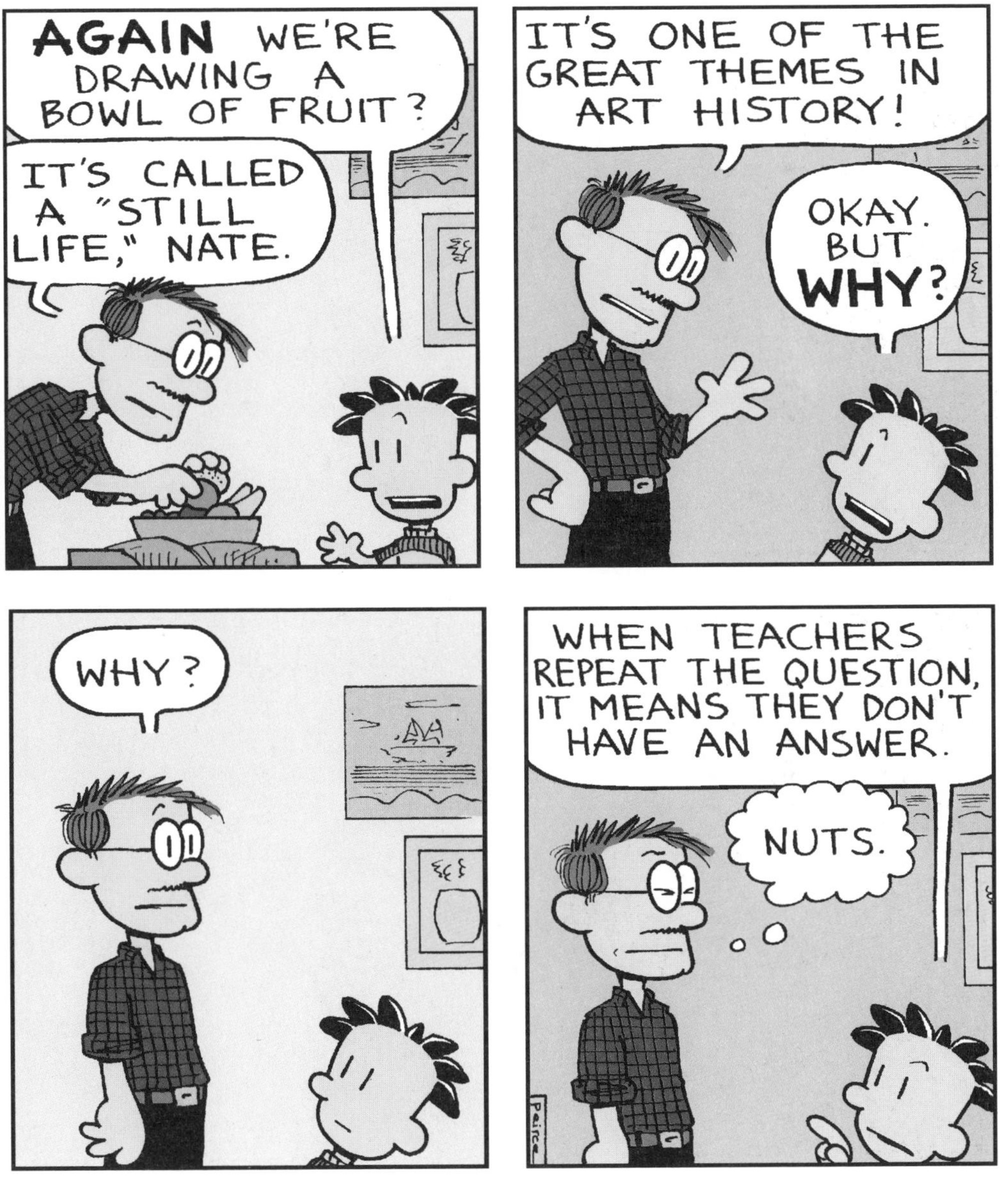
AGAIN WE'RE DRAWING A BOWL OF FRUIT?
IT'S CALLED A "STILL LIFE," NATE.
IT'S ONE OF THE GREAT THEMES IN ART HISTORY!
OKAY. BUT WHY?
WHY?
WHEN TEACHERS REPEAT THE QUESTION, IT MEANS THEY DON'T HAVE AN ANSWER.
NUTS.
Peirce

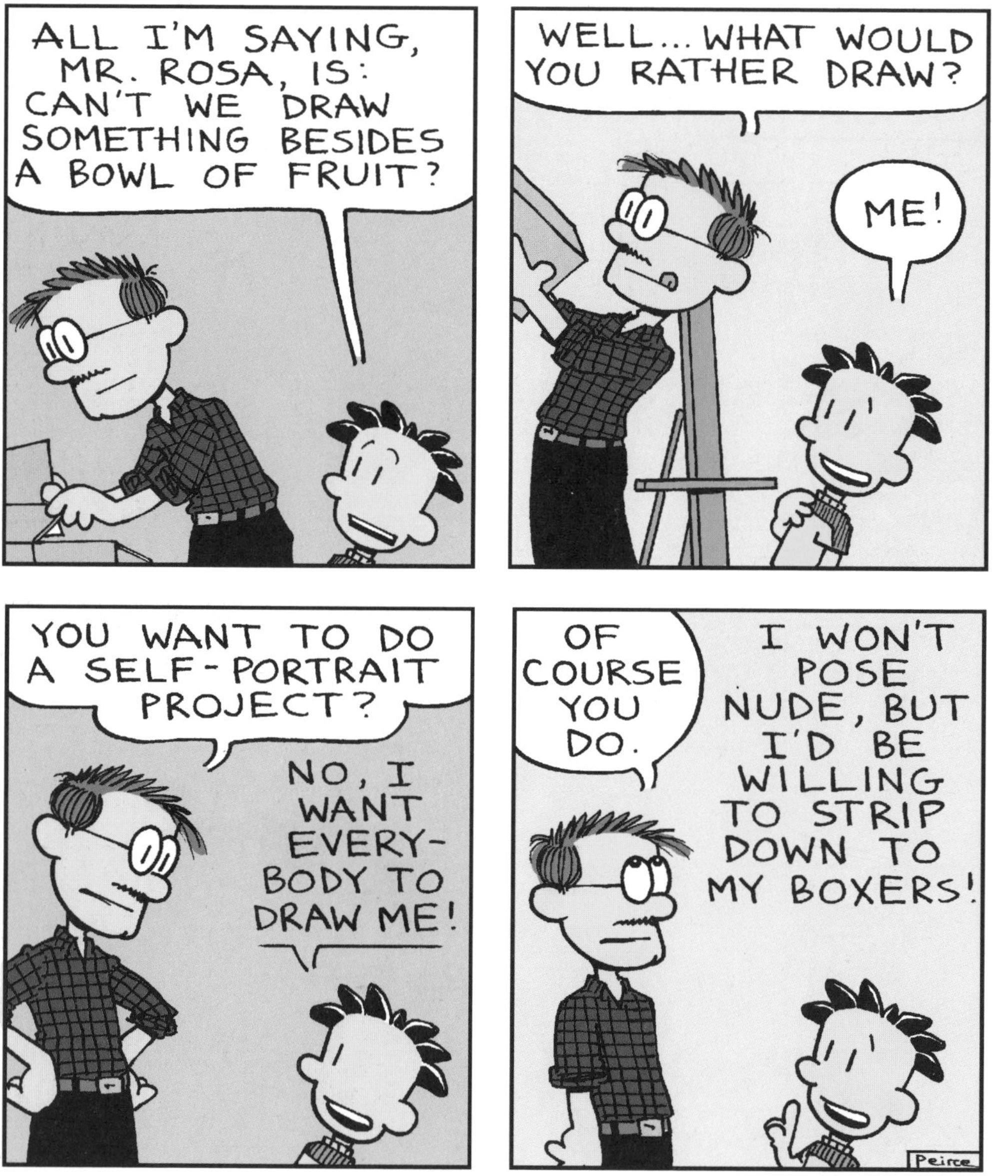
ALL I'M SAYING, MR. ROSA, IS: CAN'T WE DRAW SOMETHING BESIDES A BOWL OF FRUIT?
WELL... WHAT WOULD YOU RATHER DRAW?
ME!
YOU WANT TO DO A SELF-PORTRAIT PROJECT?
NO, I WANT EVERYBODY TO DRAW ME!
OF COURSE YOU DO.
I WON'T POSE NUDE, BUT I'D BE WILLING TO STRIP DOWN TO MY BOXERS!
Peirce

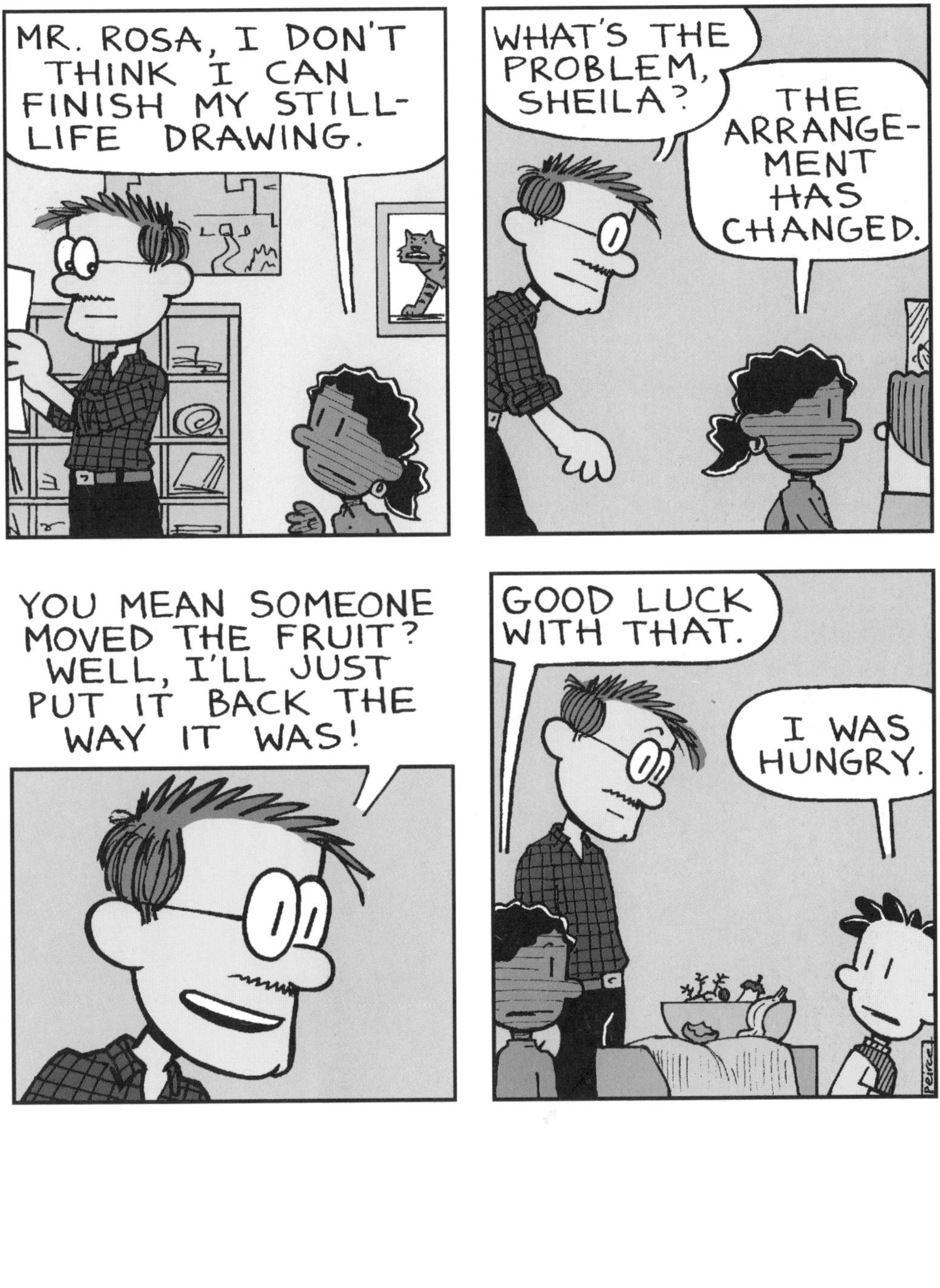
MR. ROSA, I DON'T THINK I CAN FINISH MY STILL-LIFE DRAWING.
WHAT'S THE PROBLEM, SHEILA?
THE ARRANGEMENT HAS CHANGED.
YOU MEAN SOMEONE MOVED THE FRUIT? WELL, I'LL JUST PUT IT BACK THE WAY IT WAS!
GOOD LUCK WITH THAT.
I WAS HUNGRY.
Peirce

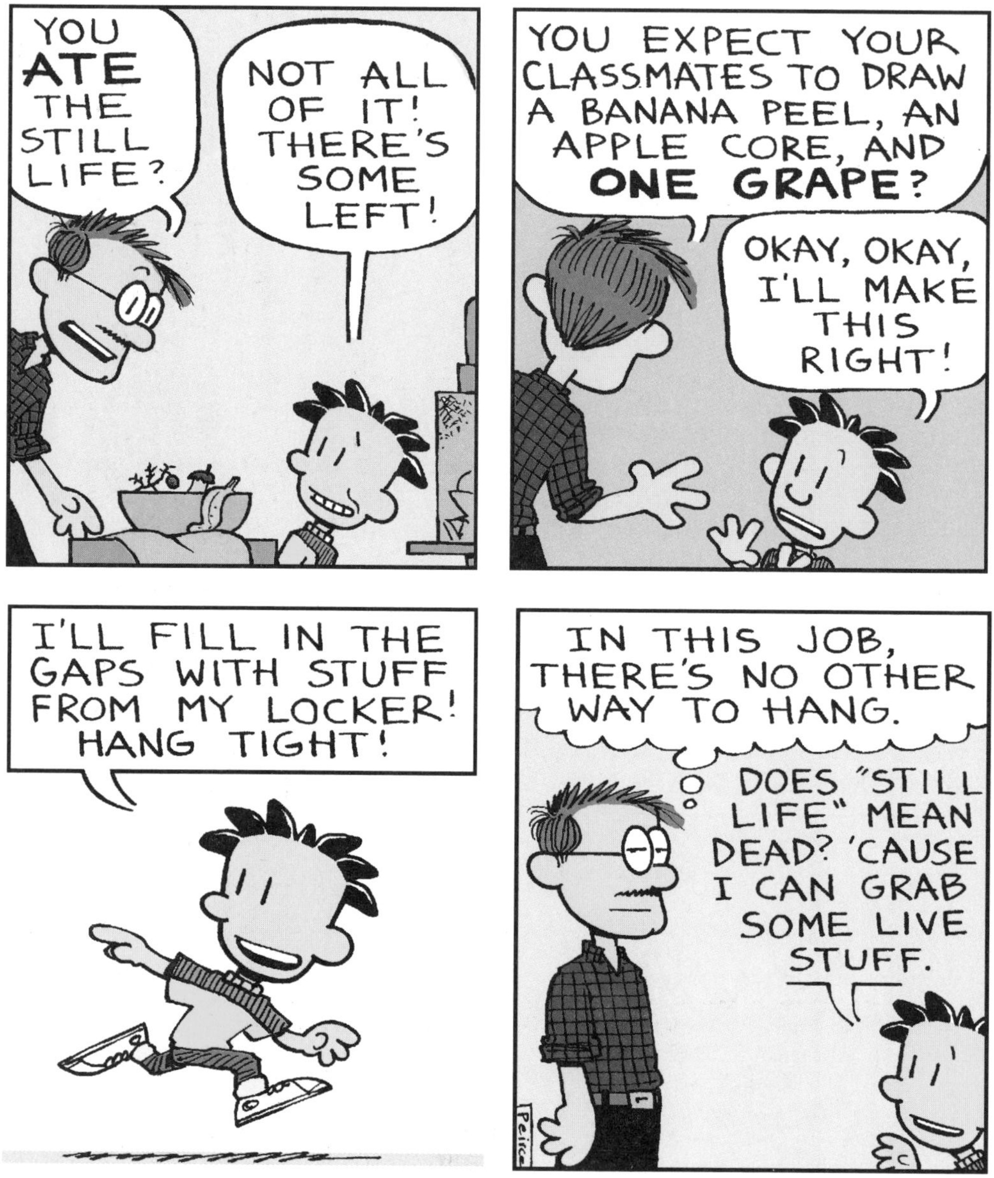
YOU ATE THE STILL LIFE?
NOT ALL OF IT! THERE'S SOME LEFT!
YOU EXPECT YOUR CLASSMATES TO DRAW A BANANA PEEL, AN APPLE CORE, AND ONE GRAPE?
OKAY, OKAY, I'LL MAKE THIS RIGHT!
I'LL FILL IN THE GAPS WITH STUFF FROM MY LOCKER! HANG TIGHT!
IN THIS JOB, THERE'S NO OTHER WAY TO HANG.
DOES "STILL LIFE" MEAN DEAD? 'CAUSE I CAN GRAB SOME LIVE STUFF.
Peirce

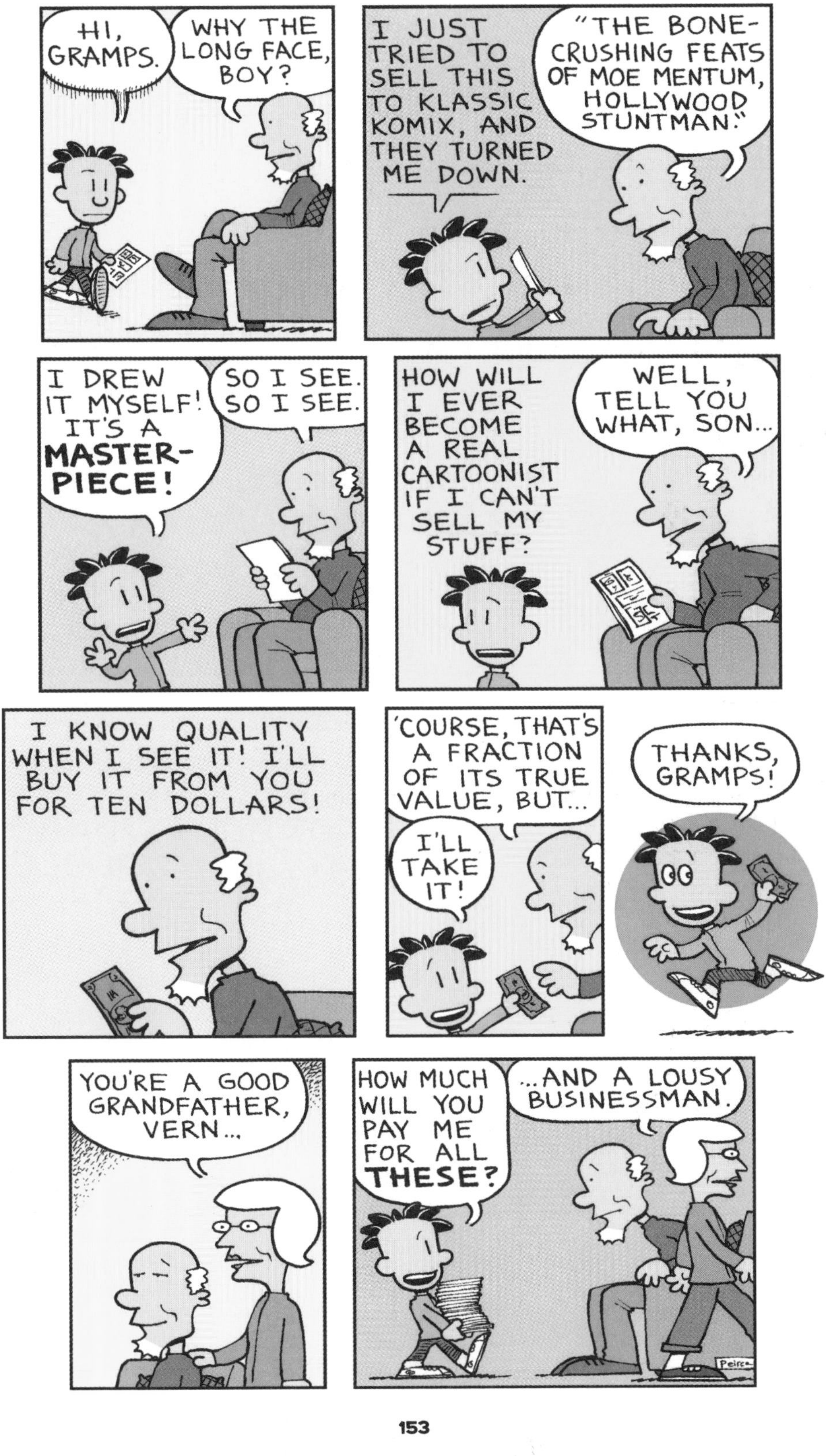
HI, GRAMPS.
WHY THE LONG FACE, BOY?
I JUST TRIED TO SELL THIS TO KLASSIC KOMIX, AND THEY TURNED ME DOWN.
"THE BONE-CRUSHING FEATS OF MOE MENTUM, HOLLYWOOD STUNTMAN."
I DREW IT MYSELF! IT'S A **MASTER-PIECE!**
SO I SEE. SO I SEE.
HOW WILL I EVER BECOME A REAL CARTOONIST IF I CAN'T SELL MY STUFF?
WELL, TELL YOU WHAT, SON...
I KNOW QUALITY WHEN I SEE IT! I'LL BUY IT FROM YOU FOR TEN DOLLARS!
'COURSE, THAT'S A FRACTION OF ITS TRUE VALUE, BUT...
I'LL TAKE IT!
THANKS, GRAMPS!
YOU'RE A GOOD GRANDFATHER, VERN...
HOW MUCH WILL YOU PAY ME FOR ALL **THESE?**
...AND A LOUSY BUSINESSMAN.
Peirce

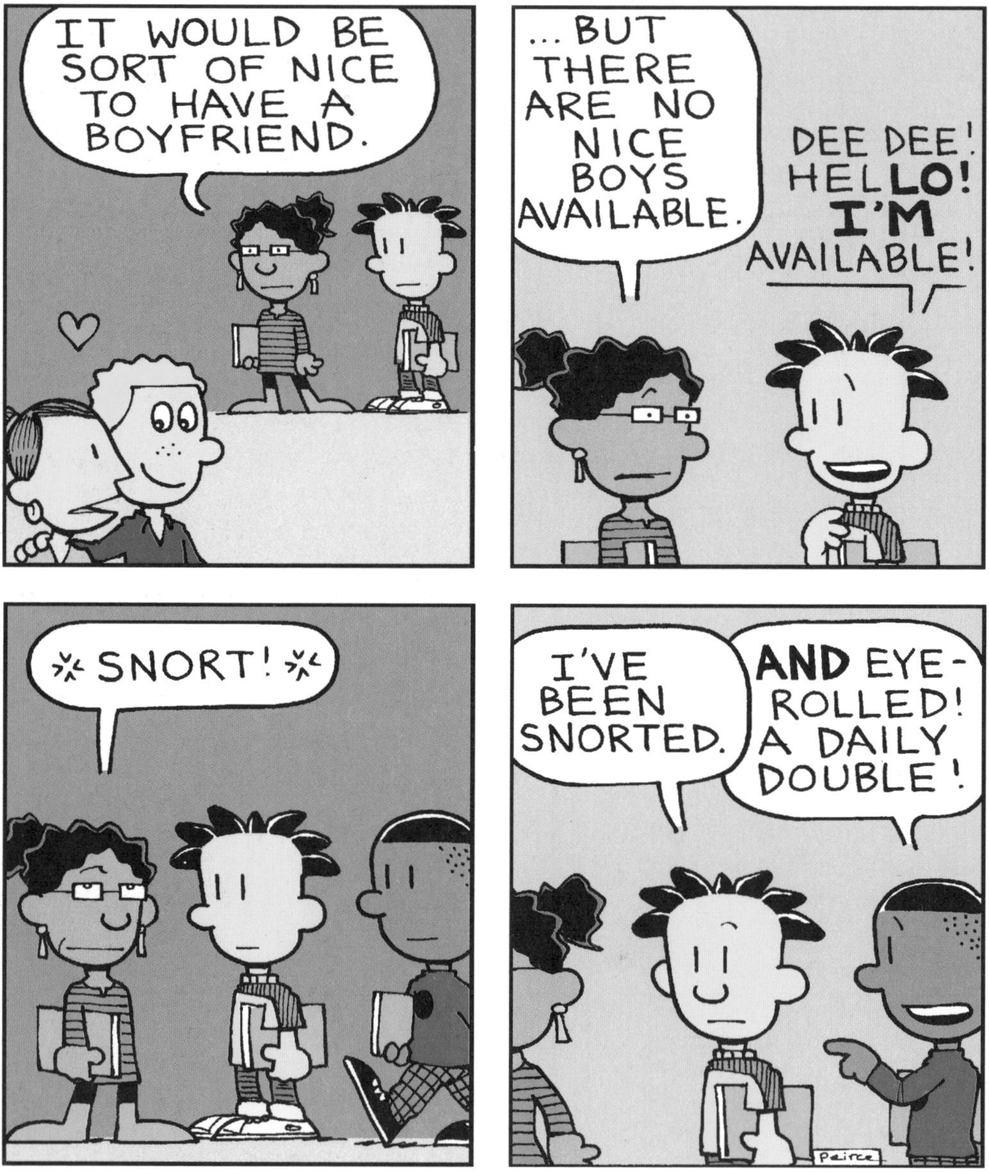
IT WOULD BE SORT OF NICE TO HAVE A BOYFRIEND.
... BUT THERE ARE NO NICE BOYS AVAILABLE.
DEE DEE! HELLO! I'M AVAILABLE!
SNORT!
I'VE BEEN SNORTED.
AND EYE-ROLLED! A DAILY DOUBLE!
Peirce

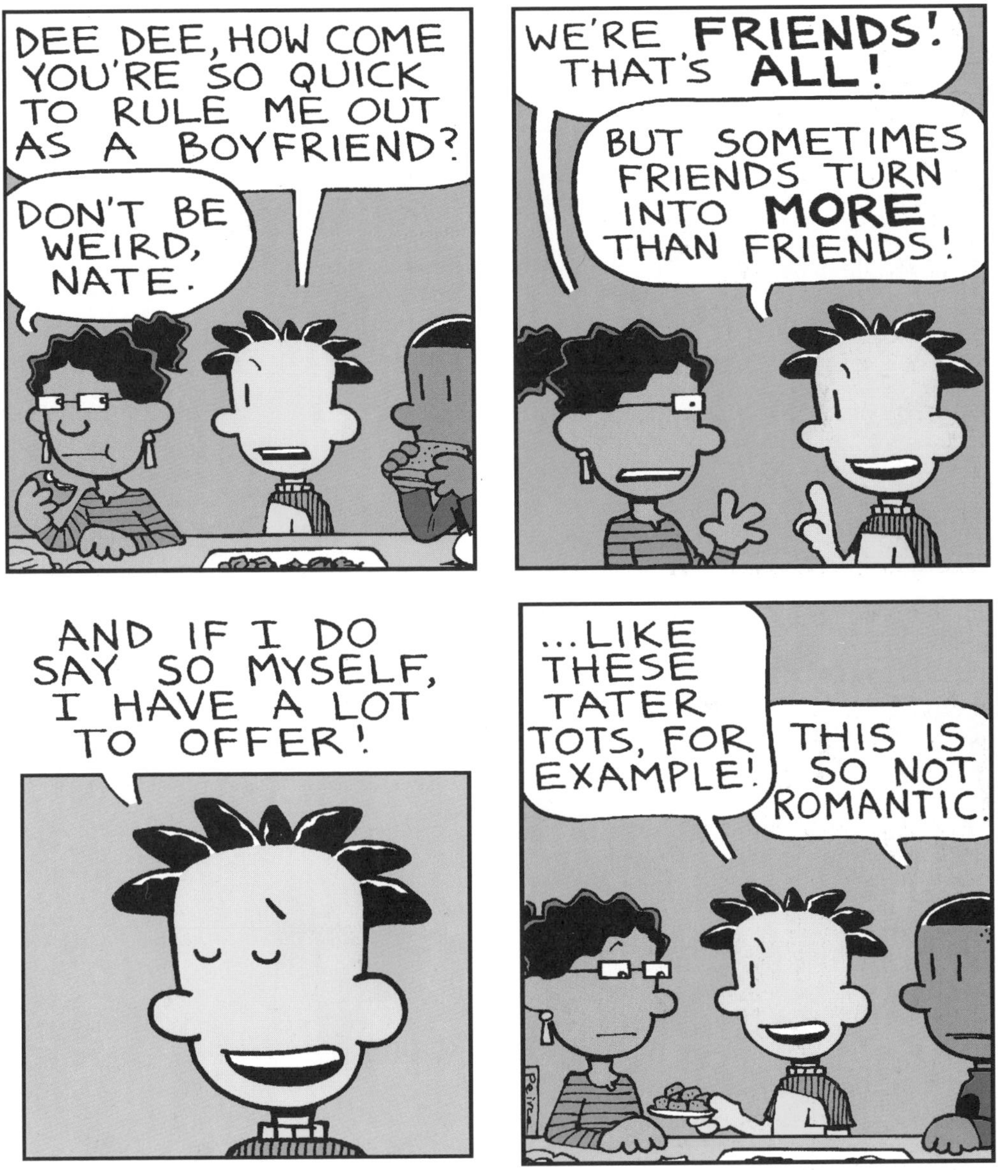
DEE DEE, HOW COME YOU'RE SO QUICK TO RULE ME OUT AS A BOYFRIEND?
DON'T BE WEIRD, NATE.
WE'RE FRIENDS! THAT'S ALL!
BUT SOMETIMES FRIENDS TURN INTO MORE THAN FRIENDS!
AND IF I DO SAY SO MYSELF, I HAVE A LOT TO OFFER!
...LIKE THESE TATER TOTS, FOR EXAMPLE!
THIS IS SO NOT ROMANTIC.
Peirce

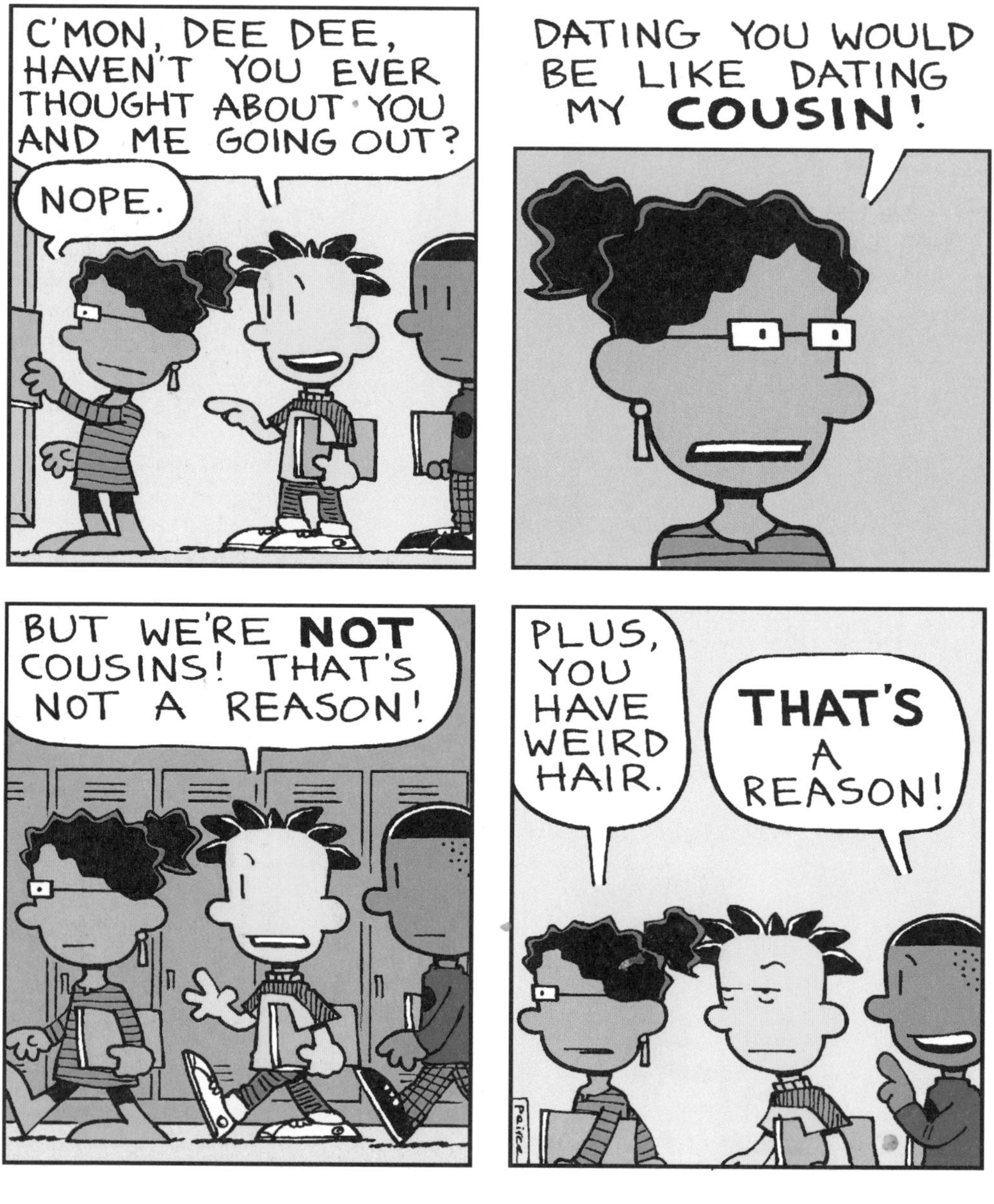
C'MON, DEE DEE, HAVEN'T YOU EVER THOUGHT ABOUT YOU AND ME GOING OUT?
NOPE.
DATING YOU WOULD BE LIKE DATING MY COUSIN!
BUT WE'RE NOT COUSINS! THAT'S NOT A REASON!
PLUS, YOU HAVE WEIRD HAIR.
THAT'S A REASON!
PEIRCE

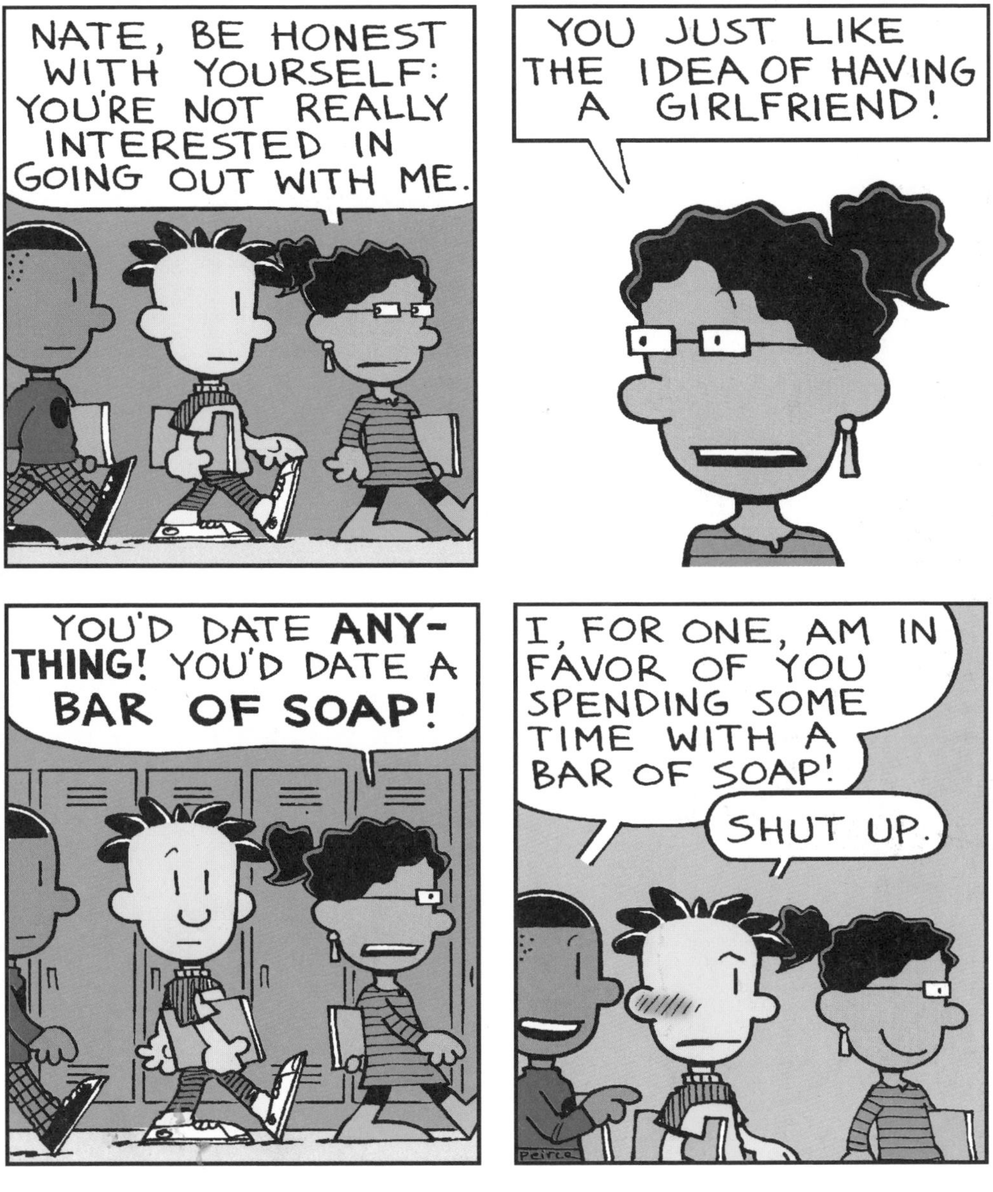
NATE, BE HONEST WITH YOURSELF: YOU'RE NOT REALLY INTERESTED IN GOING OUT WITH ME.
YOU JUST LIKE THE IDEA OF HAVING A GIRLFRIEND!
YOU'D DATE **ANY-THING**! YOU'D DATE A **BAR OF SOAP**!
I, FOR ONE, AM IN FAVOR OF YOU SPENDING SOME TIME WITH A BAR OF SOAP!
SHUT UP.
Peirce

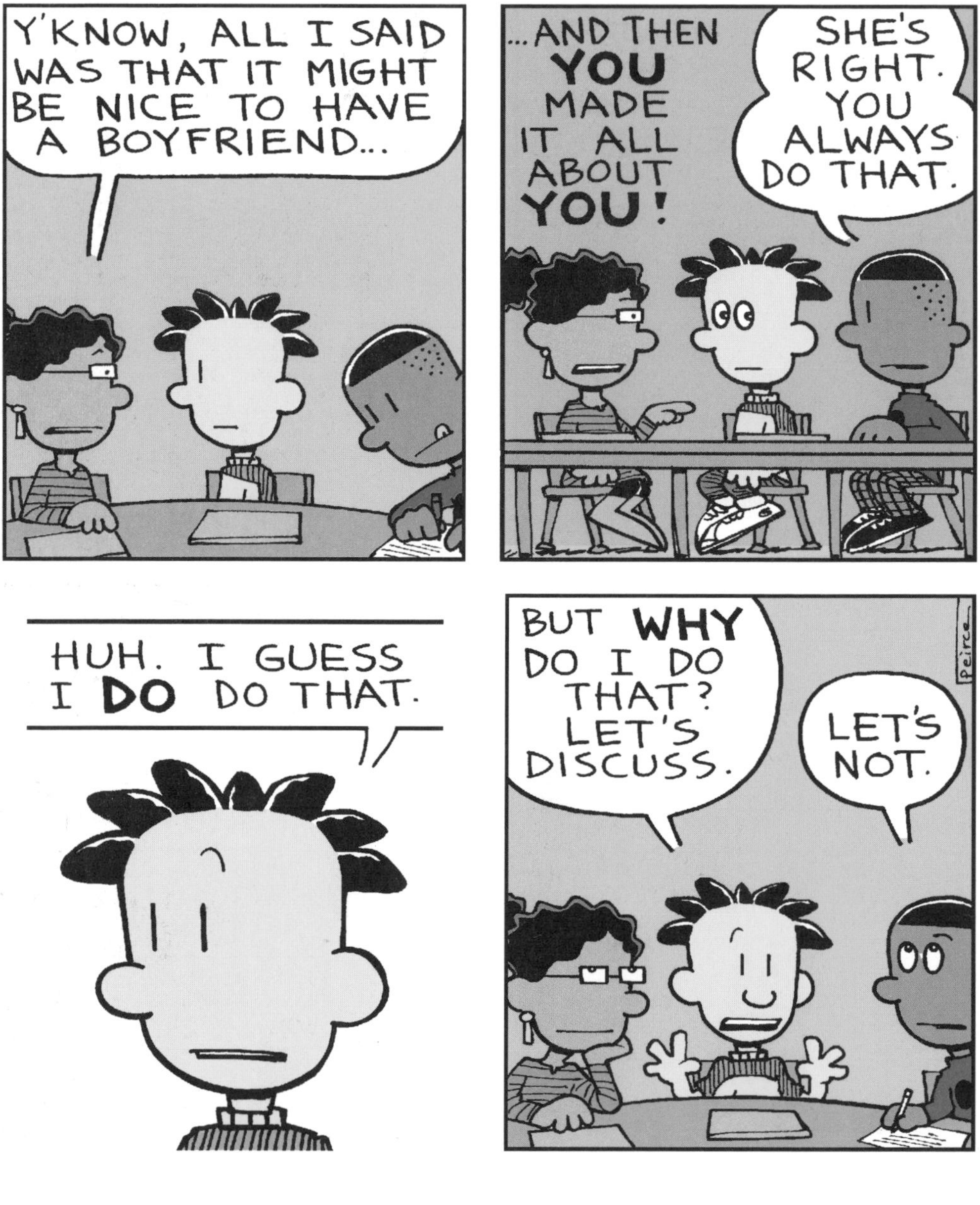
Y'KNOW, ALL I SAID WAS THAT IT MIGHT BE NICE TO HAVE A BOYFRIEND...
...AND THEN **YOU** MADE IT ALL ABOUT **YOU**!
SHE'S RIGHT. YOU ALWAYS DO THAT.
HUH. I GUESS I **DO** DO THAT.
BUT **WHY** DO I DO THAT? LET'S DISCUSS.
LET'S NOT.
Peirce

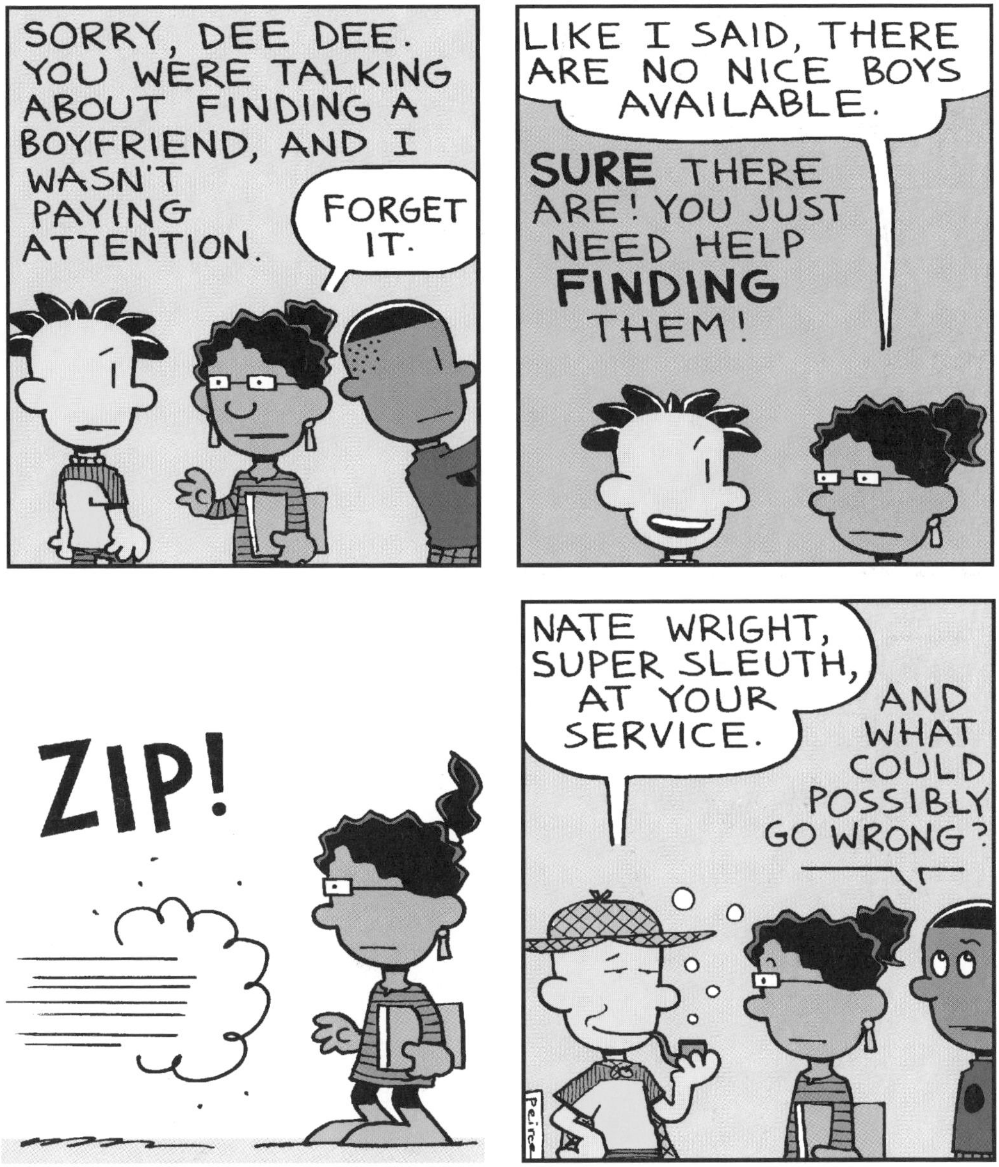
SORRY, DEE DEE. YOU WERE TALKING ABOUT FINDING A BOYFRIEND, AND I WASN'T PAYING ATTENTION.
FORGET IT.
LIKE I SAID, THERE ARE NO NICE BOYS AVAILABLE.
SURE THERE ARE! YOU JUST NEED HELP FINDING THEM!
ZIP!
NATE WRIGHT, SUPER SLEUTH, AT YOUR SERVICE.
AND WHAT COULD POSSIBLY GO WRONG?
Peirce

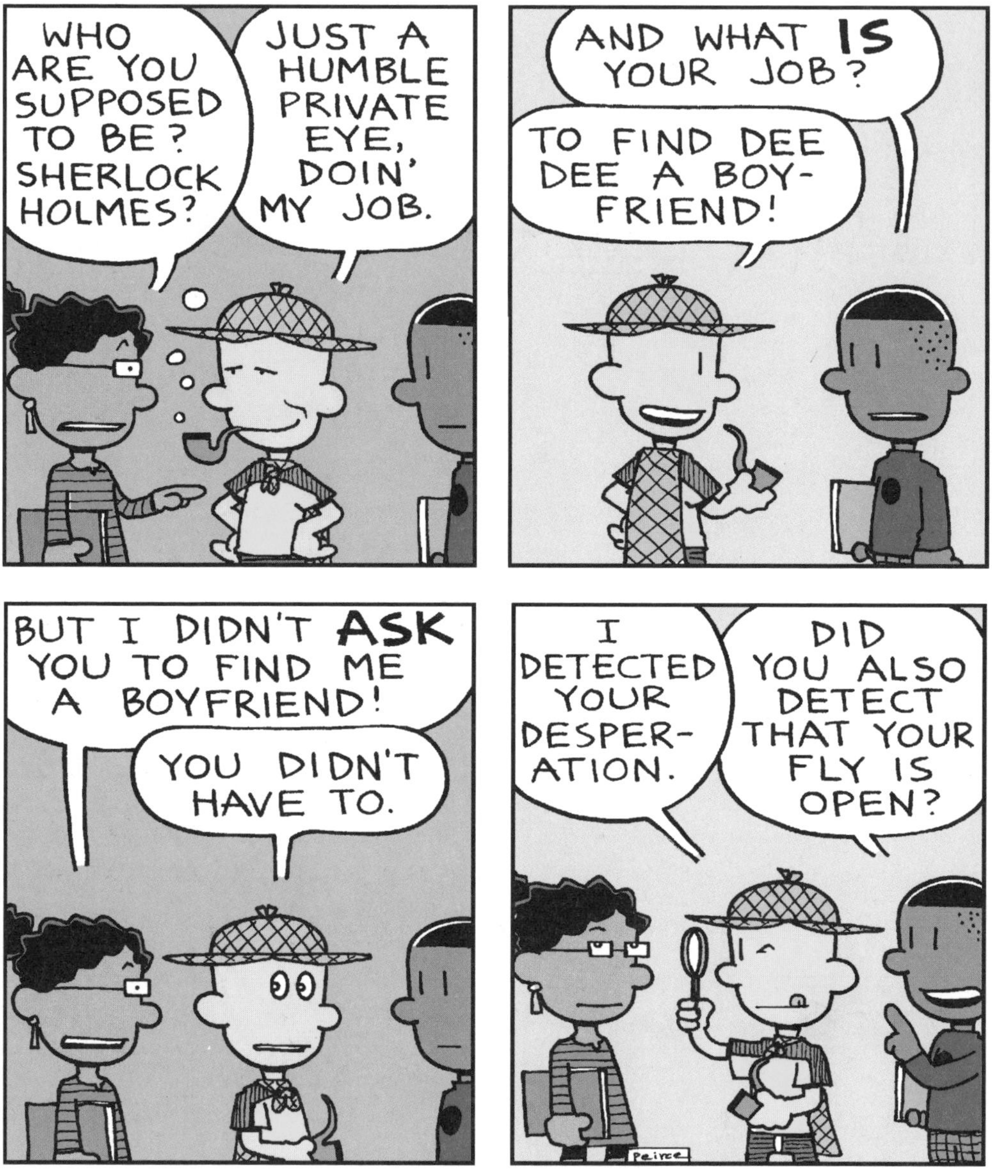
WHO ARE YOU SUPPOSED TO BE? SHERLOCK HOLMES?
JUST A HUMBLE PRIVATE EYE, DOIN' MY JOB.
AND WHAT IS YOUR JOB?
TO FIND DEE DEE A BOY-FRIEND!
BUT I DIDN'T ASK YOU TO FIND ME A BOYFRIEND!
YOU DIDN'T HAVE TO.
I DETECTED YOUR DESPER-ATION.
DID YOU ALSO DETECT THAT YOUR FLY IS OPEN?
Peirce

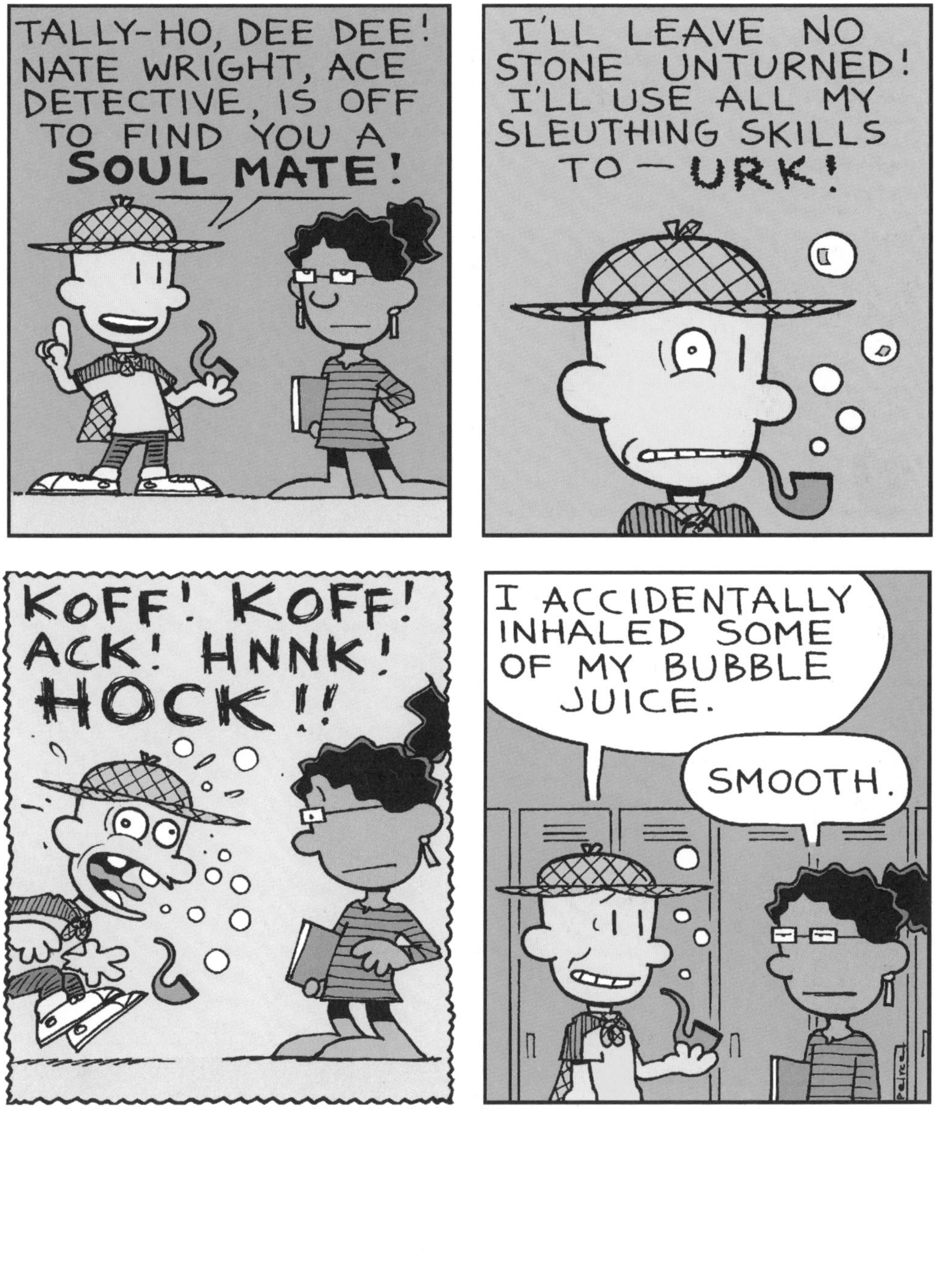
TALLY-HO, DEE DEE! NATE WRIGHT, ACE DETECTIVE, IS OFF TO FIND YOU A SOUL MATE!
I'LL LEAVE NO STONE UNTURNED! I'LL USE ALL MY SLEUTHING SKILLS TO — URK!
KOFF! KOFF! ACK! HNNK! HOCK!!
I ACCIDENTALLY INHALED SOME OF MY BUBBLE JUICE.
SMOOTH.
Peirce

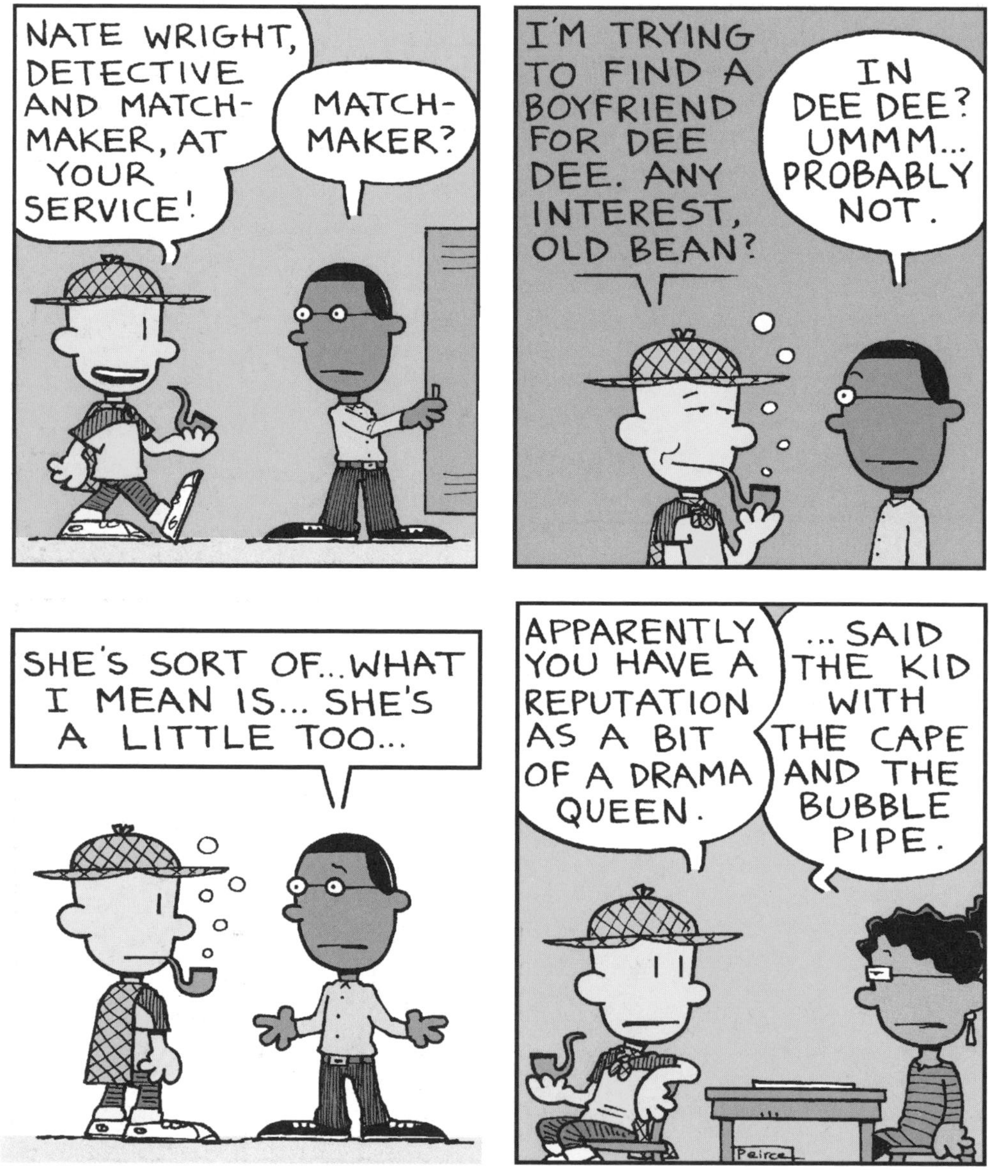
NATE WRIGHT, DETECTIVE AND MATCH-MAKER, AT YOUR SERVICE!
MATCH-MAKER?
I'M TRYING TO FIND A BOYFRIEND FOR DEE DEE. ANY INTEREST, OLD BEAN?
IN DEE DEE? UMMM... PROBABLY NOT.
SHE'S SORT OF... WHAT I MEAN IS... SHE'S A LITTLE TOO...
APPARENTLY YOU HAVE A REPUTATION AS A BIT OF A DRAMA QUEEN.
...SAID THE KID WITH THE CAPE AND THE BUBBLE PIPE.
Peirce

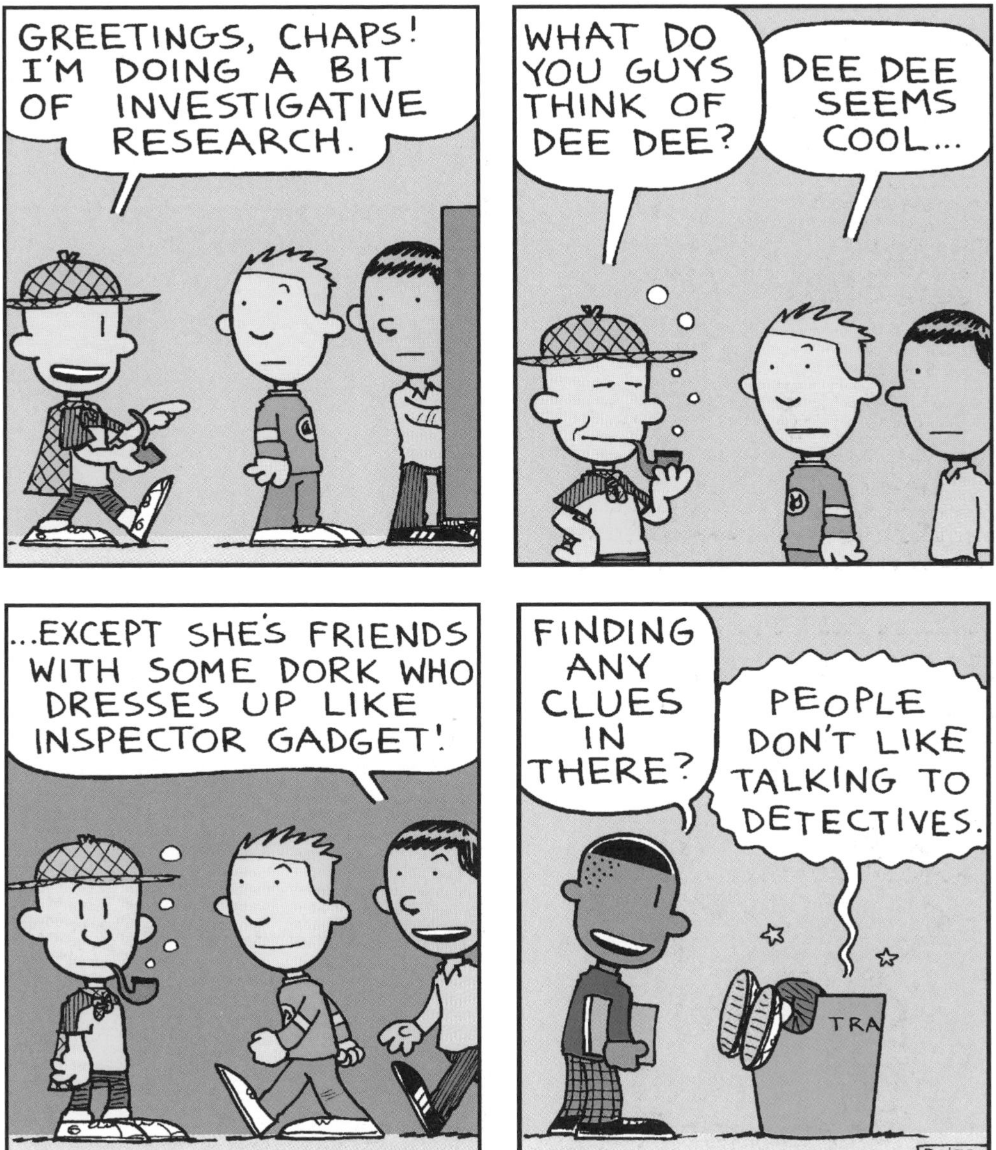
GREETINGS, CHAPS! I'M DOING A BIT OF INVESTIGATIVE RESEARCH.
WHAT DO YOU GUYS THINK OF DEE DEE?
DEE DEE SEEMS COOL...
...EXCEPT SHE'S FRIENDS WITH SOME DORK WHO DRESSES UP LIKE INSPECTOR GADGET!
FINDING ANY CLUES IN THERE?
PEOPLE DON'T LIKE TALKING TO DETECTIVES.
TRA
Peirce

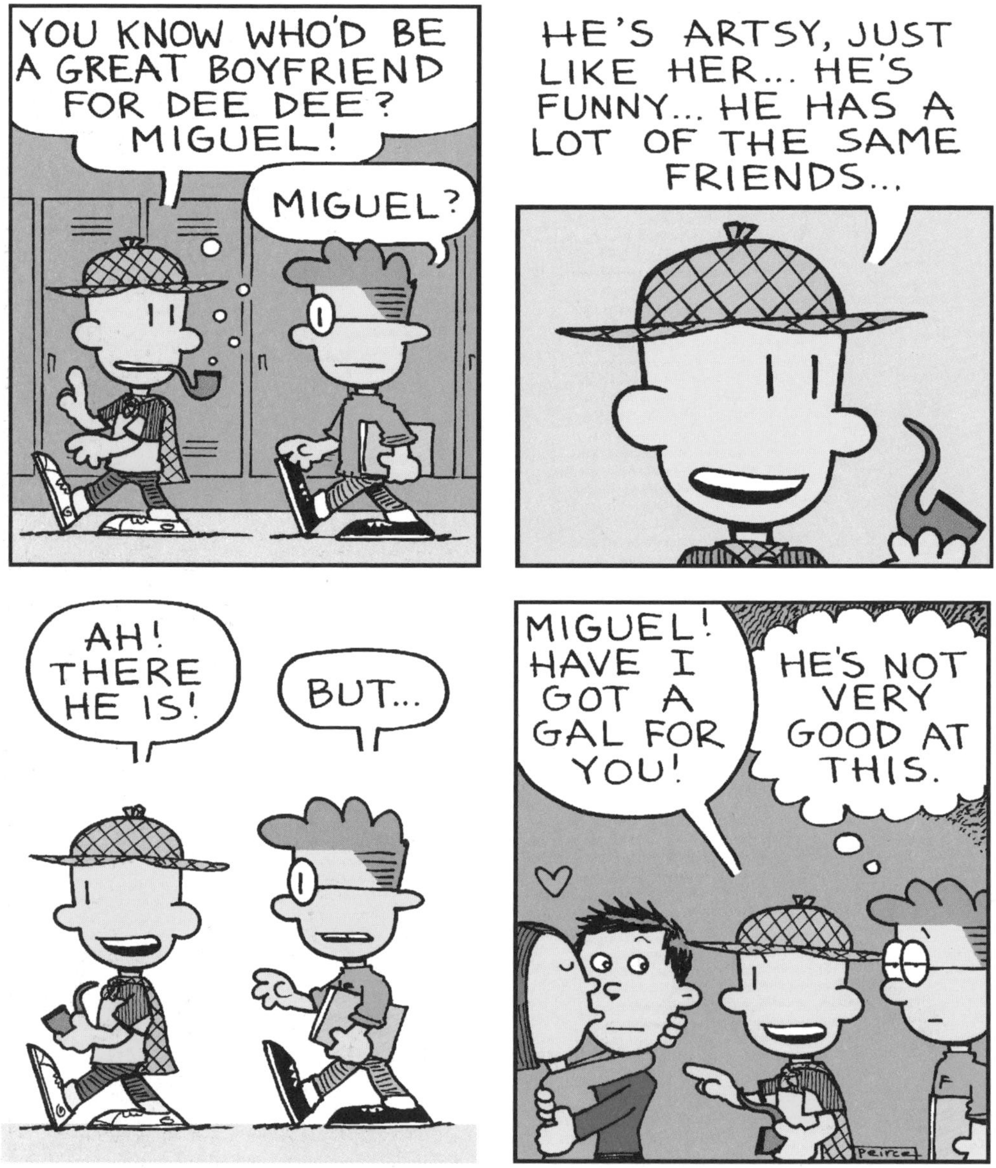
YOU KNOW WHO'D BE A GREAT BOYFRIEND FOR DEE DEE? MIGUEL!
MIGUEL?
HE'S ARTSY, JUST LIKE HER... HE'S FUNNY... HE HAS A LOT OF THE SAME FRIENDS...
AH! THERE HE IS!
BUT...
MIGUEL! HAVE I GOT A GAL FOR YOU!
HE'S NOT VERY GOOD AT THIS.
Peirce

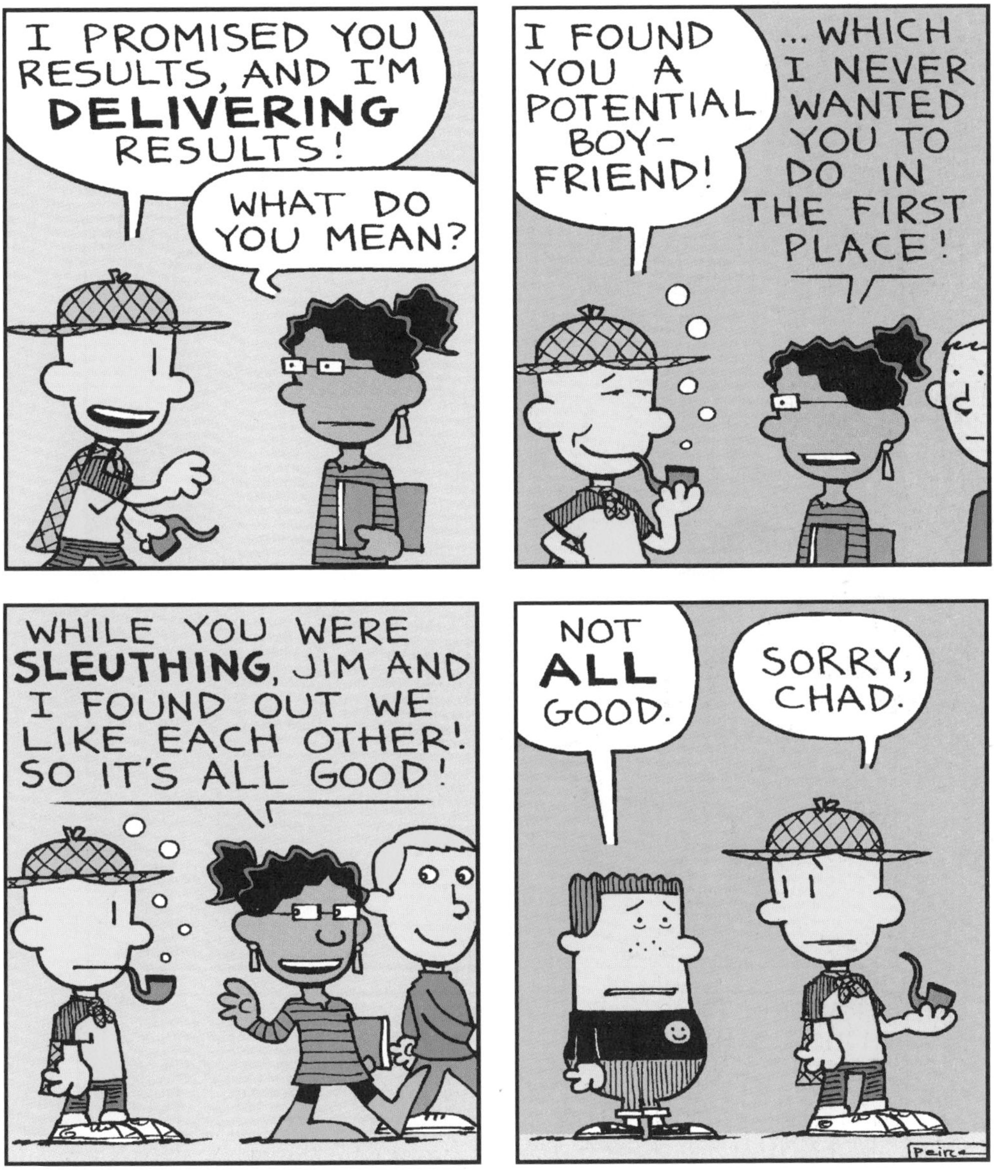

I PROMISED YOU RESULTS, AND I'M **DELIVERING** RESULTS!
WHAT DO YOU MEAN?
I FOUND YOU A POTENTIAL BOY-FRIEND!
...WHICH I NEVER WANTED YOU TO DO IN THE FIRST PLACE!
WHILE YOU WERE **SLEUTHING**, JIM AND I FOUND OUT WE LIKE EACH OTHER! SO IT'S ALL GOOD!
NOT **ALL** GOOD.
SORRY, CHAD.
Peirce

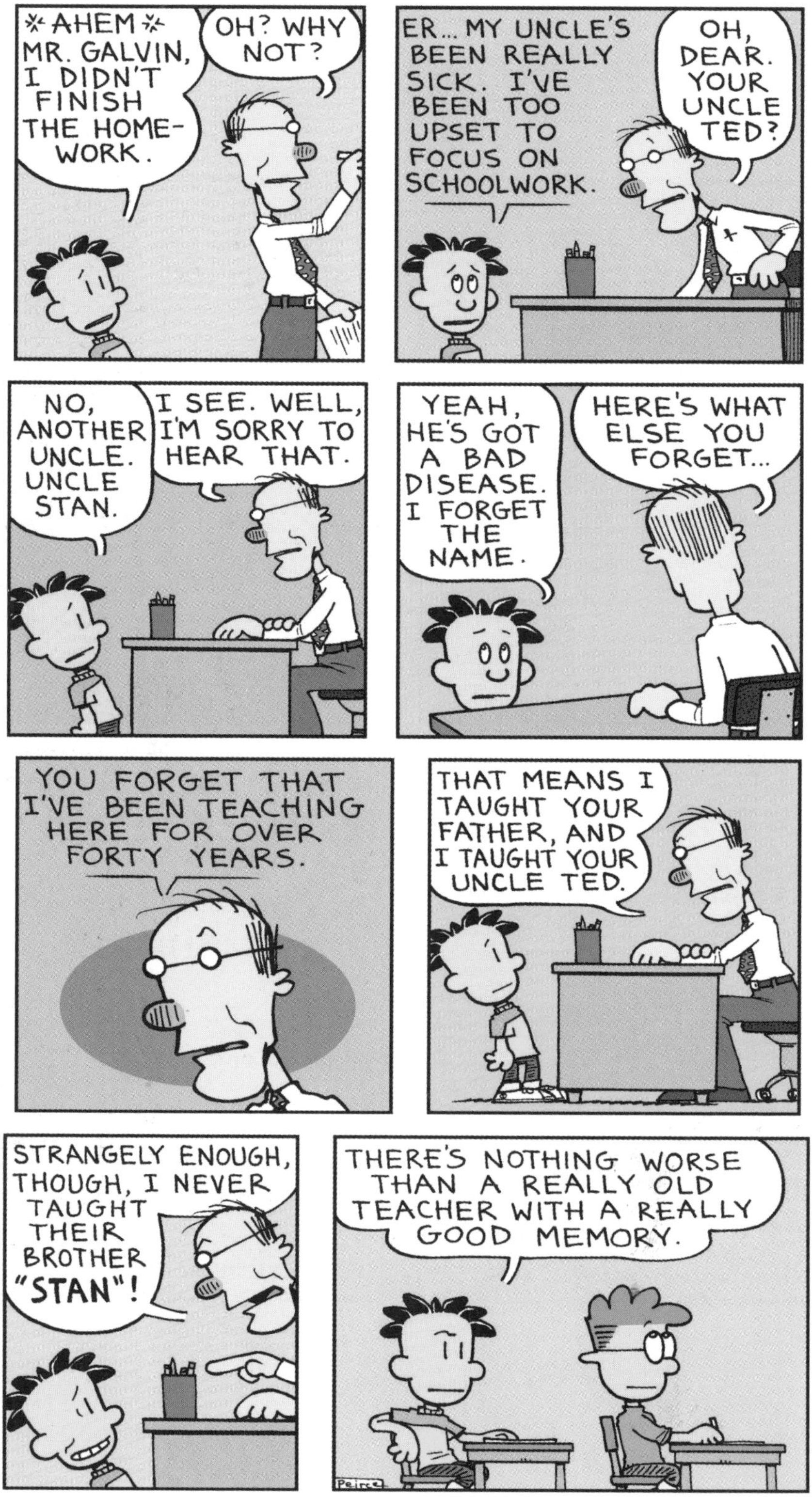
AHEM MR. GALVIN, I DIDN'T FINISH THE HOME-WORK.
OH? WHY NOT?
ER... MY UNCLE'S BEEN REALLY SICK. I'VE BEEN TOO UPSET TO FOCUS ON SCHOOLWORK.
OH, DEAR. YOUR UNCLE TED?
NO, ANOTHER UNCLE. UNCLE STAN.
I SEE. WELL, I'M SORRY TO HEAR THAT.
YEAH, HE'S GOT A BAD DISEASE. I FORGET THE NAME.
HERE'S WHAT ELSE YOU FORGET...
YOU FORGET THAT I'VE BEEN TEACHING HERE FOR OVER FORTY YEARS.
THAT MEANS I TAUGHT YOUR FATHER, AND I TAUGHT YOUR UNCLE TED.
STRANGELY ENOUGH, THOUGH, I NEVER TAUGHT THEIR BROTHER "STAN"!
THERE'S NOTHING WORSE THAN A REALLY OLD TEACHER WITH A REALLY GOOD MEMORY.
Peirce

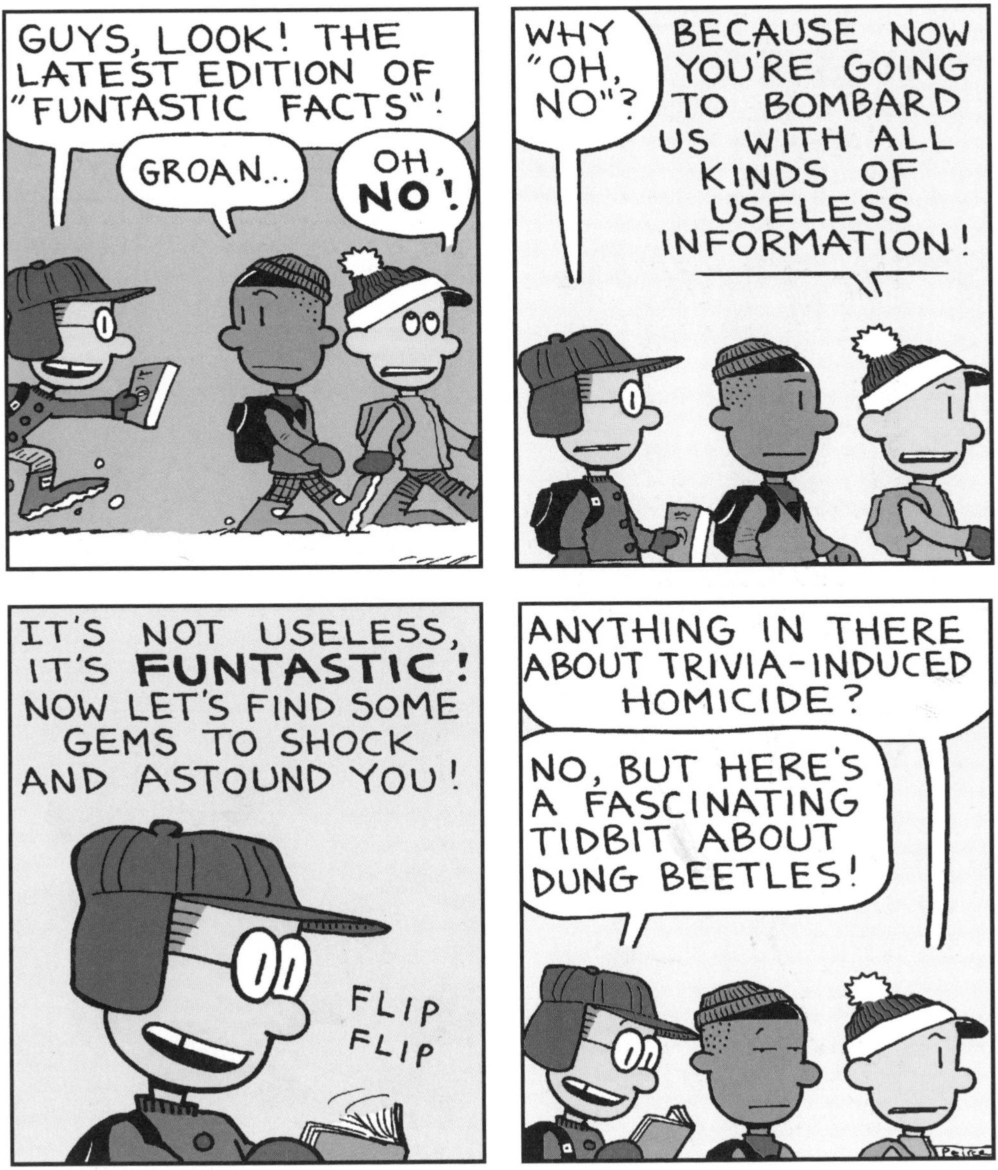
GUYS, LOOK! THE LATEST EDITION OF "FUNTASTIC FACTS"!
GROAN...
OH, NO!
WHY "OH, NO"?
BECAUSE NOW YOU'RE GOING TO BOMBARD US WITH ALL KINDS OF USELESS INFORMATION!
IT'S NOT USELESS, IT'S FUNTASTIC! NOW LET'S FIND SOME GEMS TO SHOCK AND ASTOUND YOU!
FLIP FLIP
ANYTHING IN THERE ABOUT TRIVIA-INDUCED HOMICIDE?
NO, BUT HERE'S A FASCINATING TIDBIT ABOUT DUNG BEETLES!

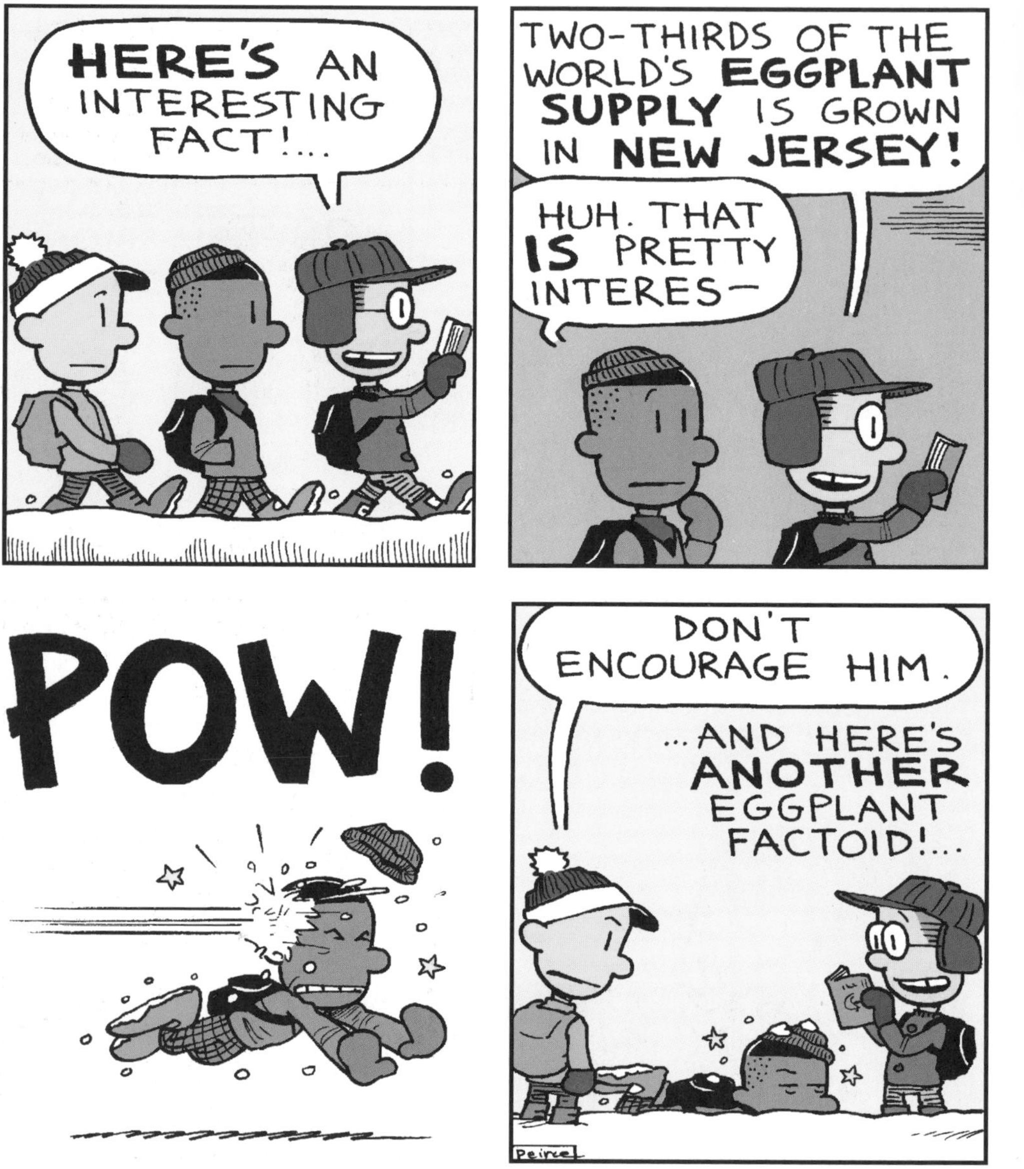
HERE'S AN INTERESTING FACT!...
TWO-THIRDS OF THE WORLD'S EGGPLANT SUPPLY IS GROWN IN NEW JERSEY!
HUH. THAT IS PRETTY INTERES—
POW!
DON'T ENCOURAGE HIM.
...AND HERE'S ANOTHER EGGPLANT FACTOID!...
Peirce

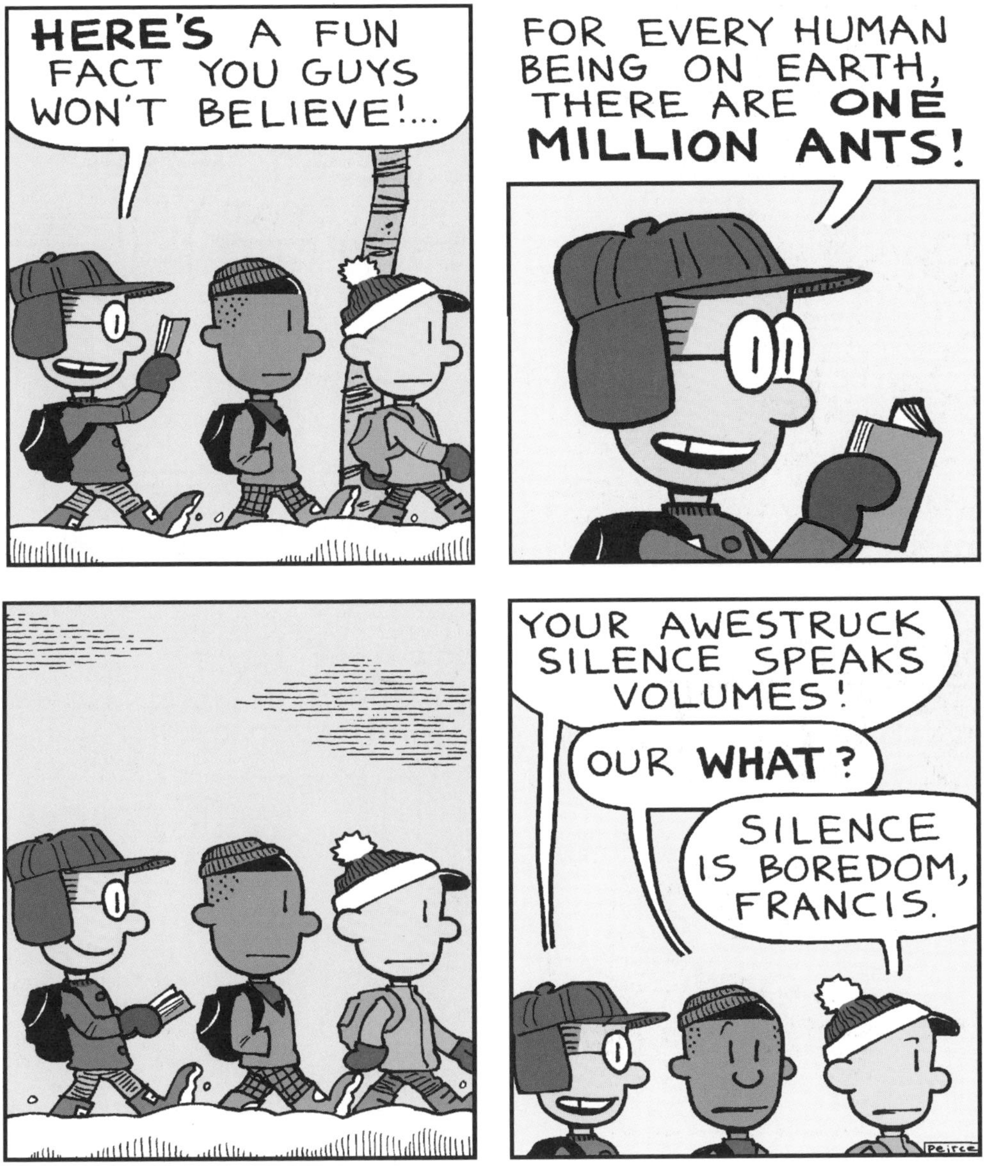

HERE'S A FUN FACT YOU GUYS WON'T BELIEVE!...
FOR EVERY HUMAN BEING ON EARTH, THERE ARE ONE MILLION ANTS!
YOUR AWESTRUCK SILENCE SPEAKS VOLUMES!
OUR WHAT?
SILENCE IS BOREDOM, FRANCIS.
Peirce

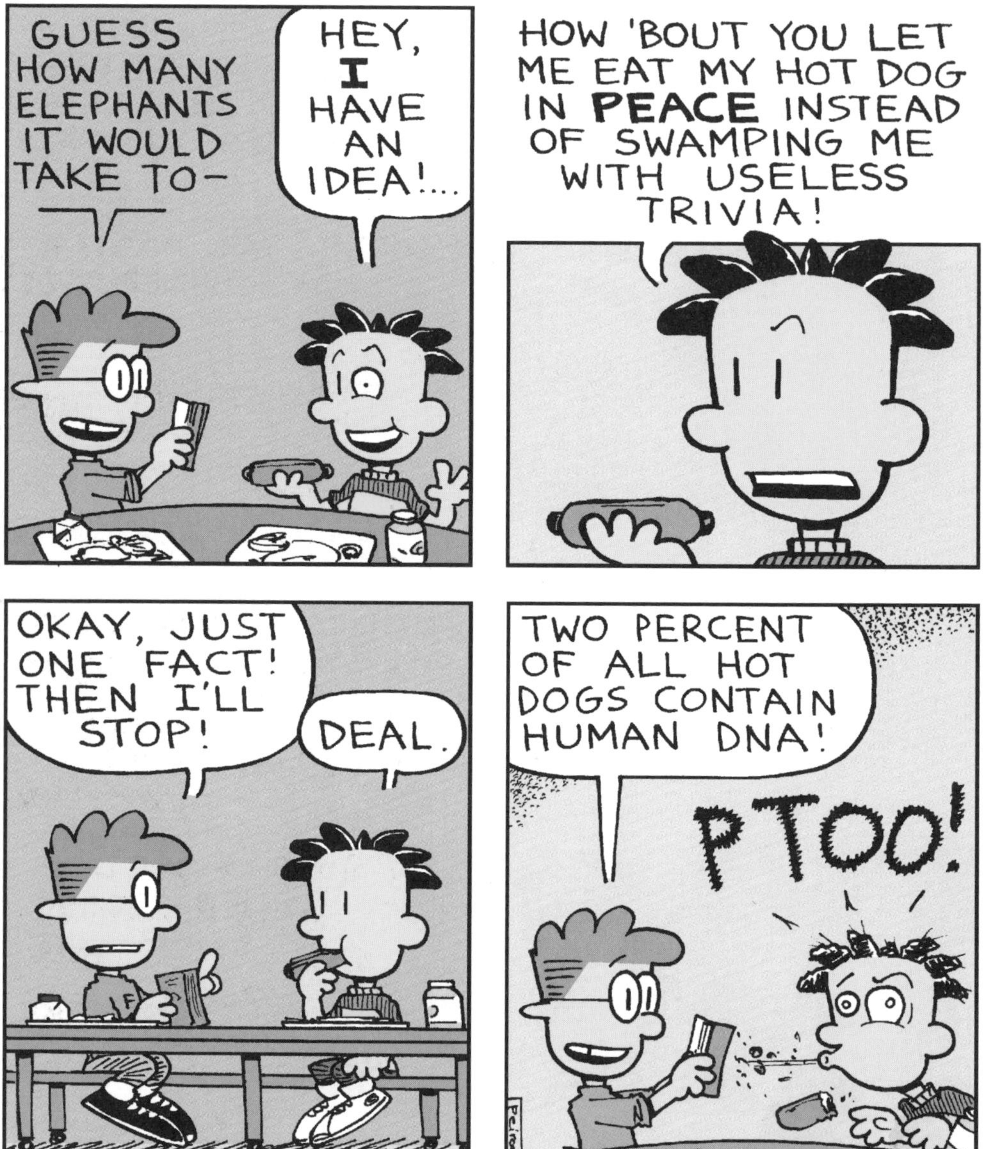
GUESS HOW MANY ELEPHANTS IT WOULD TAKE TO–
HEY, I HAVE AN IDEA!...
HOW 'BOUT YOU LET ME EAT MY HOT DOG IN PEACE INSTEAD OF SWAMPING ME WITH USELESS TRIVIA!
OKAY, JUST ONE FACT! THEN I'LL STOP!
DEAL.
TWO PERCENT OF ALL HOT DOGS CONTAIN HUMAN DNA!
PTOO!

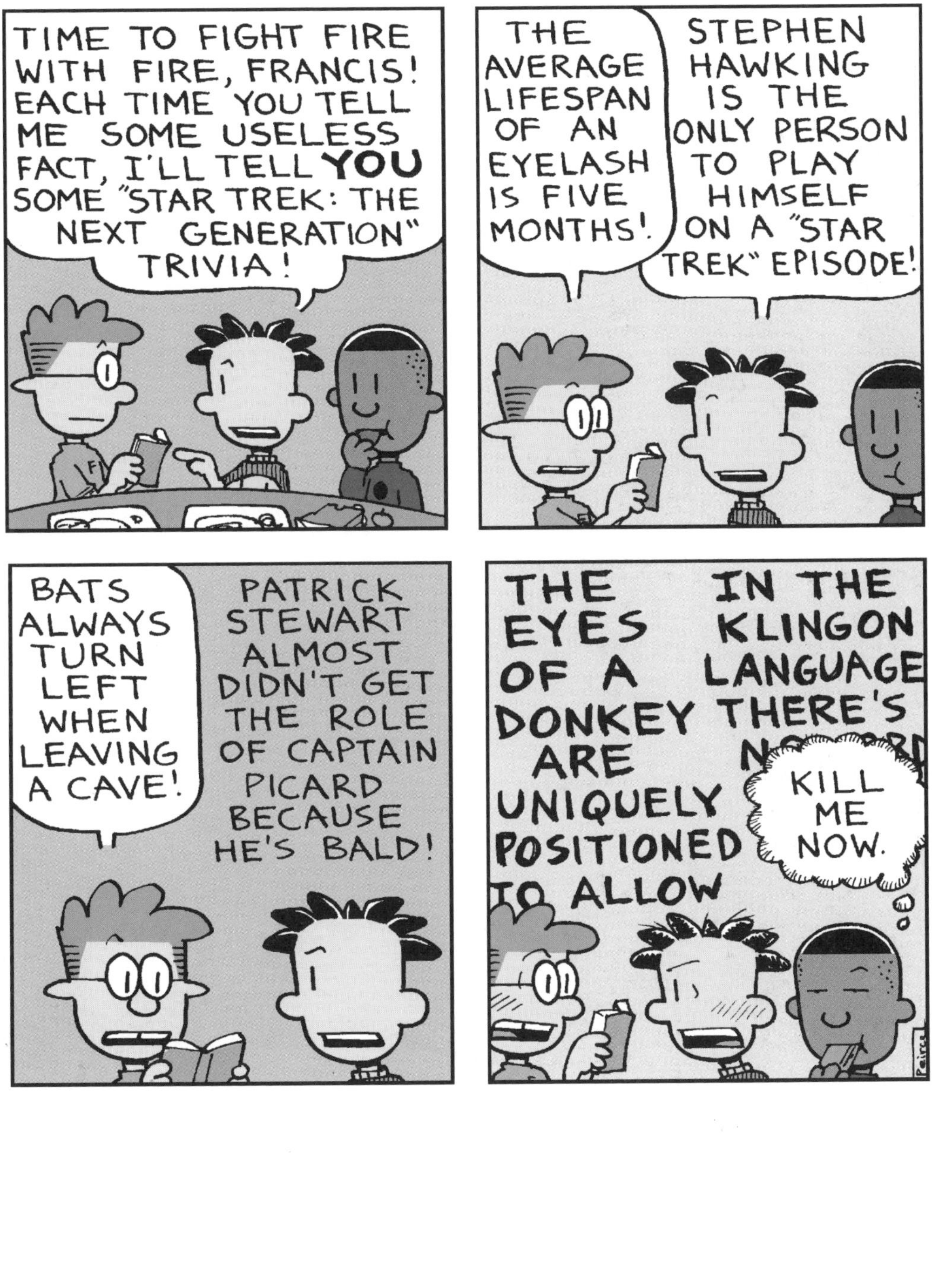
TIME TO FIGHT FIRE WITH FIRE, FRANCIS! EACH TIME YOU TELL ME SOME USELESS FACT, I'LL TELL **YOU** SOME "STAR TREK: THE NEXT GENERATION" TRIVIA!
THE AVERAGE LIFESPAN OF AN EYELASH IS FIVE MONTHS!
STEPHEN HAWKING IS THE ONLY PERSON TO PLAY HIMSELF ON A "STAR TREK" EPISODE!
BATS ALWAYS TURN LEFT WHEN LEAVING A CAVE!
PATRICK STEWART ALMOST DIDN'T GET THE ROLE OF CAPTAIN PICARD BECAUSE HE'S BALD!
THE EYES OF A DONKEY ARE UNIQUELY POSITIONED TO ALLOW
IN THE KLINGON LANGUAGE THERE'S
KILL ME NOW.
Peirce

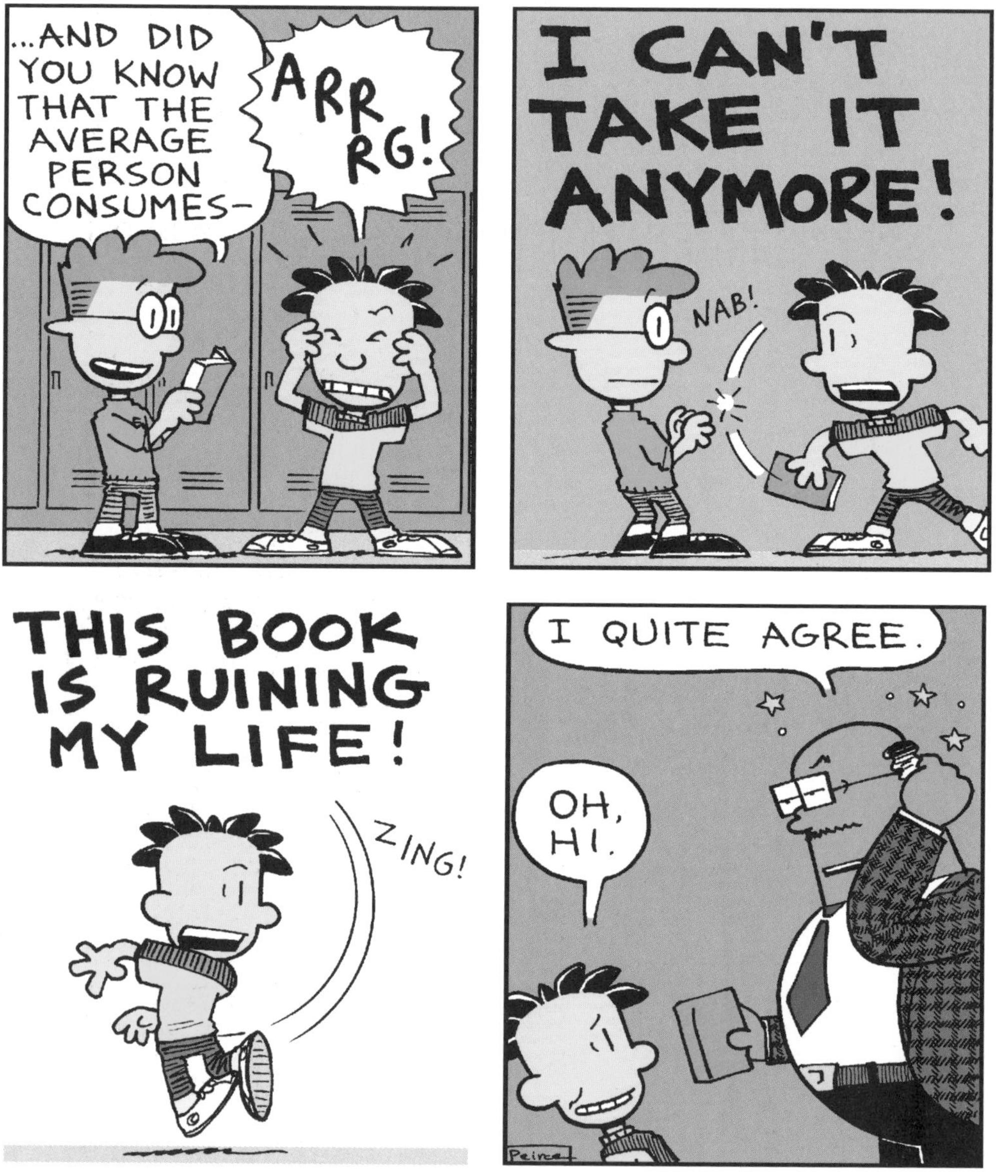
...AND DID YOU KNOW THAT THE AVERAGE PERSON CONSUMES-
ARRRG!
I CAN'T TAKE IT ANYMORE!
NAB!
THIS BOOK IS RUINING MY LIFE!
ZING!
I QUITE AGREE.
OH, HI.
Peirce

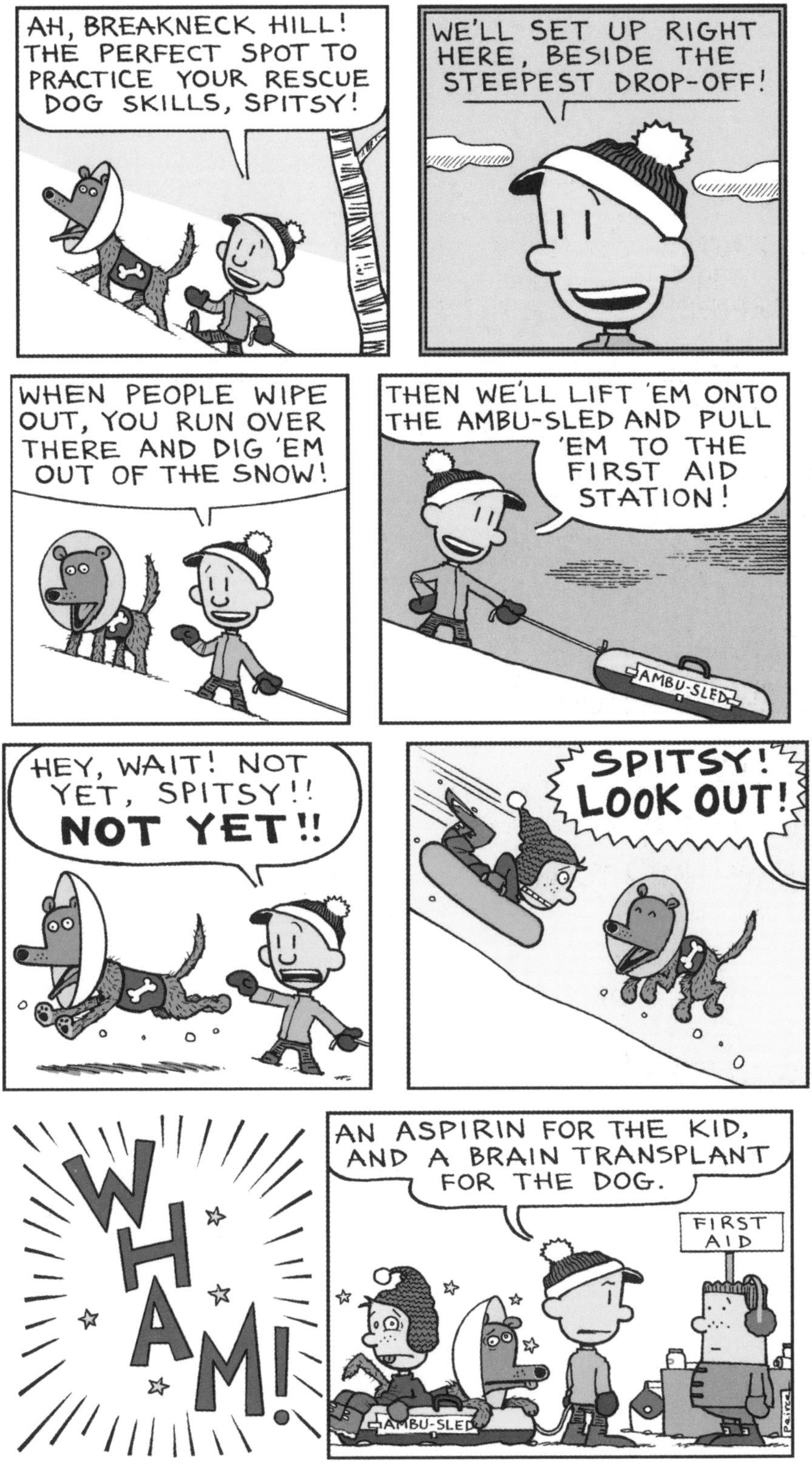
AH, BREAKNECK HILL! THE PERFECT SPOT TO PRACTICE YOUR RESCUE DOG SKILLS, SPITSY!
WE'LL SET UP RIGHT HERE, BESIDE THE STEEPEST DROP-OFF!
WHEN PEOPLE WIPE OUT, YOU RUN OVER THERE AND DIG 'EM OUT OF THE SNOW!
THEN WE'LL LIFT 'EM ONTO THE AMBU-SLED AND PULL 'EM TO THE FIRST AID STATION!
AMBU-SLED
HEY, WAIT! NOT YET, SPITSY!! NOT YET!!
SPITSY! LOOK OUT!
WHAM!
AN ASPIRIN FOR THE KID, AND A BRAIN TRANSPLANT FOR THE DOG.
FIRST AID
AMBU-SLED
Peirce

Big Nate is distributed internationally by Andrews McMeel Syndication.

Big Nate: Release the Hounds! copyright © 2022 by United Feature Syndicate, Inc. All rights reserved. Printed in China. No part of this book may be used or reproduced in any manner whatsoever without written permission except in the case of reprints in the context of reviews.

Andrews McMeel Publishing
a division of Andrews McMeel Universal
1130 Walnut Street, Kansas City, Missouri 64106

www.andrewsmcmeel.com

22 23 24 25 26 SDB 10 9 8 7 6 5 4 3 2 1

ISBN: 978-1-5248-7557-2

Library of Congress Control Number: 2022932537

Made by:
King Yip (Dongguan) Printing & Packaging Factory Ltd.
Address and location of manufacturer:
Daning Administrative District, Humen Town
Dongguan Guangdong, China 523930
1st Printing—6/13/22

These strips appeared in newspapers from September 10, 2018, through February 23, 2019.

Big Nate can be viewed on the Internet at
www.gocomics.com/big_nate.

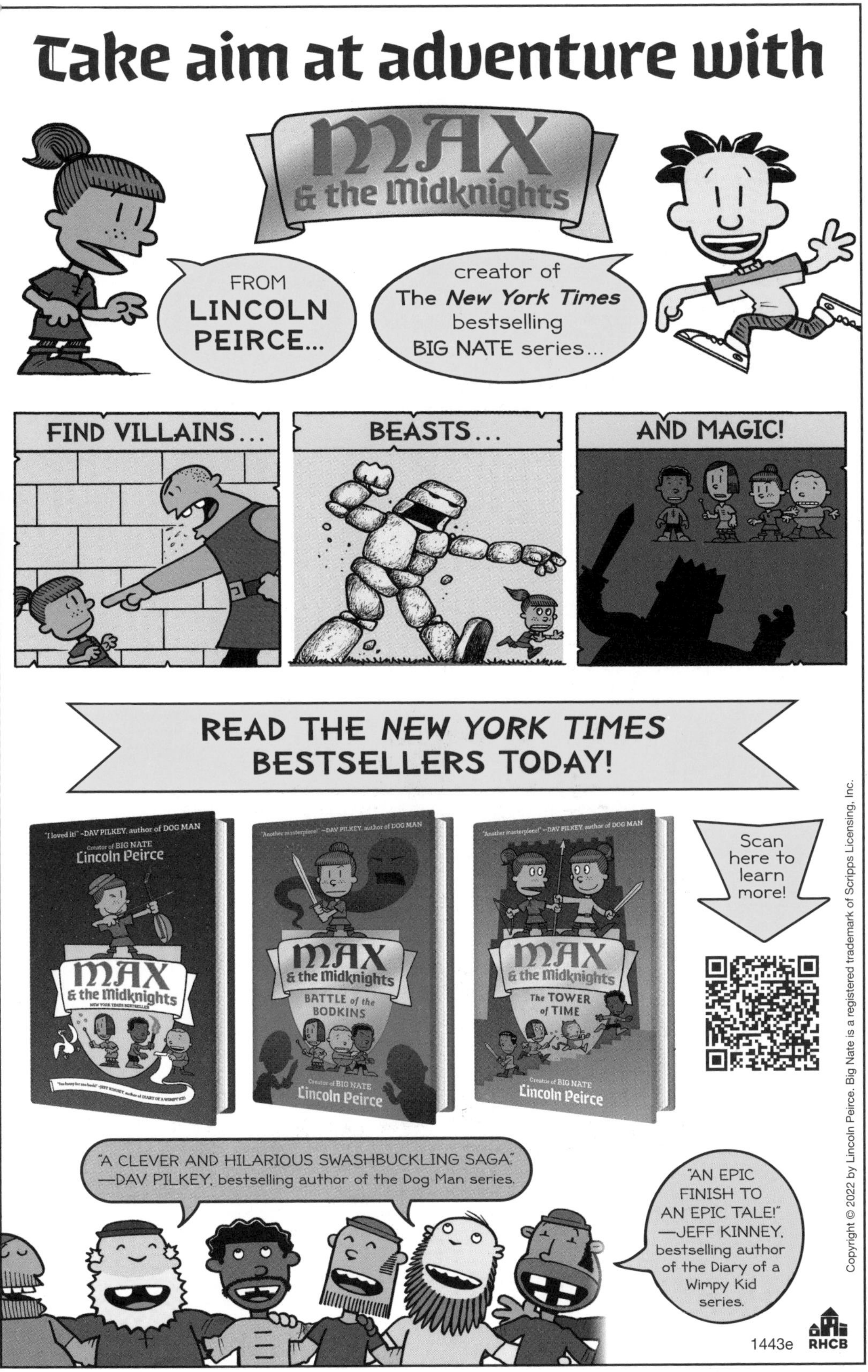
Take aim at adventure with
MAX & the Midknights
FROM LINCOLN PEIRCE...
creator of The *New York Times* bestselling BIG NATE series...
FIND VILLAINS...
BEASTS...
AND MAGIC!
READ THE *NEW YORK TIMES* BESTSELLERS TODAY!
"I loved it!" –DAV PILKEY, author of DOG MAN
Creator of BIG NATE Lincoln Peirce
MAX & the Midknights
"Another masterpiece!" –DAV PILKEY, author of DOG MAN
MAX & the Midknights BATTLE of the BODKINS
Creator of BIG NATE Lincoln Peirce
"Another masterpiece!" –DAV PILKEY, author of DOG MAN
MAX & the Midknights The TOWER of TIME
Creator of BIG NATE Lincoln Peirce
Scan here to learn more!
"A CLEVER AND HILARIOUS SWASHBUCKLING SAGA." —DAV PILKEY, bestselling author of the Dog Man series.
"AN EPIC FINISH TO AN EPIC TALE!" —JEFF KINNEY, bestselling author of the Diary of a Wimpy Kid series.
Copyright © 2022 by Lincoln Peirce. Big Nate is a registered trademark of Scripps Licensing, Inc.
1443e
RHCB

A NEW GRAPHIC NOVEL BASED ON THE HIT TV SERIES ON *Paramount+* AND **nickelodeon**™

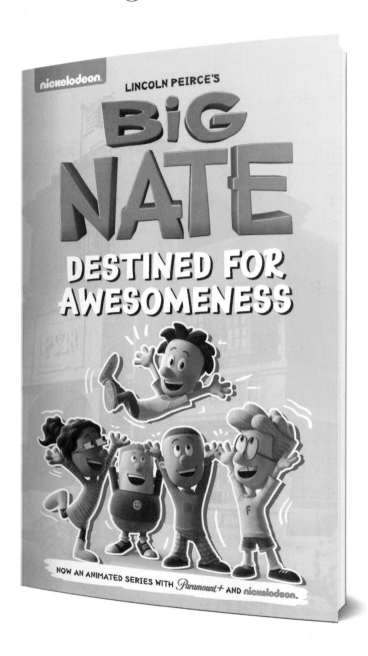